THE
MORNING
AFTER

**Center Point
Large Print**

**This Large Print Book carries the
Seal of Approval of N.A.V.H.**

LISA JACKSON

THE MORNING AFTER

Center Point Publishing
Thorndike, Maine

This Center Point Large Print edition
is published in the year 2004 by arrangement with
Zebra Books, a division of Kensington Publishing Corp.

The text of this Large Print edition is unabridged. In other
aspects, this book may vary from the original edition. Printed in
Thailand. Set in 16-point Times New Roman type.

ISBN 1-58547-468-1

Library of Congress Cataloging-in-Publication Data

Jackson, Lisa.
   The morning after / Lisa Jackson.--Center Point large print ed.
    p. cm.
   ISBN 1-58547-468-1 (lib. bdg. : alk. paper)
    1. Large type books. I. Title.

PS3560.A223M67 2004
813'.54--dc22

                                        2004001914

ACKNOWLEDGMENTS

Again, I would like to take this opportunity to thank Bucky Burnsed, Public Information Office for the Savannah Police Department. His help was insightful and invaluable in answering my many questions as well as helping me avoid some errors. In the course of the story, to make the plot work and to keep the characters true to their natures, I had to bend the rules, setting, and procedures of the Savannah Police Department.

There are other people who helped me in the writing of this book. Some helped with research, others critiqued, still others maintained my office and, of course, my friends and relatives provided emotional support.

Specifically I would like to thank Nancy Berland, Kelly Bush, Ken Bush, Nancy Bush, Matthew Crose, Michael Crose, Alexis Harrington, Danielle Katcher, Ken Melum, Roz Noonan, Ari Okano, Kathy Okano, Betty and Jack Pederson, Sally Peters, Robin Rue, Samantha Santistevan, John Scognamiglio, Michael Siedel, and Larry Sparks. If I've forgotten anyone, please accept my sincere apologies.

PROLOGUE

Oh, God, it was cold . . . so cold . . .

Bobbi shivered. She was sluggish, could barely move, her mind groggy and dull. She wanted to sleep, to ignore the vague sense of uneasiness that teased at her mind. Her eyelids were heavy. As if she'd taken too many sleeping pills. An acrid odor reached her nostrils, something foul. She cringed and realized that her room was quiet. Still. Eerily so. No sound of the hall clock ticking off the seconds, or the fan from the furnace turning the air . . . no . . . the silence was deafening.

You're not in your room.

The thought hit her hard.

You're not in your bed.

She forced an eyelid open. She was . . . where?

The rancid smell made her gag. Slowly, her mind began to clear. Where the hell was she and why couldn't she move? Her lungs were tight, the air thin, the darkness complete. Panic shot through her blood as she realized she was lying on her back, wedged against something hard, slick fabric pressed against her nose.

It was dark. Airless. She had trouble drawing a breath. And that god-awful smell . . . She nearly retched.

This was wrong, all wrong.

She tried to sit up.

Bam!

Her head cracked against something hard and she

couldn't move her arms. Not upward, not side to side. She was wedged tight in a small space, upon an uncomfortable bed . . . no not a bed, something softer and spongier and squishy, with hard points poking upward against her back. And that horrendous, rotting smell. Fear, cold as death, shrieked through her thick brain. She was crammed into some kind of tight box.

And then she knew.

With sickening clarity.

She was stuffed into a coffin?

God, no! That was impossible! Unthinkable. Her mind was just clogged, that was all. And this claustrophobic paranoia was all part of some kind of weird, macabre dream. That was it. That had to be it. But her blood was pumping frantically through her body. Sheer terror sliced through her.

No, oh, no . . . please, no . . . this has to be a dream. Wake up, Bobbi. For God's sake, wake the hell up!

She screamed and the shriek resounded in her eardrums, going nowhere, bouncing in the tight airless space.

Think. Don't panic! Oh, God, oh, God, oh, God.

Wildly she tried to kick upward, but her bare feet hit the hard surface, a toenail catching on the lining. It ripped backward. Raw pain seared up her foot and she could feel her nail hanging by a thread of flesh.

This couldn't be happening. It was a nightmare. Had to be. And yet . . . with all her might she tried to push, to climb out of this horrible confining space with its satin lining and . . . and . . . Jesus Christ, she was lying on something soft in places, hard in others, a . . . a . . .

A body! You're lying on a body!

"Noooooo! Please let me out!" She shredded the lining with her fingers, scratched, clawed and pounded, felt bones and rotting flesh and the bristle of hair against her bare skin . . . bare skin . . . dear God, was she naked? Shoved into this gruesome box without any clothes? Who had done this to her? Why? "Help! Please help me!" Her own screams echoed in her ears, ricocheting back at her. "Oh, God, oh, God . . . please, someone." Jesus Christ, was she really lying on a dead person? Her skin crawled at the thought of the rotting flesh beneath her, the lipless mouth pressed against the back of her neck, the bony ribs and hands and . . .

Maybe it's still alive—just comatose like you were.

But she knew better. The once-live padding beneath her was cold as death and reeked and was probably already decomposing and . . . *oh, please let this be a horrible, monstrous nightmare. Please let me wake up.* She heard sobbing and realized the sounds escaped from her throat. *Don't panic. Try to figure a way out of this . . . while you still have air. The fact that you're breathing means that you were probably just dropped here. Just because you're in a coffin doesn't necessarily mean you're underground . . .* But she smelled the dank earth, knew that this death box was already in a grave. It was only a matter of time before—

Snap out of it and figure a way out of this! You're a smart woman, think! THINK! If you're not buried, just trapped in here, there could still be time . . . But she knew the seconds were running out, each one bringing

9

her closer to a macabre, unthinkable death. *Please, God, don't let me die. Not like this . . . not . . . not like this.*

"Help me! Help! HELP!" she cried, shrieking and scratching wildly at the top of the coffin. She tore at the smooth satin lining, her long, manicured fingernails breaking, her skin ripping, sharp pain searing up the back of her hands. The stench was overwhelming, the air so cold and thin . . . it had to be a dream . . . *had* to. And yet the pain in her fingertips, the blood flowing under her nails convinced her that she was living a nightmare so evil she could barely imagine it.

Horror strangled her and she thought she might pass out. Screaming at the top of her lungs, she kicked, banging her knees and feet, her muscles cramping, her bare skin torn and bleeding, tears running from her eyes. "Don't let me die this way, please, oh, please, don't let me die this way . . ."

But the darkness remained. The squishy body beneath her didn't move, decaying flesh touched hers, sharp ribs poked upward against her back. She shuddered, nearly vomited, and screamed.

Above the sound of her voice she heard the chilling, resonate thud of dirt and stones raining onto the top of this hideous coffin.

"No! No!"

She pounded until her fists bled and burned, all the while pleading and crying. "Let me out! Please, please!"

Who would do this to her?

Why . . . oh, God, why . . . Who had she wronged so

horribly? There were so many she'd lied to, their faces running through her half-crazed mind, chased by panic. But who would hate her enough to torture her this way? Who would have cause? Who would be so cruel?

She gasped. The air nearly gone. She was fading. Her mind spun wildly to thoughts of the men in her life and to one in particular, one who probably didn't remember her name, one she had wronged fiercely.

Pierce Reed.

Detective with the Savannah Police Department.

A man honored, but with dark secrets of his own.

No . . . Reed wouldn't do this to her, didn't really know how deeply their lives were entwined, didn't care.

It was another man, some monster who had trapped her here.

She began to shiver and weep.

"Let me out! Let me out," she screamed, sobbing, her throat aching, her skin crawling with the thought of the decomposing human that was her bed. "Please, please, let me out of here . . . I'll do anything . . . anything, oh, please, don't do this . . . ."

But she didn't even know to whom she was begging and the shovels of dirt and pebbles kept raining on the grave.

She gasped, drawing in a ragged, burning breath of what was left of the air. Her lungs were on fire from lack of oxygen and she felt suddenly weak.

Helpless.

Doomed.

She made one last vain attempt to claw her way out of her prison, but it was no use. The blackness crashed over her, crushing the fight from her, squeezing the life from her, and her hands fell to her sides. This, then, was her tomb. Forever.

Above the gruesome silence she thought she heard laughter. It sounded far away, but she knew it was meant for her to hear. He wanted her to know. To hear him before she drew her last breath.

Whoever had done this to her was enjoying it.

CHAPTER 1

"That son of a bitch is taking me back to court!" Morrisette blazed into Reed's office and slapped some legal papers on the corner of his desk. "Can you believe it?" she demanded, her west Texas drawl all the more evident in her fury. "Bart wants to reduce my child support by thirty percent!" Bart Yelkis was Sylvie Morrisette's fourth and latest ex-husband and father of her two kids. For as long as Reed had been with the Savannah Police Department, Sylvie and Bart had been at odds over how she raised Priscilla and Toby. Sylvie was tough as dried leather and rarely kept her sarcastic sharp tongue in check. She smoked, drank, drove as if she were in the time trials for the Indy 500, swore like a sailor and dressed as if she were pushing twenty rather than thirty-five, but she was first and foremost a mother. Nothing could bristle her neck hairs faster than criticism of her kids.

"I thought he was caught up in his payments."

"He was, but it was short-lived, believe me. I should have known. It was just too effin' good to be true. Damn it all, why can't the guy be a dad, huh?" She dropped her oversize purse onto the floor and shot Reed a glance that convinced him right now all the men in Morrisette's life were suddenly considered big-time losers. Including him. Morrisette had a reputation for being tough, a woman hell-bent to do a man's job, a prickly female cop whose tongue was razor-sharp, her opinions unpopular, her patience with "good ol' boys" nil and her language as blue as any detective's on the force. She wore snakeskin boots that were far from department issue, spiked platinum hair that looked as if Billy Idol had been her hairdresser, and had an attitude that would make any young punk think twice about taking her on. Reed had suffered many a sympathetic glance from other cops who pitied him for his bad luck in the partner draw. Not that he cared. In the short time he'd been back in Savannah, Reed had learned to respect Sylvie Morrisette, even if he did have to walk on eggshells upon occasion. This morning her face was flushed a color bordering carmine and she looked as if she could spit nails.

"Can he do that—reduce the payments?" Reed had been opening his mail but, for the moment, set his letter opener on a desk that was a jungle of papers.

"If he can find himself a wimp of a judge who'll buy into his pathetic, poor-pitiful-me act. So, Bart lost his job, so what? He should get off his ass and find another means of gainful employment—you know, like normal people do? Instead, he thinks he'll cut back on me and the kids." She rolled her eyes and straightened her petite frame, from the worn heels of her boots to the top of her spiked blond hair. Her west Texas drawl was stronger than ever when she was on a tear and she was on a major one this morning. "Bastard. That's what he is! A card-carrying, dyed-in-the-wool, fucking bastard." She stalked to the window and glowered outside at the gray Savannah winter. "Jesus, it's not as if he pays us millions to begin with. And they're his kids. *His* kids. The ones he always complains about not seeing enough!" She stomped a booted foot and swore under her breath. "I need a drink."

"It's nine in the morning."

"Who cares?"

Reed wasn't too concerned. Morrisette was known to go into overdrive in the theatrics department, especially when her kids or one of her four ex-husbands was involved. Her domestic traumas reinforced his vow to remain single. Spouses were trouble and cops didn't need any more than they already had. "Can't you fight him?" Reed drained a cup of tepid coffee, then crushed the paper cup and tossed it into an overflowing wastebasket.

"Yeah, but it'll cost. I'll need a damned attorney."

"The town's lousy with them."

"That's the problem. Bart's got a friend who owes him a favor—a lawyer friend. So he called in his marker and she filed a motion or whatever the hell it is. A woman. Can you believe it? Where's the sisterhood,

14

huh? That's what I'd like to know. Isn't there supposed to be some kind of female bond where ya don't go trompin' all over another woman's child support?"

Reed didn't touch that one with a ten-foot pole. As far as he knew, Morrisette wasn't part of any sisterhood. She ran roughshod over men and women with equal vigor. He picked up his letter opener again and began slitting a plain white envelope addressed to him in care of the Savannah Police Department. The address was written in plain block letters: DETECTIVE PIERCE REED. The return address seemed familiar, but he couldn't place it.

"So, this is it," Morrisette groused. "My kids' future in the toilet because Bart built this woman a fence for her dogs a few years back and whamo—she goes after my paltry support check." Morrisette's eyes slitted. "There oughta be a law, ya know. Don't people in the legal profession, and I use the term loosely, have better things to do than file stupid lawsuits to screw little kids out of a piece of their father's paycheck?" She raked her fingers through her already unruly hair before storming back to the desk and scooping up her legal papers. Flopping into a side chair, she added, "I guess I'll be putting in for overtime, and lots of it."

"You'll get through this."

"Screw you," she spat. "The last thing I expected from you, Reed, is platitudes. Okay? So stuff 'em."

He swallowed a smile. "Whatever you say."

"Yeah, right." But she seemed to cool off a bit.

"Why don't you sue Bart for *more* money? Turn the tables on him."

"Don't think I haven't considered it, but it's the old adage of tryin' to get blood out of a damned turnip."

Reed glanced up at her and grinned. "You might not get anything but the squeezing might be fun."

"Let's not talk about it."

"You brought it up," he reminded her as he extracted a single sheet of white paper from the envelope.

"Don't remind me. My luck with men." She sighed through her nose. "If I were smart I'd become a nun."

"Oh, yeah, that would work," Reed mocked. He unfolded the single page. There was nothing on the paper save a few lines written in the same neat block letters that had been used in the envelope's address:

ONE, TWO,
THE FIRST FEW.
HEAR THEM CRY,
LISTEN TO THEM DIE.

"What the hell is this?" Reed muttered.

Morrisette was on her feet in an instant. She rounded the desk and studied the simple note. "A prank?"

"Maybe," he muttered.

"A warning?"

"For what?"

"I don't know. You think maybe this is a benign nutcase or a bonafide psychotic?" She frowned, her worries about court-ordered child support reduction seeming to have disappeared. "I don't like the mention of 'listen to them die.' God, there are some real sickos in the world." She studied the block lettering, then scru-

16

tinized the envelope. "Mailed directly to you." Her eyes narrowed on the postmark. "From here in Savannah. And the return address is downtown on Abercorn . . . Jesus, just around the corner."

"Colonial Cemetery," Reed said as it came to him.

"The cemetery. Who would send a letter from there?"

"Another crackpot. This letter's a crank," he said, frowning. "Someone who read about the Montgomery case and wants to jerk my chain." Since last summer when he'd been on the trail of a killer who had a vendetta against the Montgomery family, Reed had gotten a lot of press. Too much of the kind of publicity he abhorred. Credited with cracking the case, Pierce Reed was suddenly looked upon as a hero and sought after as an expert by other departments, by reporters who were still reliving the case, even by the attorney general in Atlanta. His reputation had been exaggerated and his personal life picked and prodded ever since capturing Atropos, a woman determined to decimate one of Savannah's wealthiest and most infamous families.

In the past six months, he'd been quoted, photographed, and interviewed more times than he wanted to think about. He'd never liked the limelight, had always been an intensely private man. He had a few demons of his own, secrets he'd rather keep hidden, but hell, who didn't. Reed would have preferred to go about his job without the inconvenience of fame. He hated all the attention, especially from those reporters who seemed fascinated with his past, who had taken it upon themselves to find out every little piece of information about him and to tell the world what made Detective Pierce Reed tick. As if they had any idea. He picked up the letter and envelope with a handkerchief, then found a plastic bag in his desk drawer. Carefully, he slipped the envelope and note into the bag. "I think it's nothing, but you never know. Better keep it in case it ends up being evidence."

"Evidence of what? That there's another looney on the loose?"

"There's always another looney on the loose. I'll keep it just in case and then send out a BOLO over the local system and through NCIC, just in case any other department in the country has gotten anything like it." He turned to his computer, accessed the National Crime Information Center run by the FBI. "Maybe we'll get lucky," he said to Morrisette. "In the meantime, I think I'll take a break and walk over to the cemetery."

"You think you'll find something?"

"Nah. Not really. But you never know." He stuffed his arms through the sleeves of his jacket. "As I said, it's probably just a crank. Someone getting his jollies by making a vague threat against the department."

"Not the department. This particular crazy has zeroed in on you." Sylvie was adjusting her shoulder holster. "I'm coming with you."

He didn't argue. It would have been useless. Sylvie was the kind of cop who followed her instincts and bent the rules—the kind of hardheaded woman who couldn't be talked out of a decision once she'd made it. He slid the plastic bag into a file drawer.

They walked outside through a side door and the

winter wind slapped Reed hard on the face. The weather, usually mild in December, had a definite bite to it, the product of a cold snap that was roaring down the East Coast and threatening crops as far south as Florida. Morrisette, fighting the stiff breeze, managed to light a cigarette as they walked the few blocks past Columbia Square. Colonial Cemetery, Savannah's oldest, was the final resting place to over seven hundred victims of the nineteenth century yellow fever epidemic and was the site of far too many duels in centuries past. General Sherman had used this plot of land in the middle of Savannah as a campground during the Civil War, or, as many of the locals referred to it, the War of Northern Aggression. Shade trees, now barren of leaves, seemed to shiver in the wind, and dry leaves skated down the pathways that cut through the ancient gravestones and historic markers where so many people believed demons resided.

It was all bunk as far as Reed was concerned. And this morning, this burial place seemed as much a park as a graveyard even though dark, thick-bellied clouds scudded overhead.

Only a few pedestrians wandered through the tombstones and nothing about them looked suspicious. An elderly couple held gloved hands as they read the markers, three teenagers who probably should have been in school smoked and clustered together as they whispered among themselves, and a middle-aged woman bundled in ski cap, parka and wool gloves was walking a scrap of a dog wearing a natty little sweater and pulling on its leash as it tried to sniff every old tombstone. No one seemed to be lurking and watching, no graves appeared disturbed, no cars with tinted windows rolled slowly past.

"Don't we have better things to do?" Sylvie asked, struggling to keep her cigarette lit. She drew hard on the filter tip.

"You'd think." Still, Reed scanned the dried grass and weathered grave markers. He thought of the cases that he was working on. One was domestic violence, pure and simple. A wife of twenty years finally had decided enough was enough and before suffering another black eye or cracked rib had shot her husband point-blank while he slept. Her attorney was crying self-defense and it was up to Reed to prove otherwise—which wasn't that hard, but didn't make him feel good. Another case involved a murder-suicide pact between lovers, in this case a couple of gay boys, one seventeen, the other almost twenty. The trigger man, the younger of the two, was still hanging on to life in the hospital. If and when he got off the ventilator and came to, he'd find himself looking at a murder charge. The third recent homicide case wasn't as defined. A body pulled out of the Savannah River two days before. No ID and not much left of her. Just another Jane Doe. No one seemed to be looking for her, no missing persons reports were on file for a black woman whom, the ME thought, was around thirty years old, had type O-positive blood, extensive dental work, and had borne at least one child.

Yeah, he did have better things to do. But as his gaze swept the cemetery that was the final resting place of

Savannahians who died two hundred and fifty years ago, a graveyard where it was rumored ghosts resided, he had the unnerving sensation that the crank letter wasn't the last he'd hear from its author.

One, two, the first few. Hear them cry, listen to them die.

What the hell did that mean?

No doubt, he'd soon find out.

"I seen him," Billy Dean Delacroix insisted excitedly, the pimples on his boyish face a brighter red in the cold wind. At fifteen he was a pistol. "That ol' buck started up over ta the hill. But he won't get far. I nailed him, I did, he'll be droppin' soon. I seen his white tail a-flashin', come on, Pres!" Billy Dean took off at a dead run, galloping through the undergrowth with the easy gait of a track star, his pappy's big-eared dog streaking beside him.

Prescott Jones, Billy's second cousin, older by six months and heavier by fifty or sixty pounds, struggled to keep up. Berry vines pulled at his old jeans, ripping at the denim while branches scratched his face, nearly knocking off his glasses as he dashed along the old deer trail that wound along the banks of Bear Creek. A raccoon, peering from behind his dark mask, waddled quickly out of the way and deep into the bracken. Overhead, a hawk slowly circled.

Prescott was panting by the time he reached the crest of the hill, sweating beneath his hunting jacket and his pa's old thermal shirt. Billy Dean, dressed head to toe in camouflage, was nowhere to be seen.

Nor was the ugly red-coated dog.

"Son of a bitch," Prescott muttered, gasping for breath. Sometimes Billy Dean could be such a bastard, running off ahead and all. He wondered if Billy had even hit the buck hard, probably just clipped him and they'd be chasing the wounded sumbitch for miles.

Prescott caught sight of some red spots on the dried grass near the trail, enough to change his mind and make him think that the deer had been wounded badly. Good. He couldn't handle much more of this fast-assed traipsing through the wilderness. Truth to tell, Prescott enjoyed everything about hunting but the actual tracking of the prey. Oh, he liked to shoot a squirrel, buck or fox as much as the next guy. Even fantasized about killing himself a bear or a gator and having it stuffed, but all in all, hunting was a lot of work and he much preferred the beer, weed and a bit of crank now and again that went along with the actual hunt. He liked campfires and making up stories about whores and big game, all the while getting high. The hunting itself, the tracking game, the wounding game, the gutting game and the hauling out of the game was kind of a pain.

"Hey! Over here! Pres! C'mon. Just over the ridge . . . What the hell?" Billy's voice came from down in a holler, one deep in shadow. Prescott followed the sound, noticed a few more splashes of fresh blood on the bent grass and curled up leaves on his way down an overgrown trail. Through tall pines and scrub oak, he eased his way down. The path was steep, cut into the side of a cliff, and precipitous enough that his hunting boots slid a time or two. Prescott's heart was thumping.

Holding on to his pa's hunting rifle with one sweaty hand, Prescott feared he might pitch himself over the cliff. But all along the way down he spied a smattering of blood. Maybe Billy hadn't lied, after all. Just because the boy was known for telling whoppers didn't mean he hadn't actually struck the whitetail in a vital organ.

Prescott eased his bulk through a thicket of saplings to a small patch of dead grass, a shadowy clearing in this dark ravine. Ringed by scraggly woods, the clearing saw very little sunlight.

Billy Dean was standing to one side of a snag that bore the charred bark of a tree hit by lightning. In front of the dead tree and Billy Dean was a thick mound. At first, Prescott thought it was the lifeless buck, but as he got closer he could see that he was wrong. Dead wrong. Billy Dean was scratching the side of his face nervously while staring down at a pile of dirt and rocks that was about seven or eight feet long and over two feet wide. Billy's dad's old dog was whining and pacing around the edge of the neat, unnatural heap.

"What is it? What you got there?" Prescott asked and noticed that the red dog held his nose up, into the wind.

"It's a grave."

"What you say?"

"A grave, man, look. And it's big enough for a human."

"No way . . ." As Prescott, breathing hard, walked closer, he saw that Billy Dean was right.

The dog whimpered, his fur shivering.

Prescott didn't like the looks of it. A grave out here in

the woods near Blood Mountain. No, he didn't like it at all. "What d' ya think we should do?"

"Dunno."

"Dig it up?"

"Maybe." Billy Dean nudged a pile of soft dirt with the barrel of his gun, something his daddy would skin him alive for if he ever caught him.

The hound was still acting weird. Jumpy. Whining and staring across the clearing. "Oh, shit."

"What?"

Billy Dean leaned down. "There's somethin' here. A ring . . . hell, yes, it's a weddin' band." He reached down and picked up a gold band with several stones. Billy wiped it on his pants and a diamond, a big sucker, winked in the poor light. Smaller red gems glittered around the diamond as the nervous old dog whined. "Jesus. Look at the size of it. Must be worth somethin'." Squinting, he studied the inside of the band. "It's got something etched into it. Listen to this: To Barbara. Love forever. Then there's a date."

"Whose is it?"

"Someone named Barbara."

"Duh! I *know* that." Sometimes Billy Dean could be so damned dense. He might be able to run like a gazelle, but Prescott figured he weren't no smarter than one of his daddy's half-breed dogs. "But Barbara who? And why's it here?"

"Who cares? Too bad, though. The inscription prob'ly means it's not worth as much."

"So what? You ain't thinkin' of stealin' it." But Prescott knew better. Billy Dean had a larcenous bent

24

to him—not that he was bad, just poor and sick to the back teeth of never havin' anything. The dog let out a low growl. Lowered his head. Prescott saw the reddish hackles rise.

"I'm not stealin' nothin'. I just found it. Tha's all." Billy pocketed the ring, then before Prescott could say anything else, let out a whoop. "Looka there. Now don't tell me this ain't my lucky day. There's the buck! Shit-o-day! Look at him. It's a damned four-point!"

Sure as shootin', the deer had dropped and breathed his last damned breath just on the other side of a pair of knotty oaks. Billy Dean had poked it to make sure it was really dead, and satisfied, was already unsheathing his knife, but Prescott didn't help. He felt a chill as cold as the devil's piss. It skittered down his spine from the base of his skull clean to his tailbone and it had nothin' to do with the wind whippin' and screamin' down the holler.

No, it was somethin' more.

A feeling, the kind that warned him of danger.

Just like ol' Red, the hound.

Prescott glanced over his shoulder, his eyes squinting behind the smudged lenses of his glasses.

Was someone watching them?

Demon eyes peering through the dark foliage near the abandoned old logging road?

Why did the damned dog keep watch, staring at the darkest part of the forest?

The spit dried in Prescott's mouth. He suddenly wanted to pee. Bad. "I think we best git outta here."

"Why?" Billy Dean was already on one knee, slitting

the buck's belly from sternum to his privates.

The dog growled again.

Low.

A warning.

"I got me a buck to gut," Billy said, "then I figure we'll dig up the grave."

"What? No way!"

"Hey, there might be more where that there ring came from."

"Maybe we should call the police."

"Why?"

"Cuz there's somethin' evil here," Prescott whispered, edgy as he eyed the other side of the clearing where the brush was dense and dusky. The dog showed his teeth and began to circle, his eyes never moving from the shadowy trees. Prescott's insides nearly turned to water. "It's somethin' we don't want to mess with."

"Speak fer yerself. I ain't goin' nowhere till I field dress this sumbitch, dig up the grave and see what's what. Maybe there's some more damned jewels—some kinda treasure."

"Why would there be?"

"Who knows?" Billy Dean rocked back on the worn heels of his boots and squinted one eye up at the sky as if to see better.

Dark clouds shifted. An omen if ever there was one.

Billy didn't seem to see it that way. "I figure this here is God payin' me back fer all the times He shit on me." Billy turned back to his work. He'd already sliced the four-point's hide just far enough not to puncture any innards. The guts rolled out on the ground in one glistening lump. "I know, I know I shouldn't talk that way about the Lord, but He never did much fer me. Till now. I figure He finally's squarin' things up a bit." Shoulders hunched, Billy worked at cutting the buck's bowel and tying it off.

"I don't reckon so," Prescott argued, fear making his skin crawl as stubborn Billy worked. "Come on, Billy Dean. We need to get out of here. Now."

"I'm not leavin' my kill. And I'm diggin' up the damned grave. What's got into you?" Billy stood, then turned, still holding his hunting knife in his left hand, blood dripping from the blade and staining his fingers. The skin across his face appeared more mottled than ever as he glared at his cousin. "Ye're scared, ain't cha? Jesus H. Christ." His voice was filled with disgust. Billy's eyes moved to the shaded woods. "What is it? What'd you see?"

"Nothin.' I ain't seen nothin', but that don't mean there ain't somethin' there." Prescott caught a movement, shadow on shadow, a bit of leaf twisting unnaturally in the wind. The dog's growl was low enough to seem unworldly. "Come on," Prescott ordered, starting back up the trail at a jog. "We need to get goin'," he yelled over his shoulder. "Now!" He didn't stop to see if Billy Dean was following him, just took off as fast as he could, running hard up the trail. The dog streaked past him on the fly, tail between his legs.

Damn it all to hell, Billy Dean had better come along. No deer or no damned ring was worth dealin' with the pure evil Prescott sensed had trod through this stretch of backwoods. The path was steep, his feet unsteady, his lungs threatening to give out as he breathed hard enough to fog his glasses. Sweat poured down his face, into his eyes, under his collar. *God, please help me git outta here alive and don't blame me for Billy Dean's attitude. He's an idiot, God, please* . . . His lungs were on fire, his heart pumping crazily as he stumbled past a fork in the path and around a steep switchback. This was the right way. Or was it? Had he passed that split oak—

Something moved . . . shifting in the hazy light filtering through the trees. Jesus! Whatever it was, slid through the undergrowth. A person? A dark figure. A man? Or the embodiment of Satan himself? Prescott's heart froze. He spun around too quickly, twisting his ankle.

Pain splintered up his leg.

Oh, shit! Prescott let out a squeal, then bit his tongue. He didn't want Lucifer to find him.

Run! Now!

He had to hide. He bolted. Up. Down. Wherever the trail led while the pain in his leg shrieked through his body.

Don't think about the pain. Don't think about Billy Dean. Just get away. Fast!

The forest, bracken, scraggly trees, scrub bush flashed by in a blur.

From the trail ahead the dog let out a frightened, painful yelp. The cry echoed through the canyons.

And then there was silence.

Deadly, empty silence.

Oh, God. Prescott felt a fear as deep as he'd ever known.

He froze, his ankle screaming in agony. He strained to see through the foggy, smeared lenses. Where was the dog? Where the hell was the damned dog? And the dark figure? Holy shit, where had that devil gone? Maybe it had all been a figment of his imagination. That was it. A trick of gloomy light in shadows? And where had it been—the black image? Higher on the ridge, or had he been turned around with the switch-backs and offshoots on the trail? He couldn't think, could barely breathe.

Oh, God, oh, God, oh, God!

He had to keep moving!

Deep in his boot, his ankle throbbed. Sweat covered his body. He was half blind. The crest of the ridge seemed hundreds of feet above him, the ravine abutting the trail a deep, dark abyss. How would he ever make it out of here? Why hadn't he tried to follow that damned old logging road? If only Billy Dean would show up and help him and . . .

Snap!

Somewhere nearby a twig broke.

He froze.

His pulse throbbed in his ears.

God help me.

Fear sliced through his heart.

Did he hear someone behind him? Footsteps on the blanket of dry leaves?

Prescott spun.

Again too fast.

Agony ripped through his ankle and it buckled.

Pebbles on the path skittered beneath his feet as he slipped toward the edge of the ravine. His arms waved frantically, but it was too late. He lost what frail footing he had. Screaming, he scrabbled wildly in the air, catching only a glimpse of a shadowy, tall man in the trees as he fell backward, pitching headfirst over the edge.

CHAPTER 2

"Come on, Nikki, give it up. Let's go out for a few drinks." Trina Boudine paused at the edge of Nikki Gillette's cubicle, stretching her model-slim black frame over the edge that separated their desks. "You know what they say about all work and no play."

"I've heard. But I don't know who 'they' are, and they probably weren't concerned about paying the rent." She glanced up at Trina. "And, just in case you haven't noticed, I'm not Johnny, and I'm not a boy."

"Details, details." Trina's dark eyes flashed as she smiled and showed off white teeth that were crooked enough to be interesting. She flipped a sleek wrist where half a dozen copper bracelets jangled. "What're you working on that's so damned intriguing? Last I heard you were doing a series on the budget cuts to the school district." She clucked her tongue. "Mighty fascinatin' stuff, that."

"Okay, okay, you've made your point." Nikki rolled

her chair away from her computer and hoped Trina didn't catch any of the text she'd written as her story had nothing to do with money, budget cuts, or public outcry over lack of school funding. Instead, she was writing another crime piece, about a woman fished out of the river two days earlier. It wasn't really her story. Norm Metzger had been given that assignment, but Nikki couldn't help herself. Crime fascinated her. It always had and it had nothing, not one little thing to do with the fact that her father was Judge Ronald "Big Ron" Gillette. She frowned at the thought of her father, then glanced up at Trina. "Okay, so I'll meet you. When and where?"

"Sevenish for drinks and hors d'oeuvres at Bridges. Aimee and Dana will be there. We're celebrating. Aimee's divorce and Dana's engagement. Kind of both ends of the romance spectrum."

"Sounds fun," Nikki muttered sarcastically.

"Well, you can see why we need a few more people. I'm hoping maybe Ned, Carl and Joanna can join us—you know, make it a party. Aimee is having some trouble getting enthusiastic about Dana's engagement, but Dana wants to celebrate."

"Even though she was married twice before?"

"You know what they say—"

"Third time's a charm, yeah, yeah. You're just full of pearls of wisdom today, aren't you?"

"Always." Trina's phone rang and she rolled her eyes as Nikki's computer screen flipped crazily.

"This damned thing," Nikki growled. "I thought Kevin was going to fix it." Kevin Deeter was the

31

editor's nephew, a part-time student and full-time electronic whiz whose sole job at the *Sentinel* was to keep all the electronics working. A loner who told weird jokes, he kept mostly to himself. Which was a blessing. She frantically punched the escape key, then rebooted and the computer came back to life.

"Kevin was by earlier."

"Did he do anything to the computer?"

"Sorry. I was busy. Didn't notice."

"Great," Nikki mumbled testily. She didn't really like Kevin, but tolerated him for his computer skills. It certainly wasn't for his sense of humor. "I swear, he messes up more than he fixes. Damn."

Trina gave a quick shake of her head, a warning that Nikki caught. From the corner of her eye Nikki spied Kevin lurking by the coatrack, earphones plugged into his cassette recorder. He probably hadn't heard her and even if he did, he needed to know that he was supposed to fix things, not make them worse. And what was with the earphones? If Tom Fink caught anyone else tuned into headphones while on the job, that employee would be out on his ass.

"I'm going to tell him to leave my equipment alone unless I'm here," Nikki vowed.

"Sure you are." Trina's phone jangled for the third time. "Duty calls." Sliding her desk chair into the booth, she answered, *"Savannah Sentinel,* Human Interest. This is Trina."

Nikki rolled her chair closer to her computer monitor. She'd been surfing the Internet, getting as much information as was available on the Jane Doe who had been found tethered to heavy barbells at the bottom of the river. Scuba divers had found her remains and the police had been called in. Detective Pierce Reed was in charge of the investigation. As usual, he had "no comment" about the case and no amount of calling on her part had even gotten her connected to the reclusive investigator.

She clicked on a picture of Reed. He looked as if he might have done time as the Marlboro man. Tall and rangy, with a craggy but handsome face and eyes that didn't miss much. She'd discovered that he was single and had told herself it was necessary to know as much as she could about him, including his marital status.

She'd also found out that he had worked for the Savannah Police Department once before, over twelve years ago and only for a short while, before he'd moved to the West Coast and joined the San Francisco Police Department where he'd eventually become an investigator.

From there on his past was a little murky, but from what she could piece together she figured that Reed had landed himself in some kind of hot water. Major trouble. A woman had been killed while he'd had her apartment under surveillance. From what Nikki could discern, Reed had seen the murder, hadn't been able to save the woman's life, nor ever capture the killer. Reed had been reprimanded, though not stripped of his badge. Nonetheless, he'd resigned and shortly thereafter, he'd returned to Savannah.

The rest, as they say, was history. Capped in the form of the Montgomery murders.

While the strains of some easy listening music filtered through the speakers set high overhead in this warehouse-turned-office building, she tapped a pencil on her desk and scowled at the image of Pierce Reed, a photograph taken thirteen years earlier when he'd still been a fresh-faced cop in Savannah. In his late twenties, but still serious, he nearly glared into the camera. She wondered what drove the man. Why uproot himself and move to California, only to return here over a decade later? Why not marry? Why no children?

She'd love to do a story on Reed and was working on an angle to sell to her editor. Something along the lines of the man behind the myth, a personal look into one of Savannah's finest . . .

Her phone jangled and she cut off speculation about the elusive detective.

"*Savannah Sentinel*," she said automatically, her attention focused on the caller. "Nikki Gillette."

"Hi, Nikki, this is Dr. Francis with the Savannah School Board. You called earlier?"

"Yes, I did," Nikki said quickly as she visualized the woman—tall, imposing, never a hair out of place, an African-American woman who had made good and at forty-two held a major position of authority in her hometown. "Thanks for calling. I'd like to interview you on the recent budget cuts," Nikki said and clicked over to her notes on the computer while holding the receiver between her shoulder and ear. "There're rumors that some of the smaller neighborhood elementary schools are going to be closed."

"Temporarily. And we prefer to call it merging.

Taking two or three schools and blending them together for everyone's benefit. We maximize our talent that way, the students are exposed to a lot of different teachers with innovative ideas, their educational experience is broadened."

"Even if they're bused out of their neighborhoods, mainly the poorer neighborhoods, and shuttled across town?"

"So that they ultimately benefit," Dr. Francis cut in with her smooth, dulcet voice. A native Savannahian, her accent was subtle and refined. She'd been a poor girl who had worked her way through the school system here, who had found scholarships, grants and work study programs to propel her through undergraduate school and a doctoral program while her single mother held down two menial jobs and raised a total of six kids. Dr. Francis was the epitome of the American dream, a philanthropist, never married, with no children, but a woman with foresight who actually seemed to care about all of the kids in Savannah. So why did Nikki have the feeling that she'd somehow sold out? Dr. Francis rambled on and on about serving the needs of the students and the community and Nikki took notes, reminding herself not to be so cynical. Maybe the woman really believed the garbage she was peddling. *And maybe it's not garbage. Just because they're closing down a school you attended years ago, doesn't make it necessarily bad.*

Nikki clicked her pen and listened, agreed to meet with Dr. Francis later in the week and hung up thinking that the story wasn't exactly Pulitzer Prize material, not even Nikki's particular cup of tea, but it might have merit and was certainly newsworthy in its own way. No, it wouldn't spark a byline in a bigger newspaper, wouldn't propel Nikki Gillette to a job at the *New York Times*, or *Chicago Tribune*, or *San Francisco Herald*, but it would help pay the bills for the month and maybe she'd learn something.

Maybe.

In the meantime she wouldn't give up on the Jane Doe pulled from the river, nor would she put her story on Detective Pierce Reed on the back burner. Nope, there was something there, something newsworthy. She could feel it. She just had to find out what it was. To do that, she needed to interview Reed, somehow get close to him.

Which was about as likely as cozying up to a porcupine. The man was bristly, grumpy and sometimes just damned rude. Which was probably why she couldn't just drop her idea about a piece on him. He was a challenge. And Nikki Gillette had never backed down from one. Never. Not the daughter of the Honorable Ron Gillette.

Somehow, some way, Nikki would ferret out everything there was to know about Detective Pierce Reed. Maybe she'd come up dry, with nothing of interest. Maybe Reed was about as interesting as a dirty gym sock. She smiled. No way. In her gut, she sensed there was a story around the elusive cop. She'd just have to uncover it, no matter how many layers deep Reed had covered it.

The life-flight chopper took off in a noisy whir of rotors as it lifted from the floor of the ravine. In a rush of winter air, it scaled the forested cliffs before disappearing over a hill. On the trail halfway up the cliff face, Detective Davis McFee turned his gaze on the young boy shivering before him. The kid was scared as hell, that much was certain, but other than the older boy might not survive, McFee didn't know much.

McFee's partner, Bud Ellis, took over. "Let's go over this again, Billy Dean. You were out hunting and something spooked your friend."

"My cousin—er, second cousin."

"Prescott Jones?"

"Yeah. Me 'n him hang out a lot."

"It's not huntin' season."

"Yeah." The pimple-faced kid had enough smarts to look down at the ground and dig his toe into the soft earth.

Jones's story was that he and his cousin had been tracking a deer, following the wounded buck down into the ravine, stumbled upon what looked like a grave and something had spooked the Jones kid. Scared spitless, he'd scrambled up the hill along with Billy Dean's dog, and by the time Billy Dean had climbed to this section of the trail, he'd discovered that his cousin had fallen down a steep precipice on the switchback.

In the fall, Jones had cracked his skull, broken three ribs and splintered his right forearm. He'd also scratched the hell out of his face and shattered his glasses. The EMT in the chopper wasn't sure, but the kid could also have a punctured spleen or some other internal injury, no doubt a concussion. McFee wasn't certain the older boy hadn't been pushed down. Maybe the two boys got into a fight, maybe they were just squirreling around, but somehow Prescott Jones had ended up fifty feet below and beat to crap.

Ellis prompted, "So you was chasin' him up the hill?"

"No, sir. I was *followin'* him and old Red, wherever the hell that mutt is. Anyway, when I got ta here, I seen him down there." He pointed down the steep hillside, into the woods below. "I couldn't get to him so I kept runnin' to the truck. His pa's got a cell phone in there and had to drive a mile for reception but then I called you all right quick. That's what happened. I swear." The kid's teeth were chattering from the cold or fear or both.

"And you found a grave down at the bottom of the holler?" Ellis asked.

"Yes, sir." Billy Dean nodded so furiously that a lock of his dirty blond hair flopped up and down between his eyebrows.

"Let's take a look-see." Ellis cast a glance at McFee and they followed the boy to the bottom of the trail where, on one side of the clearing was a gutted buck, his innards spilled onto the ground, and, nearby, just as the kid had sworn, was a mound of fresh earth, appearing for all it was worth like a grave. McFee didn't like the looks of it. He pulled out his can of tobacco and stuffed a wad near his gum. What the hell was beneath the surface? Maybe another dead deer. Maybe nothing. Maybe trash . . . though usually trash was left strewn about without much care. This was a pit that was covered, but the earth hadn't been camouflaged with leaves or sticks or foliage to hide it. Aside from the fact that the grave, if that's what it was, was tucked deep into this ravine, whoever had buried something here had left it visible to anyone who passed.

It was odd. Damned odd. "Let's see what's in there," he said to Ellis.

"Shouldn't we call the sheriff? Maybe we need a crime scene unit."

"For what crime?" McFee asked. "Who knows what's inside. We dig it up and find nothin', then what? We've called everyone out here on a wild goose chase."

"Tell ya what. I'll go up and get the shovel and make a call to the department."

"You do that. Billy Dean, here, will keep me company, won't ya, boy?"

The kid looked about to argue, but changed his mind. "Yessir."

"Good. Man, it's cold down here." McFee rubbed his arms and looked up at the sky. Gray clouds threatened rain. As Ellis hurried up the trail, McFee took out his knife and carefully moved some of the dirt to one side. The kid fidgeted and McFee guessed he knew more than what he was saying. "You ever been up here before?"

"Yep."

"Ya have?"

"Well, not right here, but around."

"You been in this holler?"

"Once. A month or so ago."

39

"You see this grave then?"

"No, sir, it weren't here."

That much McFee believed. The earth was too fresh, like turned sod in a new field. Not quite the right color of the surrounding dirt, not trampled by animals or packed by rain. There had been a downpour two days ago. Torrential. Enough to flatten this mound. But it hadn't. Because whatever was beneath the earth was fresh. McFee scraped again with his knife. He was square in the middle of the mound, centered so he wouldn't miss whatever was below. But as he dug, making a small hole, his blade went deep, deeper than the shaft of his knife, deep enough that he had to lean over and place a knee on the dirt. Deeper and deeper while the kid shifted his weight from one foot to the other, ran the back of his hand under his runny nose and jangled the keys in one pocket.

"Your dog the kind that runs off?"

"What? No, sir. Old Red, he don't go far."

"Where you reckon he is?"

"Don't know." His eyebrows pulled together in a scowl and his lips turned in on themselves as if he were worried. He bit at his lower lip and sniffed. "Pa'll skin me alive if somethin' happened to him."

"No reason to borrow trouble," McFee said. He felt certain they'd found enough as it was.

Reed's stomach growled. Acid burned up his esophagus. He glanced at his watch and realized he'd been going through paperwork, taking calls, answering E-mail and generally catching up ever since he and Morrisette had returned from the cemetery this morning. Breakfast had been coffee, lunch nonexistent and he'd been up since six A.M. It was now two forty-five. Time for a break. He rolled his neck around, trying to crack it and break up the tension in his shoulder muscles. How long had it been since he'd been to the gym and worked out. A week? Ten days? Hell, maybe longer. Tonight. No matter what came up, he'd throw on his sweats and trek over to the old athletic club where boxers sparred, weights clanged and the smell of musk and sweat wafted to the old rafters. It wasn't a typical today type club with fancy computer-linked treadmills and stair-step machines that calculated heart rate, calories burned and distance traveled. Nope. This was old school. Weights, weights and more weights. If you wanted to run, you jogged. If you need an upper body workout, you tackled a big bag, throwing punches to get rid of your aggression, or for faster, quicker movements, you worked with a sparring bag.

The real macho types could don gloves and mouthpieces and go at it in the ring while the other members of the gym looked on and placed a side wager or two. Not that it was legal, but then, what was? Reed and a few others in the department chose not to see the bets going down. He imagined drug deals were transacted on those cracked concrete floors, or behind a bank of battered lockers, but he hadn't witnessed money exchanged for meth, coke or steroids. So far. He hoped he never did.

Stretching in his chair, he considered the note he'd received this morning. The letter was probably mailed from another nutcase getting his rocks off by trying to rattle the department and get a little fame for himself. The envelope had been mailed to him as he was an easy target, the most high profile detective in the department compliments of the Montgomery case a few months ago.

Which galled him.

He reached into his top drawer, found a bottle of antacid and popped two with a swig of leftover coffee just as the phone rang for what had to have been the hundredth time today. He swung the receiver to his ear. "Detective Reed."

"Sheriff Baldwin, Lumpkin County."

Reed straightened. Not a usual call. Lumpkin County was over three hundred miles north. But familiar to him. Too familiar. "What can I do for you, Sheriff?"

"I think ya need to come up here straightaway."

"Me?" Reed asked, his stomach knotting the way it always did when he sensed something wasn't right.

"I think it would be best."

"Why's that?"

"Two boys were out huntin' with their dog, up near Blood Mountain. One boy, Billy Dean Delacroix, he got lucky and wounded a buck. The kids took off after him and followed his trail into a ravine. Found the buck dead at the edge of a clearing. And that's not all. They think they stumbled onto some kind of grave cuz of the fresh turned earth and their old hound was going apeshit. One kid, Billy Dean's cousin, Prescott Jones, got spooked and ran, said there was the devil there or somethin' and hightailed it the way they came in. Billy

Dean was pissed, thought his cousin was imaginin' things, but a few minutes later, he gets to feeling jumpy and takes off after Prescott. Just as Billy Dean's comin' over a rise, he hears a scream that scares the liver out of him. He rounds a corner and sees the Jones boy doin' a header off the cliff. Now, it's fifty feet down and there's no way to reach him, so Billy Dean, he runs to his daddy's pickup and calls for help on the cell phone—which doesn't work so hot up in the mountains. He has to drive a ways before the call actually connects."

"Jesus." Reed was doodling, writing down the kids' names on a pad, hoping the sheriff would get to the point.

"The way we figure it, the two kids were out there where they shouldn't be, probably high on somethin', and they either had an accident or one kid pushed the other." He hesitated, sounded as if he were drawing hard on a cigarette. Reed waited. Still didn't know why the sheriff had called him.

"Trouble was, it was just as the boy said. A grave was down in the holler, fancy coffin and all."

"Coffin?"

"Yep, someone went to the trouble of buryin' the bodies in a rosewood box."

"Bodies? As in more than one?"

"Ye–ep. Two, as a matter of fact. One fresh, one not so . . . The reason I'm callin' you is that we think you might know one of the victims."

"Me? Why?" Every muscle in Reed's body tensed. He quit doodling.

"We found your name in the coffin."

"What? My name?" Was the man insane? His name on the inside of the coffin? What did that mean? "*In* the coffin?"

"That's right. A note addressed to you. Along with a small microphone."

"Sheriff, hold on a minute. There was a note for me and a microphone *inside* a coffin that held two bodies up in the woods three hundred miles from Savannah?"

"You got it. A hole was bored into the box and the mike placed in a corner, near the vic's head, the note was placed at the foot, tucked into the lining."

"Any ID on the victims?" Reed's mind spun. First, the weird note this morning and then this bizarre news about bodies in Lumpkin County, the part of Georgia where he'd grown up—a place he'd rather forget.

"Both Jane Does. Maybe you should just come on up and see for yourself. I've already worked it out with the state police. They'll fly you up in a chopper. The major crime team is already up there, preserving the site, but seein' as your name was on the note, I really think you should take a look at this."

Reed was already reaching for his jacket.

Around four o'clock, Trina said, "Something major is going on up in Lumpkin County." She was on her way back from the soda machine, a sweating bottle of Diet Coke swinging from her fingers. An instrumental rendition of a Patti Page tune wafted from hidden speakers in the offices of the *Savannah Sentinel* as Nikki tried to put an interesting spin on her dry story about the school board.

"How major?" Nikki looked up from her computer monitor. She was interested in anything having to do with news even though Lumpkin County was a long way north of Atlanta, not far from the Carolina border.

Trina's forehead furrowed a bit. "I don't know. But big enough to warrant the interest of the *Sentinel*."

"Really?" Nikki was all ears.

"All I know is that Metzger was so excited, he almost forgot to gloat."

Norman Metzger was the *Sentinel*'s crime reporter. His byline accompanied nearly every story having any-thing to do with the Savannah Police Department or other police agencies in the state. It wasn't that he was such a bad guy, just inefficient in Nikki's mind and, as Trina had indicated, had a high and extremely inflated opinion of himself. "He was grabbing his jacket and barking orders to the photographer, telling Jim to get a move on.

"When I asked him 'Where's the fire?' he threw me a grin that the Cheshire Cat would have killed for and just said 'Dahlonega.' " Trina twisted off the cap from her Diet Coke and her eyebrows elevated over eyes that were charged with fire. "I figured you'd want to know."

"You figured right." Nikki scooted her chair back, looked down the hall and saw Metzger plop a wool cap on his head and jangle his keys in the pocket of his jacket. He tossed Nikki a glance down the hallway, caught her staring and gave her a mock salute as he winked at her.

Creep.

He knew she wanted his job and couldn't help but rub

it in every chance he got.

Her jaw tightened as she rolled her chair back to her desk.

"Don't let him get to you." Obviously, Trina had caught the entire exchange.

"With Metzger, it's impossible."

"Nah, it isn't. Don't play his game. Let it slide. Water off a duck's back."

"If you say so." Nikki's mind was spinning. What was it that was so important up in the north Georgia mountains? "Thanks for the tip," she said to Trina. "I owe ya one."

"Oh, you probably owe me a dozen or more, but who's counting. You can buy me a drink tonight. Remember, whatever this is, you're not bagging out on us. I'm not going to be the only piece of sanity between Dana's elation and Aimee's despair. No way, honey. You're showin' up."

"Promise."

"Yeah, yeah, I know." Trina slid into her chair and disappeared behind the partition just as her phone began to jingle. "*Savannah Sentinel,* this is Trina Boudine . . ."

Nikki didn't waste a second. She picked up her cell and called a number she knew by heart. Another cell phone. This one belonging to Cliff Siebert who worked in the detective unit of the Savannah Police Department. He made it his business to know what was going on and for some reason, he usually confided in Nikki. Maybe he was interested in her, a thought she harbored but didn't want to acknowledge right now. So far, he'd

46

never really come on to her. Well, not lately. There was a chance he opened up to her because she was Big Ronald Gillette's daughter, but, more likely it was because of a severe case of guilt.

"Hi, it's me," she said brightly when he answered.

He groaned, but it was good-natured. "What do you want?"

"Something's up. Something big if I can judge by the smile on Norm Metzger's face. He's on his way upstate. Dahlonega."

"How'd he find out about that?"

"About what? And I don't know." There was a second's hesitation, just as there always was each time Nikki pried and Detective Siebert struggled with his conscience. "Come on, Cliff. What's happening?"

"You can't find out from that end?" he asked, stalling. As he always did.

"Are you kidding? You know how my boss thinks. Tom's a good ole southern boy, who, beneath his liberal veneer, feels that all women should be a cross between Scarlett O'Hara and Heidi Fleiss."

"Careful now, I'm a good old southern boy, too."

"You know what I mean," she said with a sigh. Cliff was getting on her nerves, but then, he usually did. Always had. Cliff Siebert had been her eldest brother's best friend in high school. Andrew had gone on to Duke University. Cliff had gone through the police academy and had finished college while working at the Savannah Police Department. His family owned property outside of town, three farms that had been in their family for six generations, but Cliff had balked at becoming a farmer. He'd wanted to be a cop from the first time he'd seen a black and white cruiser patrolling the streets of the small town where they'd grown up. The weekend Andrew had died, Cliff was supposed to have visited him but had bagged out at the last minute. He'd been swimming in guilt ever since.

"Metzger really gets under your skin," he said now.

"Amen." Nikki tapped her pencil angrily. She'd had it with men who talked out of both sides of their mouths, the ones who extolled the virtues of the working woman by day, only to pull a Dr. Jekyll and Mr. Hyde routine after quitting time when they expected dinner on the table at six and their wives to act like thousand-dollar call girls—well, after the late night news and latest sports report, of course. Didn't that attitude go out in the fifties? The NINETEEN fifties?

Tom Fink, the *Sentinel*'s editor, could breathe fire, brimstone and right-wing politics all he wanted to from his side of the glass ceiling. But he wasn't going to hold Nikki Gillette back. No way, no how. She planned to bust right through that invisible barricade. The way she figured it, Fink could cut himself a whole new attitude with the shards that flew out as she rocketed past him on her way to the big time. All she needed was the right story. Just one. She sensed that whatever was happening up in Lumpkin County might just be it. "Come on, give. What's going on?"

There was a heavy sigh, a loud creak, as if he'd turned in his chair, and then a lowering of Cliff's voice. "Okay, okay. Listen. All I know is that Pierce Reed roared out of here. Fit to be tied. On his way to the

48

sheriff's department in Lumpkin County, if you can believe that. He left about twenty minutes ago. I don't know what that was about, but I did hear that a kid was life-flighted from the backwoods in that part of the mountains, fell down a cliff or something, and he's on his way to Mason Hospital in Atlanta. I don't know all the details, don't even know the extent of the kid's injuries or how the whole mess is connected to Reed, but from what I can piece together all this came down about half an hour before Reed got the call." He fell silent for a minute. "You know, Nikki. You didn't hear it from me."

"I never do." Nikki glanced at the clock. "Thanks, Cliff," she said, mentally on her way to north Georgia. "I won't forget this."

"Do—forget it. Okay? I didn't tell you anything. If you spout off, it could cost me my job. So, remember, how you found out about this—you picked it up on the police band or something."

"Right."

"And Nikki?"

"Yeah?" She was reaching inside her purse for her keys.

"Say hi to your mom for me."

Nikki stopped cold. Just as she always did when she thought of her mother these days. Her fingers brushed the metal of her car keys and they felt suddenly icy. "I will, Cliff," she promised, then hung up. In her mind's eye she caught a fleeting glimpse of her mother, now frail, unhappily married, dependent upon a big bear of a man who, if he didn't love her, at least wasn't unfaithful. Well, as far as anyone knew. From outward appearances, Judge Ronald Gillette was the epitome of propriety, ever the doting husband to a sickly wife who was often confined to her bedroom.

As Nikki shot to her feet she tried to shake off the sadness that settled like a blanket over her soul whenever she thought of her mother too long.

At the reception desk, she marked herself out for the rest of the day and pushed all thoughts of her family out of her head. Holding her jacket tight around her, she hurried outside where the wind caught in her hair, blowing wild red-blond strands over her eyes and slapping at her face. The day was already dark, twilight pressing in as she dashed across the street to her little hatchback parked beneath a street lamp.

What the devil was Pierce Reed doing in Lumpkin County, so far out of his jurisdiction? It smelled like a story, but she tried not to get her hopes up. Maybe this was all a wild goose chase. Yeah, well, if that was the case, then why was Norm Metzger hot on Reed's trail? No, there was definitely a story there. Ramming her car into gear she sped toward I-16, pushing the speed limit. It would take her at least five hours to get to Dahlonega, and then what? Even if she caught up with Reed, what were the chances that he'd fill her in?

Slim and none.

Nada and zilch.

Unless she found a way to get to the man.

She maneuvered through town to the interstate while half listening to news radio. She also had the police band on and heard about traffic violations and a robbery at a convenience store on the south end of Savannah, but nothing about whatever it was Reed was involved in. Nothing at all.

She passed a semi hauling something flammable and pressed her foot hard on the accelerator. The trucker honked and she gave him a cursory lift of the hand as she flew by like the proverbial bat out of hell. She didn't know what she'd find in Lumpkin County, but she figured it was ten times more interesting than the latest action by the Savannah School Board. Anything surrounding Detective Reed was.

Handsome, stoic, all business, Pierce Reed was a prickly one, a detective who never let anyone too close, a man who totally clammed up when it came to dealing with the press.

But that was about to change.

Reed just didn't know it yet.

"So, this is what we make of it. Whoever brought the coffin up here used this old logging road." Sheriff Baldwin pointed to a fork in the twin ruts and angled the nose of his Jeep to the right. "We figure he probably used a truck with a lift and a winch. I've got a detective already talking to the DMV about possible owners of that kind of truck. We're also lookin' for any that might have been stolen."

"Good idea," Reed said, unbuttoning his jacket. Baldwin was in his late fifties, but as lean as when he'd been a drill sergeant in the army some thirty years earlier. A no-nonsense man with a craggy face, sharp eyes and thick gray moustache, he had the heater cranked up, and it rumbled as it blew hot air onto the windshield and into the interior of the department-issued vehicle. The police band crackled with static and the engine whined as the rig bucked up the hill.

"It's a start. But not much of one. Hell, I've worked for the county for twenty years. Never seen somethin' like this." Baldwin shifted into a lower gear. The Jeep's headlights slashed through the gloom, beams bouncing off dried grass, sparse gravel and the rough trunks of scrub oak and pine. An opossum appeared from beneath a scraggly bush, its eyes shining, then it turned and lumbered awkwardly into the darkness of the surrounding brush.

"I just can't figure why anyone would go to all this trouble."

Neither could Reed. As the Jeep bounced and whined its way through the woods, he glared into the darkness. What the hell was he doing up here, near the little two-bedroom house where he'd been born? How had his name been on a note inside a damned coffin with two bodies *up here?* From the moment Baldwin had called, Reed had thought of nothing else. He'd brooded about it during the helicopter ride, and the sheriff, when Reed had met him at the courthouse, hadn't had enough answers to satisfy him. No one did.

Yet.

They'd been driving nearly forty minutes, leaving the lights of Dahlonega and civilization far behind, when Reed caught his first sight of some kind of illumination through the trees.

Here we go, Reed thought, feeling the usual rush of

adrenaline he always did when coming upon a crime scene.

"We started investigating late this afternoon, but day-light was fadin' fast. The forecast is for rain and we were afraid we might lose a lot of trace evidence if we had a real gully washer, so we hauled in some major equipment ASAP," the sheriff explained, but Reed knew the drill. Had seen it before on major cases.

Other vehicles, vans, SUVs and cruisers were parked at odd angles about a hundred feet from a gate. Head-lights, lanterns, flashlights and the glowing red tips of cigarettes cut through the gloom. Officers from several state and county agencies had already roped off the scene. The back doors of a van were open wide and crime scene investigators had already begun collecting evidence. Detectives and deputies from the county joined with the state police.

Baldwin made a couple of quick introductions, then, as one of his deputies held a fluorescent lantern aloft, he pointed to a rusted gate that consisted of one heavy bar which swung over the dried grass and dirty, sparse gravel, the remains of what had once been a road. "See how the weeds're bent, and the oil drips are visible on the grass?" Reed saw. "And the gate, here"—Baldwin pointed to the rusting bar—"had been chained and locked, but the chain's been cut clean through. Had to be heavy cutters to take care of those links." Reed squatted, bending close to observe the damage. "Who-ever did it was careful to wire the gate shut behind him . . . See, here." He swung his flashlight at a spot in the chain where the links had been severed, then reattached with something akin to coat-hanger wire. The gate had been dusted for prints and an officer was taking tire impressions. Others were scanning the weeds with flashlights and roping off the area to preserve it for morning light when they might be able to find trace evidence.

Cautiously, so as to not disturb the scene, Baldwin led Reed deeper into the woods, up a steep rise and down the other side to a clearing where klieg lights had been set up and more investigators were carefully sifting through the soil, taking samples, using digital cameras, Polaroids and video camcorders to record everything. The wind was cold as it cut through Reed's jacket and there was a threat of rain in the air, but above it all, something else lingered in the atmosphere. Something unnamed. Something dark. Evil. He sensed it. As he did with most murder scenes. Baldwin angled through a copse of spindly trees to a clearing. They passed by a dead deer, its sightless eyes catching in the beam of the flashlight, its innards spilled onto the forest floor. Dark blood pooled and thickened in the grass around the carcass and Reed felt the scavengers hiding in the dark woods. Waiting.

Baldwin came to a shallow grave. Reed's gut clenched as he spied earth piled around a rosewood and brass coffin, the wood blackened and stained, the metal no longer shiny, the lid pried open under the eerie, unnatural illumination from the klieg lights mounted on poles near the scene. Reed stepped closer, every muscle tense.

"Jesus!" Reed's voice was whispery and thin, his

curse more like a prayer. He drew a deep breath. "Why the hell didn't you tell me she was alive when the bastard tossed her inside?" Rage tore through him. "Who in God's name . . ."

Wedged into the stained satin-lined box were two bodies, one nearly hidden by the other. The smell of death, of rotting flesh, was overpowering. The bright lights seemed eerily out of place in these dark woods as they illuminated a ghastly scene. Reed stepped closer, squinting in disgust. The body on the top was that of a naked woman, her skin blue-white with death, bruises discoloring her face, arms and legs where she'd obviously tried to force herself out of this tomb.

For the love of Christ, she'd been buried alive.

He tried not to think of her horror until he studied her face.

Sweet Jesus, no . . . it couldn't be. He thought he might throw up as he looked past the bruises to the fine, cultured features, the hands where manicured nails had now been ripped off, the open, terror-riddled dead eyes of Barbara Jean Marx. "Son of a bitch," he muttered, turning away for a second and drawing in a fresh lungful of air. *Bobbi? No!*

When he turned to face the horror again, he was certain it was she. Naked, long legs bruised, perfect breasts flat against her ribs now as she rested, stripped bare, on the rotting remains of another person. She'd obviously been dead a short while, perhaps less than a day. Blood had run from her ears, and her hands were clenched into bloodied claws as if rigor mortis had set

55

in while she was still trying to scrape her way to freedom.

"Know her?" Baldwin asked.

Reed's insides clenched. His throat closed. He fought the urge to puke. "Yeah," he finally whispered, still disbelieving, his gaze riveted on the dead woman. Dear God. Was it possible? Bobbi? Vibrant, sexy, naughty Bobbi? Time seemed to stand still. The noises of the night faded. Images flashed behind his eyes, hot, erotic pictures of this woman with her sultry brown eyes, hard, well-muscled body, wispy red teddy that showed off large breasts with incredible nipples. She'd mounted him slowly, with narrow-eyed intention, her fingers grazing each of his bare ribs, nails softly raking over his chest as he'd sweated, watching, gasping for breath, his erection hard and aching. God, how he'd wanted her.

Now, staring at her pale, lifeless form, he cleared his throat and forced the sensual thoughts to disappear. They seemed nearly profane at the moment. A muscle worked in his jaw and he felt not only sad and repulsed, but suddenly weary. How had she come to this? Who had done it to her? "Her name is Bobbi Jean. Barbara Jean Marx." His voice was husky and rough, even to his own ears. He hadn't loved her, but still . . .

"How did you know her?" the sheriff asked, and there was just a hint of suspicion in the raise of his eyebrows.

Reed gritted his teeth. Took a deep breath. Felt the eyes of half a dozen cops on him. "Barbara Marx and

I?" He turned away from what had become of her and fought the rage that tore through his soul. "Yeah, I knew her." In the biblical sense. No reason to hide the truth. It was bound to come out now. "A couple of months ago we were lovers."

CHAPTER 3

"The microphone inside the coffin, does it work?"

Oh, yeah, The Survivor thought, *it works just fine. So does this little tape player. That's the beauty of high tech.*

Pierce Reed's voice was coming in with only a little distortion even though he was half a mile away. Higher on a hillside, hidden in the trees, binoculars trained on the spot where klieg lights rained illumination onto the forest floor, he listened, his recorder getting every sound. It was impossible to see much with all the vegetation blocking his view, but he felt a sense of well-being, of retribution nonetheless as he peered through the pine branches.

"We think so. The mike looks new," a male voice finally responded.

"Then the bastard could be listening in right now." Pierce Reed's voice. Even after all the intervening years The Survivor recognized it and the hairs on the back of his neck raised.

"Always that chance," one of the other voices agreed, maybe that redneck of a sheriff. For a few seconds all he heard was background noise, muffled voices. No doubt the police had turned away and were discussing the fact that they were already hunting the surrounding hills, that they had dogs and teams of officers searching through the ravines and ridges. He wasn't worried. Had expected them. But it was time to go.

"You said there was a letter." Reed's voice again.

"Here . . . tucked inside."

There was a pause. Then Reed's voice. "Tick tock, on goes the clock. Two in one, one and two."

The Survivor mouthed the words as Reed spoke them. *Figure it out, bastard.*

"What the hell does that mean?" another voice, the one they'd called Baldwin, demanded.

A thrill slithered down The Survivor's spine.

"Don't know, but I got a similar note this morning at the station."

The Survivor smiled at the note of trepidation in Reed's voice. The cop was worried. Good. *You should be, you pathetic piece of shit. For once, do your damned job!*

"What did that one say?" Baldwin again.

"One, two, the first few. Hear them cry, listen to them die."

That's right.

"Hell. Well, the guy ain't no damned Shakespeare."

The smile fell from The Survivor's face . . . What kind of comment was that?

"But you're sure it's the same guy?"

Of course it is, you insignificant hick!

"Same paper. Same handwriting." Reed again.

Solemn. A thread of anger in his voice. Perfect.

"So we got ourselves a nutcase and he's focused on you."

"Looks as if."

"And it's pretty serious if he killed your girlfriend and dropped her into a coffin that he went to the trouble of digging up. We'd better check the local cemeteries."

"And try to ID the other woman. There might be a link between them."

The Survivor licked his dry lips. Heard the rustle of the wind through the brittle branches overhead. Perhaps he'd given too much away too soon.

"Let's find out."

"Wait a minute." Reed barked out the terse command.

Time was ticking by, precious seconds where those damned curs might locate him, but The Survivor lingered, couldn't resist hearing the rest. Again, he trained his field glasses toward the light. He hoped for a glimpse of Reed, craved the chance to see pain etched upon the cop's face. Imagining Reed bending over, observing his naked lover's features in death's cold detail was sweet, sweet vengeance. His pulse accelerated in anticipation.

"Look at this! The lining's been shredded, and her fingers . . ." His voice shivered in fury and despair.

That's right Reed, she tried to claw her way out. The Survivor felt his blood quicken at the thought. Barbara Jean Marx had gotten what she'd deserved. So would the others.

A dog began baying, his excited howls echoing through the canyon.

He couldn't stay much longer. It wasn't safe. The Survivor loved dragging Reed up here to the back country where the bastard had been born. Now it was time to return to Savannah. . . . Hauling the coffin here had been dangerous; he could have been seen, but it had been worth it, just to rattle Reed. To point the cops in the wrong damned direction. But he hadn't counted on those dumb-ass kids showing up first; that had been a mistake.

He wouldn't make another.

"Why the hell didn't you tell me that she wasn't dead . . . Oh, Christ, you wanted to see my reaction, didn't you? What? You think somehow I was involved in this and that I put my own name on the note and . . ." His voice faded for a second. The Survivor imagined the cop pulling himself together. "Listen to me, you bastard, whoever you are." Now the voice was clear, as if Reed were speaking directly into the microphone. "You're not going to get away with this, you hear? I'll hunt you, you sick bastard. To the ground. You got that? To the damned ground. You'll never rest easy again!"

Oh, no, Reed? The Survivor gathered his pack and began quickly walking along the path toward his truck. *Just watch me.*

The needle on the speedometer slanted well over sixty as Nikki drove steadily north through the night. Her hatchback threatened to spin out on the curves, but she held the wheel steady, zipping through the hills as a thin rain began to fall. Automatically she flipped on the wipers. And noticed she was nearly out of gas.

She had her route planned out and only wished she could zap herself with a magic wand or one of those sci-fi teleporters so she could land in Lumpkin County when Reed arrived at the scene of the crime, which, if she figured right, was a double homicide. She'd caught some information on the police band, but it wasn't enough to piece together. All she knew was that she was heading for an old logging road near Blood Mountain. She'd plugged her laptop computer into the GPS and had found her route, but she needed more information. She'd tried the Lumpkin County Sheriff's Department and, naturally, was told by a recording that it was closed until the next morning. She'd called a couple of contacts she had up here, but nothing had panned out. When she'd dialed Cliff Siebert again, he hadn't picked up. No doubt he was ducking her.

She took a corner a little too fast and her wheels squealed. She really wanted to talk to Detective Pierce Reed himself, but that would be tricky. She'd tried to get close to him during the Montgomery murders, but he'd been reticent—no . . . downright bristly whenever she'd approached him. He had a reputation for not being fond of the press and she didn't blame him after the woman had died during the stakeout. It seemed that even though he'd been cleared of any wrongdoing through the San Francisco Police Department's Internal Affairs Unit, the media had crucified him.

There was a good chance her father knew more about Reed than she did.

Nikki scowled as she dimmed her lights for an approaching car. She didn't like asking "Big Ron"

Gillette for any favors. Never had. Wouldn't do it.

Sure you would, Nikki-girl. You'd do anything for the right story. She could almost hear her older brother taunting her, which was impossible as Andrew had been dead a long time. Her internal temperature seemed to drop as another car whooshed past and her wipers slapped the rain from the windshield.

Andrew, the star athlete.

Andrew, the exceptional student.

Andrew, groomed to follow his illustrious father's footsteps.

Andrew, dead from a fall from a deck thirty feet above the ground.

Andrew, body broken, blood-alcohol level in the stratosphere, traces of ecstasy and cocaine swimming in his veins.

Andrew, a victim of an accident. Or had it been suicide?

Coincidence that only the week before he'd been turned down for law school by Harvard, his father's alma mater.

Nikki set her jaw. Squinted into the night. It had been eight years since her elder brother's death and still it lingered, a dark veil appearing when she least expected it. She shook off the old feelings of disbelief and despair as her little car shot past a milepost sign indicating Dahlonega was still nearly a hundred miles away.

She pulled into the next gas station/mini mart she came across and filled her tank. Inside, the acne-faced kid behind the counter looked about fourteen, but sold

62

the guy in front of her a six-pack as if he'd done it all his short life. As she grabbed a Diet Dr. Pepper from a cooler, she overheard the customer, an unshaven guy in his late sixties with unruly gray eyebrows and a couple of teeth missing say, "What's all the fuss up ta Blood Mountain?"

The kid rang up the sale, snagged the proffered bills and handed out change. "Don't really know that much 'bout it, but a couple of hunters got spooked, one ended up fallin' or bein' pushed down a ravine. Got himself life-flighted to Mason General in Atlanta."

Nikki, edging past the Cheetos, was all ears.

"I heard the police are crawlin' all over the place. That they're findin' graves up there."

The kid wasn't about to show any interest. He lifted a shoulder and handed the customer his change.

"Ye-ep, old Scratch Diggers claims that they've already dug up two bodies."

"What would Scratch know?"

"A lot. His wife works police dispatch."

"Scratch talks too much."

"Fer sure. But he usually gets his facts straight."

Two bodies—maybe more. So what did that have to do with Pierce Reed? Nikki picked up a package of Doritos and a magazine, then perused the pages as if she were interested in the latest celebrity gossip. All the while her ear was trained on the conversation.

But it was over. The old guy was ambling toward the door with its quaint bell and high-tech video camera mounted over the jamb. "See ya later, Woodie. Say hi ta yer folks."

"I will," the kid promised as the bell rang and the customer left.

Nikki made her way to the checkout stand. "Is that true?" she asked, feigning innocence as she searched through her handbag for her wallet. "I couldn't help but overhear what you were talking about. Are there really some bodies buried on Blood Mountain?"

"I don't know. I was watchin' the news a little while ago"—he hitched his chin toward a small black and white TV tucked beneath the counter. The reception was bad, the image of a reality show grainy—"and there was some news about graves being found up there, but the report was, how do they say it, 'unconfirmed by police sources.'" He offered her a country-boy smile and added, "But as my daddy always said, 'where there's smoke, there's fire.'"

"Isn't that the truth?" she agreed as she found a five and he made quick change. "How far is that from here?"

"Hour, maybe an hour and a half," the clerk said as he bagged her items.

And in that time Norm Metzger and half dozen local news teams would beat her to the punch. She climbed into her car and eased onto the highway before gunning it. So the police weren't talking. That wasn't a surprise. Maybe she could get lucky. If Cliff Siebert would only tell her why Pierce Reed had been sent to the scene, then she'd have a new angle, possibly one she could use with Reed. She tapped her fingers on the wheel and bit her lip as she drove. Somehow, she had to get an exclusive with the reticent detective. There had to be a way to get to him. There always was. She just had to figure out how.

"You said you were lovers." Sheriff Baldwin had been leaning over the coffin. His back popped as he straightened. Mist was rising around them, rain threatening, and the cold mountain air seeped into Reed's bones.

"We had been. It was over."

"When?"

"The last time I saw her was a couple of months ago. I broke it off."

Baldwin was interested. He shifted from one foot to the other and in the eerie fake light from the kliegs his eyes narrowed.

"Why's that?" The sheriff cast another look into the coffin. "Good-lookin' woman."

Reed felt a muscle in his jaw jump. "Let's just say it was because of her husband. Jerome Marx. A businessman in Savannah—import/export, I think. He didn't approve."

The sheriff drew air between his teeth. "She was married?"

"She didn't think so. He did. Took offense to my being involved with his wife."

"Don't blame the man," Baldwin muttered. "You didn't know she was hitched?"

"She claimed she was separated, that the divorce was just a formality, was supposed to have been final any time."

"You didn't check? It's all a matter of public record."

65

Those dark eyes drilled into him.

"No."

"You trusted her."

"I never trusted her." But he hadn't been able to resist her. Some men relied on booze to get them through. Others used drugs. Or cigarettes. Pierce Reed's Achilles' heel was women. Usually the wrong kind. Always had been, probably always would be. He glanced down at Bobbi and his stomach soured.

"Guess we'll have to notify Marx. Have him come up and ID the body."

"Let me talk to him."

The sheriff hesitated, glanced at Detective McFee and Deputy Ray Ellis, all the while tugging thoughtfully on his lower lip. "Don't see what that would hurt, especially since he's already in Savannah. But you'd better take someone with you seein' as you know the vic. McFee," he said, nodding toward a huge man whose face was hidden by the brim of his hat. "You accompany the detective back home."

"Fine." Reed didn't care who tagged along, but he sure as hell wanted to see the look on Jerome Marx's face when he was handed the news that his wife had been buried alive.

"Hey!" a voice shouted from beyond the lights. "We've got company. The press is here."

"Great," Reed muttered under his breath as he noticed headlights through the trees. The last thing they needed was a media circus up here.

"Keep 'em away from the scene," Baldwin ordered, his scowl as deep as Reed's. To McFee, he said, "Let's give Reed a look at the other body. The one below."

Careful to disturb very little, the big man gently lifted Bobbi's head with his gloved hands.

In the klieg's glow, a partially decomposed face stared up at them, a macabre skull with features that were indistinguishable, only a layer of thin gray hair curled tight and what had once been a blue dress indicated that the body below had once been an elderly woman.

Reed shook his head and clenched his teeth. It wasn't the rotting woman that bothered him; he'd seen bodies in all stages of decay, but the thought that Bobbi had been awake, aware that she was being buried alive along with a cadaver caused bile to rise up his throat. What kind of sicko would do this? Who knew that he and Bobbi had been lovers? Who cared enough and was twisted to the point that they would do this?

Jerome Marx.

Why else address the note to Reed and leave it in the coffin?

But why would he bury her atop the other woman— who the hell was she? And surely he would know if he put a note in the coffin addressed to Reed that he would become the prime suspect. Jerome Marx was many things, many bad things, but he wasn't stupid.

The sheriff rubbed his jaw, scraping the stubble of his beard, while in the distance the dogs howled plaintively. "When we're done here, I think we should go back to the office and you can give me a statement."

By the time Nikki Gillette pulled into the Dahlonega

office of the sheriff's department, it was late, after nine P.M. She'd been on the road for hours and her bones ached. Her stomach rumbled, her head pounded and she still hadn't figured out how to get to Pierce Reed. Worse yet, she wasn't alone. Several news vans were camped out in the department lot, more parked along the street. And her heart sank when she recognized not only Norm Metzger, but Max O'Dell from WKAM, a Savannah television station. There were other reporters as well, some from Atlanta and a couple of others she knew but couldn't name. Whatever had happened up on Blood Mountain was shaping up to be the story of the week.

Some way, she had to get the inside track.

Norm spotted her and climbed out of his car. "What're you doing up here?"

"Same as you."

"Mike put you onto the story?" he asked, arching an eyebrow above his rimless glasses. The photographer had slid from behind the passenger side and joined a growing throng of reporters huddled around the police station.

"I just thought I'd come up and check things out," she said.

"It's a pretty long trip for a joyride," Norm observed.

"I was interested, okay?"

"So you found out about the bodies."

"Yeah."

"And that Pierce Reed was called up here."

She nodded as Norm pulled on a pair of gloves. "He doesn't like you, you know."

68

"He doesn't like any reporters."

"But you in particular. You really got on his nerves during the Montgomery case."

"Is that right? Did he tell you that?"

"He didn't have to. I saw the way he bristled every time you approached him."

"He's a bristly kind of guy."

"Especially when you're around." The main door to the sheriff's department opened and Sheriff Baldwin along with several detectives, including Pierce Reed, appeared on the concrete steps.

The sheriff, without the aid of a microphone, asked everyone to "Listen up." The shuffling, whispering and general speculating stopped and everyone poised, pen, recorder, or pencil in hand. Cameras were pointed at the group of officers. "We're all tired here, and I suppose you are, so I'm going to make this short. This afternoon there was an emergency call to 911. It sounded like a hunting accident involving two youths. When we got to the scene, we life-flighted one of the young men to Mason Hospital in Atlanta, while the other one gave us a statement. The two had found what appeared to be a grave up near Blood Mountain, so we went up to investigate. Sure enough we found a grave and not one, but two bodies. At this time, pending ID of the bodies and notification of next of kin, we'll give out no further information, but we are looking into the situation as a possible homicide. That's all."

But the reporters wanted answers. Several began shouting at once.

"Sheriff Baldwin? Do you expect to find any more bodies?"

"How long had the victims been there?"

"Why did you call in a detective from Savannah?"

"Is the hunter going to survive?"

"I said, that's all," Baldwin reiterated in a voice that was firm and bordered on belligerent. He looked weary but determined as he raked his gaze along the crowd. "We'll have more information in the morning. For now, you all best get some rest." He waved off any more questions and disappeared inside. Nikki edged closer and thought she caught Reed's eye, but if he saw her, he made no sign of acknowledgment, no indication that he recognized her. The door swung shut behind him and lest any reporter be so bold as to follow, a deputy was posted at the door.

"So, now what?" Norm said, sidling closer.

"Now, I guess, we wait," Nikki said, though she had no intention of sitting around and waiting for parceled-out information. Not when she lived only a few streets away from Pierce Reed.

"Two bodies in one coffin?" Sylvie Morrisette wrinkled her nose as she flopped into one of the side chairs in Reed's office the next morning. Her platinum hair seemed even more spiked than before and there was the faint, ever-present smell of cigarettes that wafted across the desk. "That's a new one. Someone couldn't afford his own accommodations?"

"Hers," Reed clarified, not amused at her attempt at humor. He wasn't in the mood. He'd spent half the night in northern Georgia knowing that the sheriff and a couple of the detectives considered him a suspect, then had grabbed a couple hours of sleep before walking nearly comatose through the shower and landing behind this desk around six-thirty. He was surviving on coffee, Tums and Excedrin. A half-eaten doughnut was in his wastebasket, the only reminder of his last meal. He wasn't in the mood for jokes.

"One of the vics is Barbara Jean Marx. The other is still a Jane Doe."

"Barbara Jean Marx?" Morrisette's eyebrows puckered together, showing off her most recent silver stud. "I've heard the name somewhere."

"Married to Jerome Marx until recently." He gritted his teeth at the thought of how easily she'd lied to him and how he'd so willingly believed her. "Marx owns an import/export business downtown. I thought I'd go pay him a visit and give him the news personally."

"You know him?" Morrisette asked as she scrounged in her purse and dragged out a piece of gum. "Cuz it seems like you do."

He hesitated. Decided he may as well confide in her. "I knew Bobbi Jean. We were involved."

"And *you're* going to talk to the ex? Isn't that against department policy?"

"A detective from Lumpkin County—Davis McFee—will be with me."

Morrisette lifted an eyebrow. "You got yourself your own police escort?"

"Very funny," he mocked, though the thought rankled. Obviously, Baldwin didn't trust him. *Would you?*

Come on! *Baldwin's just covering his ass.* "I thought maybe you'd want to tag along."

"Wouldn't miss it for the world." She unwrapped a disfigured stick of gum and popped it into her mouth. "So, fill me in."

Reed told her everything he remembered, from the chopper ride upstate through the grisly discoveries in the grave to the meeting in which Sheriff Baldwin 'for the sake of department integrity' had decided to send McFee to lead the investigation. The fact that he was allowing Reed, an ex-lover of Bobbi Jean's, to tag along, severely bent the rules. When he'd finished, Morrisette whistled. "Jesus, Reed, what a mess. You think the note in the coffin is connected with the one delivered here yesterday?"

"Seems like too much of a coincidence not to. And it looks identical. Same paper, same handwriting. The lab is comparing the two as well as checking for prints."

"We should get so lucky," Morrisette muttered as the phone rang.

Reed held up a finger, silently asking her to wait, and picked up. Though he was hoping for information on Bobbi and the other woman in the coffin, it was another case in which a couple of kids were playing with their father's revolver and one ended up dead. A depressing way to start an already bad morning.

While he was on the call, Morrisette's beeper went off and she grabbed her cell phone from her fringed purse and disappeared out the door. She returned before he hung up, but didn't slide into the chair again. Instead, she propped her slim butt on the windowsill and waited until he hung up. The door to his office was ajar and he heard voices and footsteps, officers and staff arriving for the day shift.

"So, when are you visiting the deceased's husband to give him the news?" Morrisette asked as a telephone jangled down the hallway.

"Ex-husband. As soon as the detective from Lumpkin County gets here."

"What about the autopsy?"

"Done in Atlanta, sometime today, probably. It's got priority. But first they want someone besides me to ID the body."

"Who knew you were involved with the woman?"

"Aside from Marx, no one."

"No one that you knew. She could have spilled the beans to a friend."

"Or Marx could have."

"When was the last time you saw her?"

"Six, maybe seven weeks ago."

"That when you called it off?"

"Yep."

"Learned that she wasn't quite divorced."

"Mmm."

"When was she reported missing?"

"She wasn't. I checked with Rita in Missing Persons." He loosened the top button on his collar and yanked at his tie. "But then, she hadn't been dead all that long. The coroner thinks less than twelve hours when we found her. We're starting to work backward from then, find out who saw her last, what she was doing." He glanced at the clock. "I thought I'd check with the jewelry store where she worked."

"You know any of her friends?"

He thought, and shook his head, then thought that he'd really not even known her. Their affair had been sexual, yes, but not much more than that. And yet . . . the killer had linked them and it soured his stomach to think that she might have died such a horrid death because of her link to him.

As if Sylvie Morrisette had read his mind, she said, "Don't beat yourself up. I see it in your eyes. You think this woman is dead because of you. Because of the notes."

"Don't you?"

"I don't know. Not yet. Neither do you." She hopped off the sill. "Let's stay objective."

Reed wondered if that were possible.

He had the distinct feeling it might not be.

The phone jangled and he picked it up just as Detective McFee arrived. The big man dwarfed Morrisette and Reed couldn't help but think of Lurch of the *Addams Family* on seeing McFee in the morning light. Not only was he large and rawboned, but his skin was sallow and his eyes deep-set. Reed introduced the two detectives, noticed how Morrisette gave McFee the once-over, and mentally chastised himself. Why was it Sylvie "tough-as-nails" Morrisette, four times divorced, still sized up every man she met as if they might be the candidate for number five?

Grabbing his jacket, he decided he'd never figure it out.

A slow smile crept across The Survivor's face as he watched the morning news. The late-night reports had been sketchy, but as the day had broken, more information was surfacing about the discovery in the ravine near Blood Mountain. It was the lead story.

Balancing on the edge of his ottoman, he recorded and watched five different screens, all with different reporters, but all telling essentially the same tale. There was footage of the grave site, taken from helicopters that had hovered above the bottom of the ravine as dawn crept over the forest floor. Crime scene workers were still searching the ground for evidence. The area around the grave had been marked in a grid, and the workers painstakingly sifted through every inch of soil, dead leaves and dry grass. As if they'd find anything.

His blood quickened at the thought that he'd caused this confusion. That all these people were working because of him. That Pierce Reed's life had been disturbed and he'd been dragged up north to the place he'd been born. Reed had spent the first few years of his life in a two bedroom house outside of Dahlonega. A bonafide, dyed-in-the-wool Georgia cracker, though most people assumed he'd started life somewhere in the Midwest and Reed did little to disavow this misinformation. The man was a fake. A phony. A slimeball.

But he was about to get his comeuppance.

One of the screens flickered with the image of the dead buck—the deer that lunatic kid had killed. Some of The Survivor's joy diminished . . . He hadn't counted on the hunters. Had thought he was alone along the windswept deer trails.

He climbed to his feet and could barely stand up in this small room where the televisions dominated one brick wall and their flickering screens offered the only light. One wall was all shelves, floor to ceiling filled with all of his electronic equipment. Microphones. Video cameras. Surveillance gear. And hundreds of movies he'd purchased on tape and DVD. Movies about heroes who had beat the odds, who had survived and avenged, who had taken justice into their own hands, who had meted out their own kind of payback.

Charles Bronson.
Bruce Lee.
Clint Eastwood.
Mel Gibson.
Keanu Reeves.

Actors who had portrayed tough men were his idols. Stories that told of men enduring horrid pain, then wreaking vengeance. Mad Max, Rambo, The Matrix . . . those were the films that made his blood run hot.

He had few clothes hidden here, though, in his other life, the one he let the world see, he had suits and jeans, dress shirts, Dockers and even polo shirts. But here, his needs were simple. Basic. Hooks held his camouflage outfit and wet suit. A steel door hid a closet he'd fashioned himself, small, confining, dark. With no doorknob on the interior side. A perfect place to keep someone alive. His furniture was sparse—a worktable, a battered chair and ottoman facing the screens and his prize, an antique dresser and mirror he'd salvaged from his mother's home.

He walked to the bureau and saw his reflection in the cracked oval mirror. Backlit by the flickering screens, he studied his image. Icy eyes stared back at him—eyes that had been labeled troubled, or sexy, or bedroom or cold. Rimmed with spiky lashes and protected by thick brows, one of which was split and bore a small scar. Even that imperfection had added to his allure with women; some considered him thrilling and dangerous.

Sensual.

A brooding, quiet man with secrets.

If they only knew.

He saw his upper body, strong from working out—army style. Fingertip push-ups and hundreds of chin-ups and sit-ups. Swimming. Running. Exertion. Perfection. Every muscle honed.

How else would he have survived?

He opened the second drawer and looked at the clothes within. A lacy black slip, bra and panties . . . the whore Barbara Jean Marx's underclothes. There were other scraps as well, rotting fabric that had been covering the dead woman's privates. Nasty, dirty, now encased in a plastic sack. He needed the old underwear, of course, so that his collection would be complete, but didn't want the torn, filthy, rotting fabric to touch the silken perfection of Barbara Jean Marx's expensive panties, slip and bra.

Touching the whore's underthings, running the silk through his fingers brought a welcome warmth to his blood and he closed his eyes for a second, lifted the panties to his nostrils, felt the thickening in his groin. As much as he'd hated her, he'd lusted after her. All normal men did.

And what do you think is normal about you, you useless, stupid sack of shit?

The voice withered his erection and he forced himself not to hear the taunts that still reverberated through his mind. He folded Barbara Jean's underclothes and slipped them into their plastic sack, then gave himself a swift mental kick for losing the ring . . . damn it all to hell, he'd wanted that ring, fancied himself fondling the glittering stones as he'd watched the news about Barbara Jean Marx, ex-model, rich wife's bizarre death. But somehow, he'd lost the damned ring. Another mistake. His jaw tightened.

Slipping her clothes into the second drawer, he noticed the drops of dried blood on the bureau and touched them lightly with the pad of his thumb. As he often did. Just to remember. But he was careful not to wipe the drops too hard, needed them to stay where they were, even the ones that ran down the side. A few dark stains settled over the lip of the top drawer and around the keyhole, but he didn't open it. Would never. That private space was sacred. Could not be violated. He touched the chain at his neck and the small key that hung from it.

Sometimes it was tempting to take off the links of worn gold and slip the key into its lock and listen as it clicked. The old drawer would open slowly, sealed from the blood that had once been sticky, and then he would . . .

Not! He would never open the drawer.

All the recording lights were glowing. He could leave. Assume his other life. He licked his lips and tried to slow the rapid beat of his heart as he took one last look at the news and the havoc he'd caused. Because of a whore's gruesome death. Again, he imagined her waking in the coffin, terror riddling her body. He could have hauled the coffin to the surface, been her hero and taken her then. She would have done anything for him. Spread her legs. Sucked his cock. Anything.

He felt a rush of desire, a jet of lust running through his bloodstream, and he imagined Pierce Reed in bed with her.

Bastard.

The Survivor's mouth was suddenly dry. He couldn't pull up any spit as he stared at the televisions and remembered plunging the needle into her arm. . . . She'd collapsed, crying out as she lost consciousness and . . . A series of beeps brought him out of his reverie. He snapped back to the moment and realized he was running out of time. Quickly he clicked off the alarm on his watch, slid out of the room and, as the recorders taped every moment of the news, walked quietly through the dark corridors that were little more than tunnels. He braced himself to face the cold winter morning and the new day.

Finally, his time had come.

CHAPTER 4

Quietly he stole through the shadows. It was just twilight and he was dead tired and if he were caught, he'd probably lose his job, but Reed slipped through the back gate and, finding a spare key where Bobbi had always kept one behind the hose bib, he let himself into the garage, stepped out of his shoes and walked into her kitchen. The shades were pulled down and the light over the stove was burning softly, just as always. He hadn't been in the cottage in months and yet it was familiar. The only reason he'd risked visiting her house was that he was certain he'd be thrown off the case. The second the D.A. caught wind that he'd been intimate with a victim, Reed would be diverted to other cases and all the information on Bobbi's death would be off-limits to him. Which galled the hell out of him.

He walked in stockinged feet across the worn hardwood, through a small eating space to the living room, arranged just as he remembered, with overstuffed furniture, colorful throws and plants growing in every corner. Newspaper sections were scattered on the coffee table. He didn't disturb them, but noted that it was the morning edition of the *Savannah Sentinel,* dated two days earlier. Bobbi, or whoever had been in the cottage, had been reading about the local news. The boldest headline was about a reconstruction project in the historic district and the byline was Nikki Gillette. One of the most irritating women he'd ever met, one of those dogged, do-anything-for-a-story reporters who was ever trying to get ahead. She had the looks for it. Curly red-blond hair, bright eyes, tight ass, but she was trouble. Not only an aggressive reporter, but the daughter of the Honorable Judge Ronald Gillette.

Reed carefully swung his penlight past the paper to a plate with a nearly burned, half-eaten piece of toast. Jelly congealed in one corner of the plate, and a cup of coffee, again half drunk, showed lipstick stains on its rim. Breakfast. Two days earlier.

He walked into the master bedroom. The sheets were rumpled, half off the bed, a pillow on the floor, but he knew from experience that it wasn't a sign of a struggle. Bobbi always left her bed in disarray. "I think it's sexy that way, don't you?" she'd asked him once as she stood on her tiptoes and kissed the bend of his neck. "That way the bedroom always looks like you've just made love and are ready to go at it again."

She'd never seen his military-sharp bed or austere room with a single dresser, thirteen-inch TV, half-mirror and rowing machine.

The closet door was open. He swept the penlight through the interior. Dirty clothes were falling out of a basket on the floor, dresses hung neatly above. Using a cloth he opened the dresser drawers and found under-clothes, sachets, T-shirts and shorts. Nothing out of the ordinary. Her nightstand gave up a vibrator, creams, Kleenex, a broken picture of her dressed as a bride and a worn copy of the Bible. Nothing unusual. Nothing incriminating.

The bath was as untidy and smelled of a perfume he

recognized. Bottles of makeup, hair products, aspirin and lotion littered the small counter. A hairbrush, filled with dark hair, was pushed against one of those magnifying mirrors that lit up. In the medicine chest were the usual ointments, creams, feminine products, fingernail polishes and medications: Vicodin, Percocet and a full month's supply of birth control pills.

Obviously not used for quite a while.

The claw-footed tub with its recently added showerhead needed to be scrubbed.

But there was nothing out of the ordinary.

The second bedroom, used as a study and general catch-all, was a mess, but not out of the ordinary for Barbara Jean Marx. This cottage was "temporary" she'd told Reed on the last morning he'd seen her. They were lying in the bed, tangled in sheets, with the smell of sex hanging heavy in the air. "Just a stepping-stone to something bigger once the divorce is final."

"I thought it was," he'd said.

"We're hung up on a technicality. I want more money. He doesn't want to pay it."

"You told me it was over."

"It is."

"I mean legally." He'd been pissed. Really pissed and had thrown off the bedsheets. While she was trying to explain, he'd pulled on his clothes and left. He remembered walking outside into the middle of a September downpour, the rain heavy, steamy and hot.

Now, he walked through the rooms one last time, taking note of the scene. He'd come back, of course, with McFee and Morrisette. If he was allowed. But he'd needed to see for himself what Bobbi's last day had been like. He walked into the kitchen and saw the answering machine. The light was blinking. It was the kind of machine with a tape and he knew how it worked. A simple machine with a great "keep as new" feature. He could play the tape and no one would be the wiser. Using a cloth, he hit the button. The machine hissed and chortled as the tape rewound. There were two hang ups before a woman's voice blasted through the kitchen.

"Hi, there. Just me." It was Bobbi herself.

Reed nearly jumped out of his skin. "Bet you didn't expect this, did you?" Christ, what was she talking about? "I'm off to meet *him* but I forgot to pick up deodorant and the dry-cleaning, and I wanted to test this new cell phone out, so this is just a reminder. Cool, huh?" She laughed, amused with herself, and Reed's skin crawled as he remembered that husky giggle. It was as if she were still alive.

Had she been calling someone who was staying here, or was she leaving the message for herself? And who was the *him* she was talking about? Jerome Marx? A new boyfriend?

There were no other messages.

Reed reset the machine so that the hang ups and Bobbi's call were "new," then he let himself out. Just as he had a dozen times before.

Pierce Reed was the key.

Nikki knew it and reminded herself of the fact as her clock radio blasted the next morning. She'd spent a useless day and night in Dahlonega, digging into Reed's past, trying to find a link between him and the grave discovered up at Blood Mountain, and had come up empty handed before finally giving up last night. What a waste of time and energy. She slapped the damned alarm quiet and groaned as she rolled out of bed. She'd tumbled between the sheets barely three hours earlier after driving for hours. Her eyes felt as if they had sand in them, her head ached and she twisted her neck only to hear it pop. Not a good sign. Reaching for the remote, she clicked on the local news just as Jennings, her yellow tabby, and the laziest creature on earth, raised his head. From the pillow next to hers, he stretched and yawned, showing off needle-sharp teeth and his pink scratchy tongue. Nikki petted his fluffy head without thinking about it as she stared at the television.

The grave with two unidentified bodies still topped the news. On every channel.

So, why was Reed involved?

A Savannah cop wasn't helicoptered over three hundred miles to the north Georgian woods just because he'd had his name splashed all over the newspapers during the Montgomery case. No. There had to be a reason, had to be more to Reed's involvement than met the eye. Nikki just had to figure out what it was. She slogged her way to the kitchen, measured Italian roast and water into the coffeemaker, then headed for the bathroom where she twisted on the shower spray. As the pipes in the old house creaked and the water heated, she edged back to the bedroom and checked with the national news. CNN had picked up the story but it was buried beneath trouble in the Middle East and the President's holiday travel schedule. She tried the local news again and determined no more information had been released by the Lumpkin County Sheriff's Department.

Good.

She wanted this story.

So bad she could taste it.

With a sense of urgency, she hurried through the shower, hoping the hot spray would wash away the cobwebs in her head and the aches in her muscles. But the water pressure on the top floor of this old house was less than invigorating. She spent less than ten minutes with her makeup and hair, moussing her wild strawberry blond curls into no particular style and inwardly groaning when she noticed the dark smudges beneath her eyes that no amount of cover-up could conceal.

No big deal.

"Who cares?" she said to Jennings, who'd managed to hop onto the edge of the pedestal sink and was watching her perform her morning routine. "Hungry?"

He jumped off the rim of the sink and ambled toward the kitchen.

"I'll take that as a 'yes.' Be there in a sec."

She stepped into black slacks, pulled on a long-sleeved tee and threw on a jacket. As she slung the strap of her purse over her shoulder, she was already considering the right angle for her story and figuring out how she'd get to Reed. Of course, she'd try the direct approach, not that it had worked in the past. Her small bedroom was only steps from the kitchen/living area of her apartment, which itself was the turret of a once-grand Victorian home. Now, the hardwood floors needed refinishing, the walls and molding could use a fresh coat of paint and the countertops needed to be replaced. But it was home. Her home. And she loved it.

In the kitchen, she quickly fed the cat, then poured a cup of coffee and sipped it as she watched more of the news on her ancient twelve-inch set, the one she'd splurged on in college. The televison and Jennings were roughly the same age, acquired her senior year when Nikki had decided she could make some decisions for herself. Decisions that had included a string of all the wrong boys to get involved with.

"It's only natural," her shrink had advised. "You've suffered a major loss. Not only you but your whole family. You're searching for someone to fill that void."

Nikki had thought the guy was a quack and had only endured one uncomfortable session. Sure, she missed her older brother. And yeah, Mom and Dad and her other brother and sister were all in mourning. But she doubted that because Andrew had died, she'd felt some need to date every loser she'd encountered at the University of Georgia. In retrospect, the television and Jennings had been two of her better decisions.

Images flashed on the screen and she turned her attention, again, to the news.

No more reports from Dahlonega.

Nor did she see any interviews with Pierce Reed— not even on the local channels. All the better.

It made things easier for her, she thought, pouring herself a second cup of coffee in a travel mug. The way she figured it, all she had to do was keep track of Reed, follow him, check with her contact on the force, find out why he went charging up north and she'd be able to piece together the mystery of the dead bodies. One way or another, she'd get her exclusive.

She was already punching out Cliff Siebert's cell number as she walked outside and paused on the upper landing. From this vantage point, she could look down the street and see over the rooftops and treetops of Forsyth Park. The city was already awake, traffic rolling down the old streets of the historic district. Not far away was the police department.

Cliff didn't pick up.

"Big surprise," Nikki muttered and figured he was still dodging her. She left a message as she hurried down the steps and felt a cool winter breeze against her wet hair. Her car was parked in her small spot and she tossed her notebook, computer and bag into the backseat and wedged her coffee cup into the holder. She slid her key into the ignition and heard the hatchback's old engine grind. "Yeah, yeah, come on, I'm tired, too," she muttered, and on the fifth try, the engine fired and caught. "See, I knew you could do it," she said as she backed up, then eased into the alley where vine-covered garages and old carriage houses lined the narrow street.

On her way to the office, she passed the police station, considered stopping and thought better of it. She needed to make an appearance at the office and get her act together before she nailed Reed.

• • •

"To what do I owe the honor of this visit?" Jerome Marx asked, standing as his secretary led the three detectives into his office. He'd been "out of town on business" until this morning. He had the decency to stand but there was hostility in his dark eyes, a tightness to the lips hidden in his goatee and the edge of irritation beneath the outright sarcasm in his words. He was dressed in a crisp navy blue suit, white shirt, wide burgundy tie and gold cuff links. His office, decorated in leather and mahogany, oozed the same genteel breeding that his wardrobe tried so desperately to convey.

It was all a front.

Reed knew that Marx was about as far from old money and southern gentility as he was. The son of a dressmaker and a used-car salesman Marx had scraped his way through college on a football scholarship to a junior college, then walked on at a small four year university where he'd earned a degree in finance. From there he'd joined the ranks of corporate America, working for car rental companies, banks and mortgage brokers until he decided to become an entrepreneur using capital he'd inherited from his wife's father. He and Barbara Jean hadn't had any children.

Considering the way things had turned out, it was just as well.

McFee introduced himself as well as Morrisette and Reed. The skin over Marx's cheekbones stretched even tighter when he met Reed's eyes.

"I'm afraid we're here with bad news," McFee said.

"What kind of bad news?" Marx was instantly on edge.

"We think we've found your wife's body."

"What?" His face drained of color. "My wife? Barbara?"

"Yes. If you've watched the news, you know about the grave we discovered up near Blood Mountain in Lumpkin County—"

"My God, you mean . . ." His gaze flew from one detective to the next. "You mean that Bobbi was . . . in that . . . in there . . ." He swallowed, then dropped into a wing-back chair positioned near his desk. "No . . . I mean, that's not possible."

"I'm afraid it is, sir. We'd like you to come down and identify the body. It's in Atlanta."

"Oh, my God . . . oh, my God." He buried his face in his hands. Clean hands. Manicured fingernails from the looks of them. He seemed genuinely shocked, though, of course, his response could be faked. "No. I don't believe it." He looked up and the grim faces must've convinced him. "Of course I'll go with you. Atlanta?"

"Where they'll do the autopsy."

"Oh, Christ! Autopsy?"

"It looks like a homicide."

"But who? Who would want to . . ." His voice trailed off. So he was finally getting it. "You think I did something to Bobbi?" He was aghast. "I would never." His eyes met Reed's again and some of the starch left him. "Sure we had our ups and downs and we were going through a divorce, but I swear, I had nothing to do with this. If you want me to identify the body, then let's do it. Now."

Trina pounced on Nikki the minute she dropped her purse into a desk drawer and clicked on her computer. "You're in big trouble." Trina peered over the top of the cubicle wall as piped-in music played instrumental renditions of Christmas carols over the clatter of computer keys and muted voices.

"I figured. Metzger probably smoked into Fink's office at the crack of dawn yesterday."

"That, too, I suppose."

"You suppose."

"I was talking about our date the other night. Since you bagged out you left me to play shrink to Dana and Aimee." Trina rolled her expressive eyes. "I spent the night swiveling my head, congratulating Dana and telling her how much fun marriage was going to be, that Todd was a great guy, a fabulous catch, then pulling a one-eighty and telling Aimee how lucky she was to be rid of her cheatin', lyin', bastard of a husband."

"Sounds like fun."

"I could have used backup."

"Sorry, I was—"

"I know, I know, chasing down the story that will send your career through the stratosphere. By the way, Dr. Francis called you. Wants to nail down an interview time as the school board is meeting next week and then won't meet again until after Christmas. She just wants to make sure you understand her position on the upcoming bond issue."

Nikki groaned. "And you know this—how?"

"Celeste routed your voice mail to me again."

Nikki forced a fake smile. "Nice," she said, her voice dripping with sarcasm. "Anything else?"

Tina's grin took on Cheshire-like proportions. "Just a message from Sean . . ."

"Sean?" Nikki's heart squeezed and she felt that old, familiar unwanted pain. "What did he say?"

"That he'd be in town and wanted to, let me see . . . what was the exact phrase? 'Hook up.' "

"Fat chance." Nikki wasn't going down that road again.

"Why not, Nik? It's been what? Ten, twelve years?"

"Almost, and I say, 'once a liar and a cheat, always a liar and a cheat.' "

"Maybe he's grown up."

What were the chances of that? "Anything else?" Nikki asked, refusing to think about Sean Hawke with his devil-may-care attitude, bad-boy smile and chiseled body. It was over. Period. She didn't believe in redemption, wouldn't take the time. Didn't want to be "friends" even if it were possible. Which it wasn't. "Any other messages?"

"Nope."

"Good." This wasn't much of a surprise as most people called her on her cell, which was just as well, considering Celeste's state of incompetence. She was twenty-four and, in Nikki's opinion, completely brainless. Why else would she be involved with Fink who had a daughter from his first marriage about Celeste's age? The fact that he was currently married to wife number two and had two kids in elementary school didn't seem to permeate Celeste's brain, either, and her continued remarks that Fink's marriage was "dead" and that he and the wife were "living separate lives" and "only staying together for the kids" turned Nikki's stomach. But then, nearly everything about Fink did.

As if he'd read her thoughts, he walked by and said, "Nikki. Come into my office when you get a minute."

Trina melted into her cubicle.

Great, Nikki thought, her headache returning with a vengeance. She grabbed her purse and followed Fink, who walked with the easy ambling gait of an ex-jock. He was still neat and trim, his once-dark hair now shot with silver, his wardrobe leaning toward khakis and polo shirts, as if he'd just come from the golf course. He opened the door to his glass-paneled room and waited for her to enter. *Ever the gentleman,* she thought sarcastically as he motioned her into one of the side chairs and took his position at the desk, one leg hoisted over the corner, hands clasped over his knee. "I heard you were up at Dahlonega the last couple of days."

It hadn't taken Metzger long to break the news. "Actually, just a little over twenty-four hours, but, yeah, I was there, right," she admitted, watching Fink's foot swing.

"Any particular reason?" He was stone-cold serious, his eyes steady, his lips a thin line.

"I wanted to know what was going on with the grave the police found."

"I gave that story to Norm."

She nodded. "And he didn't like it that I went up there."

"Let's just say he was concerned."

"Why?"

"He thinks you're trying to beat him to the punch."

"So, he's threatened?"

"I didn't say that."

Nikki was tired and angry. Her tongue got away from her. "You implied it. Look, I don't see what it hurts that I drove up there. My work hasn't suffered. Metzger still has his story. What's the problem?"

"Maybe there isn't one," Fink said, though his expression didn't change. "I didn't call you in here to tell you to back off or to remind you to be careful of stepping on someone's toes. Not at all. In fact, I think a little competition is good as long as you remember that you and Norm are on the same team. What I want from you as well as him is the best story possible."

"So, you're not telling me to leave it alone."

"It's Norm's piece. You know that. Respect it. But, no, you don't have to leave it alone. As long as you don't ignore your own work."

"That's it?" she asked, dumbstruck.

"That's it." The corner of his mouth lifted. "What? You thought I was going to ream you out?"

"At least."

He snorted as he eased off the desk. "For pushing Metzger?" he asked and shook his head. "Nah. As I said, a little good old competition doesn't hurt anyone."

"So, I've got the green light to investigate the story?"

"As long as you don't get in Metzger's way." Fink

was nodding, his head keeping time with his moving foot.

"What about him getting in my way?"

"Now, you're pushing it, Gillette."

She held up both hands beside her head as if in surrender. "Just checkin' the boundaries."

"Now, you know them." He stood and she took it as her cue to do the same.

She was nearly at the door when he said, "And play this one straight, okay? Nothing that would get the paper into any trouble, legal or otherwise."

Reflexively her spine straightened. She knew what he was talking about. The Chevalier case. Long dead, but one that would haunt her for the rest of her life. She'd been young and green at the time and had compromised nearly everyone she knew, including her father, all for the sake of a story. She'd learned her lesson. A long time ago. Turning to face him again, she inched her chin up and said icily, "Trust me, everything I get will be on the up-and-up. You and the *Sentinel* will be able to bank on my story."

Fink offered his almost-a-smile. "That's all I need to know."

Amen, she thought, but didn't say it. No reason to tick him off. Not when he'd finally agreed to let her do something with more meat to it than school board agendas and interviews with the historic preservation committee. It crossed her mind as she zigzagged through the cubicles that she shouldn't trust him, but she put the feeling aside. She could access her suspicions later. For now, she was finally able to prove herself. With Fink's blessing. Things were looking up. She'd spend a few hours here, catching up on some of the stories she had in the works, then she'd pick up where she left off. That meant tracking down Detective Pierce Reed.

Finding him wouldn't be tough but getting him to open up would be something else altogether. She'd tried to interview him before and he'd always responded to her as if she were a pariah. His attitude toward the press and the people's right to know needed a serious adjustment and Nikki figured she knew just how to do that.

No doubt Reed had a skeleton or two in his closet— a dirty little secret that he'd rather not have anyone know about.

This is close to blackmail, Nikki, that damned voice in her head chided, but she wasn't listening. Not today. She'd be careful with whatever information she dug up. She just needed a little firepower, something to get him to confide in her. Her conscience pricked again. *How would you like Reed digging into your past?*

Ignoring the question, she made her way to her cubicle and before she called Dr. Francis back or finished her story on the school board, she connected to the Internet and her favorite search engine where she typed in *Detective Pierce Reed.* As she waited for the links about Reed to appear, she made a mental note to check on his marital status and any more information about what had happened to him in San Francisco. And what about the fact that he'd spent the first few years of his life in Northern Georgia, up near Blood Mountain and the site of the graves before his parents had split and his mother had hauled him to Chicago before eventually landing on the West Coast. Despite all that Reed kept returning to Savannah, once about fifteen years or so ago and then again recently. Why? She made a note to herself to dig deeper in Lumpkin County, to talk to the sheriff, the kid who was hurt, his cousin, and anyone else who knew Reed growing up. There had to be a reason that Reed went all the way up there.

The computer screen flickered and she smiled. Detective Pierce Reed had dozens of links of information about him. There was a veritable wealth of data, much of it tagged to the *Savannah Sentinel*. But there were other bits of info, including a series of articles in San Francisco and Oakland, California newspapers.

With a click of the mouse, Nikki Gillette got a glimpse inside the personal and professional life of Detective Pierce Reed. She saw pictures of him as a much younger man and decided that as handsome as he'd been back then, he looked better now. At least, he was more appealing to her. He'd filled out, his hair was dusted with a bit of gray, but his bold features and hawkish eyes seemed to fit better into a craggy face where squint lines and beard shadow dared appear. The disappointment and suspicion that guarded his gaze these days only added to his allure.

You're a sick woman, she told herself. *And always get involved with the wrong type. Sean Hawke is a case in point. As attractive as Reed may be, remember that any interest you have in him is singularly and totally professional. You have a story to write, a career to bolster, and what you don't need by any stretch of the imagination is a romantic entanglement.*

She nearly laughed out loud. Romance? With Pierce Reed? The quintessential hater of the fourth estate? What a joke!

"I want to find out who was the last person to see Bobbi Jean alive," Reed growled at Morrisette and McFee as they drove away from Marx's office. It was dark, nearly nine o'clock, the streetlights keeping the night at bay and Morrisette, driving with her usual lead foot, was at the wheel. Reed was riding shotgun and McFee was in the backseat of the cruiser. They'd spent the day driving to Atlanta and observing as an ashen-faced Jerome Marx had identified his estranged wife. He'd never broken down, hadn't allowed one solitary tear to track from his eyes and hadn't seemed overly grief-stricken, but he had appeared shocked to learn of her death and that trauma hadn't worn off when he'd viewed the body. He'd watched as the sheet was lifted, every muscle in his body stiffening. "It's her," he'd whispered and turned away as if he couldn't bear the sight of her.

Reed hadn't determined if his revulsion was because she was dead, or because he'd been divorcing her. Whatever the reason, if Jerome Marx had thrown her alive and screaming into that coffin, he was doing a damned fine job of hiding his guilt. He'd talked freely to them and agreed to a polygraph test. He'd asked where her ring was, the one he'd given her for an anniversary, then said she'd probably taken it off because of the divorce proceedings that had been pending. When asked if they could search his premises, he'd not even batted an eye, nor asked to speak to his attorney. For all practical purposes, Marx was acting as if he had nothing to hide. But Reed wasn't buying it.

"And I want all her phone records and—"

"Yeah, yeah, the usual, I know," Morrisette said as she drove. "Friends. Relatives."

"Bobbi's got a brother somewhere around New Orleans, I think, but her parents are deceased."

"Kids?" Morrisette asked as she reached for a crumpled pack of Marlboro Lights. She managed to shake out the last cigarette and negotiate a turn near the river.

"None that I know of." Reed's mind was working overtime and he was barking orders. "We'll work backward from there. We'll check with her job, her landlady, her friends. Someone must know something. I've had her house watched, just to see if anyone shows up." When Morrisette cast a glance in his direction, he added, "Until the body was positively ID'd we couldn't get a search warrant."

"You ID'd the body," she said.

"It wasn't as official as her husband's."

"So now you're going by the book?" she asked.

"Strictly by the book."

"Yeah, right. Not you, Reed."

"Let's stop by her house. See if the crime scene team is there yet." He rattled off Bobbi's address and Morrisette managed a police U-turn at the next alley. Then they were speeding south through the historic district, past refurbished homes with high porches, wide windows and gleaming shutters, around the park-like squares with their benches, statues and lush vegetation.

"There might be a little problem with you being on the case," Morrisette pointed out as she lit up and cracked the window. The smell of Old Savannah wafted into the cruiser as it drew out the smoke.

"I worked it out with the sheriff."

"That's right," McFee chimed in. The "silent one" finally spoke as Morrisette turned onto a side street.

"Yeah, in Lumpkin County. Okano might see it differently. She's a stickler for details." Morrisette held her cigarette in her teeth as she negotiated a tight corner.

Reed scowled into the night.

"That's the trouble with lawyers." Morrisette checked the rearview mirror as the police band crackled. "Always on the lookout for a lawsuit."

"No, the trouble with lawyers is that they're paranoid," Reed grumbled, but he knew he was walking on thin ice. Katherine Okano, the D.A., was usually on his side and had been known to bend the rules a bit, but when she found out that he and Bobbi had been involved, she would likely pull the plug on his participation in the case. Morrisette hung a left at the next corner and drove up to Bobbi's driveway. Several cruisers were parked on the street and crime-scene tape was being stretched across the yard. A K9 unit was included. Morrisette parked in the driveway and squashed her cigarette in the tray. All three detectives made their way through a team collecting evidence and into the house.

Aside from the buzz of activity, the place looked the same as it had the last time Reed stepped through the door. He made his way outside, ensured that his footprints, should there be casts made, were accounted for. "What have you found?" he asked Diane Moses, who was in charge of the crime scene team in Savannah. An African-American who had fought her way through the trenches, Diane was smart and tough. The running joke in the department was that if she wanted to, she could not only part the Red Sea, but divide it into a grid.

"Not much. Still collecting. The big news is no forced entry. But then, her car is missing. She must have met the killer somewhere, either by accident or intent."

"Not an accident. This murder was planned."

"If you say so."

"No one goes to the trouble of digging up a coffin just on the off chance he runs across a victim." *Nor does he address a note specifically to a cop.*

"Well, it looks like our gal was into sex and God. Fun *and* religion. All sorts of sex toys in the bedroom, but her reading material was spiritual. Go figure."

The place was being photographed and videotaped, though there was no evidence of a crime. Every part of Barbara Jean Marx's life was about to be opened up to the public. Including questions about her relationships. His name was bound to come up.

"Did you check her computer? E-mail? Her phone?"

"We're taking the hard drive with us and there were no messages left on her phone. No trace of Caller ID for the numbers coming in."

"You're certain?" he asked, glancing at the phone. "No messages?"

Diane looked up from her clipboard. "That's what I said, no messages."

"What about hang ups?"

Frown lines pulled her eyebrows together. "Nothing. Nada. The tape on the machine was empty. If she had a cell phone or a purse, we haven't found either. Anything else?" she asked. "Because if not, I've got work to do." At that moment, the photographer asked her a question and Reed backed off. He walked to the telephone and looked at it. The message light was not blinking. So someone else had been here, *after* his evening visit.

They left after another ten minutes and Morrisette took the wheel again as they headed back to the station. The night seemed darker, headlights bright as they flashed by, street lamps giving off a false blue sheen. A few Christmas lights adorned houses lining the streets, and every once in a while he caught a glimpse of a decorated tree, festively aglow in a large window.

He'd forgotten it was the yule season.

Not that it mattered.

Morrisette gunned the engine as they whipped by Colonial Cemetery. The graveyard looked barren and bleak with its ancient headstones and dry grass. And this was the return address for the missive he'd received yesterday morning. As if whoever had penned the note had been here. "We need to check with all the local cemeteries," he said, eyeing the few leafless trees planted between the old grave markers. "See if any of the graves have been disturbed."

"You think whoever planted the coffin up in the mountains got it from down here?" McFee asked.

"It's possible," he thought aloud, but then, anything was. Glancing through the back window he wondered if he was being followed. Had Bobbi's killer been watching him? Seen him walk familiarly through the house? Or had he been hiding in the shadows, in a tiny nook or cranny, and Reed had walked right by him? Or was it someone else who had the key to Bobbi's place and had come looking for her? What about her husband? Jerome Marx had still been paying her bills. As far as Reed knew, Bobbi's part-time job wouldn't pay her Visa bill.

Morrisette wheeled into the parking lot at the station. "I'll start calling around, checking with everyone who knew Barbara Jean." She stood on the brakes and the cruiser slid into its spot. McFee was staying on another couple of days, sending his reports by fax and E-mail to the Lumpkin County Sheriff's Department and, in Reed's opinion, generally getting in the way. He wanted to take the bull by the proverbial horns and run the investigation, but he couldn't. Morrisette was right. He had to watch his step.

Outside, the night was cold and damp, the air thick with the feel of rain about to fall.

"Christ, it's cold," Morrisette muttered as she jabbed the rest of her cigarette into a canister of sand near the door.

"It's winter," McFee said.

"Yeah, but doesn't Mother Nature know this is the South?"

Reed shouldered opened the door, held it for her and McFee, then walked with them up the stairs, their boots ringing on the steps as they made their way to the second floor. McFee peeled off at the temporary desk he'd been assigned while Morrisette followed Reed into his office. "I've got to get home," she said, almost apologizing. "I haven't seen much of the kids lately."

Reed glanced at his watch. "Aren't they in bed?"

"I forgot, you don't have children. Lucky you . . . or maybe, lucky them."

"Very funny," he countered, taking off his jacket. The inside of the station was warm, over seventy, even though it was night and the offices were relatively deserted. Only a few diehards like himself, mostly those without families, were at their desks. He felt a sense of melancholy about his solitary state, but it was fleeting. He wasn't the kind to settle down. All his relationships had failed, including the one that had mattered in San Francisco. Helen had been a schoolteacher and professed to love him, but it hadn't been enough to keep him in the city after the tragedy. Nothing could have. So he'd returned to Savannah and the few relationships, if you could call them that, had been fleeting, including his short-lived affair with Bobbi Marx. "Go home to your kids."

"I will," she said, and walked out the door just as her pager went off. "See. The sitter's tracking me down as we speak. I'll see ya tomorrow."

"Right," he replied, but she'd already disappeared

103

beyond the desks and down the stairs. He was left alone in his office. He skimmed his E-mail, didn't see anything of interest and figured he could read through the messages in the morning. He was bone tired and the thought of his recliner, a hot shower and a cold beer was inviting.

Maybe he should just go home. Get a fresh start on everything in the morning. He reached for his jacket as his phone rang. He snagged the receiver before it could jingle again. "Detective Reed," he said automatically.

"You're still there. Thought I'd probably get your voice mail this late."

Reed recognized the voice as belonging to Gerard St. Claire, the ME. "Look, I've got a preliminary report on the case up north. I've been on the horn with the examiner in Atlanta."

"Already?" Reed's exhaustion dissipated.

"As I said, preliminary. Very preliminary, but we were told to put a rush on it. We already called Lumpkin County. But I thought you'd like to hear what we've got."

"What is it?"

"We don't know too much. Yet. The unidentified woman looks like she had a heart attack. We haven't come up with anything that suggests homicide, although if she was originally stuffed in that box and buried alive, she could have had a coronary. We're still checking but decomposition has set in and from the state of it, we're thinking she's been dead close to ten weeks."

Reed was taking notes. Listening.

"The other woman is easier."

Reed's gut tightened.

"Cause of death for the more recent victim, the one identified as Barbara Jean Marx, was probably asphyxiation, but we're still checking her blood and body for other wounds. Nothing's come up as yet. She probably just suffocated in that box. Rigor indicates she was dead less than twenty-four hours. The body wasn't moved, which is consistent with her dying in the coffin. No visible wounds, no blood aside from scrapes on her fingers from trying to claw her way out. One tattoo of a rose climbing up her spine."

Reed remembered. Had traced the body art with his fingers. Jesus.

"She has a few bruises as well—we're checking those out. It's still too early to tell if there was a struggle. We're looking at what she had under her fingernails, but as I said, no visible wounds." The ME hesitated, but Reed sensed there was something more.

"Anything else?"

"Yeah. There's something I thought you should know about the Marx woman."

"I'm listening." Reed sensed bad news was coming. Real bad. His skin tightened over his muscles and his fingers clenched around the receiver.

"She was pregnant."

Reed sucked in a breath. "Pregnant?" *No!*

"Eleven, maybe twelve weeks along."

Reed didn't move. His breath stopped for a heartbeat.

"Could give you a motive."

"Uh-huh," he forced out, his pulse pounding in his brain. Bobbi? Pregnant? *Three months* pregnant? All the spit dried in his mouth. He remembered her in the hotel room on the island. Gauzy curtains fluttering on a breeze that smelled of the ocean. Her tousled dark hair, upturned nose, eyes smoldering with desire. "Was it good for you," she'd cooed, her body still glistening with sweat. "Cuz, honey, if it wasn't, we can try again." She'd nibbled at his ear. Ever playful and blatantly sexual. She'd gotten to him. It had been early September . . . Labor Day weekend. He'd been able to look through the open window to the bay where sailboats skimmed the smooth water, their sails brilliant against an incredibly blue sky.

"We'll x-ray the bodies and open 'em up while the lab work's being done," St. Claire was saying, cutting into the memory. "And we'll try to get an ID on the other body."

"Good." Reed was barely listening. "Send me the report."

"Will do." St. Claire hung up and Reed dropped the receiver in its cradle. He swung his head around to look out the window where a street lamp glowed eerily and he noticed rain had begun to fall. The street glistened as a dark figure—little more than a shadow—darted across the street.

He ran a hand over his eyes and the shadow was gone. Maybe it had been his imagination. Or just someone outrunning the rain that was beginning to fall in fat drops. Damn it all, there was a good chance that Bobbi Marx's unborn baby was his. Some sick son of a bitch had not only killed Bobbi, but the fetus as well.

Why?

Who?

Was she dead because of the pregnancy, or was that an accident?

Two in one, one and two.

Two in one—Holy Jesus, is that what the killer meant? He'd killed two in one? The baby and Bobbi. Had the bastard *known* she was pregnant? Reed's jaw clamped so hard it ached.

He glanced at the digital display on his watch. Red numbers glowed on his wrist.

Tick tock, on goes the clock.

A clue. It had to be. They were racing against time . . . and the rest . . .

One, two, the first few. Hear them cry, listen to them die.

The sick bastard had to be indicating the victims. That these two were only the first . . . the few . . . how many more? Would he know them?

Sick inside, he realized that this was a taunt, probably written while Bobbi was alive. The murderer had been proud, cocky. Wanted to show off. Reed wondered if there had been time to rescue Bobbi from that hellish death if Reed had only been smarter.

There was no way . . . he'd received the letter and she'd already been buried alive. His fists clenched impotently. The letter had been addressed to him. Whatever was happening, it was personal. Between the killer and him.

Suddenly, Reed needed a drink. A stiff one.
Two in one, one and two.
What the hell did that mean?
Whatever it was, it wasn't good.

CHAPTER 5

Reed hadn't answered her calls.

Nikki had left three voice mail messages in the span of four days at the police station. Detective Pierce Reed hadn't seen fit to call her back. She'd gotten nothing. She'd even E-mailed, to no avail. The man was avoiding her, she decided as she finished her coffee and threw the dregs down her kitchen sink.

Things weren't much better in Dahlonega. She'd driven back there, snooped around, talked to a sheriff who just plain stonewalled her and returned to Savannah with not much more than she'd started with. She'd figured that there was something important up by Blood Mountain, that Reed's roots were the reason he'd been called up there to the killing ground . . . but so far, she'd been disappointed.

Her only consolation was that Norm Metzger, who had been rapid to be up in Lumpkin County, had come back pretty much empty-handed as well.

"Desperate times call for desperate measures," she'd confided to Jennings as she dressed. The cat was curled in the folds of her duvet while the seldom-used heater rumbled noisily, vainly attempting to warm the cold morning air that had seeped through the old windows of her apartment. Shivering, Nikki pulled on a black skirt and khaki sweater, then stepped into suede boots. She topped the outfit off with a suede jacket and decided she looked as good as she was going to. "If Mohammed won't come to the mountain," she said to the cat, "then the mountain will come . . . I guess I'm using every one of the old adages today. Booorrring, right?"

Jennings didn't seem to notice or care. He leapt off the four-poster and trotted, tail high, to his food dish in the kitchen.

"You know, a compliment or two wouldn't hurt," she admonished as she added some dry kiblets and a forkful of bargain brand canned food into his dish. The concoction smelled as bad as it looked but Jennings, verging on obese, relished it and ate noisily.

Nikki packed her laptop and purse, then wrapped a scarf around her neck. "No time to waste," she muttered to the cat. "Opportunity knocks once at one man's, or woman's, door." Hiking the strap of her computer over her shoulder, she said, "That's another little pearl of wisdom my dad used to say all the time."

The cat ignored her.

"Well, I believe it. Tom Fink isn't known for his patience. If I can nail this story, then watch out. I'll be up for a raise and you and I will tell old Fink to shove it. We'll be moving to a big city with a major market." She reached down and patted Jennings's tawny head. "How would you like to move to New York? No? Dallas? Hmmm, what about L.A.? You know, I can see you on Sunset Boulevard. We'll get a convertible and expensive shades and . . ." She glanced at her watch and realized she was stalling. ". . . and I gotta go."

She was out the door and stepping into the wet morning before she could second-guess what she was about to do. It was still dark outside, but the moon, thankfully, was obscured, so she didn't have to rearrange her body clock and remind herself it really was morning. The steps were slippery as she hurried down two flights to the fenced yard. No other windows in the apartment house showed any hint of illumination through their pulled shades. The other tenants seemed to realize that five-thirty in the morning was really the dead of night.

But then, the other tenants weren't chasing Pierce Reed.

Probably because they're sane.

She was tired, had been up half the night searching for information on Reed, including checking all public records. She'd discovered that he wasn't married and never had been, and she knew about his trouble during his tenure at the SFPD. He'd had a steady girlfriend, but she'd ended up marrying someone else after the botched case.

Reed had returned to Savannah, the city where he'd started with the police force nearly fifteen years earlier.

Nikki hadn't learned much more, but she'd only started scratching the surface. Sooner or later she'd figure out what made the elusive detective tick. She unlocked her hatchback and slid inside.

Her little car coughed and rattled before starting, but finally fired. Nikki sped out of the parking lot and drove the few blocks to Reed's apartment building, another ancient home cut into smaller living units.

His El Dorado, a Cadillac nearly old enough to be considered a classic and beat up enough to ensure it never would be, was sitting in its usual space. Good. Nikki had been by before. During the Montgomery case when she was chasing the story, she'd cruised by. She'd even gone so far as to figure out which unit was Reed's, though she'd never had the guts to knock on his door. Until today.

Sure enough, there was a light glowing through what she'd surmised was Reed's frosted-glass bathroom window. Either he slept with a nightlight, or the detective was up and about, soon to start his day.

Circling the block, she found a parking space across an alley and pulled in. Her heart hammered at her own boldness—she'd never accosted a police officer in his home before. She had little doubt of Reed's reaction—he'd be furious, probably. So what good would that do? Her fingers tapped nervously on the steering wheel as she waited, listening to the radio and the police band, her ears pricked for any information about the grave found in northern Georgia. She didn't want to piss Reed off; she just needed information. A few other lights snapped on in the apartment building and within twenty minutes Reed appeared, his dark hair wet and pushed away from his face, a white shirt crisp beneath a sport coat as he crossed the small parking lot. Tall and lanky, with a jaw square enough to befit a Hollywood stunt man, he tossed a briefcase into the backseat of his boat of a car, slipped behind the wheel and eased the El Dorado out of its spot.

Nikki didn't even start her hatchback's engine until his big car passed and turned the corner two blocks down. Then she followed. As she wheeled around the turn she saw his car make a left a quarter of a mile up the street. She felt a moment's satisfaction. He was headed to his favorite morning haunt, a deli not far from the I-16 entrance.

She'd give him time to sit down and order, then show up while he was trapped waiting for his meal. If he didn't want to be interrupted he'd let her know.

Pulling into the lot of a nearby bank, she gave him five minutes. That should be plenty. With her notepad and recorder tucked into her purse, she dashed across the wet pavement and thought she saw something move in the thicket of live oaks near the back door. She paused, looked again, but saw nothing. Yet the smell of cigarette smoke lingered in the air. Her gaze searched the shadows, then she told herself she was being silly. So a cook from the diner stepped outside for a smoke. So what? She hurried toward the entrance. Two men already leaving held the door for her and she slipped quietly inside.

The diner was warm. At six in the morning, a gaggle of locals were already huddled around the counter that surrounded the kitchen. Farmers, delivery men, truckers and the like swapped stories and jokes, sipped java and plowed into massive breakfasts of ham, grits, fried eggs and toast. Paddle fans pushed the smoke-laden air around while bacon sizzled on a grill, and pies, freshly baked and already on display, rotated slowly in a refrigerated case.

She glanced around the tables.

Reed was in a back booth, nursing a cup of coffee and eyeing a newspaper.

It's now or never, she thought, girding herself for the inevitable brush-off. Anytime she had tried to get information out of him, he'd become an impenetrable granite wall, offering little, his responses oftentimes bordering on rude. Well, at least, tough.

She *had* to write this story. Especially now that Tom Fink had given her his blessing. Who knew when that would change?

Ignoring the *Please Wait To Be Seated* sign, she walked up to Reed's booth and slid across from him. He didn't even look up. "Detective Reed?"

His gaze climbed from the open newspaper to her face. His expression didn't change. Light brown eyes assessed her. "I don't remember asking you to sit down."

"I know. I tried to reach you at the station and you didn't call me back."

"I've been busy."

"Of course. But I just want to ask you some questions." She was reaching into her purse, fumbling for her recorder and notepad. She pushed the record button half expecting him to reach across the table and click the machine off.

He raised a dark eyebrow. "You always want to ask questions."

She ignored the remark and plowed on. "You went up to Dahlonega."

"So did you."

So, he'd seen her. She'd thought so. "Yes, I'm working on the story."

"Is that so?" His voice was steady, without a trace of amusement.

"Yes, and—"

The waitress, a tall, slim twenty-some-year-old with Nicole Kidman curls and a name tag that read Jo came by to take their orders. "Have you decided?" she asked, smiling widely as she held a steaming carafe in each hand.

Quickly, Nikki grabbed a menu from its hiding spot between a plastic ketchup container and a metal syrup carousel.

"Regular or decaf?"

"Regular," Nikki said automatically.

Jo turned over a cup on the table and filled it.

"The usual," Reed said, lines of irritation etching his forehead. "Number Four. Ham, eggs over easy, wheat toast and grits. Hot sauce."

"Got it. You?" Jo turned doe-brown eyes on Nikki.

"Just coffee, oh, and a slice of pie. Pecan."

"That's all?"

"Right."

"Ice cream? It comes with it."

"None, thanks. Just the pie." Nikki wasn't really hungry, didn't want anything but high-octane coffee, but she needed a reason to stick around. Otherwise she was certain Reed would give her the boot. Fast. That he hadn't rebuffed her in the first thirty seconds of their conversation was a record.

"I'll be back in a sec," Jo promised without jotting anything down, then bustled off to the next table.

"So." Nikki set her recorder on the table.

Reed glanced at it derisively. "I'm not going to tell you anything about the case in Lumpkin County or any other ongoing investigation, for that matter." He picked up his cup and stared at her over the rim. "You may as well get your pie for the road."

"I just want some background information."

"Don't have any."

"But—"

"The department issues statements to the press. So does the Lumpkin County Sheriff's Department and the FBI. You can wait for them like everyone else."

"The FBI has been called in?" she asked, her pulse jumping. If that were the case—

"Not yet." He drank a long swallow of coffee.

"But they will be."

"I was just giving you an example."

She wasn't convinced. "Maybe you were trying to give me a tip."

He laughed and the corners of his eyes crinkled sarcastically, not softening his harsh features in the least. "Oh, yeah, *that's* what I was trying to do." He stared straight at her. "But not just one. I think I want to be the leak in the department, you know, give you every bit of evidence that comes down the pipe. That way it'll be in the papers and the murderer will know exactly what we've got on him. And so will every nutcase who wants to make his own splash and take credit for a crime he didn't commit. You'd be surprised how many yahoos want that kind of attention. Sifting through them all would cost the department a lot of time and money. It's a waste of manpower and really muddies the water, which allows the real killer to go about his business." He took another sip of coffee, then set his near-empty cup on the table. "Just call me Deep Throat." Mockery flared in his eyes as he added, "Maybe you're too young to recall the Watergate insider who confided to Woodward and Bernstein."

"My dad's a judge. I grew up hearing about that Deep Throat as well as about the X-rated movie he was named for."

"Really?" Reed reached inside his jacket pocket for his wallet. "The way I heard it, your old man wasn't talking to you, either. Not since you compromised his case."

Her throat tightened. Heat washed up the back of her neck. But she stared him down. "That was a long time ago, Reed. He got over it."

"I wouldn't. Not if you crucified me the way you did your own father. Believe me, I'd never forgive you," he said as the waitress returned carrying a variety of platters. Reed pulled his gaze from Nikki's and offered Jo a humorless smile. "I think Miss Gillette neglected to tell you she wanted her pie 'to go.'"

"Oh." The girl was suddenly flustered. No doubt she'd heard the tail end of the conversation. "I'm sorry, let me wrap your order up." Quickly, as if she couldn't make tracks fast enough, she slid Reed's platters onto the table and swept the slice of pie back to the kitchen.

Reed turned his attention to Nikki again. "Now, listen to me, Miss Gillette. The only tip I'm giving today is to Jo, for serving me this." He jabbed a fork at his grits. "I have nothing to say to you but 'no comment,' and no matter how many E-mails or voice mails or any kind of messages you leave me, I won't have anything to say until the department issues a statement, and probably not then. You'll have to live with what the rest of the reporters in town get."

She felt her back going up. "You know, Reed," she said, "I never figured you for sticking to the company line. I thought you had more guts. More class. That you'd form your own opinions."

"And tell them to you?" he asked, jaw sliding to one side.

"I always heard you were a rogue cop, someone who bent the rules to get to the truth."

"You heard wrong."

"Did I?" she challenged. "Why did you go up to Lumpkin County? A detective from Savannah. Were you called in to give your expertise? Or did you have some connection to the place? To the killing? Why you?"

He didn't answer but there was the tiniest of flickers in his eyes, a shadow slipping quickly through them. "I don't know."

"Of course you do."

A muscle worked in his jaw. "Leave it alone, Nikki. This is police business."

"What the hell happened up on Blood Mountain?"

His lips tightened. "Since you're here, I have some advice for you."

"Good. I'm listening." She flicked a glance at her recorder silently taping the entire conversation.

"The next time you stake out someone's apartment and tail them, you might be a little more discreet."

"I guess I should take a lesson on stakeouts from you, right?" she shot back and immediately regretted the dig.

His jaw clamped. His eyes narrowed and he slowly set his fork down with such precision that she knew he was holding back his rage. "This interview is over."

"It never began."

"That's right." He reached over and pressed a button on the recorder. The tape player clicked off. Reed glared her down.

Jo picked that moment to return with a Styrofoam box. "Here ya go, hon."

Nikki reached for her purse, but Reed's hand shot across the table, catching her wrist. Strong fingers tightened. "It's on me." As quickly as he'd grabbed her, he let go. Turning to the waitress he managed a needle-thin smile. "Add Miss Gillette's order to my bill."

"Will do," Jo said, her eyes moving quickly to Nikki, then back to Reed. She dropped the receipt onto the table, then turned on her heel and headed for a nearby table where a group of men in hunting coats and hats were settling in.

Nikki tried to backtrack, to salvage some kind of relationship with the man. "Look, Detective Reed, I'm sorry if we got started on the wrong foot."

"We didn't get started at all."

"What is it you dislike about me so?"

"It's not personal."

"Oh, yeah?"

"It's your profession. I really don't like any reporters. Any of 'em. They just get in the way."

"Sometimes we help. You need the public to be informed."

"Rarely. What you really do is rile people up, start making assumptions, scare the hell out of the public, print stories that aren't always double-checked . . . it's a real pain in the ass. But don't quote me. That's 'off the record.' "

"You just don't like having watchdogs. The media keeps you honest."

"The media is a pain in the ass." He glanced down at his uneaten meal, frowned, and reached for his wallet. "I changed my mind. You can stay. I'm not hungry anymore." He slapped a twenty onto the table and slid out of the booth. *"Bon appétit!"*

"Hey! Wait a minute." She took off after him, flying out the door as he strode to his El Dorado. Cold air slapped her in the face as she dashed across the parking lot. He had already unlocked the car when she reached him. "Okay, okay, I'm sorry about the dig about the stakeout," she apologized. "I blew it. I shouldn't have brought up what happened in San Francisco. And I know I went too far defending my profession. I know there are reporters that would . . . sensationalize a story just to make a big splash, okay? I blew it. I shouldn't have mentioned it. I just want this story. I don't expect you to compromise the investigation. I wouldn't ask for that. And I don't expect special consideration, but I want a new angle. I mean, here we are in Savannah and you went all the way upstate to another jurisdiction."

"So?"

"Why? What's it to you? What's going on?" He didn't respond, just stood there. "Look, I want to work with you, not against you," she tried again, but he just stared at her. It was still dark, rain was collecting on his dark hair and his expression in the bluish glow from the diner's neon sign was hard. Uncompromising. Damn near pissed off.

"You people," he said in a voice so low she barely heard it. "You just never know when to give up, do you?"

"No more than you do. If you gave up, no cases would ever be solved."

"It's not the same."

"We both have jobs to do."

"That's right. And I need to get to mine." He climbed into the huge car, jabbed the keys at the ignition and fired up the engine.

Furious with herself, Nikki stepped back and watched as he wheeled out of the lot.

"Great," she muttered under her breath. "Just damned wonderful. Some kind of investigative reporter you are, Gillette." Hiking her collar against the rain, she walked back to the bank's parking lot and slid behind the wheel of her car. So much for getting closer to Reed. That had backfired. Big time. So it was back to square one.

Again. But there was a reason Reed was called up to Lumpkin County. Something important. His expertise? His connections? The fact that he'd been born up there? What? She'd checked and double-checked, couldn't find any reason other than he'd spent a few years there as a child and that lead had fizzled into nothing.

Fuming, she drummed her fingers on the steering wheel and told herself she wasn't going to figure it out here in the damned empty parking lot. She had some serious digging to do. She pumped the gas and twisted the ignition. As the engine sparked, she looked over her shoulder to back out of her spot when she noticed something move near the hedge surrounding the parking lot, a shadow duck away from the glow of the street lamp.

Her heart clutched.

She glanced in the rearview mirror. Nothing.

Another look over her shoulder showed the hedge undisturbed.

"It's nothing," she told herself just as she caught a glimpse of a man standing on the other side of the hedge, still out of the glow of the street lamp. She couldn't distinguish his features but knew he was staring at her. Watching her.

Had he been waiting?

The same man she'd seen before her meeting with Reed?

Her throat went dry as she threw the car into reverse. So what if a man had been lingering near the diner? Big deal. It wasn't a crime and it was damned near rush hour. Dawn was already casting gray light into the city.

Maybe the guy was waiting for a ride, looking for a bus, on his way to work . . .

Or maybe not.

There was something about the way he stood, just out of the light, that made him seem different. She'd sensed his eyes upon her. Observing. Her skin crawled instinctively. "Pervert," she muttered, glancing again at her rearview mirror.

He was gone.

Not a trace of him anywhere near the street.

Vanished swiftly, as if she'd dreamed him.

"Come on, Nikki. Get a grip." Maybe her imagination was just working overtime and she saw evil lurking where there was none. All the talk about graves and dead bodies and murder was probably just getting to her. "Oh, that's good," she thought aloud. "The would-be crime reporter creeped out because of a guy who was probably just waiting for a bus." What was wrong with her? One confrontation with Reed and she was suddenly jelly? That wasn't like her. She rammed the car into gear and drove out of the parking lot. There was no one watching her, following her. It was nothing. Nothing!

And yet . . .

She looked in the mirror once more. Was he there? Just out of the lamplight? Silently spying from the shadowy foliage? Was there a bit of movement?

Cold sweat appeared on her skin as she stepped on the accelerator.

A horn blasted.

She stood on the brakes, narrowly missing a taxi that

was roaring by on her right. She hadn't even seen the cab. Adrenaline pumping, fingers damp on the wheel, she told herself to pull it together. She couldn't afford to blow the opportunity of cracking this story wide open. Not when she'd waited for it all of her life.

She gunned it and the hatchback squealed onto the street.

One last peek at the mirror, but she saw no one. No one at all.

Run, bitch, The Survivor thought from the dense foliage on the other side of the hedge. Between the leaves he observed the red taillights as Nikki Gillette's car disappeared around a corner. *You'll never get away. Not from me.*

A thrill skittered down his spine. Anticipation sang through his blood. She was hooked and her interest would ensure more media attention, not just from the rag of a newspaper that she worked for, but from the television and radio stations as well. Not just in that hick town up north, but in Atlanta and here in Savannah as well. The national media would pick it up . . . yes . . .

As he'd expected, Nikki Gillette had tailed Reed to this diner and confronted the cop. From outside the window, The Survivor had watched their exchange. It had gone perfectly, according to plan. Standing in the cold air he'd heard nothing of the conversation, but, from their expressions, and by reading their lips, he'd watched the argument ensue.

She wanted a scoop.

Reed wouldn't tell her a thing.

Which would spur her into delving deeper. It was her nature. Nikki didn't like to lose.

Now, cop and reporter were both involved.

Perfect.

Their nerves were already stretched tight.

The Survivor smiled. Licked his lips with the tip of his tongue.

For this was just the beginning.

CHAPTER 6

"Okay, Cliff, so give," Nikki said when he'd finally answered his cell phone. She'd spent the morning in the office, catching up as quickly as she could on her other work, leaving a message for her sister, listening to a little office gossip, but for the most part concentrating on the two bodies found in the single grave in the northern Georgia woods. She'd tried all her contacts in Lumpkin County and a friend with the AP who worked out of Atlanta, but what little information had been given to the press from the sheriff's department was already widespread. It didn't give her the edge she needed. Now, seated at her desk, doodling on a notepad, she spoke softly, hoping no one, including Trina, would overhear. "What's happening with the case up in Dahlonega? Why's Reed involved?"

"Hell, Nikki, why don't you ask him?" Cliff was irritated.

"I tried. This morning. Let's just say he wasn't overly communicative."

"Sounds like him."

"So, why him? Why did he chopper up there? What was the connection?"

"I can't say."

"But there was a connection."

"I said, I can't—"

"Why not?"

He didn't answer, but she'd guessed the reason when Reed had been sent up to Dahlonega. "Because somehow Reed's involved. Either with the victim or the killer or he's a suspect or—"

"Whoa. Slow down. Don't overspeculate."

"But there has to be a reason. Do you know who the victims are yet?"

He hesitated.

"I take that as a yes."

"I didn't say that."

"Come on, Cliff. You guys are going to release the names as soon as the next of kin have been notified."

"It'll happen this afternoon."

"So, give me a little bit of a head start."

He sighed through his nose, and Nikki felt a second's relief. Cliff always let out his breath before spilling significant beans. "I guess it wouldn't hurt. There are two women, one older and decomposing badly—we don't know who she is. The other one is younger, obviously been in the coffin a short while."

"How short?"

"Less than a day."

125

"Who is she?" Nikki asked

"Her name is Barbara Jean Marx. Goes by Bobbi. Native Savannahian. Look, that's all I can tell you, really. I've got to go."

Nikki wrote down the victim's name. It was a start. "How did she die?"

Hesitation. Nikki put a question mark by the name.

"What about the other one?"

"I'll leave it at homicide, at least in Bobbi's case, but I really can't discuss it any further. It could injure the investigation."

"That's department mumbo jumbo and you know it." Nikki wrote Reed's name beside the victims and put another question mark by *Who is the other victim? How related?*

"For now, it's all I can say."

Bobbi could tell Cliff wasn't about to be swayed on the cause of death issue, so she tried another tack. "So, who is she? And I'm not talking about her name."

"I'm not at liberty to say."

"You're beginning to sound like a broken record."

"Good."

Hearing the finality in his tone and knowing he was about to ring off, she quickly asked, "Why would the department send Reed? Or did the Lumpkin County Sheriff's Department request him?"

A beat. No answer. He was clamming up. She had to work fast. "Was it because he lived up there once, or because he's got some special skills, or just because he was the cop on duty?"

"Figure it out, Nikki," Siebert growled. "It ain't

rocket science." He hung up with a loud, final click.

"Damn," she muttered, but tore the piece of paper from her notepad and stuffed it into her purse. She didn't waste a minute. This was her chance. Her BIG chance. One she wasn't going to share with Norm Metzger. No way. No how. No matter what Tom Fink wanted. She wouldn't take a chance that somehow someone in the office might discover what she was researching, so she packed up her laptop, logged out and drove home. Even though she might freeze as the insulation in her turret apartment was nearly nonexistent, she did have cable Internet and a password that would allow her into news archives at the *Sentinel* and its sister newspaper in Atlanta. Whatever there was to know about Barbara Jean Marx, Nikki would discover it this afternoon, then start the legwork to check out "Bobbi's" home, her workplace, her friends. And maybe in so doing she'd figure out why the woman was murdered.

"What do they know up at the sheriff's department?" Reed asked when McFee entered his office around three. Reed had worked all morning, catching up on other cases, tracking down the lab to see if they'd gotten any latent fingerprints off the note he'd received the other day, calling St. Claire and asking about more information on the victims in the grave. The ME had faxed over the preliminary reports and Reed was reading them now. Everything St. Claire had told him had proved true. Barbara Jean Marx had died of asphyxiation, she had a high blood alcohol level and traces of a sedative, Ativan, in her blood. Her fingers were scraped raw, her knees bruised, her forehead bloodied, presumably from hitting her head on the inside top of the coffin. She'd lost fingernails and toenails while trying to claw her way to freedom. And she'd been about eleven weeks pregnant. His gut clenched as McFee settled into a side chair. "You talked to Baldwin?"

"A couple of times, but we still haven't got much more information than we had a couple of days ago," the big detective admitted. His scowl was more pronounced as he ran a hand over his jaw. He reached into his pocket and pulled out a small notepad. "Prescott Jones, the kid who was hurt up at the mountain, he's still critical. Baldwin went up to talk to him and find out what he saw, but didn't get much out of him and the doctors and nurses weren't happy to have anyone disturbing him. The boy's old man wasn't any help. Seems to think the kid can sell his story to a tabloid. Baldwin's still working on him, though. He talked to the other boy."

"Delacroix?"

"Right. But his story hasn't changed and he can't remember any more details. There was something about him, though . . . he seemed to be holding back."

"Maybe cops scare him. They do a lot of kids. So the boy clams up rather than get himself into what he thinks will be deeper trouble."

"I'll check with him again." McFee made a note to himself. "Or maybe the sheriff can get whatever it is out of him."

"Maybe," Reed allowed.

"I also talked to the lead investigator for the crime scene and they've got a serial number on the coffin, along with soil samples. You were right, some of the dirt on the coffin didn't match the soil where it was found. Too much sand."

Boots beating a sharp tattoo announced Morrisette before she appeared in the doorway. Her blond hair projected in all directions and she was dressed head to toe in denim jeans, shirt, and jacket. Along with her snakeskin boots that she'd bought long ago in El Paso. "Did I miss anything?" she asked and offered McFee a smile that could easily be construed as flirty. Jesus, would she *never* learn?

"McFee was just filling me in on what they found up north."

"The crime scene team got a serial number on the casket and soil that doesn't match the surrounding dirt."

"So, the coffin came from somewhere else."

"Looks like," McFee said. "They're checking and comparing."

Morrisette propped her rear on the windowsill. Behind her, on the other side of the glass, a winter sun was forcing rays through thick clouds. "They might see if it matches the silt around Stonewall Cemetery."

"Why?" McFee asked.

"They had a disturbance the other night."

Reed turned all his attention to his partner. "A coffin missing?"

"You got it. Not just the coffin, but the body inside."

"Let me guess—a sixty-year-old woman?"

"Pauline Alexander."

McFee snorted. "That works. The coffin was made in Jackson, Mississippi, and sold to Beauford Alexander, for his wife. Just about two months ago."

"Pauline Alexander died at home, a heart attack while she was in the kitchen making jam or jelly or preserves or the like." Morrisette shrugged. "I didn't know anyone did that sort of thing anymore. Anyway Beauford came in from hunting, found her on the floor and called 911. But it was too late."

Reed scanned the autopsy on the older woman, looking for anything that would have caused a heart attack, but there was nothing, at least so far, that would indicate foul play. "So, we have one woman who died of natural causes and another who was murdered, left alive in the casket to die," he said, then glanced up. "And she was pregnant."

"Shit, no!" Morrisette pushed up from the windowsill.

McFee's expression hardened. "A baby?"

"The victim was around two months along."

"You think the murderer knew?" Morrisette demanded. "Jesus H. Christ, what kind of sick, perverted wacko would off a pregnant woman? Who would be so angry? Hell, it's probably the father. The husband."

"If he was the father," Reed said, his guts roiling. "We'll need a DNA test."

"You said you were involved with her." Across the desk, McFee was staring suspiciously at Reed.

"What? Wait a minute." Morrisette's mouth dropped open. "*You, the father?* Oh, Christ, wait till Okano gets wind of this. Your ass will be off this case in a heartbeat."

"Any news on who saw Bobbi last?" Reed asked.

"Maybe you should tell me." Morrisette was pacing, running her fingers nervously through her already electric-shock-styled hair. "Why didn't you say anything?" She was angry, her cheeks flaming. "You know, Reed, we're partners. You know everything about my life, my kids, my exes and . . . oh, hell." She flung herself back against the sill in exasperation. "Got any other little secrets you want to air?"

"Not now."

"Well, let me know, would ya?"

"What we need to figure out is if Barbara Jean Marx knew Pauline Alexander."

"That, and a whole lot more," Morrisette muttered.

"Yes, but is there a connection? Was Pauline's coffin exhumed randomly or was the killer giving us another clue? The note mentions two."

"Are you fuckin' for real?" Morrisette muttered. "Or do you have ice water in your veins? You just found out that your lover was tossed into a coffin, buried alive, possibly carrying your child and you . . . you sit there calmly and ask if she knew the other woman?" She rolled her eyes and threw up a hand. "I can't believe it."

Reed leaned back in his chair. "The best thing we can do is solve this."

"But—"

"He's right," McFee cut in. "And you don't have

much time." He was staring at Reed, but hitched a thumb toward Morrisette. "Because she's right, too. Your ass is gonna be thrown off this case. Pronto."

Nikki's cell phone chirped as she pulled up to the curb in front of Jerome Marx's business. Caller ID verified that her friend Simone was on the other end of the connection. "Hey, what's up?" Nikki asked, eyeing the doorway to the redbrick building situated a few blocks from the Cotton Exchange.

"Kickboxing tomorrow night, seven o'clock. Remember?"

Inwardly Nikki groaned. She had hours of research ahead of her tonight and tomorrow, and a story to write. "No."

"You missed the last class."

"I know, I know, but I'm caught up in something really big."

"Don't tell me," Simone said and Nikki could hear the smile in her voice. "The story of a lifetime. Your chance to make it in the big time, your big break, the scoop of the century, the—"

"Okay, okay, so you've heard it all before."

"Mmhmm. I thought we could go kick some butt, then get barbecue or go out for drinks or something fun."

"I don't know if I can make it."

"Come on, Nikki, this class was your idea."

Nikki glanced at her watch. Five-thirty. Where was Marx? "I don't know."

"You'll feel so much better."

Simone was right about that. A little exercise couldn't hurt, and after class Nikki usually felt wired, ready to take on the world. "Okay, I'll meet you at the gym, but I'm not sure about anything else."

"I guess I'll just have to talk you into it. Maybe we can talk Jake into going out for something afterwards."

Jake Vaughn was their instructor. Tall, dark, handsome, with muscles straight out of a Mr. Universe competition. Also, Nikki suspected, gay. All the women and some of the men in the class drooled over him. Jake didn't give off any of those sexual vibes of most thirty-something jocks. Simone didn't seem to notice or care. She'd been harboring a crush on Jake since the first class in September. "You can try."

"I will."

Nikki's eyes were on the building's doorway where she spied Jerome Marx exiting. He was wearing an overcoat and walking briskly to a parking structure. "Look, Simone, I've got to run. I'll see ya later."

"I'm counting on it. Tomorrow." Simone hung up. Nikki clicked off her cell phone, dropped it into her purse and was out of the car in one swift motion. Darkness was already descending as she hurried up the street and caught up with him at the building's staircase. "Mr. Marx?"

The guy turned to face her and a bit of a smile touched his lips. Not exactly the grieving husband.

"Nikki Gillette, the *Savannah Sentinel*. I heard about your wife. My condolences."

"My ex-wife," he clarified, his smile sliding away to reveal the hard line of his mouth. "Well, at least, soon-to-be ex, but thank you."

"If you have a minute or two, I'd love to speak with you about what happened." She was nearly jogging to close the distance between them.

"What's to say? Bobbi was murdered. Some creep threw her in a coffin and buried her alive with a dead woman. I hope to God the police catch the bastard." He started up the concrete steps.

Nikki stopped short. "Alive?" she repeated, shocked, her blood turning to ice water. In Nikki's mind she envisioned being in a tight space, running out of air, no escape. "She was alive?" As horrified as she was, she felt a thrill of excitement. She'd not only learned the ID of one victim, but the unique method of the killing. "Was she awake? Or . . . or drugged? Did she know what was happening to her?"

He blanched. Realized he'd said too much. "That was off the record."

"You didn't mention anything being restricted."

"Quote me and I'll sue," he said over his shoulder, but it didn't matter. Nikki was jazzed. This was it! The story she'd been waiting for. She had two sources saying that Barbara Jean Marx was the victim. She'd double check with Cliff about two bodies in one coffin, about Barbara Jean being buried alive, but she had her scoop.

"Do you know who the other woman was?" she asked, her mind already spinning to her angle.

"No."

"Did your wife have any enemies?"

"Too many to count, and this interview is over—not

134

that it really began." He shouldered open the door to the third level. Nikki caught the door and was through it as he made his way to a black Mercedes.

"Do you have any idea who would want to harm Barbara?"

He paused at the sleek car's fender. "Ask Pierce Reed," he said angrily. "Now, if you'll excuse me." He unlocked the car and was behind the wheel before she could respond. With one final glower, he backed out of his parking space and drove down the ramp.

Wind howled through the open spaces of the parking garage and Nikki stood on the concrete between oil stains and tire marks. The lot was empty except for a few cars. Nikki's boots slapped on the dirty concrete as she headed to the stairs. Barbara Jean Marx was left for dead in the coffin. With another body? The gruesome thought turned Nikki's stomach and for a second she felt the victim's fear. Nikki was claustrophobic by nature, preferred wide open spaces to tight closets or elevator cars, or small rooms. The thought of waking up forced into a coffin between a dead woman and the lid or floor . . . oh, God, it was too gruesome to consider. Who would do such a thing? How passionately could one person hate another to place them in such a grisly situation?

Nikki walked to the staircase and started down.

Ask Pierce Reed.

Of course she'd ask Reed. He was involved in the investigation.

And yet, the way Jerome Marx had spit out the suggestion, as if it were an invective, was odd. As if there were something more to it. *You're making more of it; your imagination is working overtime. Again.*

She heard a door slam from a floor above her and the soles of shoes scraping on the stairs.

But why was Reed called in on the investigation?

And why did the name Barbara Marx ring some sort of distant bell with her? From the moment she'd heard the name it seemed familiar. Maybe it was a movie star or other celebrity, a famous person she'd read about in a gossip column or the credits of a movie, but she had the feeling . . .

The footsteps overhead were gaining on her and she considered the dark figure she'd seen this morning, the stranger in the shadows. Her pulse quickened a bit; the stairway wasn't all that well lit, and she increased her pace, hustling to the first floor as the footsteps rang ever closer. She threw open the door to the street and put some distance between herself and the parking garage, glancing over her shoulder in time to see a man in an overcoat dash away from her, as if he were in a hurry of his own. He didn't even as much as look in her direction as she reached her car, but her heart was drumming a hundred beats a minute as she unlocked the door.

She nearly climbed inside when she noticed the piece of paper tucked under her windshield wiper. Inwardly she groaned. Great. A parking ticket. But it was after hours, right? And it really didn't appear to be a citation. Oh, God, someone had hit her car. That was it. And they left the scene. She ripped the note from beneath the wipers and opened the folded page. She'd expected to find a name and phone number. Instead, there was one word:

Tonight.

What the hell did that mean?

The wind kicked up and dry leaves skittered down the street. A car passed and Nikki glanced around, looking for the person who'd left the note. No one was close by. No one lurking and watching that she could see. The few pedestrians visible seemed like office workers hurrying through the dusk to their own vehicles or homes. There was a kid on a skateboard, a woman pushing a carriage, an older man walking his dog, a teenaged couple cuddling and laughing as they jaywalked across the street. She looked back to the parking area . . . the door was closing . . . the hairs on the back of her neck raised, though there was really no reason.

She shoved the note into her purse and scooted into her car. She was usually pretty fearless, but there was something in the air today, something that put her on edge, and the thought of Bobbi Jean Marx crammed into a coffin with a dead, decomposing woman bothered her. She was a reporter. She'd become inured to a lot of the pain and suffering in the world, but when the suffering was children or animals, it got to her. Big time. Anyone who inflicted harm on the innocents should be locked away forever or worse. The same went for any creep that threw a living, breathing woman into a coffin with a corpse. What death could be worse? She shuddered and drove away from the curb.

Tonight.

Tonight, *what?*

"What in God's name were you thinking?" Katherine Okano was standing behind her desk, staring out the window as Reed knocked on her partially opened door, then entered. The District Attorney's arms were crossed under her breasts, the fingers of one hand tapping angrily on the opposite arm's sleeve. Thin, imperative and determined, she nailed Reed. "You *knew* Barbara Jean Marx, a victim in a homicide investigation, and you requested to be on the case?" Before he could answer, she added, "And she was pregnant. The child could be yours. Do you see that there is a conflict of interest here?" Her voice dripped sarcasm.

"I want to find her killer."

"No doubt, but you're off the investigation." She looked over the tops of her wire-rimmed glasses. A no-nonsense woman in her mid forties, she sported a blond bob, quick mind, and a stare that could cut a person to the bone.

"I knew Barbara."

"You're prejudiced. And by the way, the woman was married. The department doesn't need this kind of bad publicity. The press would have a field day with this."

She pulled out her desk chair and settled into it as if the subject were closed. "No more discussions, Reed. You're out."

"The letter in the coffin was directed to me. I got another one in the mail the other morning with a fake postmark, Colonial Cemetery. I think they're from the same person. Whoever this creep is, he's trying to engage me."

She looked up at him. "All the more reason."

"Kathy, you know I can handle this. I'll be objective and yet I'll have an inside view of the case."

"Give it up, Reed. No way."

"But—"

"And I suggest you give up a DNA sample voluntarily."

"Already done."

"Good. Then leave it, Reed. We're doing this one by the book." She blinked once. "Got it?"

"Got it."

"Fine. But if you have any ideas of doing something behind my back, remember, it's your job we're talking about. I stuck my neck out for you when you left San Francisco. Don't make me look like a fool."

"Wouldn't dream of it."

"Good." She offered him the first sincere smile of the day. "Then you won't object to a paternity test and an interview with Detective McFee."

"Not at all," Reed said, though he was fuming inside. He knew that she wasn't accusing him of anything, probably didn't suspect him of any wrongdoing, but it galled him nonetheless. He walked to the door and as he was leaving she said, "Thanks, Pierce. I know this isn't easy and . . . well . . . my condolences if . . . you know."

If the child turns out to be yours.

"Yeah. I do know." He left her office and wound his

way back to his own desk. His child. Was it possible? Damn, what a mess.

She was in the kitchen. Small, with white hair piled high on her head, exposing a dowager's hump beneath her dressing gown, the woman was busy at her stove, heating water for tea. Just as she did every Tuesday night, the only evening the maid didn't stay in. The old house was dark except for the bluish glow from the television she'd left on in her bedroom and the warm patches of light from the kitchen.

The Survivor watched her from the outside. Hungered for what was to come. He saw it in his mind's eye, the killing, and a rush stole through his blood. Hidden in the shadows of a huge magnolia tree, he petted the huge tabby cat in his arms and glanced up to the sky. The quarter moon was high, barely visible through the web of branches and the thin layer of clouds that hung above the city. The cat was nervous, trying to get away. No such luck.

The tea kettle whistled. The Survivor heard its shriek even through the watery panes. Good. The cat jumped, but couldn't get away. It was almost time. Sweat broke out on his skin. He must be patient. A few more seconds.

The back door opened a crack. The old woman stepped into the porch light's beam. "Maximus?" she called in her cackly voice. "Come, boy."

The cat squirmed.

Adrenaline pumped through his veins. The time was near.

Wait. Not yet.

"Here, kitty, kitty . . . Maximus, you little devil . . . where are you? Come, boy, come kitty, kitty, kitty." Her voice edgy with concern, she shuffled from one end of the porch to the other and peered into the darkness and the dense foliage of her garden.

In his arms the tabby tried to scrabble free.

Not yet. Not quite yet. His blood thundered in his ears. Rushing. He didn't move. Didn't make a sound.

"Oh, for pity's sake, you naughty boy, now you come in . . ."

Now!

In one silent movement, he hurled the cat over the fence.

The tabby screeched.

"Maximus? What the devil?" she asked and hurried down the steps . . . onto the brick path . . . her slippers rustling as she made her way to the gate.

He reached into his pocket. Gloved fingers found the waiting syringe.

"Come here, boy. Kitty, kitty, are you hurt?" She was fumbling with the latch when he leapt from the shadows. She started to scream.

With one hand, he covered her mouth.

She struggled, surprisingly strong for an old bony thing. "Time to meet God, Roberta," he whispered roughly against her ear and she struggled more fiercely, her body writhing wildly. But she was no match for him.

With his free hand, he plunged his deadly needle into her scrawny arm, through the silky fabric of her dressing gown. She fought, twisting her neck backward and staring into his face. There was a moment of recognition, of astonishment and anguish as she bit into the glove. Hard. Teeth piercing the leather.

Pain shot through his palm. "Bitch!" he snarled.

Her last-ditch effort to save herself was too late.

The damage was done.

Her eyes rolled back in her head. Her jaw slackened. Her body sagged.

He threw her over his shoulder as the cat, hissing, darted through the shadows to stare at him with angry malevolent eyes. His only witness. And an unwitting partner. The stupid creature didn't realize he'd never see his mistress alive again.

No one would.

CHAPTER 7

"You're calling the guy 'the Grave Robber?'" Tom Fink asked as he adjusted his reading glasses and studied the final draft of Nikki's article on the crime scene in Lumpkin County. It was late at night, the morning edition was about to be put to bed, and Nikki shifted from one foot to the other in front of Fink's desk. He stood on the other side. Her article was faceup between them.

"Right. It's got a nice ring to it, don't you think?" Nikki was jazzed to think that finally she would see her byline on the front page. She imagined the story in print. Bold headlines would declare: "Grave Robber Strikes, Baffles Police."

If Fink went for it.

"Your sources are impeccable?" He raised a skeptical eyebrow.

"Of course."

"Don't bullshit me. You've talked to Reed?" Fink pointed to the detective's name in the second paragraph.

"I've tried. He's not too cooperative. But I have a source close to the investigation—"

"Who?" he demanded.

"Uh-uh. I don't reveal my sources. Not even to you."

"You're willing to take the stand to that effect."

"If I have to. But I won't. I spoke to both victims' husbands to corroborate."

"Wait a minute," he clarified. "One victim. The old lady, Pauline Alexander, died of natural causes."

She really had Fink's attention now. Good. "So it appears. But no one's certain."

"Curiouser and curiouser?" he asked.

"Very."

Some of his grim demeanor faded as he skimmed her article for the third time. "You've shown this to Metzger?"

Nikki couldn't lie. Even if she wanted to. Which she didn't. Fink would find out soon enough. "No. I haven't spoken to him."

Fink looked over the top of his reading glasses and he didn't look pleased. "Why not? I thought I said you two were to work together."

Lifting a shoulder, Nikki said, "I work better alone. I think if you asked Norm, he would say the same about himself."

"So you've gone off half-cocked." He straightened, crossing his arms over his chest, his frown deepening into crevices all over again. "I told you—"

"Do you want to run this or not?" she demanded, taking the offensive. "Right now, we've scooped the competition. In six hours, everything in here"—she rapped the pages with an impatient finger—"will be splashed across every newspaper in the southeast and on TV and radio. Right now, we have the scoop, unless we blow it, and as to this article's validity, I'm standing behind what's in here one hundred percent."

"I expect you to do that for every story."

"Then make it a hundred and fifty percent, or two hundred. I'm telling you, Tom, this is hot. It's damned near an exclusive."

He snorted. Looked dubious. Chewed on the inside of his lip as if this were some kind of world debate or something when, in Nikki's estimation, this was a slam dunk.

"Tom, really. Trust me."

He glanced up at her. His eyes said silently, *I did once before and you blew it with the Chevalier trial.* But he didn't utter the words because for over a decade, ever since that debacle, her work had been impeccable. Yet, he hesitated. And she knew why. It bugged the hell out of him that he didn't know any of Nikki's contacts. It had been a source of friction between them for years.

"I spent the past three hours double-checking the facts."

Cliff Siebert had been reticent with the details, but he'd confirmed everything she'd learned from Jerome Marx. When she'd asked about Reed, Cliff had informed her that she'd better talk to the brusque detective herself. Like she hadn't tried that already. She'd left more messages, gotten no response and decided to mention his name in the article, about how he'd been called up to Lumpkin County, that *he* was the connection to the murders.

"All right, we'll run it. Page one." Tom rubbed the back of his neck and she expected him to warn her that her job was on the line. Instead, he muttered, "Good work."

Nikki couldn't believe it. A compliment from Tom the Terrible? Things were definitely looking up. Before he could change his mind, she grabbed her things and was out the door where the night had settled deep into the city. Mist hovered over the street lamps and stoplights as she climbed into her car. She cranked on the ignition and the engine sputtered, coughed and died. "Come on," she muttered. Not tonight. Her little Subaru couldn't give out on her now. She twisted the key again and this time the reticent engine roared to life. "That's better." Sighing in relief, she patted the dash and drove out of the lot.

The streets were quiet. Eerily empty. Only an occasional car passed by as she drove home. She thought of the man who she'd seen after her aborted meeting with Reed, and as she pulled into her parking space at her house, she scrounged in her purse and found the note that had been left on her car. Its singular message was clear in the pale light from the security lamps.

Tonight.

Meaning this very night, right?

Was it a warning?

A threat?

Or a harmless prank?

The hairs on the back of her neck raised and she glanced in the rearview mirror. Nothing seemed out of place, though the old house was as dark as it had been when she'd left over eighteen hours earlier. She was tired, that was it. Overreacting.

Nerves strung tight, she yanked her briefcase and purse from the car and hurried along the walk to the gate. Unlatched and swinging free, as if someone had been in too much of a hurry to bother shutting it, it creaked in the wind. Nikki slid through the opening and slammed the wrought-iron latch closed behind her.

Heart hammering, she made her way along a brick path to the exterior stairs, all the while telling herself she was a fool. What was she afraid of? The night? For God's sake, this was ridiculous! She had no time for paranoia.

Her boots clattered as she climbed, and on the final landing she saw movement, something slipping through the shadows. She nearly screamed before she recognized Jennings. "Oh, for the love of God, what're you doing out here?" she asked as the cat pounced onto the steps and, tail aloft, raced up the final steps to her apartment. Nikki followed. Though she could have

146

sworn she'd locked the tabby inside.

Or had she?

Maybe she'd left the bathroom window open to vent out the steam from her shower . . . or maybe he'd slipped past her on her way out this morning. Either way, he was meowing and pacing in front of her door. "Okay, okay, I know," she said, scrabbling in her purse for her keys. "It's cold out here." She found the damned things and went to stick her house key into the lock but as she did she realized the apartment door hadn't quite latched behind her. No wonder the cat had escaped. But . . . the door wasn't ajar, either, just not quite shut. As if someone had intended to close it but had been in a hurry.

Like you. This morning.

She remembered flying out of the apartment, wearing her boots and scarf, hell-bent to tail Reed and confront him. But the door had slammed shut behind her. She was certain she'd heard the latch click. It would have locked.

And the gate would have latched.

Her lungs constricted. Fear slid through her blood at the thought that someone had been inside, was possibly still in her home. Heart in her throat, she cautiously reached into the interior, her fingers searching the wall until she found the light switch and flipped it on. The living room was suddenly ablaze with light. Jennings shot through the door before Nikki could catch him.

No one was hiding in the corners or tucked behind the curtains.

The apartment looked undisturbed.

Still nervous, Nikki walked slowly from one room to the next. Everything, down to the cat's partially consumed food, was just as she'd left it. Cold coffee sat in the pot, her slippers were against the bureau where she'd kicked them, some of her makeup bottles still rested on the counter.

"False alarm," she told the cat and breathed a sigh of relief as she locked the door and double-checked the windows, all of which were shut. "So why didn't the front door latch?" she wondered aloud as she stripped out of her clothes and turned on the radio.

A syndicated talk show, *Midnight Confessions*, was being aired. The host was Dr. Sam, a New Orleans radio psychologist who was currently dispensing advice to any nutcase who had a phone. Nikki remembered the notoriety of the show a few years back when a serial killer stalked the streets of New Orleans and called Dr. Sam while she was on the air. Tonight she was talking to a woman who was thinking about starting a physical affair with a man with whom she'd had cybersex, whatever the hell that was, over the Internet. "Just what we need," Nikki muttered, crawling into bed and petting the cat. "Other people's perversions." Jennings began to purr so loudly Nikki barely heard the next radio caller whining that her current husband didn't get along with her fifteen-year-old daughter. "Big surprise. I didn't get along with my dad, either." She pulled the duvet to her neck and closed her mind to her own rebellious teenage years and her incredibly dysfunctional family. With a pang of guilt she realized she hadn't spoken to her mother in almost a week. "Tomorrow," she promised, making a mental note as she turned off the light and settled deeper under the covers. The room was chilly, the winter night seeming to seep through the window, and shadows played against the walls. Nikki closed her eyes and rolled over, her hand slipping under the pillow, her fingers touching something foreign and stiff—paper, no, an envelope.

What in the world?

She shot out of the bed, snapped on the light and tossed the pillow to one side. Jennings streaked under the bed.

There, on the blue sheets, was an envelope.

Reminding her of the note she'd found on her windshield.

"Oh, God," she whispered, terror driving straight to her heart.

She jumped away from the bed, every muscle tense. Quickly she scanned the bedroom again, rechecking under the bed and in the closet, knowing that someone, some stranger, had been in her house. Her ears strained: She heard nothing but the sound of the wind outside and the old house groaning. *Calm down, Nikki. There is no one, no one inside your apartment. You checked. The door is locked. The bolt is thrown. The windows are latched.*

And yet she was shaking in the middle of the floor.

Someone had been in earlier.

And had left a message.

Trembling, she eased toward the bed, as if she expected someone to leap out from under it when she

149

already knew no one was there. So scared she couldn't think straight, she picked up the envelope and slowly opened it. The message leaped out at her:

IT'S DONE.

She repeated the phrase aloud. "It's done. What? What's done?" What the hell was this all about? How had someone gotten into her apartment? She walked to the front door, opened it slowly and looked for signs that the lock had been forced. Nothing. But she had no doubt someone had gotten in through that door and inadvertently let the cat out. Some unknown person had been in here. In her bedroom, touching her bed, lifting her pillows. Her heart was thundering. Fear and anger stormed through her. Who would do this? Who had a key? Why would someone go to so much trouble to leave her a note—no, that wasn't it; whoever did it intended to terrorize her as well.

Trying to keep panic at bay, she tried to think logically. Someone was trying to tell her something . . . something important. *TONIGHT* and *IT'S DONE*. Someone had accomplished his mission, whatever that was. Deep inside, she knew it was something bad, something dark and evil. She remembered the figure in the street . . . early in the morning . . . watching her . . . with Reed.

Dear God, could it have something to do with Pierce Reed? That seemed farfetched and yet the notes had started after this whole Grave Robber thing began. *No way. You're leaping to conclusions that don't make sense. Think rationally, not from fear. Who would do this to you? An enemy? Who has a key besides you and the landlord? A friend you loaned one to?* She ticked off the list of people she'd given a key to, but, unless someone had made a copy, she'd always gotten her keys back. Simone had borrowed her car on occasion, and she'd asked her sister Lily to watch her apartment and Jennings when she was out of town; there was her old boyfriend, Sean Hawkes, and her father . . . Trina had borrowed her car and her house key had been on the ring . . . Dear God, there had been too many to count.

Right now, Nikki was too tired to think and didn't believe that anyone she knew or trusted would be involved, unless they were careless and someone had made a copy. Slowly, she made her way back to bed and threw off the covers. If he'd left the note, he could have left something else as well. Something far worse. She spent the next hour going over every inch of her apartment, but found nothing else disturbed, no other indications that anyone had been inside. Only then did she prop a desk in front of the door and try to resume her life.

You should call the police.

And do what? Tell them she'd gotten two notes that meant nothing?

They do not mean nothing and you know it.

Maybe in the morning. She'd look like a fool. Tough reporter Nikki Gillette, frightened by a couple of notes.

She couldn't sleep in the bed as it was . . . The thought that some pervert had been in it was too much to bear. She carried her duvet into the living room area and curled onto the couch, wondering if she would ever feel safe in the bed or this apartment again. She'd always considered this tower room as her personal haven. Now, it had been violated. "Bastard," she muttered, her nerves stretched to the breaking point. Burrowing deep under the covers, she closed her eyes. Her ears strained to hear the tiniest noise that seemed out of sync in her home, but she heard only the sighing of the wind and a rumble of the furnace.

Who the hell was leaving the notes?

And why?

The cemetery was dark, illuminated by a slice of moon hiding behind thin, wispy clouds. A chill wind whistled through the bleached white gravestones and rattled the branches of the trees where Spanish moss danced and swayed.

The city was quiet and The Survivor heard nothing but the beating of his heart and his own ragged breathing as he hauled the old lady to her final resting place. She was in a bag, motionless but heavier than she looked. With silent footsteps he made his way unerringly to the waiting grave, a black yawning pit that already held one body. Waiting for the second. He'd already pried the casket open and inserted the microphone. He slid the body bag into the pit, then crawled in himself. Damp earth surrounded him. The scent filled his nostrils and the darkness folded around him as he worked, removing her from the bag and shoving her into the coffin. Despite the cold, he was sweating by the time he'd closed the lid and climbed out again. He began to fill the hole, dirt and rocks raining down on the coffin's lid. Shovel after shovel. He'd expected to hear her by now. Thought she'd begin screaming, but he heard nothing as he buried her. Nothing through the ever deepening dirt, not a sound from the microphone to the receiver in his ear. "Come on, wake up you old bitch," he ground out, working quickly, filling the damned hole as quickly and silently as possible. The cemetery was deserted, locked at night, but there was always the chance that someone was about, a security guard or kids looking for the thrill of breaking into a graveyard at midnight.

Still, there was no sound from within the damned coffin.

This was not good.

She needed to wake up.

To realize her fate.

To understand that it was payback time.

His entire body was drenched by the time the hole was filled. He considered sprinkling leaves and debris over the freshly turned soil, trying to make it blend in, but there really wasn't any reason to. Reed would be here tomorrow anyway.

Quickly, still holding his shovel and the now-empty bag, he scaled the fence and dropped into the foliage at the rear of the cemetery near an access road. His truck was parked right where he'd left it, deep in the shadows of a live oak tree. Undisturbed. So far, so good, he thought as he opened the canopy and placed his shovel into the bed of the pickup.

Headlights flashed behind him, twin beams cutting through the darkness. Bearing down on him. On his truck.

"Shit."

Quickly he climbed into the pickup, started it and shoved the rig into gear. The headlights rounded a corner, nearly blinding him in his rearview mirror. He made a fast U-turn and passed the oncoming vehicle, a battered old station wagon, in a blur. He kept his face averted as he gunned the engine and blew by the intruders. Who the hell would be on this road this late at night? Teenagers looking for a place to drink, smoke weed or make out, probably.

Damn the luck.

But at least it wasn't a cop car.

He licked his lips, checked his mirrors and was satisfied that the wagon hadn't turned around and followed him.

He turned off the access road and tried to stay calm. Sweat ran down his face, encased his body. He couldn't mess this up. It was his one chance at retribution . . . He was The Survivor. He checked his rearview mirror and his gut clenched when he spied a police cruiser turning onto the street behind him.

Maybe whoever was in the beat-up old wagon had called the police.

But why?

Maybe someone had been in the cemetery and seen him.

Maybe—

The cruiser's lights flashed on.

154

Son of a bitch!

He heard a low-sounding moan, then a pitiful cry. "Help me . . . oh, God, where am I?" And then a shriek of terror split through his eardrum. The old lady had finally woken up. She was sobbing, clawing, screaming and he couldn't enjoy it. Not now.

The cop was gaining.

He couldn't outrun a cruiser. But if he was stopped and the cop found the equipment and bag in the back, he'd be found out. Before he'd finished his mission. No way. Not now. He was too close and he'd waited too long.

The cruiser's sirens screamed through the night. The lights were nearly blinding.

His breath was shallow, his pulse ticking wildly, his mouth dry as a desert.

"Help, me! Oh, God!" He ripped the receiver from his ear. Stuffed it into his pocket. The cop car was nearly riding up his ass. He couldn't take the chance that the policeman, if he pulled him over, might hear the cries coming from the receiver.

The Survivor's hands tightened over the wheel as he edged to the side of the road. He had a gun. If the cop stopped him, he could blow the pig away. Easy. Then ditch the truck. It wasn't registered to him. He could still make it. Still fulfill his mission

Siren screeching, lights pulsing, the cruiser blew by him doing eighty. The cop at the wheel didn't so much as give him a second look.

He was safe.

For now.

• • •

"Help!" Roberta cried, her heart pounding so frantically she was certain it would explode. She was waking up, her mind still fuzzy, but she knew she was in trouble. Some kind of unthinkable, horrible trouble. Or maybe it was a dream. A nightmare.

Yes. That was it.

Wake up. Wake up now.

She shivered and placed her hands against the tattered cloth of the lid of the box that held her. It didn't budge. She pushed hard. Still nothing.

Terror raced through her blood.

Wake up. Wake up and you'll be in your own bed.

She dragged in a breath of stale air . . . but it was so hard to breathe and . . . and . . . this had to be a nightmare of the worst kind.

Wake up, Roberta! For pity's sake, wake up!

She forced her eyes open.

Blackness.

Total, Stygian darkness.

Something was terribly, vitally wrong. Her throat went dry. Her fear congealed into pure, undiluted horror.

Do something. Get out! For God's sake, get out of here!

She pushed upward.

Nothing.

Again. Harder.

Her hands ached.

Her wrists felt as if they might snap.

This was no dream. It was real. She was trapped. Like

a sardine packed in a tiny can. Oh, sweet Jesus, no.

Her mind cleared and she realized she was naked. Not a stitch on her body.

And her back was pressed against something that contoured to . . . no . . . oh . . . NO! The squishy thing beneath her was a body. The top of the box was actually a lid of a casket and she was no doubt being buried alive.

Like that poor other woman.

"Help me! Please, someone!" She began screaming and kicking, banging her naked knees, scraping at the coffin's lid, yelling until her voice ached.

She didn't dare think of what was beneath her—the metal of a belt buckle pressed into her back, the feel of bones beneath tattered clothing against her rump, bony ribs touching her shoulders. She screamed again and again, over her own sobs and the acrid stench of rotting flesh. "Help me! Help me, oooooh . . . God . . . pleeeease." She was crying now, scraping her fingers raw, her lungs tortured and burning, her mind shrieking with fear. She couldn't die like this, not squished against a dead corpse whose fetid skin and tissues were sticking to her hair and skin. Her flesh crawled and she imagined worms and maggots and all sorts of vile creatures crawling through the stringy, decaying muscles and innards beneath her.

"Let me out. Please, please . . . lct me out of here!"

Half-crazed, propelled by adrenaline, she kicked harder.

Bam! She heard a sickening snap. Pain jarred up her leg. She was gasping, drawing in thin, wretched air.

It was no use. She couldn't escape. "Why?" she cried, sobbing. "Why me?"

Calm yourself, Roberta. Remember your faith. Reach out to the Father. He will help you. He is with you. He has not forsaken you.

She scaled her own ribs upward, past her bare breasts to the hollow of her throat, to find her cross, but as her bloodied fingers searched her neck, she realized that her chain and cross were missing. Whoever had stripped her had taken off her necklace as well as stripped her of her precious wedding ring.

"You sick bastard," she hissed. Tears of despair streamed from her eyes. She began to cough. Fear congealed her blood and an odd pain started up her arm. A tingling and worse, something squeezing her, deep in her chest.

Trust in the Lord God. He is with you. Roberta, keep your faith!

The pain burned through her, but she clung to the words that had comforted her as a child. Quietly she began to murmur, "Jesus loves me, this I know, 'cause the Bible tells me so . . ."

What the hell was that?

Singing? The old lady was singing? The Survivor adjusted his earpiece once again as he guided his truck into the dark alley behind his house. No lights glowed in the upper stories and the basement was dark as death. He cut the engine behind a gray van with moss growing on it.

"For little ones to Him belong. They are weak but He

is strong . . ." Roberta Peters trilled.

As if it would do any good.

The Survivor listened to her surprisingly strong, clear voice, the sound of a woman no longer wailing in fear but loudly proclaiming her faith in a song she'd no doubt learned as a child.

As if she was ready to accept death and meet her Maker.

The Survivor's upper lip curled back in disgust. He recognized the lyrics and tune. Had sung the song himself. How many times had he been forced to warble that pathetic little ditty after a particularly brutal beating? And what good had it done?

Where had God been when he'd been in pain?

Listening and ready to save him?

Not that The Survivor remembered.

"Go ahead," he muttered in disgust, as if the old woman could hear him. "Sing your pathetic lungs out."

"Yes, Jesus loves me . . ." Roberta Peters's clear voice cracked. "Yes, Jesus loves . . ."

And then there was nothing.

She didn't cry out again.

Didn't beg for mercy.

Didn't sob uncontrollably.

The skin over his face tightened painfully. He rolled down the window and spat. Who would have thought the old woman would so docilely accept her fate, probably even looking forward to slipping into the next realm, hoping to sail smiling through the Pearly Gates?

The Survivor felt empty inside. Furious, he yanked out his earpiece. For this, he had worked so hard? For her acceptance and compliance, he'd plotted and planned? Shit! Aside from the first gasps and cries of terror and a few bangs when she'd tried to free herself, Roberta Peters's reaction had been a bust.

Not nearly as satisfying as Barbara Marx. Listening to Bobbi Jean, as she'd called herself, had been exhilarating, even bordering on sexually stimulating. The fact that she'd been such a lusty, sensual woman had added to the thrill of her death. Even now, thinking of her wails, he felt his body respond.

But this . . . the pathetic crying and singing of a childish Bible school song had left him feeling empty inside.

Don't worry about it. The old lady had to pay. As had the others. There will be more. You know there will be and some of those will be even more rewarding than Barbara Jean. Be patient.

He slid from his truck, locked it, then walked unerringly through the shadows to the back entrance of the old home where he resided. Along the broken brick path to the basement, the vines were thick, fronds of ferns slapping at him, the smell of the earth filling his nostrils as he withdrew his keys and slipped through the door into the dark interior. To his private space. No one suspected he dwelled deep within the bowels of this old mansion, even the owners didn't realize he had the keys to this particular part. Which was perfect.

He didn't snap on any lights, felt with his fingers along the old shelves and brick walls.

Tonight he would listen to the tapes again. Compare them. Time them . . . see how long it took each of his victims to die. As he ducked through the doorway and slipped into his private space, he turned on the lamps and walked to his bureau where he deposited Roberta Peters's underpants—voluminous panties for a scrawny woman. But not white, no, lavender and smelling a bit of the same as if she'd kept them in a drawer with sachet. They were silky, no doubt expensive.

He removed the tape recorder from his pocket and slid the cassette into his player. Once again he heard her whispering cries, oh, there was some begging involved and he smiled to himself as he thought of the others . . . how he would draw out their torment so that he wasn't disappointed again. There was so much work to be done, so many more who would pay, and the notes, he had to write them carefully, guiding the police down one path before veering sharply. He smiled as he pulled out his album and looked at the remaining victims. Their terror would be complete. They would know how they had failed him. They would understand why they were doomed to their own private hells.

He would make certain of it.

CHAPTER 8

"You got the name of a good attorney?" Morrisette asked the next morning as she strode into Reed's office.

"You plan on suing someone?"

"Bart. I've had it, and that yo-yo dumb-assed lawyer

I've used in the past hasn't done diddly-squat. If Bart wants to take me to court, so be it, but the gloves are comin' off, let me tell you." She flung herself into a side chair, crossed her legs and scowled. One booted foot bobbed in anger. "He's the kids' father for Christ's sake. What makes him think he can get away with not payin' me?"

Before Reed could respond, she said, "And then *he* has the balls to take *me* to court? What the hell did I do to deserve that jerk? Lowlife, no-damned-good son of a bitch, that's what he is. How many men do y'all reckon there are in the world? What—three, maybe four billion, and of all of those potential mates, he's the bastard I picked to have kids with. I should have my head examined." She shoved a hand through her spiked hair and let the air out of her lungs slowly, as if she were intent on exhaling her anger. A second later, a lot more calmly, she added, "Okay, enough about my so-called personal life. What's new besides you getting your ass kicked off the Grave Robber case?"

"Grave Robber? So you've seen the *Sentinel*." It was a statement. The entire town, or, for that matter, county, had probably read the article on the front page. He reached into his desk drawer for his roll of antacids and popped a couple.

"Nikki Gillette at her finest." Morrisette scowled. "God, I hate the press."

Reed didn't comment. His views on the fourth estate were well documented. As for Nikki Gillette, she was something else altogether. Had she not been a reporter, he might have found her attractive. Built like an athlete,

162

with a tight ass, small breasts and lean legs, she was bullheaded and determined. Never mind that he'd noticed she had pale green eyes and eyebrows that could arch cynically in a heartbeat.

"How'd she get her information?"

"You were mentioned."

He snorted. "There's a leak in the department."

"Are you kidding? This office is a veritable sieve. Where's McFee?"

"Don't know. I'm not on the case anymore."

Morrisette cracked her first smile of the morning. "My ass. You're not *officially* on the case, but that's not gonna stop you."

"Sure it is," he deadpanned. "I go strictly by the book."

"Save me." She twisted in her chair and kicked the door closed. As it slammed shut, Morrisette became dead serious. "Barbara Marx was pregnant. Was the kid yours?"

His chest tightened. He looked away. "Don't know."

"But it could've been."

"Yeah." A muscle worked in his jaw. He didn't want to think about it.

"Jesus H. Christ, Reed, what were you thinkin'? In today's world? You didn't use a condom?"

He didn't answer, just glanced out the window where morning light was filtering through the dirty panes and pigeons were roosting on the sill.

"Men!" She sighed audibly and jabbed at her hair with her fingers. "Damn, I could use a cigarette."

You and me both.

"Okay, okay, so you don't need a lecture."

"That's right. I don't."

She shook her head. "Okay, so what do you want me to do?" Suddenly she was all business again. Composed. Her little jaw set, her mouth a line of determination.

He was two steps ahead of her. They were an odd team. There had been bets by some of the other detectives about how long their pairing would last. Odds were against it. But so far, it had worked. "You'll need to handle the official stuff. Requests that require signatures. Phone calls to and from the department. That sort of thing."

"And what'll you do?"

"Work on other cases, of course."

"Give me a break." Morrisette snorted. "Okay, okay, so that's the way we'll play it. Okano will have your badge if she finds out you're still working on this. Even in an advisory capacity."

"But I'm not working on it."

"My ass."

Reed didn't argue as a matronly clerk rapped on the door, entered and dropped a bundle of mail into his box. "Mornin'."

"Morning," Reed replied. "How's it going, Agnes?"

"Same old, same old." Her eyes slid to the desk. "I see you're gettin' yourself some press."

"It's hell to be popular."

"Ain't that the truth?" Chuckling, she left.

Reed grimaced as he snapped the rubber band off the bundle and began shuffling through the small stack.

"I'll want to know when we can talk to the kid in the hospital."

"Prescott Jones?"

"Yeah. Check on his condition and if he's allowed visitors. See if we can get in to talk to him for a few minutes."

"You mean see if *I* can get in to see him."

Reed grimaced. "That's right. There's a good chance he's seen the killer. And so far, he's the only one. Take a picture of Marx up there with you and flash it at the kid. Then double check Jerome Marx's alibi." Reed continued sorting through his mail as he talked. "Have you talked with anyone where Barbara Jean worked— Hexler's Jewelry Store near the Cotton Exchange?"

"Already looking into it. And I've started with a list of her friends. What about relatives?"

"There's a brother, I think. Maybe an aunt. The brother's name is"—he flipped through the envelopes—"Vic or Val or . . ."

"Vin. Vincent Lassiter. That one I've checked out, but he's MIA. His phone was disconnected a week ago and he did some time. Car theft, solicitation and possession, nothing violent that I've come up with."

"Hell's bells, aren't you the efficient one?" Reed looked up from the mail.

"Just doin' my job," she quipped. "I thought you might want to put a friendly call in to Detective Montoya in New Orleans, to double check on Lassiter. Unofficially, of course."

"Of course."

"See what he knows about Lassiter."

"Good idea." He glanced down at the mail and saw the envelope.

An average white envelope, handwritten, addressed to him.

"Shit."

The return address was out of town on Heritage Road. No name. He stopped sorting and slit the envelope open. A single page was enclosed. It read:

ONE, TWO, THREE, FOUR . . .
SO, NOW, DON'T YOU WONDER HOW
MANY MORE?

He froze. Reread the damning words over and over again.

"What?" Morrisette said. She was on her feet in an instant. Looking over his shoulder, she read the message. "Oh, Jesus." She moved her gaze to stare straight at Reed. "This son of a bitch means business."

"What the hell do you think you're doing?" Norm Metzger was so angry the moustache above his goatee quivered with rage. He slapped a folded copy of this morning's paper onto Nikki's desk. She'd expected the explosion, had caught his angry glances all morning, and seen him beeline into Tom Fink's office as soon as the editor had shown up this morning.

"I found an angle and ran with it." She leaned back in her chair and stared up at him, not giving in an inch. She was tired, had barely slept a wink because of the note in her apartment, and wasn't about to take any of

Metzger's guff. Not today.

Hooking a thumb at his chest, he growled, "It was supposed to be my story."

"Take it up with Fink."

"I have. But you already know that." Metzger leaned over her desk, pushing his face close enough that she could smell the coffee on his breath. "You've been trying to muscle in on my territory for years, Nikki, and it's just not going to work."

"'Muscle in on your territory?' Oh, come on, Norm. Who are you? James Cagney in some old tough-guy black and white movie from the forties?" She managed a smile and noticed the corners of his mouth were so tight his lips had paled. "As I said, I saw an angle and ran with it. I talked it over with Tom and he decided to go with the story."

"You could have run it by me."

"Why? Would you have if you were in my position?"

He straightened. Looked up at the ceiling. "No."

"I didn't think so."

"So you want to work with me on this?" he asked as if granting her a great favor. When she was the one with the source and the scoop.

"I work better alone."

He snorted. "You don't prescribe to the two heads are better than one theory?"

"Only a man, because of his anatomy, would think that."

He slid her a glance that was meant to be glacial. "You know, Nikki, you act tough, but you'd better be careful. This is a small newspaper in a town with a long memory. You got yourself into trouble a while back, so you'd better be sure you don't make the same mistake twice."

"I won't," she said with more confidence than she felt as he walked back to his desk.

Trina slid her chair back. "Ouch. Looks like someone's fragile male ego has just been bruised."

"And battered, but not broken." She glanced down the hallway. Metzger was grabbing his coat and wool cap, making a big exit and a bigger point. "He's just ticked cuz I aced him."

"And he won't forget it. I wouldn't want to be on Metzger's bad side."

"Is there a good one?"

"My, my, look who's full of herself today." Trina laughed and winked as her phone rang and she rolled her desk chair into her cubicle.

Nikki called her landlord and had the locks of her apartment changed. Fortunately, the man who owned the building loved doing handyman tasks and he promised that he'd change the dead bolt, tumblers, and have the entire project done by the time she got home. She could pick up her new set of keys at his apartment on the main floor this evening. When he asked why she wanted them changed, she told him about an ex-boyfriend who was bothering her and there were no further questions. She spent the rest of the day avoiding Metzger, putting together her story on Dr. Francis and the school board, while doing research on the Grave Robber case. The sheriff's department in Lumpkin County offered up a few more details, the hospital in Atlanta wouldn't let her talk to the kid in the accident and the other kid was off-limits, his old man insisting on payment for any interview with Billy Dean Delacroix. Frustrated, Nikki put a call into Cliff again, then tried to locate any information she could on the two women in the grave. Barbara Jean Marx's husband wouldn't speak to her and the employees at Hexler's Jewelry Store were close-mouthed as well.

But Nikki wasn't about to give up.

Nor did she forget about the two notes she'd received.

TONIGHT.

And

IT'S DONE.

Whatever happened last night was now a fait accompli.

The headline was worth the trouble.

"Grave Robber Strikes, Baffles Police."

Oh, yeah!

Though he was tired, The Survivor tingled inside as he smoothed page one of the *Savannah Sentinel* on his table. Carefully, making certain that he was cutting in a perfectly straight line, he sliced the article from the rest of the page and discarded the remainder of the paper. The clipping would go in his scrapbook with the pictures. His televisions were all glowing bright, anchormen and -women mouthing words in hushed voices since he kept the sound down until he heard something he wanted, then he'd up the volume. His tape players were recording every segment of the news, cable stations from all over the country. Later, after a few hours of sorely needed sleep, he would edit out all the unwanted pieces before adding to his personal tape library.

The Grave Robber.

Nikki Gillette had come up with a name for him, as if she'd anticipated that he would strike again. If only she knew how close she was to the truth, to him. Humming softly to himself, he walked to one amplifier on the long wall and upped the volume . . . nothing . . . she must've already gone to work. No matter. He had last night's tape. He pushed the play button, heard the mini tape rewind and then Nikki Gillette's voice, clear over the sound of the talk-radio program. He'd marked the part he liked, the precise moment when she'd read the note.

"What? What's done?" her voice screeched.

Again, The Survivor tingled, felt an erotic heat warming his blood, but pressed the pause button. He walked to the bureau and reached into the second drawer. There, he withdrew a pair of lacy black panties, barely more than a thong. Oh, Nikki was a naughty girl. He smiled and rubbed the sheer scrap of fabric against his cheek, hearing his beard stubble catch on the fine silk. She didn't even know they were missing. He'd purloined them far too early, he supposed. Taking them wasn't part of his usual ritual; she was, after all, still very much alive, not yet locked in a coffin with a corpse. Nonetheless, he couldn't resist stealing her personal, sexy piece of lingerie.

He clicked on the recorder again. It began to play. A

gentle hiss of the tape, then, as he fondled Nikki's panties, she began to talk to him directly, not knowing that he'd planted a tiny microphone in her bedroom, that anything she said or did in that room would be recorded . . . just for him. . . . He waited, heard her moving through her apartment, felt her fear as she reentered the bedroom. Licking his lips in anticipation, he listened as the antique four-poster bed creaked under her weight. He imagined she was climbing into her bed, stretching upon the silky blue sheets and thick duvet. The spit dried in his mouth as he called up the image. Oh, yes . . . he remembered running the tips of his fingers over the smooth fabrics that smelled faintly of her. It had been erotic then and was doubly so now. He imagined her flesh. Hot. Wanting. Feeling like silk beneath his fingertips.

His blood pounded in his ears, his cock rock-hard in anticipation as he listened hard, hearing her change of movement as she second-guessed herself, her footsteps retreating. "That's it, baby, talk to me," he said, unzipping his pants and seeing his disjointed reflection in the splintered mirror.

Soon, Nikki would speak to him. Directly. In an angry hiss. He held his breath for a second, the flimsy lace touching his erection as lightly as a moth's wings, toying and teasing with his dick as he waited. "Come on, Nikki, talk to me. Come on." He could barely hold back. His breathing was ragged, his heart hammering, pumping blood through his veins.

Finally, just when he thought he might explode, her voice filled the room.

"Bastard!" she hissed from the recording.

He let go.

Filled her panties with that special part of him.

CHAPTER 9

"Call the caretaker for Heritage Cemetery. See if there've been any disturbances." Reed was already reaching for his jacket. "If so, send a unit to secure the scene."

"You're off the case, remember?" Morrisette reminded him as he yanked open the door and started through the cubicles and desks where computers hummed, phones rang and prisoners in handcuffs sat insolently in chairs at desks while officers took statements and filled out reports.

"How could I forget?" But he didn't break stride and hurried down the stairs. Morrisette was at his heels. "I'll drive." He shouldered open a side door and they stepped into a gray day. The rain that had been threatening all morning was falling in thick drops that puddled on the pavement and ran from the gutters.

Before Morrisette could put up any kind of protest, Reed claimed the steering wheel. As he pulled out of the lot, Morrisette was on the phone to the dispatcher then the caretaker of the cemetery. She managed to light a cigarette and juggle the receiver as he turned on the lights and sped through the town, turning onto Victory Drive, passing palm trees and shivering azaleas as they headed toward the old graveyard situated on the outskirts of the city.

The police band crackled, traffic hummed, the wipers slapped raindrops off the windshield and Morrisette worked the phone. ". . . that's right," she was saying. "Okay, have the officer secure the scene. We'll be there in ten, maybe fifteen." She hung up and glanced at Reed through a cloud of smoke. Her face was set. "You're right. Someone messed with a grave last night. Visitors saw it this morning. Alerted the city, which found the caretaker who called in the situation just before we did. A unit was only two blocks away and should be on the scene by now."

Reed's jaw clenched. "Damn it all to hell."

"Looks like 'the Grave Robber'—or whoever you want to call him—is back in action. Serial?" She lifted an eyebrow and drew hard on her Marlboro Light.

"Could be."

"Jesus, we'll have to call the Feds."

"Okano probably already has."

The contents of the note echoed through his brain.

ONE, TWO, THREE, FOUR . . .

SO, NOW, DON'T YOU WONDER HOW MANY MORE?

Reed hated to think.

"So, why has this guy singled you out? Why the messages to you?" she asked, flicking ash out the window she'd cracked.

"I knew Bobbi."

"So, you think you're gonna know the next one?"

Reed's gut churned. His jaw clenched so hard it

173

ached. Christ, he couldn't imagine that all of the victims were people he'd known. Oh, Jesus, no. "I hope not," he said fervently. Would some nutcase, someone he'd made an enemy of, hate him enough to kill the people he cared about, people he knew?

Who would hate him so much?

Someone he'd offended?

Some criminal he'd sent up the river?

Hell. He turned onto the county road and followed it to the cemetery where not one, but two patrol cars were parked. The gates had been roped off with yellow crime scene tape and a few gawkers had stopped to stand in the rain and peer past the ancient headstones, hoping for a peek of the tragedy.

A white van with WKAM emblazoned upon its sides in deep blue letters was parked near the curb. The press had arrived.

"Damned three-ring circus already." Reed opened the car door as Morrisette squashed her cigarette and left the smoldering butt in the ashtray. "Let's go."

Before the reporters could get to them, they flashed their badges at a uniformed cop, then slid beneath the yellow tape. The grass was wet, the wind cold with the rain as they made their way to the back of the cemetery where a crowd had gathered. Pictures were being taken. Soil samples already being bagged. Debris collected. Impressions in the ground studied. The crime scene team, headed by Diane Moses, was already at work. Reed noticed a gate in the wrought-iron fence line that bordered the cemetery. It was wide enough for a vehicle to pass through and opened to an access road running behind the graveyard. Probably used for hearses and the digging equipment needed to excavate graves. Through the trees, far enough away from the gate so as not to disturb any evidence that might have been left, the crime scene team's van, back doors open, was parked.

"How long will it be before we can start digging?" one of the officers asked. He was wearing rain gear, and along with several of the other uniforms, was equipped with shovels and picks.

"Until we're done," Diane snapped. "Ask him." She hitched her chin in Reed's direction.

"We'll wait," he said.

"Damned straight you will," Diane grumbled as she snapped on a pair of latex gloves and picked up her clipboard. "At least we've already got permission to dig it up, but you just wait until I give the word."

"Man, did you get up on the wrong side of the bed, or what?" the officer taking pictures asked.

Diane didn't answer. But her mouth compressed into a thin line of irritation as she made a quick note, then walked closer to the grave site to converse with a man taking soil samples.

The rain seemed colder as Reed stared at the freshly turned earth. The gravestone had weathered and read: Thomas Alfred Massey, beloved husband and father. Thomas's dates of birth and death had been etched beneath his name. From the looks of it, Massey had been eighty when he'd been buried seven years earlier.

If he was in the coffin.

Until they dug it up, no one knew for certain.

Reed didn't know the man, but the name rang a far-off bell. He thought hard as raindrops ran down his nose, but couldn't conjure up an image of the guy or even put his finger on where he'd heard the name before.

At least he wasn't someone he knew.

Reed only hoped that if there was another victim, he or she was a stranger as well. He reached into his pocket for his roll of antacids. His stomach was churning from bad coffee and not much else.

Mud oozed around his shoes as Diane Moses conferred with members of her staff and the wind kicked up. He glanced at a nearby gravestone, read the name and simple message cut into the granite:

Rest In Peace.

Fat chance.

Not with the Grave Robber on the loose.

". . . so you, like, won't use my name, will you?" From across the table in the little coffee shop, the waif-like girl beseeched Nikki. Lindsay Newell was twenty-seven, but didn't look a day older than eighteen. "You know Mr. Hexler; he doesn't want any trouble or hint of a scandal at the store. He thinks it's bad for business."

"I'll be discreet and of course, if you don't want me to, I won't quote you directly," Nikki assured the jewelry clerk who had worked with Bobbi Jean Marx.

Nikki had dressed down this morning, wearing her weathered jeans and a sweater in order to help the jewelry clerk relax and feel more likely to share secrets.

176

Like they were best girlfriends or something. Nikki had bought her the coffee and a croissant, but Lindsay had only picked at the pastry. While spoons clinked in cups and conversation buzzed around them, Nikki tried to make Bobbi Jean's coworker feel at ease. None of her ploys worked. Lindsay was edgy. Customers of the Caffeine Bean came and went, the bell over the door tinkling as they entered. Each time the door opened, Lindsay visibly jumped, as if she were certain her boss would walk into the shop and spy her spilling her guts to a reporter.

"Please don't quote me. I can't afford to lose my job." The girl bit at the corner of her glossed lips nervously and checked her watch for the third time as soft jazz emanated from the speakers and the aproned cashiers behind the counter called out orders. Lindsay was on her morning coffee break and already jumpy. The triple shot of espresso in her nonfat latte wouldn't help calm her down. She'd refused to open up to a tape recorder but had allowed Nikki to take notes.

"Okay, I won't. No names. I promise. So, tell me about Bobbi Jean. When did you last see her?"

"Two mornings before I found out that she . . ." Lindsay gulped. ". . . that she was dead . . . God, that's *so* horrible. I mean, to be buried alive . . . with some decaying corpse, trapped in a coffin." She shuddered and reached for her coffee with a trembling hand. "I already talked to the police, you know, and I told them everything I know about her, which isn't a whole lot." Anxiously, she licked the foam from her lips. "Except . . ."

"Except what?" Nikki saw the hesitation in the girl's eyes. As if she had a secret she wanted to unburden.

"Oh . . . God . . . I . . . I caught her throwing up one morning just after we opened. It was just about a week ago. I had to run the store by myself for about half an hour. When she came out of the bathroom she was so pale. White as a ghost." Lindsay leaned closer, across the table, and whispered, "I mean, like, I was sure she had the flu or something and that she should go home, but when I suggested she call someone in to cover for her, she wouldn't hear of it. She said a day in bed wouldn't help her at all, in fact, that's what had started the problem. I didn't get it . . . not really, but I suspected . . . I'd seen an opened pregnancy test package in the garbage a few weeks ago, but didn't know who it belonged to. We have a lot of girls working there, so it could have been anyone's. But now . . ." She lifted a slim shoulder. "I, um, I think it was Bobbi's."

"But she was separated from her husband," Nikki said, adrenaline shooting through her blood. The victim had been pregnant at the time of her death? This was news that hadn't come out of the police department, something they were holding back. If it was true.

"Yeah, I know, but sometimes people get back together."

"Had they?"

Lindsay cast a look through the window to the sidewalk outside. Pedestrians were walking quickly, umbrellas open, coats pulled tight to their collars. "Not that I know of, and Bobbi . . . well, she dated other guys."

Nikki nearly came out of her chair. She scribbled quickly. "Do you know their names?"

"Uh-uh. I don't think anyone did because Bobbi was in the middle of her divorce and didn't want to screw up her chances of getting money from her ex—well, her husband, well, you know, Jerome."

"But surely the men would call her at the store."

Blank eyes blinked. Twirled a finger in her dark ringlets. "I guess."

"You didn't take any of the calls?"

"Not that I know of. Guys called all the time, you know, to shop for their wives or girlfriends." Lindsay pursed her lips and her eyebrows drew together as if she were really thinking hard. Meanwhile, the loud-speaker called out, "Double fudge mocha nonfat with whipped cream."

"No one special?"

"No . . . but . . . you know, I just had this feeling that one of the guys was a cop."

"Why?" *A cop? Who?*

"Little remarks, I guess. She teased about handcuffs and being frisked and guys with big nightsticks and . . . all that double entendre stuff." She really twisted on the curl now. "Oh, maybe I was just imagining things. I shouldn't have said anything. What does it matter? She's dead. But that's why I couldn't talk to the police—I didn't know who he was, didn't want to get anyone into trouble. It was just too fucked up, y'know?" Lindsay chewed on her lower lip for a second, forsook the lock of hair to pick up her paper coffee cup and said, "Look, I really have to go. My break is over and I don't know anything else." She scooted out her chair as quickly as if she expected an angry god to hurl a lightning bolt through the table if she stayed a second longer.

"Call me if you think of anything else," Nikki called, catching up with her at the door and handing her the business card she'd tucked into the pocket of her jeans.

Lindsay stared at the card as if Satan's name and phone number were engraved beneath *Savannah Sentinel*. "No, I don't know anything else. Really." She was backing toward the door and nearly ran into a guy trying to fold his umbrella. Raindrops littered the floor. "Oh! Sorry," Lindsay mumbled quickly and was out the door. She jaywalked toward the square opposite the jewelry store.

Nikki didn't waste any time. She grabbed her cup and walked into the gloom. Though it was late morning, the winter day was dark. Somber. Rain pouring off the awning. She splashed her way to her car, climbed inside and tried to start it. The engine didn't catch. "Oh, no, ya don't," she said under her breath, but the hatchback only coughed twice. "Come on, come on . . . no need to be temperamental." Lord, she *had* to take the little car into the shop. It was in severe need of regular maintenance.

The police band crackled, but she didn't catch the call.

On the third try the old engine fired and Nikki checked her side view mirror before pulling away from the curb. Her cell phone jangled at the next stoplight and she fumbled in her purse before finding the damned thing and catching it on the third chirp. "This is Nikki," she said, negotiating the turn while juggling her coffee.

"Hi, babe."

Her heart plummeted and she nearly dropped the coffee as she imagined her ex-boyfriend's face—strong jaw, dark beard shadow, even darker eyes. Mysterious eyes. Lying eyes. Nearly black hair long enough to scrape his collar. "Sean. I heard you were in town."

"You didn't call me back."

Did he sound pouty? Hurt? Sean? No way! She took a sip of her drink, then managed to force it into her cup holder with only a minimum of spillage. "I really didn't see a reason to phone." The light changed, but another car flew through the intersection. "Idiot!"

Sean chuckled. Low and sexy. "That's me."

No, that was me. I was an idiot for you!

"Look, Sean, I'm busy. Is there something you wanted?" she asked as she heard something on the police band that caught her attention. Some units had been sent to a location on Heritage Road. It didn't sound like an accident.

"I thought we could get together."

"I don't think so."

"Nikki, I need to see you."

"Now?" She couldn't believe her ears. Sean was the one who had wanted out, the one who hadn't been happy in the relationship. He'd peddled her some crap about her not being his "soul mate," whatever that meant.

"What about tonight?"

"I can't."

"Tomorrow?"

"I . . . I don't know." There had been a time when she would have reveled in hearing him utter just those words. But that had been a while back. "I don't think so."

"Nikki." His voice was low. The timbre the same she remembered. Deep. Sexy. Nearly guttural. "You're avoiding me."

"You're right. Wait a minute," she added, thinking about the note she'd found in her bed. "Do you still have a key to my apartment?"

"Maybe." He was teasing her now. Flirting. Oh, for God's sake.

"I'm serious, Sean."

"No, babe, you made me give it back, remember?"

Vaguely she remembered him removing the key from the ring that held his own set. They'd been in his old "classic" Jaguar and she'd been fighting not to break down.

"That's right. But you could have made a copy."

"Why would I do that?"

"Why do you do anything."

"Low blow, Gillette."

"So I'm not 'babe' anymore? Good." More police cars were being directed to Heritage Road. She caught the address, held the phone with her shoulder and found her city map from the overflowing glove box. "I don't have time for this now," she said and hung up. Who the hell did he think he was, anyway? He was the one who had dumped her. And now she should drop everything for him?

No way!

But there had been a desperate tone to his voice . . . Oh, God, he probably wanted money. He already owed her fifteen hundred dollars. He wasn't going to get another dime.

She thought about the night before. The note in her bed. The note on her car . . . Could Sean have left them? It really wasn't his style . . . and yet . . . "Don't think about it now," she scolded. She couldn't afford to waste another minute on a free spirit who, she'd learned later, had also been a small-time hood.

At the next light she stopped and checked the map. Oh, God. Her heart thudded. The address was for Heritage Cemetery. She felt a zing of anticipation.

No doubt the Grave Robber had struck again.

A loud honk alerted her that the light had turned green. She didn't hesitate, but turned a corner and headed out of town.

Toward her next cover story.

CHAPTER 10

Reed stared down at the open coffin. Not one body, but two were crammed into it. Just like before. Only the naked, bruised body on top was that of an old woman, the one below decomposed, but from the clothing that remained—a man's dark suit—and from the tufts of gray hair still visible, Reed guessed the other occupant was Thomas Massey.

"Jesus H. Christ," Morrisette whispered, her face ashen, her gaze riveted to the open casket. The crime scene had been cordoned off, swept over quickly by the crime scene investigators while a huge tent had been erected over the grave to preserve any evidence left at the scene. The tarp held a dual purpose. It protected the scene from the elements as well as from the prying eyes of photographers with long-lensed cameras or television stations with state-of-the-art equipment including low-flying helicopters. Until the next of kin were notified and the police had figured out if they had a serial killer on the loose, they would be careful giving out any information to the press that might panic the public or sabotage the investigation.

"We'd better check with Missing Persons and find out who she is. Call Rita and see if any reports have been filed on a missing white woman in her late fifties or early sixties."

"Don't need to." Morrisette's spiky hairdo was melting in the rain and she was shaking, visibly quaking as she stared into the grave. "Anyone got a smoke?" she demanded, yanking her gaze away and scanning the faces of her fellows.

"Right here." Fletcher, one of the uniformed cops, reached into his pocket, found a crumpled pack of Camel Straights and shook out a cigarette. With trembling fingers, Morrisette tried to light up, her lighter clicking but refusing to spark.

"You know her?" Reed asked, taking the lighter and

flicking it so that a steady flame appeared.

Morrisette drew hard on the Camel. Smoke streamed out her nostrils. "Mrs. Peters. Don't know her first name but she was a volunteer at the library. Widow, I think, but I'm not sure." Morrisette took another calming drag. Some of the color came back to her face. "Mrs. Peters helped out with story hour last summer. My kids went there every Thursday afternoon and listened to her read from one of the Harry Potter books." Angrily she hissed, "Goddam it, who would do this? What kind of sicko jerk-off would stuff an old lady into an already occupied coffin and"—she leaned forward again, staring at the dead woman's fingers—"and leave her in there alive? Shit!" She looked away and, holding her smoke in her left hand, made a quick sign of the cross with her right. It was the first time Reed had seen her do anything the least bit religious.

"The same son of a bitch who did Bobbi Jean." Reed, too, noticed the faded coffin lining, shredded and bloodied, the manicured fingernails now broken and smeared with dried blood, a bruise on the forehead, all evidence that Mrs. Peters, part-time library volunteer, had gone through the same excruciating terror as had Barbara Jean Marx.

"Kinda rules out Jerome Marx," Morrisette thought aloud. She plucked a piece of tobacco from her tongue as the wind caught against the sides of the tent, causing the plastic to flap.

"Unless it's a copycat," Fletcher offered.

"Let's not go there." Reed's thoughts were dark as

185

hell itself. It was bad enough that Bobbi and the baby had been killed, but now, another murder? One that was too much the same to be dismissed as separate. Obviously, there was a psychotic on the loose. Again. His thoughts turned back to last summer when in the sweltering heat he'd tracked down a killer who was knocking off members of a prominent Savannah family. Now, this new horror. Barely six months later. "We'll need to find out how, if at all, the victims were related," he said to Morrisette. "Did they know each other? What about the people already in the coffin? Why were they chosen. Was it random or is there a connection?" Rubbing the back of his neck, he spied the microphone. "Hell. Look at this." He squatted next to the casket and pointed to where a hole had been drilled through the rotting wood. The nearly invisible microphone was tucked inside.

"Yeah, we've already noted the make and model," said the investigator who had been cleared to bag Mrs. Peters's hands to preserve any evidence under her fingernails.

Diane Moses's team had already carefully gone over the coffin in search of fingerprints, tool marks, fibers, hairs, any piece of evidence. Just as the crime scene team had in Lumpkin County.

This murder is identical to Bobbi Jean's.

Except that you don't know this woman.

The back of Reed's neck tightened. "Did you find anything else? A note inside the coffin somewhere?"

"Note?" The investigator looked over his shoulder. His expression accused Reed of being a nutcase.

"There was no note in here. Nothing besides two stiffs and the microphone. We've already searched."

Reed relaxed a bit. At least the killer wasn't contacting him.

He heard the whir of helicopter blades and stepped outside to look up at the cloud-swollen sky. A chopper was hovering above the trees not a hundred feet away and a cameraman was hanging out of the open door. The press was trying to get a bird's-eye view of the scene. It rankled him as well as Diane Moses, who, dressed in a yellow slicker, walked to the outside of the tent, looked up and swore under her breath. "Goddamned newsmongers."

News at eleven, Reed thought. He considered the note he'd received at the station this morning. It had indicated there would be more killings. Random? Specific? Did the creep know his victims? Play with them? A bad feeling settled deep in the pit of Reed's stomach.

"What have you got so far?" he asked Moses.

"Not enough. This is all preliminary, but we're thinking the perp parked over there"—she pointed to the access road—"and either climbed the fence or had a key. The lock was intact. He would have had to have carried her, so he's a big guy or at least a strong guy. No drag marks, not even any real impressions that we can cast. The rain hasn't helped, but it only makes sense as the main road would be too visible. We'll know more later and I'll fill you in."

"Thanks," Reed said.

"Don't mention it." They walked into the tent and she

turned her attention to the department's cameraman. "You get everything you need? I want shots of the entire area and the top of the coffin as well as what's in it . . ."

"Let's go," Reed said to Morrisette, who seemed to have composed herself. "We'll get all the reports, but I think I'd better take the note that came to Okano."

"She'll bust your ass for coming out here."

"I was just along for the ride," he said as they walked across the long grass.

"Like she'll buy in to that."

He lifted a shoulder and felt rain slide down his collar. The graveyard wasn't overly tended, most of the graves a hundred years old, only a few, such as Thomas Massey's final resting place, more recent. Weeds dotted the grass and some of the bushes were unkempt. Why had the killer used this cemetery? Was it significant or unplanned—by chance? What about the grave? Did the killer choose Thomas Massey for convenience or to make a point?

He glared at the threatening horizon, dark clouds scudding across the rooftops of church spires and highest branches of the palms and live oaks that lined the streets. Why was Roberta Peters, an elderly woman, about as far from Bobbi Jean as one could be, the second victim?

Morrisette was at his side, the tops of her snakeskin boots wet from the grass and rain. As they approached the main gate, he sensed rather than saw the flock of reporters and curious onlookers gathered on the other side of the crime scene tape.

"Detective! Can you tell us what's going on?" a male voice demanded.

"I have nothing to say at this point in the investigation," Reed said automatically. He was headed for the cruiser.

"Is this another Grave Robber case?"

Reed recognized the voice. "Grave Robber?" he repeated, looking up and spying Nikki Gillette standing front and center, ever eager for a story. Her red-blond hair was pulled back in a ponytail that was dripping in the rain, her eyes were bright, her cheeks flushed in the cold. She seemed younger, less of an adversary in her oversize coat, jeans and wet sneakers. In any other circumstance Reed would have found her attractive. Today, she was just another pushy newswoman, a real pain in the ass. In one hand she held a recorder, in the other a pen and paper. The notepad was soggy, the pen dripping from the rain, and everything about her was getting wetter by the minute. Nonetheless, she was as eager as ever.

"Is this the work of the same criminal who put a second body in a grave and buried them both up at Blood Mountain?" she asked.

"It's too early to determine."

"But the M.O.?" Gillette pushed forward, never one to give up.

"I'm not going to speculate or say anything that might jeopardize the investigation." He managed a thin, impatient smile.

"It seems more than just coincidence." Nikki wasn't giving an inch. But then, she never did.

Other reporters fired their questions.

"We noticed you digging. Was another grave found?" Max O'Dell, brandishing a microphone, demanded.

"Did you find an empty coffin?" another reporter demanded.

"Or was the grave robbed?"

"Or was there a coffin with a second body stuffed into it?"

"Please," Reed said, trying to keep his temper in check. "Let us do our job. We'll answer your questions later when we know more."

"When will that be?" Nikki Gillette again, scribbling wildly, a lock of wild hair blowing in front of her face.

"We'll issue a statement."

"No press conference?" she demanded, rain drizzling down her face and pointed chin.

He bit back a sharp retort. "That's not for me to decide. Thank you." Raising a hand in a half wave, he moved away from the group of reporters and headed for the cruiser. "Let's get out of here."

"The sooner the better," Morrisette said, more subdued than usual. "When we get back to the station, we'd better fill in Okano." She slid a glance in his direction as she scrounged through her purse for her cigarettes. Keys and coins jangled within the voluminous leather pouch. "Tell you this much. She ain't gonna like it." Cracking the window, she added, "But then, I don't like it, either. Who the hell would kill an old lady who helps out at the library?" She flicked her lighter several times, swore, and dug in her purse before she found another one and finally managed to get a flame.

"He didn't just kill her," Reed growled. "He buried her alive with a corpse."

CHAPTER 11

"I need to talk to you," Nikki insisted, driving with one hand, holding her cell phone with the other. She was headed back to the office, skimming through traffic and had finally managed to connect with Cliff Siebert, an accomplishment she considered a minor miracle. "Let's meet." Easing off the accelerator she took a corner onto Victory Drive. After spending nearly two hours at Heritage Cemetery she was chilled to the bone. In that time the rain had let up and the sky was showing hints of blue through the clouds, but not before she'd been soaked to the skin. Her hair was a frizzy, damp mess that had escaped from her ponytail, her coat damp, her Nikes squishy, her socks clinging and feeling as if she'd been wading through ice water. She considered telling Cliff about her intruder, about the notes, but knew he'd tell her it was probably just a prank. Like once before. When she'd thought Corey Sellwood was stalking her. She'd made a fool of herself then. No, she had to keep what happened last night to herself.

"Meet where?" Cliff asked.

"I could come by your place tonight," she offered,

forcing some enthusiasm she didn't feel. "Or wherever you want to hook up." Trying to keep things light, she switched lanes. "What time do you get off work?"

"Going to my apartment wouldn't be a good idea." She heard the indecision in his voice and she imagined him jangling his keys nervously in the pocket of his tan Dockers. With curly, flaming red hair cropped short, Cliff was clean shaven and usually wore polo shirts. To Nikki, he looked more like a pro golfer than a cop.

"Then pick another spot." She wasn't letting him off the hook.

"I don't know . . ."

"Oh, come on, Cliff." She *needed* to talk to him. "How about somewhere out of town?"

He sighed loudly, as if he were about to make the biggest mistake of his life and was regretting it already. "All right. Tonight."

"You name the place and time and I'll be there." She turned toward the river and the offices of the *Sentinel*. She felt like something the cat had dragged in and then discarded, but she didn't have time for a shower or change of clothes. The school board article was due this afternoon and she had more work to do on the Grave Robber story. Lots more work. The bombshell Lindsay Newell had dropped earlier this morning, about Bobbi Jean Marx being pregnant and involved with a cop, gnawed at Nikki.

Cliff still hadn't answered her. "Cat got your tongue?"

"It should have."

"Oh, Cliff, give it up, would ya? Where do you want to meet?"

He hesitated a second. "Weaver Brothers. You know the place I'm talkin' about? It's a truck stop off Ninety-Five just across the Carolina border. They've got a diner that's pretty quiet."

"I've heard of it," she said, trying to picture the place on the interstate. "What time?"

"Eight, eight-thirty?"

"That'll work. I'll even buy you dinner."

"I couldn't allow that."

"Why not?"

"You're a woman."

"Oh, for God's sake. We're far into a new millennium, remember? Those antebellum days of genteel southern charm have gone the way of the dodo, Siebert."

"Not in my book. There's always room to treat a lady like a lady." Inwardly she groaned and noticed that there was no lilt to his voice, none of the exuberance of the Cliff Siebert who had been her brother's best friend, the boy who had flirted outrageously with her, the teenager who had gone squirrel hunting with Andrew. Those easygoing days and Cliff's happy-go-lucky personality had also been eroded by the passing of time and tragedy.

"I'm not a lady, Cliff. Not tonight. I'm an old family friend."

"Is that what you call it?"

"Yeah. It is. I'll see ya later." She hung up and felt a

nagging sense of guilt. She'd known Cliff had been interested in her for years. It had been his running gag while growing up. All too vividly she remembered a hot summer day when she'd come in from playing tennis. She'd been wearing shorts and a sweat-drenched T-shirt, her hair pulled into a ponytail, a visor shading her eyes. Cliff and Andrew had returned to her parents' home early from squirrel hunting. As she'd arrived she'd found them sitting at a patio table in the shade of a wide blue umbrella, happily guzzling Big Ron's stash of beer.

"You're savin' yourself for me, ain't ya, Nikki-gal?" Cliff had teased, all piss and vinegar in his early twenties, that long-ago summer before Andrew had died. Cliff's eyes had sparkled, his grin sliding from one side of his jaw to the other with easy, country-boy charm.

"In your dreams, Siebert," she'd joked back, laughing and wiping the sweat from her forehead.

"So you know about those dreams, do you?" He'd winked slowly. "Kinda X-rated, aren't they?"

"You're sick." She'd walked past them as Andrew had opened long-necked bottles and sent the caps whizzing into the thickets of magnolia, pine and jas-mine.

"Oh, honey, if you only knew . . ." Cliff had admitted, the sound of his voice trailing after her. It hadn't been the first time she'd realized that he'd only been half kidding when he'd flirted with her.

It was sad, she thought now, as she wheeled into a parking lot not far from the newspaper's offices, how that boyish bravado and her innocence had both been destroyed with Andrew's death. So many things had changed.

None for the better.

Roberta Peters's home looked more like a museum than a house. Constructed of apricot-colored stucco and flanked by a wrought-iron fence drowning in ivy, the house looked like something from the Italian country-side. It boasted porches front and back complete with balconies, floor-to-ceiling windows that were accented by gleaming black shutters, and gardens thick with lush shrubbery, even in early December. Two Christmas wreaths hung on the double front doors.

An officer had been posted at the gate, but Diane's team was already inside and Reed and Morrisette, careful not to disturb anything, walked cautiously through rooms filled with historical artifacts, furniture, and in Reed's estimation, just plain clutter.

"Shit, I wonder who her cleaning lady is," Morrisette remarked as she eyed shiny knickknacks arranged on glass shelves. "I could use her number."

"Probably a full-time maid. We need to talk to her."

"And the gardener and the guy who fixes the plumbing."

"And the people at the library."

"No rest for the weary, is there?"

"Never," Reed muttered.

So far, no one from the press had arrived. But that wouldn't be for long. Meanwhile, members of the crime scene unit were photographing, dusting, vacu-uming. The trash had been collected and the old house was being searched for any kind of evidence. No blood trail or spatter was detected, but then, Roberta Peters hadn't had any visible wounds other than the bump on her head, probably from trying to sit up in the coffin, and the raw tips of her fingers. She'd been moved to the morgue, and they were waiting for an autopsy report, which could take days. Not that it mattered all that much. Reed figured because of the condition of her hands, that Roberta Peters had suffered the same fate as Bobbi Jean.

Except it's an odds-on shot that she wasn't pregnant.

He'd suspected that the killer had been targeting him and feared that Bobbi had met her fate because of her relationship with him. Had some creep he'd sent up the river been released and decided to get back at him? He'd already started going through records of those prisoners who had been released or escaped, but now . . . he was rethinking the crimes. He'd never met Roberta Peters in his life. At least, not that he could remember.

But the killer's still contacting you.

There has to be a reason.

Unless Reed had been chosen randomly, perhaps because he'd gotten so much press last summer. He'd been a target for nutcases ever since.

Disturbing nothing, carefully walking around crime scene investigators, Reed and Morrisette walked through the refurbished home with its carved wood banisters polished to a high gloss and faded rugs that, he suspected, had been handmade in the Middle East. Upstairs were four bedrooms, the largest obviously belonging to Roberta Peters. Framed, fading pictures of the woman and a man, presumably her husband, were set on tables and mounted over the fireplace. Her clothes were in the bureau and closets, her pills and toiletries tucked away in her private bath. The second and third rooms were obviously for show and guests. Antique beds appeared never to have been slept in, the bureaus empty. The fourth and smallest bedroom was filled with personal items, clothes in the closet and bureau, bottles of face and body creams, makeup and other toiletries on the bedside table. But the owner was absent. Reed made a mental note, then took a second set of steps, the servants' stairs, down to the kitchen where Diane Moses was once again keeping a log of what was done and found at the crime scene.

"Send me all the reports ASAP," Reed said.

"I was told you were off the case." Diane, gloved, had been ordering the photographer to take more shots of the kitchen where a teapot sat on the stove and dishes for an animal were sitting on a small rug near the pantry. Reed felt all eyes turned in his direction. Diane wasn't being her usual razor-sharp cynical self as she collected evidence and made notes in the crime scene log. She was just telling it like it was.

"Send the reports to Morrisette," Reed said as the photographer snapped some more photos with a .35 millimeter camera as well as a state-of-the-art digital cam. Morrisette walked over to the bowls on the floor. "So, where's the dog or cat?"

"Haven't found it yet," Moses replied.

"Looks like the bowl was just filled."

"So, maybe the cat's on a diet," the dour-faced photographer muttered.

"Yeah, and she was making tea." The porcelain cup and saucer still sat on the marble counter. Empty and clean. A tea bag was still steeping into now-cold water tinted a deep, impenetrable brown. Two shortbread cookies sat uneaten on a tiny glass plate. "Stove was off. Kitchen lights were on, stairs, back porch and main bedroom lights were on, all others off. All the doors and windows except this one"—she pointed a gloved finger at the back door—"were locked. This one was left ajar."

"Forced?" Reed eyed the door, lock and jamb.

"Nu-uh. And no signs of a struggle. We've already gone over this room, the porch and backyard. Looks like she was turning in and didn't make it. We'll check the tea and water in the pot for possible toxins, but I doubt she even had a sip."

"Any messages?"

"No phone machine, pager or computer, nor voice mail," Diane said. "Lots of books. *Tons* of books, only one TV, tuned to a local channel that broadcasts religious stuff twenty-four seven."

"What about who she called?"

"The last number dialed is a Phoenix area code."

"She didn't live alone, though," Reed said.

"No. Someone's MIA."

Footsteps sounded on the back steps. Reed looked up and found a uniformed rookie named Willie Armstrong crossing the porch. "Found the cat," he announced. A long red scratch showed on his cheek. "Hiding under the porch. Won't come out."

"But he got a piece of you," Morrisette said.

The young cop blushed to the tips of his large ears. "Yeah. He's really freaked out. Either scared shitless or wounded. I've called animal control."

"Animal control?" Morrisette repeated. "Jesus Christ, Willie, are you a policeman or a pussy? Can't you get the damned cat out yourself?"

"Hey, I tried. The damned thing nearly took my face off!" Armstrong seemed offended by Morrisette's remarks, but then, he hadn't been with the department very long. He'd get used to it.

He was still explaining and rubbing a finger on his cheek. "The stupid thing wants to claw the hell out of me. And I didn't want to disturb the scene. Something else might be under there."

"You're right," Diane said.

"I can get the cat." Morrisette eyed Armstrong as if he were either stupid, a wimp or both. "It's not brain surgery and you don't have to be a bear wrassler." She rolled her eyes at his expense. "You don't even have to use tear gas, Willie. It's a cat, for God's sake."

"Leave it. Armstrong's right." Diane was reaching for her collection kit. "And you know it, Morrisette. Give the guy a break."

"Why should he be any different than the rest?" another cop muttered and Morrisette shot him a look guaranteed to castrate.

Young and green, Armstrong made a hasty exit down the stairs to a backyard that was fenced, private and lush with thick shrubs.

"As soon as we get something, we'll get it to you, Morrisette," Moses said pointedly. But she glanced at Reed from the corner of her eye and gave a curt nod, then went about her work.

"So everyone knows you've been booted from the case."

"I guess."

"Looks like you're gaining yourself a reputation," Morrisette remarked as they walked along a brick path to the cruiser.

Reed opened the door and slid inside. "Already had one."

CHAPTER 12

"So, you think we've got a serial killer on our hands?" Katherine Okano asked as she studied the note Reed had received through her bifocals. Her gray wool suit reflected her mood. Her demeanor was stern, her mouth set it an uncompromising line.

"Looks like." Reed was seated in one of the side chairs, Morrisette standing near the window.

"Just what we need." She settled into her chair. "Okay, what have you got."

They'd brought the D.A. up to speed on the events at Heritage Cemetery and Roberta Peters's home. They'd interviewed neighbors, one of whom had remembered they'd heard Roberta calling for her cat around ten, another who informed them that the woman who lived with Roberta was a maid named Angelina Something-Or-Other who lived in with the elderly lady and had one night off a week.

"You haven't talked to the maid yet?"

"Haven't located her."

Okano's frown deepened.

"And the press hasn't got wind of this?"

"We've had a few inquiries," Reed admitted, thinking of the phone calls and E-mail he'd received—two voice mail messages and one E-mail message from Nikki Gillette alone. She hadn't been the only one, just the most determined. And she'd made it a point to try to reach Reed. While Morrisette and Cliff Siebert and Red Demarco had gotten calls from other reporters, Gillette had zeroed in on Reed. "The press is putting it together."

Okano frowned and sat back in her chair. Her lips rolled in on themselves; behind her wire-rimmed glasses her greenish eyes had darkened. She wasn't pleased. "We'll have to make a statement, but I need more facts first."

"We're waiting for the reports from the crime scene team and the ME," Reed said, and when Okano shot him a dark look he added, "Look, you and I both know I'm not officially on the case, but the killer keeps dragging me into it by sending me letters."

"I'm in charge," Morrisette insisted. "I've already started interviewing Roberta Peters's neighbors and friends. It's a long list. She not only was active volunteering in the library, but played bridge with the same women every week, was on the board of the garden club and was a dues paying member at two country clubs. Pretty high profile."

"So the press will be all over us ASAP." Okano's eyes narrowed. "And you knew her?" she asked Morrisette.

"I knew *of* her. I probably said ten words to her last summer, most of which were 'Hi,' or 'How're ya'll doin'.' I don't know anything about her other than she helped out with story time."

Okano picked up a glass of some coffee concoction that was sweating on a corner of her desk. "Okay, you can stay, but Reed, you're off. Officially and unofficially. If the killer contacts you again, let Morrisette know, and you"—she hitched her chin to the policewoman—"you keep me up on the investigation." She tapped a long finger beside the note from the killer. "Send this to the lab, have it compared to the other letters you got, and keep me posted. Meanwhile, I'll contact the FBI."

Reed nodded but didn't make any comments about the Feds. Usually a pain in the butt, they nonetheless knew their stuff and had access to resources that were otherwise unavailable to the Savannah police. The Feds could help, and right now, the department needed all the help it could get.

"We'll have to make a statement, warn the public," Okano thought aloud. "Without causing a panic." She glanced at both of them before her gaze settled on Morrisette. "Nail this bastard, and quick."

Reed and Morrisette left the D.A.'s office together, dropped the note off at the lab, then headed back to Homicide where things were still geared up. Detectives sat at computer screens, hung onto the phone or worked on the mounds of paperwork that accompanied each case.

"I've got some phone calls to make. I'll catch up with you later," Morrisette said and peeled off to her desk.

Reed settled into his desk chair as the ancient heating system blasted him with air hot enough to bring a sweat to his brow. Outside the temperature was hovering around fifty, inside, closer to ninety. Sweltering. Like the dog days of summer. He yanked on his tie and turned toward his computer monitor. He had other cases to consider, but the Grave Robber or whatever they were going to call it was top priority. God, he hated that name—the Grave Robber. Leave it to Nikki Gillette to come up with something like that. He ignored Okano's directive that he remove himself from the investigation. He was in it knee-deep whether he liked it or not. The killer saw to that.

Why?

What was his connection to the psychotic monster who was out ripping up cemeteries and dumping live women into occupied coffins? Not just that, but why move one coffin three hundred miles north? What sense did that make? Was it some kind of statement? A clue he was missing? He clicked on his computer screen, pulled up the Grave Robber case and brought pictures of the victims to the fore. His insides clenched as he looked at Bobbi Jean. . . . She'd been so beautiful and now she'd been reduced to an ashen-skinned corpse.

He looked at the other bodies, two of which were

decomposing. What did these people have in common? How were they linked to him? Were they? Or was that all just smoke and mirrors? Had the Grave Robber known him . . . or had the creep picked Reed's name out of the paper due to all the press he'd gotten last summer? Who knew? He was still fiddling around with the information when there was a tap at the door. Swiveling in his chair Reed spied Detective McFee filling the doorway.

"Just wanted to say bye," the big man said.

"Goin' home?"

"For a while. I went over all the information on the new one this morning." His high forehead wrinkled. "Looks like we got ourselves a real nutcase on the loose. I'd like to stay, but there's not much reason. The sheriff wants me to report in."

"But you'll be back?"

"I reckon. Until this case is solved, we're all in it together."

Reed nodded. "Need a ride to the airport?"

McFee shook his head. "Got one." He crossed the short span of linoleum and shoved a hand across Reed's desk. They shook. "Be seein' ya. Good luck."

"Same to you."

"I'll let you know if we come up with anything."

"I appreciate it."

With a nod, McFee turned and headed toward the exit. Through the open door Reed watched him leave and wasn't too surprised to see Sylvie Morrisette catch up with him. The big man visibly brightened at the sight of her and for once Morrisette had abandoned her dark visage. She actually smiled up at McFee, flirted with him, appeared incredibly feminine. The big detective glanced over his shoulder, met Reed's gaze, and one side of his mouth lifted almost smugly. As if to say, *This happens all the time, Reed. Take notes. The quiet country-boy charm can get you into a woman's pants faster than a bottle of Chablis.*

They disappeared down the stairs and Reed picked up the phone. Cradling the receiver on his shoulder, he found the number he'd written down earlier, then punched out the digits. It had been the last call Roberta Peters had made . . . no, it had been the last call made from Roberta Peters's telephone. Either she had called Phoenix, or someone else had used her phone.

After three rings, a sweet-voiced woman answered. "Hello, this is Glenda of Faith Gospel Mission. May God be with you. How can I direct your call?"

Reed identified himself, stated his business and was redirected to several different voices, none of which deigned to give him any information. All soon gave up any sign of friendliness and the "May God be with you" greeting was dropped the minute he mentioned that he was with the police. His final connection was to "Reverend Joe," who flatly told him that they didn't give out any information about members of the mission's flock, then summarily hung up. Reed checked with the Better Business Bureau and the Phoenix Police Department, making inquiries about Faith Gospel Mission and specifically about Reverend Joe. According to all sources, the good preacher and his institution were clean as a whistle. Reverend Joe hadn't been charged with so much as a traffic citation. Almost too clean. Reed didn't trust the man right from the get-go. Didn't like the fact that he didn't use a surname. Maybe old Joe was enough of a celebrity with the God-fearing crowd that he didn't need one. Like Cher or Madonna or Liberace. Just Reverend Joe.

Despite his feelings, the call was a waste and brought him to another dead end. Strike one.

He took the time to grab a Coke out of the vending machine down the hall, then put in a call to the New Orleans Police Department. He was hoping to catch up with Detective Reuben Montoya, a young buck of a detective who had worked with him last summer on the Montgomery case, but was informed by a secretary that Montoya had left the department a few months earlier. Reed was referred to a detective named Rick Bentz, whose voice mail answered and Reed remembered having worked with Bentz in the past. He would have to do. Reed left a brief message inquiring about Bobbi Jean's brother, Vince Lassiter, then left his number and hung up.

Strike two.

He finished his Coke, answered a few calls and caught up on some paperwork, but all the while the Grave Robber case scratched at the edges of his brain. As afternoon eased toward evening, he was still turning the case over in his mind. He was missing something, he thought, something vital. The damned killer was teasing him with notes, brazenly mailing some kind of clues to him and Reed wasn't getting it. He pulled out a yellow legal pad, clicked his pen and started making notes. He started with the notes from the killer. Though they were already being analyzed by the lab and a police psychologist and probably an FBI profiler by now, Reed decided to mentally grapple with them himself. This was his communication with the killer. His link. There had to be something in the letters addressed to him that only he would understand. He wrote down the contents of the first letter, the one he'd received at the office with the return address of Colonial Cemetery on the envelope.

> ONE, TWO,
> THE FIRST FEW.
> HEAR THEM CRY,
> LISTEN TO THEM DIE.

This had been his introduction to the case. The killer was telling him that he was going to find two victims, even though Pauline Alexander had been buried for years and had died of natural causes. The way Reed read it, the killer was taunting him, not offering any information other than that these two were the first of what were sure to be more. Both Bobbi Jean and Pauline were victims of a sort.

> TICK TOCK,
> ON GOES THE CLOCK.
> TWO IN ONE,
> ONE AND TWO.

Again, the references to two victims, or . . . did the

killer know about the baby?

If so, there would be three . . . one and two adding up to three . . . But at that point there had only been two bodies—unless it was a reference to Thomas Massey, who was already dead at that point. If Massey were part of the killer's scheme, and not a random grave that the killer had happened upon.

"Think, Reed, think," he growled. There was something else in here, something that had to do with time. What? Was the killer on some kind of schedule? Was he that organized? Why contact Reed?

"Come on, you son of a bitch, figure it out," he growled as he wrote down the contents of the third note:

ONE, TWO, THREE, FOUR . . .
SO, NOW, DON'T YOU WONDER HOW
MANY MORE?

More taunting. The killer was playing with him. And feeling superior. Speaking to him directly with the "you" in the second line. But there was something about the configuration of the last note that seemed off. Something that bothered Reed. "One, two, three, four." Almost like a nursery rhyme, but it was obviously a reference to the bodies as well. Four victims, meaning that not only Barbara Jean Marx and Roberta Peters were victims, but also Pauline Alexander and Thomas Massey. Otherwise, why count up to four? *Unless the killer's playing with you and there are two other victims stashed in occupied graves that you haven't yet*

208

unearthed. "Hell," he muttered and was glad he could hand the note to the FBI's psychological profiler. The Feds would have a heyday with this one.

He drummed his fingers on the desk, looked over all the reports and evidence again and searched his E-mail where he found the preliminary report on Thomas Massey. An African-American who had four children flung to the far corners of the country and an elderly wife living in a small house outside of the city. Massey had been a janitor for a private school years ago as well as a deacon in his church. His wife, Bea, had worked part-time as a bookkeeper while raising the kids. From all early accounts, Massey hadn't had any run-ins with the law and he and his wife had been married forty-five years at the time of his death.

Then, there was Roberta Peters, sixty-three, a widow. No children. Lived alone in the old home she and her husband had occupied since 1956. He'd died four years earlier.

So what was the connection between the victims. Or was there one?

. . . don't you wonder how many more?

Reed's jaw tightened. Obviously the murderer wasn't about to stop. Reed wondered if there was a finite number involved. Probably not. The question was rhetorical. The bastard wouldn't quit his deadly game until the police either cuffed or killed him and Reed was hoping for the latter.

Maybe he'd get lucky and could do the honors himself.

CHAPTER 13

"You don't want to stay for dinner?" Charlene Gillette asked. Barely a hundred pounds, her skin pale, but her makeup impeccable, she was perched on the cushions of the window seat overlooking the terraced grounds of the Gillette estate. It was dark outside, the shrubbery illuminated by lamps strategically placed near the brick walls. On the kitchen table, near a bouquet of birds-of-paradise, was the morning's edition of the *Sentinel*, laid flat, Nikki's story visible, forgotten reading glasses mounted over the headlines.

"It has nothing to do with wanting, Mom," Nikki said, her stomach nearly growling at the savory smells of pot roast emanating from the oven. Pecan pie cooled on the counter and potatoes boiled on the stove. Sandra, the sometimes maid, sometimes caretaker, was tossing a spinach salad with pears and blue cheese. Nikki stood near the counter, picking at pieces of chopped hazelnuts that hadn't yet made it into the bowl.

"You're always on the go. Would it hurt you to sit down and share a meal with us?"

"Of course not." But Nikki was already thinking ahead, that she had to get the new key to her apartment, that someone had broken in, a little secret she'd keep from her parents. Otherwise they'd be worried sick and insist she go to the police or stay and live with them . . . neither being an option.

"I don't know when you've relaxed," Charlene observed.

"It's not my nature."

"Like your father."

Sandra lifted an eyebrow as she scooped up a handful of the hazelnuts and sprinkled them atop the spinach leaves.

"Is that so bad?"

Her mother didn't answer directly. Instead, she snapped her fingers as if she'd just remembered something important. "Oh, honey, by the way, guess who stopped by earlier today?"

"I couldn't," Nikki said honestly. "You know too many people around here."

"Not me. Someone you know, er, knew."

"Who?" Nikki asked, not really caring.

"Sean," she said with a little glimmer in her eye, and Nikki inwardly groaned.

"Sean Hawke? What was he doing here?"

"He just stopped by to see me. His mother and I did go to school together, you know."

Nikki remembered. Though she didn't want to.

"He asked about you."

"I already talked to him."

"And?" One of her mother's eyebrows rose.

"And nothing. He wanted to get together. I thought it was a bad idea."

"Really? But I always liked Sean." She lifted her hands to the sides of her head as if to ward off a blow. "I know, I know. It didn't work out. He was interested in someone else, but you know, you were both too young, then. Maybe now—"

"Never, Mom, and I can't believe you're saying this. Sean was and is a snake. End of subject." Nikki couldn't help but be irritated. Charlene seemed to think she was an old maid just because she was over thirty. Which was ridiculous. "Dad never liked him," she pointed out and thought she saw, from the corner of her eye, a curt nod of Sandra's head.

"Your father is suspicious of everyone." Charlene folded her arms under her small breasts. Her jaw was set in that hard, uncompromising line Nikki had seen all too often. "That attitude comes from being involved with the law and seeing the dark side of life every day."

Nikki heard the garage door open. "Speak of the devil."

Her mother's spine stiffened slightly, as if she were bracing herself, and Nikki felt a pang of wistfulness. What had happened to her parents, who, when they were younger, had danced and laughed, their eyes crinkling at each other's jokes, each trying to outdo the other? They had seemed devoted, yet independent, and above all else, respectful of each other. They had been kind. They had been happy. They had been in love, even after four children and over two decades together. Their happiness had eroded over the years, worn away by Andrew's death and their own perceptions of ever-nearing mortality. Age and sorrow had sapped Charlene of her wit and her vitality, while those same two demons had embittered her father.

Sandra swept away the final crumbs of the nuts as the retired Honorable Judge Ronald Gillette opened the door from the garage and stepped into the warm light of the kitchen.

His cheeks were ruddy, his nose always red these days, his blue eyes sparkling despite too many visible veins. Some people thought he looked like Santa Claus, but he reminded Nikki of Burl Ives's portrayal of Big Daddy in an old movie version of *Cat On A Hot Tin Roof*. "Hey, Firecracker!" he boomed and gave his youngest child the bear hug she'd come to expect. He smelled of cigar smoke, rye whiskey and rain. "So, you finally made page one! Congratulations!" Another squeeze.

Nikki was grinning ear to ear as the embrace ended. "Finally being the integral word in that sentence."

Big Ron chuckled. "It's not as if you're over the hill."

"Yet."

"Well, maybe we should have a drink to celebrate. Char—?"

"No." She shook her head and tried to hide the knots of disapproval pinching the corners of her mouth.

"You will, though?" he asked Nikki.

She thought of her scheduled meeting with Cliff. "I'll have to take a rain check, Dad. I've got work to do."

"It's only one drink." He was already walking toward the den. Her mother turned her attention toward the darkened windows and Nikki caught sight of Charlene's pale reflection in the glass, saw the pain and disapproval in that ghostly image.

"You okay, Mom?"

Charlene blinked, managed a smile. "Right as rain."

"You wouldn't lie to me, would ya?" Nikki plopped

onto the cushion next to her and hugged her mother. Charlene smelled of Estee Lauder and powder. "You saw the doctor yesterday. What did he say?"

"What he always does. That everything is all in my head." With a glance toward the hallway where her husband disappeared, she added, "He suggested I visit a psychiatrist."

Nikki took her mother's hand and was surprised that it felt bony and small. Her rings were so loose the stones kept sliding toward her palm. "Would that be so bad?"

For a second Charlene's chin wobbled, then she looked into her daughter's eyes. "So, you think I'm crazy, too."

"Not crazy. Depressed."

"Isn't it the same thing?"

"Not at all. There's a big difference." Nikki tried to be kind. But it was tough when the truth had to be said. "It's just that you seem so unhappy, Mom."

"Well, there's a brilliant observation," Charlene snapped angrily, then caught herself and extracted her fingers from Nikki's grasp. "I'm fine. Fine. Don't worry. Please."

Heavy footsteps sounded in the hallway and again her mother's lips pursed slightly, as if she could barely stand to be in the same room with her husband. She managed a tight, forced smile just as Big Ron walked into the room carrying two short glasses. Ice cubes clinked in a pale gold liquid. "Here ya go," he said, handing one glass to Nikki.

"She said she didn't want a drink," Charlene said.

"Did she?" He winked at his daughter. "Guess I didn't hear that." Clicking the rim of his glass to Nikki's, he said, "Here's to more big scoops and bylines on the front page."

"Thanks." She took a tentative sip, found the drink tolerable, and tried to ignore the tension in the air.

To mollify her mother and because she was starved, she stayed for dinner, listening to her father's golf stories and fishing stories and trying to lure Charlene into conversation to no avail. They took dessert in the family room, eating the pie and sipping coffee while Nikki tried not to notice how late it was getting. She'd nearly finished when it hit her that she'd forgotten all about Simone. Again. Good Lord, she was turning into one of those flaky friends she hated. "Oh, geez, I've got to run," she said, leaving half a piece of pie and all her coffee on an end table.

"Where's the fire?" Her father was seated in his favorite worn leather recliner. His legs were raised, his shirt unbuttoned and he'd lifted a pant leg to unbuckle the holster he wore at his ankle. He'd always carried a hidden weapon after an attempt had been made on his life, the result of a particularly unpopular courtroom decision.

"I told Simone I would meet her at the gym," Nikki explained as she picked up her purse. She glanced at her watch. "If I hurry, I can still make it."

"But we never get to see you," Charlene complained as Big Ron rubbed his calf muscle. He'd placed his holster and pistol upon the coffee table.

"Pick that damned thing up," Charlene said, jabbing

a finger at the gun. "The last time you left it out Lily came over with Ophelia!"

Big Ron didn't move except to change the channel on the big screen with his remote.

"Oh, for the love of God." Charlene's mouth drew into an unhappy, persecuted line.

Nikki hated to leave. A fight was brewing. "I'll be back. Soon. Promise." She dropped a kiss on her mother's head, then gave her father another hug before streaking out of the house. Her parents had come to an uneasy truce. They'd be okay. Yet, she crossed her fingers.

How had she forgotten her friend? As ambitious as she was, she didn't believe in work to the exclusion of all else. Family and friends were important. And yet she was ditching out on her folks, hadn't called her sister back in two days, had left Trina to deal with Aimee and Dana the other night and now had nearly stood up her best friend. "Oh, yeah, Gillette," she reprimanded, "you're a great friend."

She drove home pushing the speed limit, stopped by the owner's apartment where she was handed two shiny new keys and was told that the new locks were "guaranteed to keep unwanted boyfriends out."

"Thanks," she'd said, flashing a smile and racing up the stairs. She hesitated as she slid one key into the new lock, but the door swung open and her cozy little apartment was just as she'd left it. At least, she thought so. Agilely, Jennings hopped down from the kitchen counter to rub around her legs. She took the time to pet him, give him some new food, and change. She then called Cliff Siebert on his cell and explained that she'd meet him at the Weaver Brothers truck stop, but that she was running late because of her date with Simone. Then, with only a modicum of guilt at leaving the cat again, she locked the door securely behind her before flying down the stairs. She had five minutes to get to the gym before the class started.

Unfortunately, it was a twenty-minute drive.

CHAPTER 14

". . . that's it for tonight. Thank you." Jake Vaughn bowed, clapped his hands together and smiled at the class as he straightened. Nikki, her body drenched in sweat, felt muscles she hadn't remembered existed. She'd gotten to the kickboxing class ten minutes late and missed stretching, but had managed to squeeze into a vacant spot next to Simone as her friend had worked out and ogled the instructor.

"You're embarrassing," Nikki said, swiping at her face with a towel as most of the other class members gathered their gear and walked out of the gym with its gleaming hardwood floors, high ceilings and basketball hoops.

"You think?" Simone laughed. Her black hair was pulled atop her head in a loose, seemingly casual knot that Nikki suspected took half an hour to get just right. Her skin was a natural golden tone, her cheeks flushed from the exertion of the workout, or from being so close to Jake, Nikki wasn't sure which. "I didn't think anything could embarrass you," she said, dabbing at her forehead with the ends of the towel she'd draped around her neck.

"You were wrong."

"Then, prepare yourself for being mortified." After shooting a "watch this" look at Nikki, Simone walked boldly over to Jake who was stowing some of his athletic gear into a nylon Nike bag.

Nikki couldn't hear the conversation but assumed Simone was asking him out. He was smiling broadly, nodding, then shaking his head. Letting Simone down easy. What was wrong with the guy? Simone was a knockout in her leotard and tight little shorts. Jake *had* to be gay. Why else would Simone be interested in him? She was always attracted to the guys who were unavailable—either married, recently divorced, or somehow emotionally damaged. This was the first time that Simone had been interested in someone who wasn't physically interested in her. A real blow to her ego. Except the guy was probably just not interested in women.

Nikki slung her towel over her neck as Simone and Jake parted ways. "He's busy," Simone said, her good mood replaced by confusion. Her dark brows were knit, her lips compressed.

"Because he's gay."

"You don't know that."

"Bet?"

Simone sighed dramatically. "No! That's a dumb bet. But since Jake can't join me, how 'bout you? Dinner?"

"I love to be second choice," Nikki mocked.

"Oh, for the love of God, Nikki, that's not fair. You're always blowing me off for some other person, usually not even a cute guy—just some"—she made air quotes at this point—"big, and I mean really, really big, assignment."

"Okay, okay, I get it. I've been a flake, okay?" Nikki glanced at her watch. She had to meet Cliff in less than an hour.

"Right. So make it up to me. And don't complain about being my second choice. Besides, you've got to eat. You can convince me that Jake's all wrong for me over shrimp and fries."

"I thought you wanted barbecue."

"Yeah, well, I thought I wanted Jake, too. A girl can change her mind, can't she?"

"I had dinner at my folks'."

"Then, keep me company."

"For a while," Nikki acquiesced.

They drove in separate cars to the Bijou, a little hole in the wall off the waterfront. The atmosphere was lousy, the place noisy and crowded, but, as Nikki knew from experience, the shrimp, oysters and crab cakes were to die for. A dozen tables with red and white oil-cloth covers were wedged into a small room where ceiling fans, now decorated with Christmas lights, swirled overhead. Semi-private booths with high backs and coat hooks rimmed the perimeter of the establishment. Three teenagers were just leaving when they arrived, so Nikki and Simone grabbed their small, vacated table near the kitchen.

Minutes later their order had been taken by a waitress with purple streaks in her hair and several rings in her eyebrows. Before Nikki could convince Simone that Jake, their kickboxing teacher, was off-limits, Simone's seafood platter and Nikki's iced tea were deposited in front of them.

"Sure you don't want a bite?" Simone asked, dredging a strip of clam through a trough of hot sauce.

"I'm stuffed, really."

Nikki nursed her tea and tried not to look at her watch every five minutes as her friend devoured coleslaw, French fries, shrimp, clams and crab cakes. "Jingle Bell Rock" played for the second time.

"Okay, so I can't have Jake. I can live with that," Simone said philosophically. "I got over Andrew, didn't I?"

"Better than most of us." They rarely talked about Andrew or the fact that he'd broken up with Simone one week before he died. Nikki was far from certain that her friend had gotten through the experience emotionally unscathed, but she wasn't in the mood to argue.

"What about you? Why are you always holed up in your apartment or at work? I'm beginning to think you've got some secret lover squirreled away somewhere."

Nikki almost laughed out loud. It had been several months since she'd had a date, a long time since she'd split with Sean, her last serious boyfriend. "Go on thinking that. It makes me sound intriguing."

"You are."

"Me?" Nikki shook her head and stole a French fry.

"I'm an open book."

"An open book that works way too much," Simone said as the waitress refilled Nikki's glass and someone played an old Jimmy Buffett tune on the jukebox. The strains of "Margaritaville" played over the rattle of silverware and the buzz of conversation.

"Some of us don't have cushy jobs with the city planning department."

"Bo-ring, cushy jobs listening to city planners fight and haggle and . . . I don't know, it's just not how I want to spend the rest of my life. At least you love what you do." Simone set her fork on the table. "Okay, I guess I'd better tell you what's going on with me."

"Besides trying to convert a gay man straight." Nikki finished her tea and crushed an ice cube in her teeth.

Simone ignored the jibe. "I'm thinking of moving."

"What?" Stunned, Nikki set down her glass. Nearly choked on the ice.

"You heard me."

"But where and why?"

"I'm not sure where I want to land. But somewhere else. Richmond, maybe."

"Richmond?" Nikki couldn't believe her ears. Never had Simone mentioned leaving Savannah.

Simone began picking at the tail of a shrimp. Avoiding Nikki's eyes. "Or Charleston."

"Where did this come from?" she asked as the couple at the next table scooted back their chairs noisily.

"Oh, come on, Nikki, you know what I mean. You've been talking of leaving for years. New York or Chicago or San Francisco or L.A. I'm not talking about a cross-country move. I want to be close enough to visit my folks when I want to, but far enough away to have some space, my own space. I've got to face it, Nikki, I'm in a rut here. I have been since Andrew died. I need a change."

She had a point. Not only was Simone the only child of a wealthy old-money Savannah family, but she'd also been the beneficiary of Andrew's estate. Andrew had owned land he'd inherited from Nana and a healthy bank account. It had always been a sore spot between the families that Simone, rather than Andrew's parents, had ended up with part of the family fortune, but it had never bothered Nikki.

"I figured you'd understand," Simone was saying. "You're always on the lookout for something exciting. You get that rush through your work."

"Oh, yeah, writing such hot stories as what the historical society's next project is or who's been elected to the school board is a real high."

"You helped bust Dickie Ray Biscayne."

"And the world is better off," Nikki mocked, remembering the bastard cousin to the Montgomerys. A lowlife bottom feeder if ever there was one.

"It is," Simone insisted as a busboy neatly pocketed the tip left at the neighboring table before picking up the dishes and swiping the oilcloth with a wet towel. "Dickie Ray was organizing dogfights." She shuddered. "Awful stuff. You did the world a favor. And now you're on the trail of that Grave Robber, right?" Simone's eyes brightened. "I read the article this morning. You're on to something," she said with a smile, then leaned across the table as if about to share a secret. "I'm no investigative reporter, but I'm willing to bet from the way you've been checking your watch and cell phone you've got something more going, some-place you need to be, right?"

"Am I that obvious?"

"Yeah. I'm willing to bet it has to do with the mur-ders, right?"

Nikki hedged. "I can't say much, but for the first time in a long, long time I get the chance to prove myself to Tom Fink and I'm not going to blow it."

"Oh . . ." Simone nodded as she bit into a shrimp. "So, that's it. You know, Nikki, the Chevalier trial was a long time ago."

"It seems like yesterday."

"A lot longer than that. More like ten or twelve years. I was there. I remember." She shuddered and Nikki noticed goose bumps raise on her forearms. "I heard Chevalier was getting out or had gotten out a few weeks ago. Can you believe it? The psycho hacks up his girlfriend and most of her family, gets sent to prison and then gets released on some kind of technicality?" Simone was suddenly serious as death, her face pale. "You know, there is definitely something wrong with the system, if something like that can happen."

Nikki couldn't agree more, didn't want to think about LeRoy Chevalier and his brutal crime, or how she'd nearly jeopardized the case against him by reporting information she'd heard from her father, the judge overseeing the trial. She'd nearly cost her father his job, probably had ruined any political ambitions he might have harbored. And now Chevalier was a free man. She agreed with Simone; it just wasn't right. She checked the time and apologized to Simone. "I'm sorry, but I really do have to run."

"I know, there's a big story out there just begging Nikki Gillette to write it."

Nikki smiled as she opened her wallet, then groaned. In her haste to get home and pick up the new keys, she hadn't run to the bank. She didn't have a dime on her. "You won't believe this."

Simone laughed. "Don't worry about it. The tea's on me. Besides, when you become a Pulitzer Prize–winning journalist, you can buy!" Simone raised her hand, intending to flag down the waitress, but stopped. Her smile faded and her eyebrows slammed together. "Who's that guy?"

"What guy?"

"The guy that was in the booth over there . . ." She hitched her chin toward a corner booth located close to a side door that was swinging shut. "He was seated facing me and I caught him looking our way a couple of times. . . . I thought I recognized him, but . . ." Little lines of frustration showed between her eyebrows. "Oh, maybe it was nothing."

Nikki's mouth went dry. She stared through the glass door, peering through the panes into the darkness, but saw only the darkened, empty sidewalk beyond. Her gaze moved quickly to the bank of windows in the front of the restaurant, but again didn't catch a glimpse of anyone loitering just outside the window's warm light. No partially hidden figure. "He was watching us?"

"Oh, maybe not." Lines of frustration creased Simone's brow. "I'm probably imagining things. I've been jumpy lately."

"Why?"

"I don't know. Lately, I've just had this feeling . . ." her voice trailed off and she sighed. "I really do have to get out of this town."

"What kind of feeling?"

Simone pulled her purse from under her chair and slung the strap over her shoulder. "It's nothing." When Nikki didn't seem convinced, she added, "Really. Remember, I'm so screwed up that now I'm chasing gay guys."

Nikki thought about the note that had been left on her bed and her skin crawled just at the thought of it. If she confided in Simone now, she'd only upset her friend further. "If there's something bothering you . . ."

"It's probably just the time of year. Christmas and all. Andrew and I got together about this time of year . . . but that was a long time ago, too, wasn't it? Nearly thirteen years. You know, the weird thing is that you and I could have been sisters-in-law . . . you might have been my kids' aunt. Auntie Nik, how does that sound?"

"Familiar. Lily's daughter calls me something like that."

Obviously Simone hadn't dealt with Andrew's death any better than had the rest of the family. Maybe she *should* get away for a while. Away from the memories. Away from her best friend who just happened to be the sister of the man she'd loved. Away from the ghosts of the past.

The waitress finally caught on, sauntered over to the table and Simone asked for the check while Nikki asked about the guy who'd been sitting in the corner booth.

"Never seen him before. But then, I just started last week."

"Thanks."

"It was probably nothing," Simone said as she eyed the bill.

"Next time, it's my treat. *Really.*" Nikki gathered her purse.

"I've heard that one before. Besides, you're a cheap date. One glass of tea." Simone dropped bills onto the table and they walked together to their cars. Nikki's beat-up hatchback was parked two spaces down the street from Simone's six-month-old BMW convertible.

The cobblestone street was deserted and dark, but Nikki saw no one hiding in the shadows. Nonetheless, she was edgy, a little nervous, so she checked the interior of her car before climbing in and starting the engine. It died. Again. Pumping the accelerator, she twisted the ignition and watched Simone pull away from the curb. "Oh, for Pete's sake." She tried again and the engine coughed before sputtering and dying. Simone's taillights became distant points of red. Nikki was starting to sweat. Remembered the guy Simone had said was staring at them from the corner booth in the Bijou. But she wasn't alone; there were other patrons coming out of the building and she had her cell. She wrenched on the key again, and the engine fired. Carefully, Nikki gave the car some gas and then pulled away from the curb. Relief settled over her until she tried to negotiate the next corner and took it a little fast.

She was running late, as usual.

No matter what, she didn't want to miss her meeting with Cliff Siebert.

The Subaru wobbled in the middle of the turn. Felt out of kilter. The steering all wrong . . .

"Damn it all." Nikki pulled over to the curb and climbed out of the car to spy the problem. Her rear left tire was flat as a fritter. The others were losing air fast. "Son of a—" She kicked the flat tire and swore under her breath. She was going to miss her meeting with Cliff. No way could she make it now.

Of all the luck.

She whipped out her phone and punched in the numbers of his cell. It was dark, but she knew how to use a jack and change a tire. But she couldn't change all four.

One ring.

No answer.

Two rings. "Come on, come on!"

Or she could call AAA . . . or maybe Cliff would offer . . .

Three rings. "Oh, for crying out loud—" A van pulled up beside her and a guy in a baseball hat rolled down his window.

"Trouble?"

Four rings.

"A flat. Actually four flats."

"Want some help?"

"No . . . I'll be fine. My, uh, my husband is on his way," she lied, hoping he didn't notice her ringless fingers.

The cell phone clicked and Cliff's stock message about leaving a message at the tone played.

"I could stay with you and wait until he gets here." The stranger smiled and a gold capped tooth winked eerily in the streetlights.

"No, that's fine. He's on the phone and only a few blocks away. What?" she said into the cell. "Oh, no, it's just a guy offering help. No, that's fine. I'll tell him it'll only be a minute or two. . . . I love you, too." Glancing back at the van's driver, she forced a smile she hoped didn't wobble. "He'll be here in a second." Her throat was tight and she was shaking inside as she thought about the men who had been lurking in the streets, the break-in of her apartment, the notes she'd received, and the serial murderer stalking Savannah. Her blood turned to ice. "Thanks."

Another car pulled up behind the van and the driver touched the brim of his hat in a mock tip. "Whatever you want, honey."

Her skin crawled as he pulled away. *Honey*. Lord, why would he call her that? Intent on identifying him, she glared at his license plate as he drove off, but there was no light on the back of his van and the letters and numbers were too dark to read. All she knew was that it was a navy blue Dodge Caravan with Georgia plates. Which wasn't much.

And he could have just been a Good Samaritan.

Yeah, right.

Her cell was still in her hand. She hung up and dialed Triple A, giving the dispatcher the location of her car and explained that she'd meet the repairman at the Bijou. It was less than half a mile down the street and at least there it would be well lit and crowded.

Safe.

She started jogging.

Sweating on the outside, deathly cold inside, Nikki picked up the pace. Traffic lights blurred, the darkened shrubbery seemed sinister and she felt completely alone.

For the first time in her life Nikki Gillette felt fear—dark, mind-numbing fear.

CHAPTER 15

Reed tossed his keys and mail onto the desk in his apartment, three joined rooms on the first floor of what had once been a grand old home. He was lucky enough to end up with a bay window, tiled fireplace surrounded by bookshelves, and the original hardwood floors. In exchange he'd ended up with a minuscule kitchen and a bedroom that barely housed his bed and bureau, not that he needed much more space. Tonight he was bone tired, his body crying for sleep, his mind far too wired to even consider it. Try as he might he couldn't shake the image of Bobbi Jean in that coffin, nor dispel the terror she had to have felt. The horrid panic.

And she'd been pregnant.

Maybe with your kid.

"Jesus," he muttered as he picked up the remote, flipped on the television to the news, and hoped to quiet the demons screaming in his head. He found a pizza in the freezer, turned on the oven and popped a beer. Who would want to kill Bobbi? Who would hate her enough to throw her in an occupied coffin and bury her alive? The same sicko who did it to Roberta Peters. So the killer wasn't Jerome Marx. Unless he was cagey enough to kill another person in the same manner just as a decoy. But why go to all the trouble of burying the person alive? That was an act of rage . . . deep-seated hatred and premeditation. Then, there was the microphone. Whoever had killed them had listened to them die. Gotten his twisted rocks off by the sheer panic he'd created.

"Bastard."

The preheat button on the oven dinged. Reed tossed his frozen pizza, ice crystals and all, onto the rack, then walked back to the living area where he hoisted his laptop onto the desk. With a flick of a switch the computer hummed to life as he half listened to the television. A newscaster was summing up the basketball scores. The Miami Heat had lost, but Atlanta had pulled out a nail-biter. Reed scooted his desk chair closer and went directly to his E-mail where he had over thirty messages waiting for him.

Sifting through the spam and a couple of stale jokes that had been recycled a few times, he finished his beer and came to an E-mail with a subject line that read: GRAVE ROBBER ON A ROLL.

"What the hell?"

He clicked on the E-mail and read:

NOW, WE HAVE NUMBER FOUR.
ONE THIRD DONE,
WILL THERE BE MORE?

"Shit!" Reed hit the print button. The buzzer on the stove went off. An error message flashed and he realized he wasn't hooked up to his printer. Quickly connecting the printer cable, he hit the print key just as weird, ghost-like images appeared. Photos of Barbara Jean Marx, Pauline Alexander, Thomas Massey and Roberta Peters. The pictures of the victims floated eerily over the screen, then turned to dust and skeletons before Reed's eyes. "Holy shit." His blood froze in his veins. *One third done?* Four victims already. Meaning there would be *twelve* total?

The printer began spewing out a page and Reed hurried into the kitchen, turned off the timer and the oven, then left the pizza. He was back at the computer in an instant, reading the pages, checking the E-mail address, knowing it was phony.

Twelve victims?

Why tell him? Why would the killer tip his hand? What did the four have in common and who were the remaining eight? How were they linked?

Jaw set, he responded to the E-mail.

Doubted he'd get a response.

Forwarded everything to Bentley, a guy in the office who was a computer specialist for the department, then sent a copy to Morrisette.

Grabbing his phone, he punched in Morrisette's home number. On the third ring she answered, her voice thick with sleep. "Hullo?"

"It's me. The Grave Robber contacted me again."

"What?"

"E-mail. I've forwarded it to Bentley and to you. Check it out."

"I will. Give me five and I'll call you back." Suddenly awake, she hung up. Reed kept looking at the E-mail, hoping that there was a return path that would lead him to the killer. Was the guy that stupid? Or just that bold?

The phone chirped.

He snapped it up. "Reed."

"Jesus H. Christ, what's this fucker up to?" Morrisette said, and he could tell that she was lighting a cigarette as she spoke.

"I wish I knew."

"Twelve? Goddamn it, what does that mean?"

"I don't know, but we'd better figure it out, and fast. Do what you can, I'll see you in the morning."

"Right." She hung up again and Reed was left to stare at his computer screen and the sick images twisting and turning like leaves in the wind.

If only the bastard would slip up. Reed would nail his sorry hide. And love doing it.

WILL THERE BE MORE?

Not if Reed had anything to do with it.

"Where the hell did you git this?"

"Wh-what?" Billy Dean opened a bleary eye and made out the silhouette of his pa looming over his bed. The old man's face was set and hard and his outstretched hand held the ring—the damned ring Billy Dean had found at the grave.

"This here ring, that's what!"

"I dunno what ye're talkin' 'bout," Billy lied and knew he was making a mistake. No one lied to Merle Delacroix and got away with it.

"And I don't s'pose ya know anythin' about this neither?" He reached into the front pocket of tight, worn jeans and pulled out Billy's little blue pipe—specially tooled for weed.

Crap!

Slowly, Billy pulled himself to a sitting position and tried to think. Fast. But he was scared. "You bin lookin' through my things?"

"No shit, Sherlock. That's exactly what I've been doin' and don't give me any sass about your private stuff, cuz it won't hold water with me. No, sir. You live under my roof, you live under my rules, and my rules are damned explicit when it comes to stealin' and smokin' dope. God only knows what else ya been doin'." He glanced around Billy's messy room, the one he shared with the old dog. Merle ran a hand through his thin hair and snorted his loathing. "This here is a pigsty."

"You shouldn't go through my stuff," Billy Dean said under his breath.

"And you shouldn't be stealin'. Don't you know it's agin the law and God's commandments. You do

233

remember, 'thou shalt not steal,' don't ya?" So angry he was quivering in rage, Merle dropped the pipe onto the old comforter covering Billy's bed. "You know what you are, a liar and a sneak and a thief."

This was trouble. Big trouble.

"I didn't—"

Quick as a rattler striking, Merle grabbed Billy by the back of his T-shirt and hauled him to his feet. "Now, you looka here, boy. I ain't takin' no lies from you, nor any of that smart-assed back talk. If you want to keep on livin' here, you tell me what the hell this is all about."

Billy nearly peed his pants. "I found the ring."

His father yanked harder on the shirt and gave him a shake hard enough that his eyeballs seemed to rattle. "Yeah, you found it, all right. In some old lady's dresser."

"No!"

Another yank and this time his old man twisted on the fabric so that it tightened around Billy's neck. "Don't you lie to me."

"I ain't!" Billy insisted, gasping for breath. "I . . . I found the ring . . . Really . . . at that grave. Honest to God."

His father's eyes narrowed suspiciously. "At the grave?"

"Yeah, it was there in the dirt and I . . . I took it. Didn't figure it would harm nothin.' "

"But it weren't yours and that's tamperin' with evidence or somethin'. Goddamn it, boy, I swear, sometimes you have shit for brains. You're a fool. A damned, slow, sorry-assed fool! Hell." Disgusted, he let go of the T-shirt and Billy coughed as he pulled in a lungful of air. "I s'pose you found that pipe there, too."

The old man was baiting him. Billy didn't fall for the trap. "No, sir."

"It's yours?"

"No . . ."

"I warned you. No lies."

"It . . . belongs to one of my friends."

"Which one?"

"I can't say."

"Oh, yeah, you can, and you will." Big muscles bunched under his plaid shirt. Merle's nostrils flared and his eyes were dark as the obsidian ring he wore. His fists curled, showing huge knuckles.

"Pa, please . . ."

"Who?"

Merle's fists tightened.

"Crap."

"You got a name for me, Billy?"

Billy Dean swallowed hard and lied through his teeth. "It's Preston's, Pa."

Merle's jaw worked. "Shoulda known," he muttered. Sighing, he relaxed his hands. "Well, I s'pose that boy has all the trouble he needs right now, all busted up in the hospital the way he is. The good Lord saw fit to punish him right. But what about you and what're we gonna do 'bout this here ring?"

"I dunno."

"What say we call the sheriff's department in the morning?"

"If we have ta."

"Don't you think it would be the right thing to do?"

Billy Dean nodded. Felt bad about lying about Preston but figured it didn't hurt anything.

"Thought so." His old man pocketed the ring and winked before shutting off the light. "G'night, boy."

"Night, Pa," Billy Dean said, and as the door closed, he pounded his fist into his pillow. He shoulda sold that ring right away, gotten rid of it and made a few bucks. As it was now, he was shit outta luck. Seemed as if his old man was right. He was a damned fool.

Heart drumming, sweat drenching his body, The Survivor slid into the side entrance of his home, an old house in a respectable, if not expensive, part of town. Without turning on a light, he hurried down rickety stairs to the basement with its cobweb-strewn beams and low ceiling. It was damp down here, smelling of the earth that surrounded it, the few high windows covered with bars on the inside and vines on the outside.

He was getting careless.

And he couldn't afford to.

Not now.

Not when he was so close to accomplishing everything he'd planned for so long.

Nikki Gillette's friend had seen him. Perhaps recognized him.

Stupid. Stupid. Stupid.

When he'd been so careful for so long.

That was two mistakes. . . . First, the kid in the woods, and now, this encounter in the restaurant. No more . . . He couldn't afford another one. As it was, he'd have to deal with the problem up north with the kid who'd looked him in the eye and now . . . He gritted his teeth. How had he been so foolish, so heedlessly bold?

But it had been so tempting, a seduction he couldn't resist when, after sending the E-mail to Reed, he'd realized he'd have time to follow Nikki . . .

And then, he'd messed up.

He slapped his head.

Hard.

The voice came, then . . . with agonizing precision. It seemed to reverberate through this tiny cellar and straight to his soul.

What are ya, a girl? Damned dumb-assed cunt, that's what you are. Can't do anything right! Stupid little shit!

The insults cracked through his brain, ricocheting through his skull, causing fear to jet through his blood. In his mind's eye he viewed a thin lip curled into a disgusted sneer, witnessed a long, wicked belt snaking out of dirty denim loops, pulled by thick, hairy fingers with big knuckles and bitten-down nails, a strap of well-worn leather ready to slash welts into his backside.

"No!" he yelled, tasting the salt of sweat on his lips, focusing on the here and now and what he had to do. He was smart. A smart man. Not a girl. A man! Not a cunt.

"No, no, no!" Tears of shame burned his eyes even though he told himself that those ancient insults held no water, that they'd just been spouted from the mouth of an ignorant, useless and mean son of a bitch. Yet his breath came in short, scared bursts and the taunts he'd carried with him for a dozen years preyed like demons in his mind.

He'd prove they were wrong. That everyone had been wrong about him. He wasn't stupid. He wasn't a girl . . . he wasn't shit!

On unsteady legs he moved the bookcase with its boxes of old, forgotten junk and stooped to enter his private room, the space he'd devoted to his other self, his private self. The strong self.

Just stepping into his private hideaway, he felt more stable. In control.

The Survivor.

And Grave Robber.

Smarter than the rest.

From one shelf he extracted his scrapbook, then laid the album open on his homemade table. Yellowed newsprint with grainy pictures and faded text was pressed flat between clear plastic sheets. His eyes devoured the articles that he knew by heart.

Slowly, he flipped the pages until he reached the back of the book where the photographs he'd collected stared up at him. All the faces, some smiling, some grim, others distracted, were innocently unaware that they would face the same fate.

But they would learn.

He had survived.

They would not.

Because they were weak. And stupid.

He left the album on the table and walked to the bureau. Inside the second drawer were more pieces of lingerie. Some old, some new . . . but nothing as pretty as Bobbi Jean's slip or Nikki Gillette's panties. He opened the bags and touched his treasures, then closed the drawer firmly. He had no time for this. He touched the drops of dried blood on the dresser top and reminded himself of his mission.

It would all be over soon.

He would prove himself strong.

And then he could rest.

CHAPTER 16

"Do you know what the hell time it is?" Cliff Siebert grumbled, his voice sounding as if he'd just woken up.

"Yeah, I know, and I'm sorry," she said, driving toward his place south of the historic district. The car was running fine now that her slashed tires had been replaced with retreads she'd bought after her car had been towed to a local garage. The whole process of locating four tires she could afford and that would fit on her car had taken several hours, but she was up and running again and just burned that some thug had vandalized the Subaru and now her credit card was maxed out. Worse yet, she felt certain that her car was targeted on purpose. The crime was unlikely indiscriminate because of the notes she'd received. . . . Someone knew which car was hers, as well as where she lived. That thought chilled her to the bone. The fact that she'd used all the credit left on her card also ticked her off. "I still need to talk to you," she insisted, holding onto the cell phone as she took a corner a little wide.

"Whoa, honey. You had your chance and you stood me up."

"I left a message on your cell and explained all that," Nikki said. She glanced in her rearview mirror. Headlights appeared as a car swung around the same corner she'd just negotiated. "Someone slashed my tires, Cliff. And I think I apologized and groveled enough that you could forgive me."

He sighed and muttered something unintelligible under his breath about hardheaded career women.

"I really need to talk to you and I could be at your house in fifteen minutes."

"No!" he said emphatically. "I can't take the chance that someone sees you or your car here."

"Then meet me where we originally planned. Weaver Brothers truck stop."

He hesitated, but she knew that he lived only minutes from the place.

"Please, Cliff. I don't want to print something that's not right." The car behind her turned off and she let out a sigh.

"Something wrong?"

"You could say that."

"What?"

"I'll tell you when I see you."

"I should be shot for even listening to you. Okay. I can be there in half an hour."

"I'll owe you."

"Oh, darlin', you're in debt to your eyeballs as it is."

"I'll see you in a few." With the police band crackling, she turned around and headed toward Weaver Brothers and told herself to be wary, just not so paranoid that she was paralyzed. She thought about the three-year-old Mace in her purse, the kickboxing lessons that she was always missing, the alarm system she didn't have, and made a mental note to improve the security in her life.

Even after a quick stop at an ATM, she made it to the truck stop in less than half an hour.

Cliff's truck was parked near the back entrance, between a semi and a van. It was after midnight, there was only one solitary rig in the parking lot. As Nikki entered, she noticed a few patrons who idled at the counter, or sat at a sprinkling of tables. Cigarette smoke vied with the aromas of sizzling steaks and day-old grease from a deep-fat fryer.

Nikki spied Cliff in a high-backed booth near the swinging doors to the kitchen. He was wearing a baseball cap pulled low over his eyes, a jean jacket with the collar turned up and glasses that were tinted a light gray. He pretended to examine a menu that nearly covered his face.

"Hi." She slid onto the tufted faux-leather bench across from him.

"I shouldn't be seen with you."

"So, who's seen you?" Her gaze swept the restaurant. It was nearly deserted. Not even the waitress glanced in their direction. She was too busy flirting with two customers up front. "Besides, we're old friends."

"Is that what we are?" he asked and she inwardly

cringed at the bitterness in his tone. He was obviously out of sorts. Agitated. Distant.

"Of course." She smiled despite his chilly attitude. "We've known each other forever."

"Humph."

"You're my favorite cop."

"Because I spill my guts."

"Hardly."

The waitress, a thin woman with permanent laugh lines finally took notice and swung by. "Can I get you anything to drink to get you started?"

"Coffee for me. Regular."

"Seven and seven." Cliff barely looked up even while the thin woman rattled off the specials in a raspy voice that hinted of too many cigarettes.

"I'm not hungry," Nikki said. "Just the coffee."

Cliff glanced at the plastic-ensconced menu. "I'll have the chicken fried steak, fries and biscuits."

"That's it?" The waitress scribbled on a pad and looked skeptically at Nikki.

"Think so."

"Then, I'll be back with those drinks in a sec." She whipped off the top sheet from the pad as she headed to the kitchen.

"What's this about your tires being slashed."

"Just that." Nikki explained about her evening and the scowl on Cliff's face darkened.

"Geez, you've got to be careful. Probably just punk kids."

Nikki didn't correct him. Didn't voice her fears. She thought of the note she'd received, but decided this wasn't the time. She'd only worry him.

"Let me buy you dinner," he offered.

"It's too late for me to eat and besides, I was out at the folks' tonight for dinner. Even though it was hours ago, they force-fed me. I'm still stuffed."

Some of Cliff's hostility melted. "How are they?"

"About the same. Mom's frail. Dad doesn't seem to notice or doesn't want to. They get along all right, but sometimes I wonder. It seems . . . well, you know. Strained, I guess." She shrugged. Didn't want to think of the disintegration of what had once been such a vibrant family. "Kyle avoids Mom and Dad like the proverbial plague. I think it has to do with him being the only boy once Andrew died. He never stepped into Andrew's shoes, well, none of us did, you know that, but Kyle resented that he was expected to be an athlete and scholar and all that tripe. He's kind of a loner, puts in sprinkler systems and doesn't even date as far as I know. Mom worries that he's gay, Dad won't address the issue, and I just wish he'd find someone to be happy with." She sighed. Wished she'd been closer to her younger brother; knew she never would be.

"As for Lily, she sees the folks more than I do. She seems to have mended some of those fences she shattered with Mom and Dad, probably because of Phee, I mean Ophelia, my niece. After the initial shock that Lily was having a baby sans husband, Mom and Dad regrouped. The baby came and they turned to mush, which, all things considered is a good thing."

"A very good thing."

The waitress appeared, dropped off their drinks and

caught the high-sign from a customer in a cowboy hat who'd slid onto a stool at the counter. When she was out of earshot, Cliff folded his arms over the edge of the table. "You know, Nikki, I can't keep this up. If I keep giving you inside information, it'll cost me my job."

"You're just informing the public of their right—"

"Yeah, yeah, I've heard it a million times before. Can it. It's not about rights or the public or any of that other crap. I tell you stuff because I'm pissed off and need to let off steam. You print it because you want a story no matter what." A muscle worked alongside his jaw as the waitress swept by on her way to the kitchen. When Cliff spoke again, his voice was hushed. "You're using me, Nikki."

"We're using each other." She stirred cream into her coffee.

One of his eyebrows lifted. "Not the way I'd like."

She paused for a minute, then put her spoon down. "I know, but we've been over this before. It would be messy. Emotionally, way too messy."

His lips tightened. "It already is."

"Not if you don't let it."

He took a long sip of his drink and eyed her over the rim of his glasses. Through those gray lenses his eyes seemed colder, more distant than she'd ever noticed before. "What's in this for me?"

Here we go again. "You get to unload your conscience."

"My conscience is clear."

"Then, as you said, you get to blow off steam."

"Maybe that's not enough."

"Okay, so what is it you want?"

His eyes darkened for a second and she braced herself, but whatever was on his mind didn't make it to his lips. At times he was unreadable, as if he could erect a wall between them at will.

Dishes rattled on the other side of the door as she tasted her coffee. "What's going on?"

He hesitated, but only a second. "Reed's off the case."

"What?" Surely she hadn't heard right. "But I saw him this morning at the cemetery."

Cliff lifted a shoulder. "Okano gave him the boot. He knew one of the victims."

"Jesus. Who?"

"Bobbi Jean Marx."

In her mind, she conjured up a mental image of the woman. "How did he know her?"

"Figure it out," he said, and drained his drink.

Reed and Bobbi Jean? Lovers? And Bobbi Jean might have been pregnant? Nikki could barely remain seated. This was news. *Big* news. No wonder Reed had been avoiding her calls and had appeared distant, nearly haunted this morning at the cemetery.

The waitress, whose name tag indicated she was Toni, placed Cliff's order in front of him. The French fries glistened and the steak couldn't breathe because of the creamy gravy that spilled onto a bed of mixed vegetables. The peas and carrots looked suspiciously as if they'd come from a can. "Anything else?" Toni offered.

"This should do it." Cliff looked over the platter at Nikki. "Sure you don't want anything?"

"Nah, thanks. I'm fine," Nikki said even though she was anything but fine. Bobbi Jean and Reed? What a story! Just the angle she was looking for. And yet . . . she felt a few qualms about going public with Reed's private life and a part of her balked at the thought of Reed with the victim, of him being involved with a woman . . . a married woman. It didn't seem his style. Or, that stupid, romantic part of her she tried so vainly to repress hoped it wasn't. As the waitress left, Nikki leaned across the table. She kept her voice hushed and calm even though adrenaline was jetting through her bloodstream. This was it. Another page one story. Ignoring the twinge of guilt she felt that she was capitalizing on someone else's pain, she said, "You think Reed was romantically involved with Bobbi Jean?" She conjured up a mental image of Barbara Jean Marx and Pierce Reed and felt an unlikely jab of jealousy. Which was ridiculous. She didn't even know Reed, not really, though she'd been trying to get close to the reticent cop for years. "That's it, that's what's bugging you about this case, isn't it?"

Cliff squirted ketchup all over his fries. "There's a lot that bugs me about the case."

Nikki leaned closer and whispered, "Was she pregnant?"

His head snapped up and behind the tinted glasses his eyes narrowed. "You know about that?"

"I talked to a friend of hers who thought she might be."

Cliff, as if stabbed by a sudden shaft of conscience, didn't answer.

"The baby could be Reed's."

"It could be anyone's," he said quickly. Too quickly. "We don't know for sure. Not yet."

"Maybe even the husband's."

"*Ex*-husband, and unlikely." Cliff began sawing at his meat with his knife. "They weren't on the best of terms."

"Some people don't get along except in bed."

"Speaking from experience?" He pronged a slice of steak and took a bite.

"Low blow, Siebert."

"You're right. I'm just pissed. Besides, Jerome Marx is sterile. Had himself a vasectomy years ago."

"How do you know this?"

"Strangest thing. Marx called me up and told me. Didn't want to share the information with Reed and you can understand that, so I double-checked. Gave the information to Okano. You can probably understand this, Nikki. I could use being on this investigation. If I catch this guy, it would be a real feather in my cap."

"I suppose," she said, feeling uneasy. Cliff? Ambitious? Enough to go behind Reed's back. "Reed doesn't know?"

"About the vasectomy?" Cliff raised his shoulders. "Don't think so. Unless Okano told him." Talking around the food, he added, "Whoever's behind this Grave Robber case—your name, right?" When she nodded, he actually smiled. "Well, the name's sticking. Anyway, whoever this creep is, he's jerking us around. Making the department look foolish. He's even sending Reed notes and toying with him. Practically laughing in

247

our faces. We need to nail him, and quick."

"Sending him notes?" she said, her insides turning to water.

Cliff's head snapped up. "That's off the record."

Tonight.

It's done.

She swallowed hard. Maybe it was nothing . . . or maybe somehow the killer had zeroed in on her. Heart hammering, she considered telling Cliff.

"Are you okay?" he asked.

"Yes . . . yes . . . just tired and rattled, you know, because of the tires being slashed." *By the same guy who broke into my house?* "I've . . . I've had some trouble at my place. The other night someone broke in."

"And you reported it. Right?" Cliff said.

"Not yet."

"Why the hell not?"

"I . . . um . . . it's stupid, but remember years ago, when I thought I had a stalker and I called the police and it turned out to be . . . nothing . . . just Corey Sellwood, the kid next door who was just hanging out in my backyard where he met his buddies to smoke weed or drink. Everyone got into trouble and . . . well . . ."

"You were a laughingstock."

"Right. And the kid got into major trouble. I felt like a fool. I liked the boy and to this day he avoids me when we meet on the street."

"He's not a kid any longer."

"But he was just smokin' and jokin' and tokin' and he got into tons of trouble. He never forgave me." She thought of Corey, a boy with long hair, disturbed blue

248

eyes and a tattoo of barbed wire around one of his biceps. He'd been fourteen at the time, now was closer to twenty-six or twenty-seven. The incident had happened right around the time Andrew had died, when Nikki had been edgy. She'd never lived it down.

"Nonetheless, you report the break-in," Cliff insisted. "And don't forget to include the fact that your tires were slashed tonight. It could just tie together, Nikki." He polished off a bite of steak. "You're high profile, being the daughter of a judge and all. Now you've got your name splashed all over the front page of the *Sentinel* chasing down the Grave Robber." He pointed his knife at her. "Take care of business. Report both incidents and anything else that doesn't seem right."

"I will."

"I mean it. Don't you believe in 'Better safe than sorry'?"

"Of course. Okay. You've made your point," she said, more nervous than ever. He was right. She knew it. And she knew exactly to whom she'd make the report. Tonight, however, she had to concentrate on the story she was writing.

Stealing a French fry, she asked, "So, how did the victims die?"

"Nu-uh, Nik." He shook his head.

"Come on, Cliff."

"You know the rules, some things are kept within the department."

"But the cause of death—"

"—is off-limits to the public. End of story. You keep

pushing me on this, Nikki, and we've got nothin' else to talk about."

"Okay, okay," she agreed and ate the fry. Cliff was too valuable a source to tick off and risk never using again.

"So, the Grave Robber, you think he's a serial killer?"

"He struck again, didn't he? Two more bodies in one box. And that's all I'm tellin' you. That's enough."

"So it was the Grave Robber this morning."

A serial killer! On the streets of Savannah.

"Don't know for sure, but I'd bet my mother's life savings that it is."

"Dear God." Her mind was spinning. This was so much information. *New* information. *Exclusive* information. Page one again. She saw the headline: "Serial Killer Stalks The Streets Of Savannah." And in smaller, yet bold type: "Grave Robber Strikes Again." Tom Fink would run the story, she knew it. All she had to do was write it and it was already coming together in her head. Except that the pregnancy really bothered her. Barbara Jean Marx's death was horrible enough, and to think that she'd been carrying a child. That was the worst. Nikki felt a moment's regret that she would profit from the victims' terror. She thought of Phee, her innocent little niece, Ophelia, and shuddered inside when she considered Bobbi Jean's unborn baby. *Maybe Reed's child.* Her stomach turned sour. Perhaps she shouldn't write the story, not capitalize on another's sorrow. But didn't the public have a right to know, to be warned? Clearing her throat, she asked, "The victims, did they know each other?"

Cliff was eating, mopping the remains of his biscuit through his gravy. He ate the last piece and shook his head. "Can't find a connection." He swallowed. "Yet."

"But you think there is one. These aren't random?"

"He picked the victims and the already dead people . . . Random?" He dunked another piece of steak in the gravy and forked it into his mouth. "Nah, I don't think so. I guess we'll find out. Soon. The bastard won't get away with this."

"Are there any suspects? Persons of interest?" she asked.

"Nothing official," he said, and she felt a trickle of dread drip down her spine. Her eyes met Cliff's but he looked away quickly.

"Surely, Pierce Reed isn't a suspect."

Siebert stared out the window.

"Cliff?" she prompted, feeling a mixture of horror and excitement. Pierce Reed, having solved the Montgomery case last summer, had been nearly venerated by the public. He was a local hero here, though, she knew from her research, he wasn't considered a saint in San Francisco. In fact, he'd been vilified by the press on the West Coast. Condemned for not being able to save the life of a woman he'd been staking out. "Is Reed a suspect?"

Siebert's eyebrows slammed together as he focused on her again. He pointed his greasy knife at Nikki's nose. "Be careful what you write, okay?"

"Always am," she said and dropped a twenty onto the tabletop as she scooted out of the booth. She knew enough about the cop who had been her brother's friend to understand that the conversation was over. She saw him pick up the money and begin to protest. "Don't even argue with me. As you pointed out, it's after midnight and I woke you up. Thanks, Cliff. I'll be calling you."

"Don't. This is it. I'm out of it," he hissed under his breath. The twenty in his fist, he scowled harshly at her through his lenses. Again, the wall was erected. "If this is gonna be my investigation, then you can damn well get someone else to be your snitch!"

CHAPTER 17

"You just can't keep your name out of the papers, now, can ya?" Morrisette waltzed in and slapped a copy of the *Savannah Sentinel* onto his desk. Her face was red from the cold outside and she yanked off a pair of gloves. "It's effin' freezin' in here. Don't tell me the heat's out again."

Scanning the newspaper, Reed grimaced and felt a twinge of a headache when he saw his name in print. Page one headlines shrieked "Serial Killer Stalks Savannah."

"Subtle, isn't she?" Morrisette rubbed her hands together.

"None of 'em are." He'd gotten the paper at home and read the article. Twice. Saw his name in print, along with the story that Barbara Jean Marx had been pregnant at the time of her death. Nikki Gillette's article stated that he'd been "removed from the case due to personal involvement with one of the victims," then surmised that a serial killer was on the loose. On his way out of his apartment, he'd dropped his copy of the newspaper into a Dumpster.

"Where the hell does that woman get her information?" Morrisette asked.

"Don't know, but I intend to find out."

"She won't tell . . . won't give up a source."

"It comes from the department. Maybe we should figure it out here."

"Could be more than one guy," Morrisette thought aloud as she plopped into a side chair.

"Or woman."

"I meant guy in the nonsexist manner. I meant it as officer or secretary or janitor, for Christ's sake." Both her eyebrows raised. "Touchy today, aren't we?"

"Wouldn't you be?"

"I suppose."

"And don't forget about this." He slid a printed copy of the E-mail he'd received at home across the desk, carefully avoiding his half-full coffee cup and a stack of files.

She glanced at the page and sighed. "I thought about that all last night."

"Just a friendly little note from the killer," he said sarcastically. "It loses something in hard copy, though, here . . . I've got it on the screen."

"Grave Robber on a roll . . . Now we have number four. One third done, will there be more?" she read aloud, though she'd seen it herself. "So, have the nerds figured out who sent it?"

"Not yet. I tried to respond last night, but the answer kicked back at me. Not really a surprise. Bentley hopes he can go through the address and server or whatever the hell they are and find out where the E-mail came from, but I'm certain he won't be able to. He's forwarded it on to the FBI."

"Man, you've been busy this morning."

"Already talked to Okano, too. There'll be a statement."

"Did she warn you off the case again?" Morrisette cozied up to the radiator under the windowsill.

"Yeah, but she couldn't ignore the fact that this Grave Robber, whoever the hell he is, is contacting me. Here ya go . . . take another look at this."

Giving up the warmth of the heater, Morrisette leaned across the desk as Reed twisted the computer monitor so that she could view the original message from the killer and watch all the graphics, twisting pictures of the victims, their faces becoming skulls, their bodies morphing into skeletons before the bones disintegrated into rubble only to be resurrected into the original pictures again. "Who is this guy?"

"Don't know. But we'd better find out fast."

"I've cross-referenced the four victims—assuming that the already dead guys in the coffins are part of this thing. . . . Anyway, other than that they all lived in Savannah, there isn't much that ties 'em together. Barbara Jean Marx and Roberta Peters are about as different as night and day in age, interests, style . . . The only link I can find so far is that they were both patrons of the arts. They both went to charity functions and gallery openings, that sort of thing. But whereas Roberta had a real interest in the arts, Barbara just tagged along after her husband. You know, trophy wife. Well, yeah, I guess you do know."

Reed shifted uncomfortably in his chair.

"So, now there's gonna be more?"

"A total of twelve."

"Isn't that odd? To come up with a *number* of victims who are unconnected. I mean, if you're a killer, you're a killer, right? Why limit yourself?"

"Maybe he isn't limiting himself. Maybe this is just the first wave. Twelve here and then he'll move on. Or twelve just to tease us." Reed was fiddling with his pencil, tapping an eraser on the desk. He popped a couple of ibuprofen he found in the top drawer, then washed them down with cold coffee.

"So, you think he's trying to throw us off?"

"No, this is a clue to what he's doing. He's trying to engage us . . . or engage me."

"Yeah, why you?"

"Because of Bobbi."

"Nah. Doesn't wash. Unless you were having a hot affair with Roberta Peters, too," she said with the hint of a smile.

He snorted. "Too young for me."

"A skirt's a skirt."

"Yeah, right." Reed stared at the computer screen. "It could be someone I pissed off."

"Let's hope not. We'll never find him. Talk about a needle in a haystack!"

Reed sent her a look meant to kill as her cell phone went off. "I'll take the call and grab a cup of coffee and be back," she said, glancing at Caller ID. "It's Bart. Great. This can't be good news." She escaped down the hallway and Reed started thinking in terms of twelve. If Okano came in and saw him working on the case, he'd go toe to toe with her. Somehow, the creep was communicating with him, trying to get to him. He started a list of people who might want to harm him . . . starting with people who knew he had been involved with Bobbi. Jerome Marx was the only name he could come up with, though, he supposed Bobbi could have told a few people as could have Jerome. Reed didn't know Roberta Peters, had never met her. Nor Thomas Massey or Pauline Alexander. Just Bobbi Jean.

The phone jangled. Still staring at the computer screen, he picked up. "Reed."

"Yeah, glad I caught ya. It's Jed Baldwin up ta Lumpkin County."

"Sheriff," Reed said, leaning back in his desk chair until it squeaked. He imagined the craggy face of Jedidiah Baldwin.

"Detective McFee told me you were off the Grave Robber case cuz you were involved with the victim and all, but me, well, I don't put much stake in rules that just get in the way. I thought you'd like to know what's happenin' up here. Nothing new from all the forensic evidence, but early this mornin' Merle Delacroix came in with his son. You remember Billy Dean, one of the kids up ta the holler that saw the guy. Anyway, Merle's a single man whose got his hands full with that one.

Kind of a hothead, but he and the boy, they brought in a ring, inscribed, probably belongs to the vic. The old man was proud of himself, but the boy, I don't think he wanted to part with the ring."

"Was it a gold band with one diamond and some rubies?" Reed asked in a flash of memory. Her hands had been white, with long fingers, manicured nails that knew how to draw down a man's back. The ring finger of her right hand had been adorned with a ring that caught in the sunlight as they'd sailed. It had been autumn, the air crisp. The leaves on the trees near the shoreline fluttered green and gold as a salty breeze tore at Bobbi's long hair and pressed a short white skirt against her tanned legs. She'd been barefoot, her toes painted the same color as her fingernails, a color not unlike the bloodred stones in the ring.

"That would be the one," the sheriff said. "Inscribed."

"Was it? Didn't know." Reed had asked her about the ring and she'd laughed as she'd balanced against the jib. "Yes," she'd replied naughtily, one eyebrow arched when he'd asked about it. "I got it from an old boyfriend. He's gone, but I couldn't part with the diamond."

"Doesn't your husband care?"

"Ex-husband. Ex," she replied tartly. "You keep forgetting the *ex* part. And no, he didn't like it, but I never really cared what he did or didn't like." She'd smiled, then, her eyes sparkling as if she'd shared with him a secret.

"Ye-ep," the sheriff said, bringing Reed back to the here and now. "Says here, 'To Barbara. Love forever.'

257

It's got a date on it. June of last year."

"She said it was from an old boyfriend, but, now I know that she would have been married at that time."

"Um-hmm. It was her weddin' anniversary. Fifth year. Beats the hell out of wood or tin or paper or whatever the hell is traditional for five years of wedded bliss."

"I wouldn't know," Reed said.

"Me, neither, but I'll bet my wife does. Anyway, near as I can figure, her ex gave it to her. Got a call in to him."

So, she'd lied. Again. Not a surprise. Their whole relationship, if that's what it was, had been based on lies. More than he'd ever imagined. As he cradled the phone between his shoulder and ear he wondered if she'd lied to someone else and had eventually paid the ultimate price. With her life.

"Look who's gettin' a swelled head," Trina said as Nikki threw her purse under her desk. Trina rolled her chair back so that she could look Nikki in the eye. "*Two* stories on the front page." She clucked her tongue in exaggeration.

"Third time's a charm."

"You think you'll get another chance? Once Pierce Reed sees what you've written, I wouldn't be surprised if there's a gag order placed on the whole department and no one, not even your own personal Deep Throat, will talk to you anytime soon." Lowering her voice she added, "Norm Metzger is on a tear. He went screaming into Fink's office the minute Tom got here. A few minutes later he stormed out ready to spit nails."

Nikki had to swallow a smile. She didn't mind getting Norm upset. Not at all. They'd been rivals on this story, both trying to get information on or from Reed. Norm had gone to Dahlonega three times, searching and not finding the connection to the case he was looking for. Neither had Nikki. But she felt she was getting closer to the elusive detective. He wasn't quite so gruff when she was around him and she'd even caught him observing her not so much as a reporter and the enemy, but quizzically, as if he were trying to figure her out, as if he were intrigued by her womanhood. She'd seen the look before. Recognized it. And was a little flattered. Maybe a lot flattered. Reed wasn't a bad-looking man and he was sure as hell interesting.

"By the way, if you're interested, I talked to my friend over at WKAM," Trina went on. "There's been hell to pay about the serial killer angle. The station manager chewed on the news manager's ass and he passed it along to the reporters. Everyone's walking on eggshells over there." The corners of Trina's generous mouth twitched. "So, how does it feel to be the belle of the ball?"

"Good. But you know what they say," Nikki added, "you're only as good as your last story." She clicked on her computer to read her E-mail and Trina rolled her chair into her cube. Nikki rubbed the crick from her neck. Geez, she was tired, her muscles all aching. But she had to keep working. Once she'd E-mailed her story to Tom Fink, she'd finally tumbled into bed around two. She'd slept hard and when the alarm had

259

blasted this morning, she'd been tempted to swat at it and go back to bed. But she hadn't. Because she'd wanted to see her story in print and had stumbled down the stairs of her apartment building to find the morning edition waiting for her, bold headlines proclaiming the Grave Robber to be a serial killer. No doubt she'd get some heat from the police department for jumping the gun on that, but it was too late to retract now. Besides, she knew in her gut that the killer wasn't going to stop.

She scrolled down through her E-mail, a lot of it junk, either spam that hadn't been filtered out, or legitimate advertising or notes from colleagues and readers . . . almost like fan mail. She warmed under the compliments about her story, but told herself to remain objective.

"Nikki?"

She nearly jumped out of her chair at the sound of the voice so near. Turning, she spied Kevin, the techie, standing inches from the desk. He was practically wedged into the space that should only house her chair.

"Geez, Kevin, you scared me!" She couldn't keep the note of irritation from her voice.

He lifted his shoulders in somewhat of an apology.

"Can I do something for you?"

For a second she saw his eyes light up as if he were going to suggest something lewd or crude. Then, that flame quickly died as he thought better of it. Thank God. Kevin was okay, just kind of . . . odd. "I thought you had some kind of computer problems. Tom said I should figure out what was wrong."

"Oh. Right. There are a couple of things. Ever since

we got the new wireless system with the router, my Internet connection keeps kicking me off. Trina's doesn't, so I figure it must be my machine. It's irritating as hell. Then, to add insult to injury, my keyboard seems to stick every once in a while, and sometimes— it's not doing it now—there's a thin line down the middle of my monitor. You know, bisecting it"—she drew an imaginary line down the screen—"a little off center. It's random, and comes and goes. I've double-checked my settings and connections and all that, but it keeps happening. Think you can fix it?"

"Probably. But I need more information."

As he stood, arms folded over his chest, earphones dangling from his neck, baseball cap on backwards, Nikki elaborated about the ailments of her computer, all the while attempting to keep some space between her body and his. Which was difficult in normal situations. Here, at the desk, it was nearly impossible. Kevin was one of those people who stood a little too close, in her personal space, as if he couldn't hear or see well, and it bugged Nikki. She was forever backing up when he was around or just allowing a few more inches of air between them. "So . . . what do you think? Can it be fixed?" she asked when she'd finished ragging on the machine.

"Dunno till I've checked it out."

"Fine. I'll do some research in the archives," she said. "If you have any questions, call me on my cell or come get me . . . You've got the cell number?" He nodded and she felt a chill. "Did I already give it to you?" She couldn't remember that she had.

"Nah. I got it from Celeste. She keeps those kind of things on file."

Celeste the Incompetent.

"Why did you ask her for it?"

"I keep everyone's," Kevin explained. "That way, when I'm working on their computers, and they're in the field or home, I can get hold of them." He looked at her intently, as if she were a moron.

"I was just asking," she said, snagging her purse and cell phone and leaving Kevin to work out the bugs in her system. It made her uncomfortable watching him sit at her desk, adjust his earphones over his head and roll her chair into her work space, but she wanted the computer fixed and Kevin was the only tech-head on board.

"Give him time, he'll grow on you," she told herself as she bought a Diet Coke at the machine in the lunch-room, popped the top and made her way down two flights of stairs to the library, where all of the records were stored and a computer that worked far better than hers was available. She was alone in the place and it was quiet as a tomb, one fluorescent light flickering overhead, concrete walls painted a dull gray and looking for all the world like the inside of a prison. No music down here. No clatter of keyboards, ringing phones or buzz of conversation. Just a few filing cabinets and half-empty bookshelves. The place had always given her a case of the willies, and now with a serial killer on the loose, it seemed worse. Probably because it was so damned quiet. So isolated.

She settled into a squeaky chair and read through the

archives, then did an Internet search on Reed once more. He was the key. She knew it. He was the cop called up to Dahlonega, he was the man involved with Bobbi Jean, he was the detective who flew by chopper to Blood Mountain. Because of Bobbi Jean Marx? But how did anyone know he had been involved with her? She made notes on a legal pad, including a reminder to ask Cliff why Reed was specifically called up there, then made a quick call to Cliff's cell where, of course, she left a message, as he didn't answer. "He's evading you," she said out loud and was surprised at the way her voice echoed in the cavernous room. Her insides tightened and she almost laughed at her case of nerves. "Get a grip," she admonished herself. "It's not even dark in here." *Just still. Noiseless. Cool, but airless.*

Her cell phone beeped and she nearly jumped out of her skin. Caller ID showed it was the Savannah Police Department. Which surprised her. Cliff rarely called her on the department's line. He was too paranoid that he'd be found out. *Not paranoid. Cautious. He could lose his job, Nikki, all because of some misplaced sense of loyalty to Andrew and because he's interested in you. You've always known it, so face up to it.* Guilt riddled, she answered, "Nikki Gillette."

"Pierce Reed."

She froze. Reed was calling her. Quickly, she scrambled for her pen and paper. "Hello, Detective," she said calmly, though her heart was racing. "What can I do for you?"

"I've been avoiding calling you back. You've left several messages."

"Yes. I'd love to interview you. About the case."

"So you've said."

"You actually listened to the voice mails I've left?"

"All eight."

"I wanted to talk to you before I went to press with anything. But I couldn't wait forever. I've got deadlines."

"So, that's why I'm calling you now. I've changed my mind. I think we should talk."

She couldn't believe her ears. "When?"

"Tonight. After work. Say, seven, seven-thirty. Can you make it?"

"Sure." She tried not to sound too eager, even though this seemed like a gift from heaven. An interview with the elusive detective. No, make that an *exclusive* interview. "What happened?" she couldn't help but ask. "Why the change of heart?"

"I'll explain it all when I see you."

"When and where?"

He didn't miss a beat. "Johnny B's Low Country Barbecue on I-80. It's about a mile, maybe less, before you reach the bridge to Tybee Island. You know where it is?" In case she didn't, he gave her the address.

"I'll find it," she said, writing down the name of the place on a scratch pad. "Seven-thirty." She clicked off, felt a sense of elation and started to place the phone in her purse when she felt something. A change in the atmosphere, a cooler breath of air. Glancing over her shoulder she found Kevin, barely six inches from her. "Geez!" She jumped, knocking over the rest of her soda. "What is it with you always sneaking up on people?" She looked down at his crepe-soled shoes as she righted the can and dabbed at the spilled puddle of Diet Coke with a tissue she found in her purse.

"You were on the phone. I didn't want to bother you." For a second he looked wounded. But a second later, she saw a shaft of defiance in his eyes before his bland expression slipped into place. She'd always thought he was doped out, on something to keep him a little off; now, she wasn't so sure.

"It's all right. Let's go upstairs. On the way, you can tell me about the computer." Tossing the wet Kleenex into a wastebasket, she started for the steps. She didn't want to be trapped down here with the weird guy a second longer than necessary.

"It's working again." Which was all she wanted to hear, but, of course, Kevin didn't give up, began talking techno-speak all the way up the stairs to the newsroom floor. She couldn't shake him as he followed her to her desk, then spent the next twenty minutes telling her in minute detail what he'd done to fix the damned thing. She wasn't interested, but made a mental note to learn more about the machines so she didn't have to depend on him. Maybe a class, or a copy of some basic manual like the *Idiot's Guide To All Things Techincal*.

"Thanks, Kevin," she said as he finally ambled off. He flashed her a smile that seemed boyish rather than diabolical and she called herself a fool for letting her imagination get away from her when it came to Tom Fink's nephew.

Trina looked over the top of her cubicle. "*Never* leave me alone with that guy again."

265

"You weren't." Nikki scanned the rest of the news-room where reporters were plugged into their stations.

"He's off, Nikki. All the while you were gone he was humming and singing to himself, oddball lyrics that didn't make any sense. Kinda like kids' poetry. I kept thinking he was talking to me." She shuddered. "If you ask me, he's more than a couple of cans shy of a six-pack."

"I know, but he fixed my computer, that's all I care about."

"Well, next time don't run and hide."

Nikki flashed a smile. "Hey, Norm was at his desk. If Kevin put the moves on you or started acting strange, you could always rely on Metzger."

"Oh, God, this place *is* a looney bin." Trina's eyes suddenly widened.

"Uh-oh, looks like you've got company."

"What do you mean?" But she turned in her chair and spied Sean Hawke, all six feet two inches of him, standing at the front desk, leaning close to Celeste, while the flustered receptionist pointed toward Nikki's desk. Sean caught Nikki's eye and started walking toward her station. The years hadn't hurt him. He was still fit and handsome, his hair still brushing the collar of a leather jacket, a goatee decorating his chin. Though he was inside and it was December, he was wearing tinted glasses that, she suspected, were more for effect than vision. The rest of his outfit included khakis, a tight sweater, black boots and a killer smile.

"Oh, my," Trina said, and from the corner of her eye

Nikki saw her friend pretend to fan herself. "That boy's hot."

"That boy's trouble," Nikki said under her breath, then stood as Sean reached her.

"I figured I'd find you here."

"So, now you're a detective."

"And you're still as sassy as ever." He swung one leg over the top of her desk, pulling his jeans tight in his crotch, then grabbed a paperweight on her desk and began tossing it and catching it. That's always the way he'd been, a bundle of nerves wrapped up in a sexy, masculine skin.

Nikki introduced Sean to Trina, who nearly melted at the sight of him. Just as Nikki had years before.

"You haven't been returning my calls."

"Sorry—no, that's a lie. I'm not. I've been busy, Sean."

"Too busy for an old friend."

"One who dumped me twelve years ago."

"Ouch." He visibly winced. "My mistake."

"Maybe not. It all worked out for the best."

"Did it?" He looked up at her intensely with eyes that shifted in color. Years before, her heart had thumped wildly under his scrutinizing stare. Now, it bothered her in a different way. Once she'd found him sexy, now she found him troubling.

"What is it you want from me?"

"A date. Just a chance to catch up."

"No reason. I'm working here. Where I was when you left."

"But you graduated from college in the meantime.

267

Came back to Savannah and seem to be making a name for yourself."

She didn't respond.

"I thought you might have married."

"You thought wrong."

"You're not even going to ask about me, are you?" He tossed the paperweight into the air. Caught it deftly.

"I don't think there's any reason."

"Are you involved with someone?"

"Not now."

"Have you been?"

"Look, Sean, this is really none of your business and I've got work to do."

"So, let's meet for a drink when you get off."

"Don't *you* have somewhere you're supposed to be?"

His grin slid from one side of his jaw to the other. "Not today."

"This just isn't a good idea."

"One drink won't kill you." His smile was almost boyishly charming and there was the hint of the devil in his eyes, just as there had been way back when.

Her cell phone jangled and she said, "I really do have to go."

As she reached for the phone, he grabbed her wrist. "I'll call, Nikki." Then he released her and from the other side of the partition she heard Trina whisper, "Oh, my."

"You want him? You can have him," Nikki said, watching as Sean sauntered out of the building, his faded jeans tight over his buttocks, his boot heels unworn, his jacket without a scratch. He was almost too perfect. And he'd broken her heart . . . The phone rang again and she answered. The call was from one of the women with the historical society making sure that Nikki had all the facts straight on a tour of homes that would be open during the Christmas season. Nikki double-checked the information, then hung up.

Finally, she was free to log on to her computer again. She'd been halfway through her E-mail earlier and now finished reading the new messages that were waiting. She was nearly done when she clicked on one with a subject line of GRAVE ROBBER STRIKES AGAIN. Though she didn't recognize the return E-mail address, she clicked on the mail.

Her heart stopped. The newsroom faded into the background as she stared at the horrible images on her screen, pictures of four people—the victims of the Grave Robber, she felt certain—that disintegrated to bones before her eyes. The message was simple:

WILL THERE BE MORE?
UNTIL THE TWELFTH,
NO ONE CAN BE SURE.

She was suddenly as cold as if she'd been dropped into the North Atlantic.

What the hell did the message mean?

Was the Grave Robber talking to her?

Or . . . or was it a prank?

Her mind raced. Hadn't Cliff said just last night that the Grave Robber had sent Reed notes? . . . What about E-mail? Oh, God. What was the return path . . . ? She tried to respond. The message could be a hoax, of course. Lots of people these days got their jollies by sending spam, but she had a sense, an intuition that the killer was reaching out to her. Because of her stories. Because she'd named him. Paid attention. Somehow puffed up his sick ego.

Biting her lower lip, she replied, sending an E-mail asking for the sender to respond and identify himself. It bounced back nearly immediately. She printed out the E-mail, making two copies and on the second one, cutting off the message. Then she searched through the offices until she found Kevin, earphones in place, browsing the vending machines in the lunchroom. He was just punching in his selection when he saw her from the corner of his eyes.

"Don't tell me, you can't make the machine work," he said, his eyes nearly arrogant as they stared down his nose at her. The corners of his lips twisted up slightly, as if he were pleased with himself.

Because he was smarter than she?

Or because he'd expected her to chase him down?

"No. No. The system works fine. But I need a favor," she said, grateful, for once, that she'd found him alone.

He pulled down his earphones. "Another one?"

A bag of M&M peanuts dropped into the tray. Kevin snagged them up quickly, as if he thought she might snatch them from him.

"Yeah."

"It'll cost you," he said, and flashed a smile that bordered on a leer.

"Oh, right . . . look!" She handed him the E-mail address. "Can you find out who sent this to me?"

"Maybe." He scanned the paper, his eyebrows drawing together thoughtfully. "Why?"

"Because it's important, okay? Someone sent me a strange message and when I tried to reply, the E-mail bounced back." She handed him the response again, with the message cut out.

"Is it about the serial killer? That Grave Robber guy?"

She didn't want to lie and hated the fact that she needed Kevin's help. "Yes. Really."

"What's in it for me?"

"It's your job!"

"I got lots of work to do."

Frustrated, she stared at him. "What do you want, Kevin?"

He hesitated and she felt her chest tighten. Oh, Lord, he *wasn't* going to ask her for a date, was he? Or some kind of kinky sexual favor disguised as a joke?

"What?"

"Credit, okay? You and a lot of people act like I'm useless, or . . . or that I don't exist . . . or that I'm stupid . . . or that I only got the job because Tom's my uncle, but the truth of the matter is that you and Trina and Norm and everyone in this damned place need me." He hooked a thumb at his chest emphatically, the candy rattling in its bag.

"Credit?"

"Yeah."

"Okay . . ." she said, still unsure. His anger had flared

so quickly, as if it had smoldered for years. "You got it."

"I mean it, Nikki." He grabbed the paper from her hands and started reading it. "I'll get back to you."

"Fast. This is important."

His eyes flashed again. "Like I don't get it? I *know* that." Again with the undefinable smile. He left her standing there and she realized that he was the last one who'd used her computer. He knew the system inside and out. He could have sent the E-mail and inserted it between the others . . .

Oh, for the love of Mary, what was wrong with her? She was seeing everyone as a potential killer these days. She hurried back to her desk and started working up an interview for Reed. This was her shot. She might not get another chance.

CHAPTER 18

"The good Lord don't like anyone messin' with graves," Bea Massey insisted. She was a tiny, stooped black woman with teeth too big for her head. So far, she'd given Morrisette no information that could help the investigation. Nearly blind, she petted a raggedy old mutt who sat at her feet at the kitchen table. "Once a person is laid to rest, he ought to stay that way."

Amen, sister, Reed thought, but kept his viewpoint to himself as Morrisette interviewed Thomas Massey's widow. From his vantage point near the window, Reed inspected the grounds. Bantam chickens roosted on the back porch. A vegetable garden, gone fallow, was wedged behind a garage that listed badly and was home to a 1967 Buick Skylark. In the house, handmade lace cloths covered every table and surrounded the windows. Mrs. Massey swore she'd never met Jerome Marx, nor had she heard of him. "But I told Thomas that he had no business bein' buried in the city. He belonged out here in the country, but he wouldn't hear of it. Wanted to be with the rest of his family in Savannah. . . . Now look what's come of it."

They left the house with not much more information than they'd come with. Bea Massey had been the second stop. They'd already interviewed Beauford Alexander at the assisted care facility where he'd lived since his wife's death and thought that neither he, nor Pauline, had ever met anyone named Barbara Jean Marx. Or Thomas Massey. Or Roberta Peters.

"Two strikes," Reed muttered as they drove toward Savannah.

"What does it matter? You're out already." Morrisette punched in the lighter and glanced his way as she drove toward the city. "Remember?"

"I was thinking of you."

"And I'm touched," she mocked as the lighter clicked. She managed to light up and switch lanes as they neared the city.

Reed scowled out the window and watched the wind whip through the tall grass and scattered brush of the low country. The case was getting to him. He thought about it constantly, couldn't concentrate on the rest of his work, and was having a helluva time sleeping.

"I've been thinking about this twelve thing. Even checked on the Internet. A dozen as in doughnuts, or signs of the zodiac, or months in the year," Sylvie said.

"Right, I checked, too. There are boxcars in a dice game, jurors on a jury, twelve apostles, twelve inches in a foot and the Big Twelve Conference."

"What? Big Twelve?"

"Sports. College teams in the Midwest."

"I knew it sounded familiar. Bart was a sports nut." She snorted derisively. "I'm still paying on the big screen to prove it." She drew hard on her cigarette and scowl lines creased her forehead. "But I don't think this case has anything to do with sports."

"Probably not." But what did it mean? So far they'd come up dry with forensic evidence, at least nothing solid yet. No fingerprints, no shoe prints, only partial tire tracks, no blood or hairs or fibers on the victims, no hint of sexual abuse. Whoever the guy was, he got his jollies from their terror and death, maybe even jerked off as he heard them scream through the damned microphone, but he hadn't left any definite leads. Aside from the notes Reed had received.

Morrisette shot out a stream of smoke. "Okay, this much we know: the last person to see Barbara Jean Marx alive was her ex. Jerome Marx was at her house around six the night before."

"So he kidnapped her then, dug up Pauline Alexander, hauled them both by truck to Lumpkin County and buried them, then hightailed it back here."

"Trouble is, he drives a Porsche. As far as I can see he didn't rent a hearse."

"Maybe he stole one," Reed suggested. "Or a truck."

"Maybe. But he didn't know Roberta Peters or Thomas Massey." She flipped on the wipers as the rain that had been threatening all afternoon began to fall in thick drops. She cleared her throat and didn't look his way as she added, "We're supposed to get blood typing back on the baby ASAP. DNA is being rushed, but it'll take a little longer. Maybe next week."

To think that Bobbi was carrying his baby. Or Marx's. Or someone else's completely. While wearing her wedding band. Hell, he'd been a fool for that woman. But then, that was his M.O. Women, the wrong kind, had always been his downfall.

"The department is going to issue a statement today," she said, and he felt a jab of jealousy that he wasn't the one giving her the news instead of the other way around. Morrisette stubbed out her cigarette. "Yeah, explain a little more about the murders, warn the citizens, ask for their help, the same old stuff."

"And talk about a serial murderer?"

"Mmm. Looks like." She slid a glance in his direction as she took the corner and headed toward the heart of the city. She licked her finger and drew an imaginary line by her head. "Score one for Nikki Gillette."

"What do you know about her?"

"Other than that she's a major pain in the ass?"

"Yeah . . ."

Passing a slow moving truck, Morrisette said, "Now, wait a minute, you're not interested in her, are you?"

"Just curious. She's got the jump on the department."

"Yeah, but she's attractive, if you like pushy, bull-headed blondes."

"Don't know any," Reed drawled, looking at his platinum-haired partner. "You've been around here longer than I have. What's the story with Gillette?"

"Just that she's a spoiled brat who decided to become a journalist. She's never been married, that I know of, but then, I don't know all that much about her. I think she's been working for the *Sentinel* since she got out of school or maybe even in the summers while she was going to college . . . I think she got into trouble with the Chevalier trial while she was still going to college . . . you remember that. You were here then, right?"

"I helped collar the guy."

"And now he's been released. What a waste of time and effort. Anyway, about Nikki Gillette, I think she's always trying to prove herself to her old man. Somehow she never measured up to the older boy, the one who was killed or offed himself. Her older brother, oh, hell, what was his name. . . ."

"Andrew."

Morrisette slid him a glance as she slowed for a light. "So you already know. Why the hell am I running off at the mouth, then?"

"I just want your take on it."

"Well, the older brother was a star athlete and the real brain in the family. Damned apple of his father's eye. The kid breezed through college and applied to some fancy-schmancy law school, Harvard or Yale . . . whichever one of those Ivy Leaguers his father went to.

Didn't get in, even with Daddy's pull. Soon after, the kid dies. Falls off a deck. Or was pushed. Or jumped. No one saw or at least anyone who did see what happened kept his or her mouth shut."

Reed had heard most of the story, remembered some of it from his earlier years in Savannah.

"Anyway," Morrisette said, "from what I heard, the family fell apart. The Judge nearly threw in the towel and the old lady really went around the bend. The other kids, and there are a couple besides Nikki, I think, didn't seem to count. Not like the firstborn boy. Well, at least that's what I heard." She punched it as the light turned green. "I really don't keep up too much on old Nikki. I just know that she really blew it during the Chevalier trial, but you know that."

"Everyone does." Reed had been a junior detective in Savannah at the time. One of the first homicide cases he'd worked on had been the Carol Legittel murder and he'd helped collar LeRoy Chevalier, who had been the victim's boyfriend. Before being assigned to homicide he'd been out to the Chevalier home on domestic abuse calls that had never really stuck. Because of all the red tape and the fact that Carol would never press charges.

Hell, it had been a mess. So Chevalier had finally snapped and had killed her as well as two of her kids. Judge Ronald Gillette had presided and his daughter, a college kid working for the *Sentinel*, had overheard some private conversation and reported a little of it, nearly enough to blow the whole damned trial. Not that it mattered now. Chevalier was now a free man; could never be retried for those murders.

Reed had lost touch with most of the people involved. Soon after the Chevalier trial, he'd taken off for San Francisco.

"You know how the creep got out? A little while back. Some slimy attorney should be shot for that one. I don't care what those DNA reports say—the blood at the scene might have been contaminated. In those days, we just didn't have the techniques we have now. In my book Chevalier's a cold blooded murderer. He sliced and diced that poor single mother as well as her kids. Then, because of Nikki Gillette, there was nearly a mistrial. Fortunately the bastard is convicted and now . . . now he's out? What is the world coming to?"

"You tell me."

"To hell in a handbasket, that's what. Nikki Gillette was just a kid at the time, working at the paper as a stringer on her summer break from college, I think. Man, even then, she had too much ambition."

Reed grunted but didn't confide that he intended to talk to the reporter later. The less Morrisette knew about what he was doing on the side, the better, for her and her job.

He'd decided to find out how Nikki got her information and from where, though she'd probably protect her sources and pull out that First Amendment crap. And that's what it was. No one could convince Reed that the Founding Fathers' intent with Amendment One was to protect jerks who gave out bad information and jeopardized legitimate investigations of criminals. But Nikki wouldn't be easy to shake down. She was tough and dogged. Determined to do her job. Last summer during the Montgomery case, she hadn't left him alone. Tonight she expected an exclusive interview. Well, she'd get one. Only Reed was going to do the interviewing. Nikki Gillette knew too much. It compromised the investigation. And it was dangerous. For everyone. Including her.

He glanced at his watch and saw he had a few more hours before he'd meet with her. It would be an interesting conversation. If nothing else, Nikki Gillette was intelligent and easy on the eyes. Attractive and smart— a deadly combination in Reed's opinion. She was also more than a little spoiled from being born privileged, a silver spoon wedged firmly between her near-perfect teeth.

Morrisette dropped him off at the station. For the next few hours, he turned his attention to a domestic violence case where the wife had "accidently" pumped five rounds of bird shot into her husband. He might have survived the spray of BBs but one had nicked his jugular and he'd bled to death before the wife had come out of her state of "confusion, hysteria and panic" long enough to dial 911. When the first officer arrived at the scene she was calmly sitting in a chair at the dinette and smoking a cigarette. In Reed's estimation, this case was a slam dunk.

He was about to leave and was reaching for his jacket when the phone rang. "Reed."

"Rick Bentz, New Orleans Police," the caller said, identifying himself as once being Reuben Montoya's partner. "I got your message. You called about a guy named Vince Lassiter."

Reed let his jacket slide back over his chair. "That's right. He's the brother of a homicide victim. We need to locate him. Not only do we want to notify him about his sister but we'd like to check on his whereabouts on the day she disappeared."

"What happened to the sister?"

As images of Bobbi Jean teased his mind, pictures of her alive, vibrant and sexy as well as thoughts of her in the cold, dark coffin gasping for life and the very real view of her in death, Reed managed to tamp down his rage at the animal who had killed her and, as calmly as possible, filled Bentz in, ending with ". . . so we'd like to locate everyone associated with Barbara Marx."

"Don't blame you. The son of a bitch buries them alive?" Bentz swore under his breath. "We'll keep searching, but my guess is it'll be hard to reach Lassiter. He took off about three months ago. Didn't report in to his parole officer and didn't leave a forwarding address. The woman he lived with can't or won't say what happened to him and he hasn't turned up anywhere. Some of the guys at the station think he tried to run out on a bad debt, was caught and killed, his body dumped in the bayou somewhere, but that's just conjecture. I can't tell you what happened to him because we just don't know."

Another dead end. Reed drummed his fingers on the desk. "Figures. Anything else you can tell me about him?"

"I did pull his file." Reed heard pages being flipped. "He's been in and out of trouble with the law since he was fourteen, nothing serious, I think, though those records aren't available as he was a minor. When he was nineteen, he was involved in armed robbery. He sold out his friend, copped a plea, served his time and got out of prison a couple of years back. From there, he looked like he was on the straight and narrow. Got himself a job as a telemarketer selling cleaning supplies, hooked up with a woman he met through AA. Her name is . . . let's see . . . yeah, Wanda Parsons. Lassiter was a model citizen until the end of August. Then he vanished. Just didn't come home one night. Either managed a convincing disappearing act or ended up on the wrong side of a gun somewhere. We found his truck ditched near Baton Rouge. No one saw what happened.

"We checked with all the people who knew him, including the sister, in October. No one's heard word one."

"You think he was offed?"

"Me, I don't know, but that's the popular bet with the department."

"Keep me posted if anything changes and Lassiter turns up."

"Will do. And you'll do the same?"

"You got it. Thanks. And say hi to Montoya."

"I'd like to," Bentz said, "but I haven't seen him in a while. He's taken a hiatus."

"Is he coming back?"

"Don't know, but I wouldn't bet on it."

"If you see him, tell him to give me a call," Reed said.

"Will do."

Reed clicked his pen as the conversation ended. He stared out the window as afternoon shadows darkened the city. Did someone kill Vince Lassiter? Was Bobbi Jean's brother's death connected to hers? Would he turn up in the next coffin, assuming, from the killer's E-mail, that there would be more? Or had Lassiter disappeared on purpose? Was he somehow involved in the bizarre murders?

Adding information on Lassiter to his computer notes on the case, he felt, rather than heard, someone approach. He glanced over his shoulder and found Cliff Siebert standing in the door frame. Tall, fit, with close-cropped hair and a perpetual frown, Siebert was a young buck who knew his stuff but always seemed to be preoccupied. Reed never noticed Siebert joking with the rest of the detectives and thought the kid should learn to lighten up. Humor, even black humor, helped relieve the tension of an oftentimes grisly job.

"Somethin' I can do for you?" Reed asked.

"I was hoping you could give me your notes on the Grave Robber case."

"My notes?"

"I've been assigned to help with it. I'll be Morrisette's partner."

"Is that so?" Reed felt a slow burn ride up the back of his neck.

"Yeah." At least the kid seemed uncomfortable asking.

"Morrisette's got everything I do."

"But you made notes to yourself. She doesn't have those."

He felt the computer screen glowing with his own take on the killings.

"She's got everything she needs. All the facts."

"I'm talkin' about your gut feelings. You know . . . your impressions."

"You think I wrote those down?"

"Everyone does."

"I'll send 'em to Morrisette," Reed said, not wanting to give the younger detective an inch. There was just something about Cliff Siebert that rubbed Reed the wrong way, nothing he could put his finger on; Siebert had an impeccable record, still, Reed didn't trust him. He didn't trust anyone with a clear record. "Via E-mail."

Siebert looked about to argue, then, under Reed's glare, thought better of it. Serious expression unreadable, he said, "I'll get 'em from her."

Like hell, Reed thought. He'd pass along all the pertinent facts, and his assessment of that data, but his gut impressions, conjectures and theories, he'd keep to himself. They wouldn't do anyone else any good anyway. Quickly, he copied his notes to a disc, which he tucked into his briefcase. Then he edited the information on the hard drive and E-mailed it to Morrisette. When he was finished, he barely had time to meet Nikki, but he took a side journey to Katherine Okano's office where Tonya Cassidy, Okano's secretary, was cleaning up her desk for the day.

"I need to see Kathy."

"She's gone for the day."

Reed's jaw tensed; he sent Tonya a look guaranteed to paralyze. In his estimation, Tonya was forever on an authority trip. "When will she be back?"

"Monday."

Damn.

"She said you'd probably stop by and she left you this." Tonya reached into a top drawer and pulled out a sealed envelope. With a lift of her eyebrows that told him she already knew what was inside the sealed packet, she handed it to Reed.

It didn't take a rocket scientist to figure out what was inside.

Once in the hallway he ripped open the envelope and unfolded the single page.

The lab report was definite. His B-negative blood indicated with great probability that he was the father of Bobbi Marx's baby. There was a note that a DNA report was to follow as soon as all the tests were completed.

He felt a new sense of despair.

His kid.

The bastard had killed his kid.

CHAPTER 19

"I can't, not tonight," Nikki said, cradling her desk telephone between her shoulder and ear and only half listening to the conversation. She was pressed for time and had just put the finishing touches on her next story about the Grave Robber.

But her sister had problems of her own and from the sound of it, she was desperate. "Why not? Look, Nikki, it's not as if I ask you to baby-sit all that often."

That much was true, Nikki thought. "Any other night, Lily, I swear. But the police are holding a press conference on the Grave Robber in less than an hour and after that I've got an important interview. Really important."

"Take her along."

"Take a two-year-old along? Are you crazy?" Nikki misspelled a word. "Damn." She leaned back in her chair and gave up typing. "*You* take her along."

"But I have a date. I wouldn't ask, but my sitter flaked on me at the last minute."

"Okay, okay, look . . . Take Phee over to Mom and Dad's. I'll pick her up after the interview . . . say around nine-thirty or ten, haul her back to your place and work on my laptop when she goes to bed."

"I don't know—"

"If it's not good enough for you, find someone else. Call Kyle," she suggested.

"Kyle? Humph." Lily snorted in disdain at the mention of their brother. "What does he know about kids?"

"What do *I* know? Look, Lily, I've really got to run."

"Okay, I'll drop her by the folks', but it's really an inconvenience. I'm supposed to meet Mel at seven." Sighing, she added, "You know what your problem is, Nicole?"

Uh-oh, here it comes. "Why do I feel like you're determined to enlighten me?" Nikki dropped her cell phone into her bag.

"You're just like Andrew," Lily said, ignoring the dig. "Self-centered and driven. As if the world revolves around you." She hung up angrily and Nikki winced.

As much from the insult as from the loud disconnect. Leave it to Lily to hang up after a barb. From the time she was a whiney child, Lily had always had to get in the last word. A pseudo-intellectual who embraced academia, liberal politics and high fashion, she spent her days caring for her daughter, smoking thin black cigarettes and discussing literature and philosophy. She worked part-time at a coffeehouse and played a flute or sang in a jazz band. Nikki had been in the audience twice and just didn't get the music. The songs never seemed to end and had a melody that wove in and out of the general noise.

Martyr-like, Lily had never named the father of little Ophelia; the baby's paternity would probably be a secret Nikki's older sister would take to her grave. Not that it mattered. Ophelia, fatherless and straight-on adorable, had stolen Nikki's heart from the first time she'd laid eyes upon her niece in the hospital. Just thinking of the tangle-haired two-year-old brought a smile to Nikki's face.

Nikki finished the rough draft of her article, leaving room to make some changes in case she learned anything important at the press conference or her interview with Reed and had to do some revisions, then grabbed her coat and hurried outside. She nearly plowed into Norm Metzger at the door.

"Watch where you're going."

"Always the gentlemen, aren't you?" she spouted, though the last thing she needed was a confrontation with Norm. Not now. Well, not ever.

The angry look he sent her spoke volumes and she

braced herself for the forthcoming verbal onslaught. "Where the hell do you get your information?"

"What do you mean?"

"How can you be one jump ahead of the police?" He was blocking the door and she had no choice but to deal with him.

"I'm not a jump ahead."

"You wrote that story about the serial killer before the police made a statement. I just heard that there's going to be a press conference at six." He checked his watch. "In twenty minutes. What do you bet that they're going to paraphrase everything you already printed and bring up the possibility of a serial murderer?"

"I really don't know."

"Isn't that a surprise."

"So, why aren't you there, acing the competition."

"I'm on my way," he said bitterly. "I think I'm staring at the competition right now."

"Oh, Norm, give it up," she shot back and eased past him.

"You know, Gillette, you probably don't even need to bother with the press conference. Your 'source' gives you the goods before the rest of us."

"It really bugs you that I have a source, doesn't it?" she asked, bristling. She'd taken his guff long enough.

"What bugs me is that you trade on your name. Being the daughter of Big Ron Gillette opens a lot of doors for you that are closed to the rest of us working stiffs."

"You think it's my name?"

"I know it is." His smile, beneath his moustache, was as false as fool's gold.

"Well, you just go on thinking that way!" She somehow managed to bite back the hot retort that was on the tip of her tongue. "It'll get you nowhere fast." Then she was off, running across the street to the parking lot, her cheeks flaming, her ego bruised even though he hadn't said anything she hadn't heard before or even thought herself. She threw her purse and brief-case into the backseat and climbed behind the wheel of her hatchback. *Don't let him get to you,* she told herself as she wheeled out of the parking lot. *Don't give him the satisfaction of winning. You know what's true.* Maybe that was the worst part. She wasn't trading on her father's name, but she was using her brother's death and his friend's guilt to get her story. She drove like a madwoman to the police station where she squeezed into a parking lot behind the WKAM television van. It was nearly dark as the press conference was about to begin at the station steps. Streetlights glowed and the air was cool, but dry. Reporters, cameramen, and curious onlookers were milling around, held in line by several uniformed policemen.

Within minutes Norm Metzger and Jim Levitt arrived. Norm, now wearing a wool cap and trench coat, pushed his way to the front of the crowd while Jim adjusted a lens for his camera and followed in the wake Norm created. Like a damned lapdog, Nikki thought, content for once to be on the outer rim of the reporters. She thought about the E-mail she'd received from the Grave Robber and smiled to herself. That was her ace in the hole. Despite its chilling message. No matter what she heard from the police, it wouldn't compare to the direct communication she'd received from the killer. Which she intended to share with the cops. When the moment was right. After she'd published it.

The wind was cold and she adjusted her jacket as the press conference got started. A police spokeswoman named Abbey Marlow made a short statement about what was happening. She gave some broad facts about the killings, alluded to the fact that the killer would probably strike again, and could be in the Savannah area. She asked the press and public to help the police and if anyone had seen anything unusual or suspicious to report it to the police department and specifically the task force that was being assembled. She released the names of the victims and answered a few questions.

"Are the victims related or connected in any way?" a dark-haired woman from a local channel asked.

"Not that we can tell."

"Is it true two bodies are pushed into one coffin?" This time it was Norm.

"We have found two coffins, each with the original occupant and another victim."

"And they were buried alive?" Norm again.

"Yes."

"Do you have any leads?" Max O'Dell from WKAM got in his licks.

"The investigation is progressing, but we do ask everyone for any information they may have to bring it forward."

Nikki thought guiltily of the note in her purse as she

scribbled and recorded the rest of the questions and answers.

"Does the killer have an M.O.?" O'Dell persisted. "I mean, aside from burying his victims alive?"

A few sardonic chuckles erupted, then dissipated into the rising wind that pushed a lock of Abbey's reddish hair over her eyes.

"Of course, I can't comment on that because I don't want to jeopardize the investigation."

"Has the killer tried to contact you?" Nikki said and Abbey Marlow seemed to tense a bit. Her gaze drilled into Nikki's. "Again, I'm not at liberty to say."

"But isn't it common for serial killers to try to taunt the police, to initiate a game with them, to try to communicate or mislead them?"

"In some cases," Abbey agreed, and the other reporters, on the scent of some hidden information, pelted her with a few more questions before, smiling, she announced that the department had nothing further to say.

But from Abbey Marlowe's reaction to her questions, Nikki confirmed what Cliff had inadvertently told her, that the Grave Robber had contacted the Savannah police, specifically Reed. As the killer had written to her. Singled her out. Probably because of her first article on him. From her research, she also realized that killers, pretending to be helpful citizens, often tried to work with the cops, that they sometimes tried to ingratiate themselves with the detectives, that they got off on feeling smarter and superior to the officers trained to capture them, that they liked to be in on

290

the action . . . Fingers of ice seemed to touch the back of her neck. There was a good chance that the killer was here . . . near the steps of the station . . . watching . . . waiting . . . feeling superior . . . trying to blend in.

She sensed his presence in the shift of the wind . . . No, she was imagining things. Still, she glanced around quickly, past the reporters wrapping up, the cameramen with their shoulder cams, the curious onlookers in dark coats and hats blending into the shadows. Why did she feel as if she were being studied? Being singled out? Remembering the man she'd seen in the foliage the other morning at the diner, her breath caught. Several tall men seemed to fade into the background, away from the crowd and the streetlights that were just beginning to glow. Was one of them watching her, and when she looked in his direction, did he turn quickly and disappear into the coming darkness?

You really are getting jumpy, Gillette, she admonished as she clicked off her recorder.

"Get what you wanted?" a male voice whispered in her ear and she visibly started. Her heart squeezed in panic as she turned.

Norm Metzger was at her side.

"I think so." *Remain calm. He's a creep, a jealous coworker, but essentially harmless.* "You?"

"What was that question about the cops being contacted by the killer?"

"It's common enough. You know that. Or you should. After all, you're the paper's crime reporter."

"But Marlow nearly fell off the steps when you asked the question. Did your snitch tell you that the killer's called or written to the police department?"

"I just asked a normal question, that's all." She was stuffing her recorder, pen and paper into her purse. "Look, I've got to run."

His eyes, shadowed by the brim of his wool cap, narrowed. "You know something."

"Geez, Metzger, this may come as a shock to you, but I know a lot. It's kind of you to finally realize it." With that, she turned and made her way to her hatchback. She half expected him to follow, but no footsteps scuffed along behind her and as she slipped into her car, she spied Norm and Jim Levitt walking to Norm's Impala. She didn't like the fact that he'd picked up on her question and for once, thankfully, her little car started with one twist on the ignition.

Back at the office, she finished her story, turned it in, then checked her watch and realized she was running late. Metzger was still at his desk as Nikki slipped out the back door. Once in her car, she kept an eye on her rearview mirror just to make certain that Metzger, or anyone else for that matter, didn't follow her. Her interview with Pierce Reed had to be confidential. Completely confidential.

Reed glanced at his watch. Already she was five minutes late. He'd wait fifteen more and if she didn't show, it would be Nikki Gillette's funeral. So to speak.

Or his.

Seated behind the wheel of his El Dorado in the dark parking lot, he second-guessed himself. What he had planned could cost him his badge. But he had to do something. Anything to find out who had thrown Bobbi into that coffin.

The windows were beginning to fog over but through the glass, he stared at Johnny B's Low Country Barbecue—a restaurant of sorts which, according to the sizzling neon sign, offered up "world-renowned southern barbecue." The claim seemed a tad farfetched, but the parking lot was littered with pickups, campers, battered wagons and sedans. The El Dorado fit right in. Reed watched customers come and go, shouldering their way through the double doors of the low-slung 1950s-era building with its big plate-glass windows, grimy once-white walls and barely peaked roof. He'd already been inside. A take-out order sat in two brown paper bags on the bench seat beside him. Even in the darkness he saw that grease was already making stains in the paper.

"Come on, come on," he muttered, surprised at how suddenly it was imperative that he speak to Nikki Gillette. For years he'd ducked her and anyone else who was associated with the press. She was pretty, smart, sassy and brash. And she was the daughter of Judge Ronald Gillette. All reasons to avoid her like the plague.

Headlights flashed as a car raced into the pockmarked lot. The small silver vehicle squealed to a stop. Nikki Gillette's Subaru hatchback. Good. He didn't like the shot of adrenaline that spiked in his blood at the thought of her, but told himself it was just the fact that he was about to do something he didn't believe in, that he was contemplating putting his job on the line.

He opened the Cadillac's door and stepped into the wind that blew in from the Atlantic. Smelling of brine and rippling the marsh grass and sand dunes that surrounded the lot, the wind whipped his coat around his legs.

Nikki parked in a spray of gravel and was opening the car door before the Subaru's engine died. She was obviously in a hurry. As always. She'd dogged him throughout the Montgomery case last summer, getting in his way and under his skin. There was something about the pushy little woman that bothered the hell out of him. He'd lost more nights' sleep thinking about her than he'd ever admit. He'd hate to think how many times she'd entered his dreams. Sometimes as a cheeky, irritating reporter, other times as a sexy Lolita, seducing him with her firm breasts, nipped-in waist, athletic legs and taut, evocative ass. Those were the dreams that bothered him the most, because she wasn't a woman he admired, wasn't a woman he felt any tenderness for, wasn't a woman he wanted to get to know any better. Nope. She was the kind of woman to avoid. Period.

And here he was, waiting for her.

He hiked his collar against the wind as she gathered her bag from the backseat, locked the hatchback, then started walking briskly toward the front steps of the restaurant, directly behind his Caddy.

"Nikki. Over here," he called and she stopped short. A slim black coat was cinched at her waist and her hair blew over her eyes as she searched the darkness.

He approached, his feet crunching on the gravel.

Whirling, she gasped, one hand flying to her throat.

"Oh! Reed! You scared the bejesus out of me."

"Did I?" He couldn't help the amused smile he felt tugging at the corners of his mouth. For once, he'd gotten the better of her.

"Yeah, you did. And it's *not* funny."

"You're right. Listen, I think it's better if we're not seen together, so let's go for a drive."

"A drive? Now?" She glanced around the parking lot.

"Yeah."

"What is this, are you into some kind of kinky cloak and dagger stuff, or what?" she asked, but fell into step with him and muttered under her breath about feeling as if she were in a bad horror movie as she opened the car door.

"Careful. Dinner's on the front seat."

"What? Dinner? This?" She was staring at the greasy bags as he climbed behind the wheel. "Gee, Reed, you really know how to wow a girl."

"Years of practice." He eased the big car out of the lot. "And I don't think it's a good idea for us to be seen together."

She seemed a little mollified as he drove east on U.S. 80, tires singing on the pavement, dark clouds obliterating the night sky.

Headlights approached, then passed, and Reed double-checked to make sure that no one was following them. He wasn't lying. If anyone saw him with Nikki Gillette, his job would be in serious trouble.

"Sorry I was late," she said.

"You had about ten minutes to spare," he said, slowing for a red light.

"And then what? You'd take off?"

"Something like that." The light turned green and he took off again, following a few taillights toward the island.

"Real nice," she mocked, then added, "You weren't at the press conference."

"But you didn't expect me to be."

She glanced his way and he felt her eyes on him even though he continued to stare through the windshield, turning on the wipers as mist collected on the glass.

"You know I'm off the case."

"I figured. Is that why you called me?"

"Yep."

He drove across the bridge and onto Tybee Island, turning instinctively toward the eastern beach.

"You want to give me a story?" She didn't bother disguising her skepticism.

"Not give. Trade."

"Really? When you usually avoid me like the plague?"

He kept the speedometer just under the limit so as not to attract any attention. "You noticed."

"I would have had to have been deaf, dumb and blind not to. Really, Reed, you've acted like I was some kind of social pariah."

"You are. A reporter."

"Let's not get into that," she said quickly. "So, what is it you wanted to trade?"

His fingers tightened over the wheel. "Information."

"On the Grave Robber."

No reason to back out now. "That's right."

He had her attention. All of him. As Johnny B's special sauce was giving off its world famous aroma, Nikki stared at Reed as if he'd just sprouted a third eye. "Okay, but let's get something straight. Right now. If you're asking me to divulge my sources, then, no way."

He pulled onto a side street, not far from the beach's parking lot, and cut the engine. Through the windshield, Reed eyed the ocean. The black waters of the Atlantic were angry, whitecaps ruffling the dark surface. "Let's eat before this stuff gets cold." He reached into a cooler he kept behind the front seat and pulled out two bottles of beer. After uncapping them, he handed one to her, then took out the barbecued sandwiches. "Beef or pork?"

"Doesn't matter . . . pork," she added, obviously dumbfounded. "Thanks." She took the sandwich and half the dozen napkins that came with the order. "Is this some kind of peace offering?"

"Yeah, right."

"Well?" She was unwrapping the waxed paper.

"Consider it a bribe."

"I already told you, I won't name my contact—"

"I know, okay. I got it the first time." He bit into his sandwich and stared out the window, past the white sand to the inky sea. "You've got information as fast as the department does. So someone on the inside's feeding you."

"I said this isn't open for discussion."

"Oh, I see. Only you get to ask the questions. Then, I guess we don't have much to talk about." He took a long swallow of beer and noticed that she hadn't touched hers.

The silence stretched thin and she finally took a sip of her beer.

"I know that you were involved with Barbara Jean Marx. Is that why you aren't working on the investigation any longer?" When he didn't answer, she said, "Look, if you want to trade information, you've got to give as well as get," she said. "Barbara Jean Marx was pregnant when she died."

His throat tightened, but he didn't move.

"I figure you might be the father."

"She was married," he pointed out, his gut clenching.

"The guy had a vasectomy." Nikki was staring at him.

"How do you know that?" Reed had suspected as much, though Bobbi had never told him directly, but how could Nikki Gillette have found out? Hospital records?

"Uh-uh. You want to work with me, then let's do it, but I'm not giving up my sources. The way I figure it, there are only three reasons for you to bargain with me." She held up a finger. "One, you want me to name my informant." A second finger joined the first. "Or you want to know what I do as no one's confiding in you at the department." A third finger popped up. "Or both. You're probably frustrated to be kicked off the case, especially since it's so close to you, and you're hoping that if we join forces you'll have an inside track." She took a bite of her sandwich. "My question isn't what I can give you, but what, considering your position, can you give me?"

298

"I know information the public doesn't."

"And you'd let me in on it?" she asked skeptically.

He'd been turning it over in his mind. "On the condition you don't print it until the investigation is concluded."

"Meaning you've made an arrest, or the guy's been tried and found guilty."

"Obviously after the trial."

"How would that help me? I won't know anything more than the rest of the reporters in this city."

"It wouldn't. Not now. But it could be a major book deal when this is all over."

"Not good enough, Reed. I want an exclusive now. For the newspaper."

"I can't screw up the investigation."

"Then, I guess we're at an impasse." She dug into the sandwich, chewing and touching a napkin to the corners of her mouth in the dark car. "This is really good. Don't you like yours?" When he didn't answer, she sighed. "I just don't get what you want from me."

"I want what you get, the minute you get it. For that, I'll return the favor, but I have to have some say about what you publish. Final say." He'd probably end up fired, but right now, he didn't give a damn. He just wanted quick revenge against a killer poised to strike again. "But you have to agree not to print sensitive material until the case is over. Period."

"All right," she said, wiping her hands carefully. "Since we have an agreement, there's something I should show you. I was going to take it in to the station tomorrow morning anyway, but . . ." She lifted a shoulder, then reached into her purse. She withdrew several sheets of paper, all of which were encased in plastic. "These were delivered to me."

Reed snapped on the interior light and his blood turned to ice as he read the first note:

TONIGHT.

Then the second:

IT'S DONE

And finally, the third:

WILL THERE BE MORE?
UNTIL THE TWELFTH,
NO ONE CAN BE SURE.

The air froze in his lungs. The notes were from the killer. There wasn't any doubt. The first two were on the same kind of paper, the same exact handwriting of the notes he'd been receiving. The last communication was obviously an E-mail.

"When did you get these?" he demanded, his entire body tight. The killer had been communicating with Nikki Gillette as well as with him. Why?

"A couple of days ago." As he listened, Nikki explained about receiving the first note on her wind- shield and the second in her bed. The third came via E- mail.

Reed was beside himself. Fear clutched his gut. "The

maniac was in your house, in your bedroom, and you didn't go to the police?"

"I am now."

"But the killer was in your home!"

"I've had my locks changed and I'm going to call a security company to place alarms and sensors in the apartment."

"You need to leave that place. Move. Get away." His mind was racing, panic driving it. "This is no game, Nikki, the guy's bad news. Major bad news. How did he get into your apartment?"

She told him that the door hadn't been forced and gave him a rundown of what had happened when she arrived home, how the gate was unlatched, the cat outside. Immediately, he thought of Roberta Peters's tabby and how she'd ended up buried alive.

"You should have called the police," he growled. "By changing the locks you might have inadvertently destroyed evidence! This guy is focused on you, for Christ's sake. You can't go back there."

"Then I'm not safe at work or anywhere else."

"Probably not."

"So what? You think I should have round-the-clock police protection?"

"Absolutely."

"Slow down, Reed," she said, her hand touching his sleeve. "Are you volunteering for the job?"

"See, you are a smart girl." He wadded up the rest of his sandwich in its wrapper and threw the leftovers into the cooler. With a flick of his wrist, he fired the ignition.

"Where are we going?" she asked.

"Back to your place." He reached for his cell phone. "We'll meet the crime scene team there and if you insist on staying, I'll stay with you. Otherwise you're at my place."

"Wait a minute—"

He gunned the engine and headed inland. "That's the way it's gonna be, Nikki. Do we have a deal?"

"Damn."

"Do we?"

"I'm supposed to baby-sit my niece tonight."

"Forget it."

"But—"

"Do you want her in danger?" Was Nikki out of her ever-lovin' mind?

"Of course not."

"Then, leave her with her mother."

"She's with my folks." Nikki looked at her watch as the El Dorado sped toward Savannah. "I'm already late."

"Call them and ask them to keep her. Then, phone your sister. She's got a cell, right?"

"Yeah. She always carries it with her."

"Good. Then ring her up. I'm not kidding, Nikki. This is serious. Dangerous. Leave your niece where she is for the night. Believe me, it's better for you to look like a flake than to end up dead."

"Okay, okay, I get it." She rubbed her arms and as a car sped by, headlights spraying the interior of the El Dorado with blue light, he noticed the lines around her mouth, the nervous way she bit her lip. She did understand. Finally.

She reached for her phone. "So, now you're what?" she asked as the cell phone's keypad glowed and Nikki punched out a number. "My personal bodyguard?"

"You got it," he said as he pushed the speed limit and dialed Sylvie Morrisette on his cell. "Trust me, I'm not any happier about this than you are!"

Who would be next?

Glancing up at the television screens he was disappointed that there seemed to be no mention of the Grave Robber tonight. Even the stir this morning at Heritage Cemetery had ceased to be of prime interest. The press conference was long over and only a few clips of it were being shown.

Fools.

No one seemed to take him seriously.

Except for Nikki Gillette. The one her father had dubbed "Firecracker."

Probably because of her red-blond hair and quick temper. She was smart, sexy and not afraid to go after what she wanted—a woman to be reckoned with.

She wanted a story and he was going to give her one—the story of her life.

And death.

He slid into his desk chair and studied the computer screen that flickered in front of him. Images he'd created, a screen saver with the likenesses of Bobbi Jean Marx, Pauline Alexander, Thomas Massey and Roberta Peters danced over the black background, then, every three seconds their pictures turned to bones, a skeleton, then crumbled to ash, only to resurrect into the original images again. A little program alteration that he'd created.

After each successful burial, The Survivor had taken the pictures that he'd so carefully collected, scanned them into his computer and added them to the collage of images that disappeared before his eyes only to return again.

Only four, but soon, very soon, there would be additional images. He thought of the messages he'd sent earlier in the day and smiled.

His hands were damp in anticipation.

Licking his lips, he considered his next abduction.

His next kill.

Reaching for the sound system, he turned on the audiotapes and listened, first to Bobbi Jean, her terror, her fear, her screams and pleas . . . oh, that was good. His blood sang through his veins as he closed his eyes. His cock thickened in anticipation.

Then he heard the old lady's whimpers . . . The cries gave him a thrill, made his blood hot and his heartbeat quicken. He thought of Bobbi Jean. And Nikki. His breath came in short, excited bursts.

His lips were so dry he licked them.

Who would be next?

He closed his eyes and ran an anxious finger over the plastic-encased pictures in his album. "Eenie, meenie, miney, moe . . ."

His hand stopped. He opened an eye to stare down at the smiling, sultry image of a beautiful woman . . . Though the snapshot had been taken a dozen years ago, he knew that she was still as eye-catching as she had been then.

He wanted her.

God, he wanted her.

His cock began to throb and he wondered how she'd like waking up in a coffin. Imagined her terror, how her gorgeous features would contort in fear, how she'd plead and beg for her life, to no avail. Panic would nearly stop her heart. The air in the coffin would thin . . . her lungs would be on fire . . . oh, yes . . .

He felt powerful.

Strong.

Cunning.

Anticipation thrummed through his bloodstream.

He could barely wait.

"You're next, sweetheart," he whispered roughly as his erection strained against his fly. God, he'd love to fuck her. To slide into her. To show her how he could do what he wanted with her. Maybe after. Maybe before. But to dip into the hot warmth of her . . . or even into her cold, dead cunt. Either way.

He'd never fucked one of them . . . never let his fantasies take hold so deeply that he couldn't resist the temptation they presented. But maybe, this once, he could change his ritual a bit.

Anticipation quickening his pulse, he slowly lowered his face to the scrapbook, so that her beautiful, smiling image blurred. Then, without closing his eyes, he planted a wet kiss on the plastic.

CHAPTER 20

"So you're flaking out on me again, Nikki. Nice, real nice!" The sneer in Lily's voice was palpable even with the spotty reception of Nikki's cell phone.

Reed had dropped Nikki off at her car at Johnny B's and was now following her as she drove into Savannah. Nikki barely noticed the southern channel of the river, or the traffic, or the speed limit as she headed inland, the lights of Savannah beckoning in the dark night. Her concentration was on the telephone conversation with her angry sister.

"I told you it isn't safe for me to take Phee," she said for the third time. "Don't you get it? My apartment was broken into, Lily. Whoever did it left me a damned note. In my bed." She shivered, thinking of the intruder touching her linens, running his fingers over her bedposts, rummaging through her drawers.

"This is a surprise?"

"Don't you know there's a serial killer on the loose! He might have been the guy in the apartment."

"Well, gee, I wonder why he would break into your place, okay? Let's think. Could it be that you keep writing about him? Attracting his attention? No wonder you're a target. He's pissed off."

"He's not pissed off at me. He *likes* the attention I give him. He craves it. It's all part of the serial killer mentality."

"I wouldn't know. They have mentalities?"

"Yes, Lily, they do and—"

"He's killing people, for Christ's sake! It's not about 'mentalities!'" she snapped, then caught hold of her temper. "Listen, Nikki, I understand, okay? I do get it. It's your life and it's important." Obviously Lily couldn't keep the sarcasm from infecting her words. "So, I'll leave here and pick Ophelia up at the folks. Forget what I'm doing. Forget that this was a hundred dollar a plate dinner for a candidate Mel supports, that it's important to him, that it's important to me. Because it's all about you, isn't it? It always has been."

"No, Lily," Nikki retorted hotly as she turned off the Island Expressway. "It's all about you. It always has been."

Lily hung up so loudly, Nikki winced, then dropped the phone into the cup holder by the driver's seat of her hatchback. She told herself she should feel bad, but she didn't. Not for her sister. This was how Lily handled every crisis. By lashing out.

Still fuming, she wended her way through the historic district. She took a corner a little too fast to avoid stopping for a yellow light, then told herself to calm down. A fight with Lily wasn't exactly a news-breaking event. She and her sister had never gotten along. She glanced in her side-view mirror. Reed was still behind her, never letting her get too far ahead, never gunning the El Dorado past her. His being near was comforting in an odd way. She liked knowing he was so close. He'd been more approachable and she'd thought she'd heard a new tone in his voice, something softer, as if he cared about her—if only because

307

she was a person he was sworn to serve and protect.

At that thought, she nearly ran the next light. "Get over yourself," she admonished. "This is Pierce Reed you're mooning over." Disgusted with the turn of her thoughts, she pulled into her spot in the tiny parking lot. A police car was already parked in the alley that housed the Dumpsters for the apartment building. Red and blue lights strobed the old bricks, tall windows and gleaming shutters of the once-grand house that she now called home. Yellow tape was being strung to keep the onlookers at bay while more than one of her neighbors' lights were blazing. A few braver souls, clad in raincoats hastily thrown over pajamas craned their necks to stare up at her apartment and some of the bystanders had begun peppering a stoic-faced officer with questions.

"What's going on?" one woman asked. She was huddled under an umbrella with a big hulking man dressed in wrinkled sweat clothes.

"Don't really know," the police officer said. "If you'll please stand back and let us do our work, we'd appreciate it."

The big man didn't take the hint. "Whatever it is, it's the top apartment, the one in the turret." The umbrella shifted as the curious neighbors turned their noses skyward to stare at Nikki's apartment. Nikki moved back a couple of steps, behind the umbrella, where the nosy neighbors couldn't see her, and was grateful when, from the corner of her eye, she noticed Reed approaching.

"Isn't that where Nikki Gillette lives?" the woman

under the umbrella said. Nikki shrank back even farther. "She's that reporter, you know. The one who's writing all the stories about the Grave Robber . . ."

Nikki backed away from the conversation before they turned, saw, and realized who she was. She nearly bumped into Reed, who grabbed her arm and shepherded her away from the conversation. For once she was grateful to rely on someone else, to feel his strong fingers around her forearm. For the moment she felt protected, though she knew it was only a matter of time before she was spotted and recognized. More neighbors had begun collecting. Fortunately most of the onlookers stood away from the police, preferring the safety of the shadows or their own porches. Only a few vehicles passed by, rolling slowly, drivers rubbernecking, passengers pointing at the elegant old house while sirens, coming ever closer, wailed in the night.

"This is going to be a three-ring circus," Nikki muttered under her breath.

"Or four," he agreed.

"Thanks. That makes me feel so much better."

One of the uniformed officers took up traffic duty, waving the onlookers through while a damp, icy wind scraped Nikki's cheeks and tugged at the hem of her coat as vehicles crept down the street.

"We'll need a key," Reed said.

She wanted to refuse, hated the invasion of her privacy, but she dug through her purse, found her key ring and slipped the house key off.

"We'll go inside as soon as we get the okay."

"From?"

"Diane Moses. And believe me, she's aptly named. In this department, she does hand down the word of God."

Nikki chuckled despite her case of nerves. She glanced up at Reed and noticed he wasn't smiling, but his eyes seemed warmer than before, his perpetually harsh expression less severe, the hint of tenderness perceptible beneath his gruff facade.

"Hang in there," he said, dropping her arm as the crime scene van arrived along with two more police cars and the news van from WKAM. Nikki watched a reporter and cameraman emerge, while Reed spoke to a petite black woman whose face seemed set in a perpetual frown. The woman slid a curious glance in Nikki's direction, but her scowl only deepened, another fan of the press, as Reed introduced Diane Moses, then handed her Nikki's key.

"Hey, what's going on here?" Fred Cooper, the apartment manager, had finally awakened and wasn't too happy about it. Dressed in a striped bathrobe, he came charging around the corner of the apartment house like a bulldog. His thin white hair was standing on end, the bags under his eyes indicating he needed a lot more sleep. "What the hell is this?" Turning his gaze on Nikki, he stopped dead and the corners of his mouth pursed. "Why am I not surprised this has something to do with you?"

It was Nikki's turn to make hasty introductions. "Fred Cooper, the manager, Detectives Reed and Moses. They want to see my apartment. I said it was okay."

"Of course it's okay . . . but . . ." Fred, standing in the midst, was obviously confused and not happy about the situation. He stared at the ever-growing crowd of police and onlookers. "Jesus . . ."

Reed took over. The ensuing conversation was short. Reed explained what they were doing as Diane Moses climbed the stairs to Nikki's apartment.

Cooper backed off and stepped back to stand guard under the overhang of his porch. One shoulder propped against the doorjamb, he glared at the disruption of his usually predictable, neat life.

Members of the team roped off areas surrounding the walkway and gate, then carefully started examining the exterior of the house before climbing the stairs to Nikki's apartment. It was weird to see the police swarming around *her* home, searching for evidence of a crime against *her*. She hated to think how many crime scenes she'd visited, always hungry for knowledge, with fleeting thoughts of the victims, while her concentration had been on finding out who, what, when and why.

"We'll give them time to look around first," Reed said, grabbing hold of Nikki's arm again when she tried to follow an officer through the gate. "Even though it's been over twenty-four hours since the break-in, they could find something important."

"Okay, but my cat will freak."

The hand around her sleeve didn't let go. "He'll get over it."

"You don't know Jennings. He holds a grudge for weeks!" she insisted, staring up at her apartment. "This'll cost me a fortune in catnip."

He snorted a laugh and looked at her. For the first

time, she was certain, he really looked at her. Past her I'm-a-serious-reporter skin to probe beneath the surface, to search for the woman she usually kept locked away. "I think you can afford it," he observed as another police car, lights blazing, roared down the street.

With a squeal of tires, the cruiser ground to a stop.

"Morrisette," Reed said.

Cliff Siebert, his expression grave, made a hasty exit from the passenger side. He slid a look in Nikki's direction, then immediately turned his attention to Reed, who dropped her arm. Cliff's forehead was creased, his lips pursed. He looked ready to spit nails.

"You call this in?" he demanded, zeroing in on Reed.

Nikki saw the fight brewing and stepped in. "Wait a minute. *I* called Detective Reed and told him about the break-in."

"*You* called *him.*" Obviously Cliff wasn't buying it.

"Ms. Gillette has some evidence about the Grave Robber that she'd like to share with us all." "So, after we're through here, let's all go to the station."

"Hold on, Reed. You're off the case." Cliff scowled at the older detective and his lips barely moved as he added, "What the hell do you think you're doing? Okano will have your badge and your ass."

From the corner of her eye, Nikki saw Detective Morrisette approach. "Whoa, boys. Enough. Let's not go off here half-cocked."

"This is my fault," Nikki cut in. "I knew Detective Reed had been called up to Dahlonega and was close to one of the victims, so I approached him first. I've been leaving messages for Detective Reed ever since this case broke."

Cliff's gaze, when he looked at Nikki, was cold as death. "Detective Reed was removed from the case, Ms. Gillette. I assumed, as you're writing so feverishly about everything there is about the Grave Robber, that you knew that Detective Morrisette was in charge and that I'm assisting her."

"Listen, Siebert, turn down the testosterone a notch or two, okay?" Morrisette's multiple earrings caught in the light from the street lamps and her platinum spikes took on a gray-blue hue as another press van pulled into the alley. "Great. More dickhead reporters, present company excluded." A uniformed officer met the van, keeping the driver and newsman behind the barrier. It was weird being on the other side of the microphone, Nikki thought, strange being the victim rather than a voyeur looking for a story, an angle to make her story the best.

Morrisette was still reaming out Reed and Siebert. ". . . so I don't give a flying fuck who did the calling or responding on this. It just doesn't matter. So let's just get to work and figure out what's going on before we have the press crawling up our butts." She looked from Siebert to Reed. "Let's go." She was already starting for the gate.

Jaw tight, Cliff Siebert was only one step behind.

"Ms. Gillette said her apartment was broken into the other night. Whoever did it left a note with a poem. Looks like it's from the Grave Robber," Reed said.

"Holy shit." Only one step from the stairs, Morrisette

stopped dead in her tracks and spun on the heels of her snakeskin boots. "I assume you brought it."

"She gave it to me," Reed said. "I thought we'd take it down to the station and compare it to the other notes." He must've seen Cliff's reaction because he added, "And yeah, she does know that the Grave Robber's been sending us messages, too."

"Reed," Morrisette warned.

"Ms. Gillette's agreed not to print any of this until such time as the department deems is acceptable."

"Now you're making deals? For someone off the case, you sure throw your weight around," Cliff growled.

"Enough, already." Morrisette glared at the two men. "Let's just get this joker. You"—she pointed a finger at Nikki—"stay outside until we ask you in and then be careful where you step. Diane Moses—she's the lead crime scene investigator—will tell you what you can and cannot touch, and if I were you, I'd do exactly as she says. Got it?"

Nikki nodded. "Got it."

"And I'd find another place to spend the night." Morrisette's gaze swept to Reed's face, then back to Nikki's. "Somewhere safe. Maybe with your folks or a friend. Someone you can trust."

"I already changed my locks," Nikki protested.

"Not good enough. We might need more time. You can take a few of your belongings. A change of clothes."

Nikki argued, "Now wait a minute, this is my home."

"And it was violated once." Detective Morrisette's

face was without a trace of humor. "Let's not invite trouble back again. Got it?"

"Okay. Yeah . . . I got it," Nikki said, staring up at the turret apartment and feeling a chill. The Grave Robber had been inside her home. The creep who tossed living women into coffins already occupied by decomposing bodies had walked through her tiny rooms, running his hands over her counter and bureau, maybe even lying in her bed, going through her drawers. She shuddered.

Morrisette was right.

She'd stay away tonight.

At least, this night. In her peripheral vision she caught a glimpse of a shadow and the lower branches of the laurel hedge shuddered. Nikki's heart nearly stopped and she visibly jumped before she realized that her cat, spooked by the police, had darted under one of the police cruisers. His eyes were wide as he huddled behind one tire, staring out at her.

Nikki bent down on one knee. "Come on, Jen," she said, feeling some of the animal's unease. "It'll be all right."

But the cat didn't budge. In fact, when she reached for him, he hissed, baring his needle-sharp teeth, then scrambled away to the far side of the vehicle where he continued to cower and stare at the house.

As if he sensed the very essence of evil.

As if the Grave Robber were lurking nearby.

Hiding in the shadows.

Watching.

Waiting.

Nikki's throat went dry. She felt it then, that cold

damp wind that rattled through the branches of the surrounding trees, masking sounds, the night itself hiding the most hideous of murderers, the killer who had decided to contact her.

A footstep scraped on the concrete of the parking lot. She turned quickly and saw no one.

Or did she?

Was that a shadow in the foliage near the alley?

A dark figure walking by or a trick of light?

Did the fronds of a fern shiver as someone passed?

Suddenly frightened, she stepped backward and bumped into something, a person, and she nearly jumped out of her skin.

"Nikki?" Reed's voice asked. Turning quickly, she found the detective staring at her, studying her. "Are you all right?"

"Would you be?" she tried to quip back, though her voice faltered a little.

"Me? Hell, no. I'd be scared to death."

"Yeah, well, that about covers it." Shoving her hands into the pockets of her coat, she said, "Can we go inside now?"

"I think so. Come on." Once again he wrapped strong fingers around her arm and propelled her toward the walkway. As she looked ahead to the stairs that wrapped around the outside of the house she knew she'd never climb them again without a new, unwanted sense of trepidation. The Grave Robber had gotten into her home once. What was to stop him from doing it again?

· · ·

Morrisette didn't like what was going through her head as she drove through the empty, night-darkened streets of Savannah. Something wasn't right about the investigation, something major. She was tired, cranky, worried about leaving her kids in the middle of the night with a bleary-eyed sitter and didn't need this kind of gut-wrenching suspicion.

Reed and Nikki Gillette?

What was with the two of them? Were they involved . . . ? The way they hung close to each other while Gillette's apartment was searched felt odd . . . out of sync . . . like there was more to their relationship than met the eye. But Reed detested reporters, especially the pushy kind like Ms. Gillette. And yet . . .

Morrisette's feminine intuition, which was sometimes a blessing but more often a curse, was working overtime tonight. And she wasn't the only one who'd sensed the shift in the atmosphere. As she'd torn down the old Savannah streets, she'd tried not to notice that her new partner was brooding. Mad at the world. Cliff Siebert hadn't uttered one word on the short trip to the station. He'd even given her that pissy don't-ruin-my-lungs glare as she'd lit up. What a tight-ass. She turned onto Habersham and saw that Reed's El Dorado was on her tail. Nikki Gillette's little hatchback was behind him and all three of the cars rolled into the parking lot one after the other. Siebert had been watching their little parade in the side-view mirror and now, as she shoved the cruiser into park, his already grim expression darkened. He shot out of the car before Morrisette

317

could cut the engine. Yep, he was gonna be lots of fun, she thought, a regular barrel of laughs. She decided to have a much-needed smoke before facing Reed and Siebert in the interrogation room. She paused for a cigarette, noticed that Reed and Gillette were way too chummy, huddling close together against the weather as they headed inside. Morrisette lit up and took a couple of quick hits of nicotine as she walked to the doors. She squashed out her half-smoked Marlboro Light in the ash can. Why was the Grave Robber singling out Nikki Gillette and Pierce Reed? What did they have to do with twelve? Reed had been involved with one of the victims, but, as far as Morrisette knew, Nikki Gillette hadn't.

Maybe the notes would give them the clue they needed.

Inside the interrogation room, she took charge. Reed stood near the doorway, a concession to not being a part of the case, she supposed, while Siebert and Nikki Gillette claimed a couple of chairs. The station was quiet, only a few cops working graveyard. Even here, Savannah's bastion of security, the night seemed disturbed. Out of sync. Even a little eerie. But then, everything about this damned case was.

Nikki Gillette offered up a list of her friends and associates and starred those that had keys to her apartment, or had used her keys in the time that she'd rented her apartment. The list was way too long for Morrisette's way of thinking and, she imagined, incomplete, as it was put together hastily, but it was a starting point. Morrisette reminded the reporter that whatever they discussed was definitely off the record, then listened as Nikki Gillette explained about getting the notes on her car, in her house and the E-mail at work.

"It's essentially the same things I received, only with different wording," Reed said, then held up a hand to cut Morrisette off. "Ms. Gillette knows I got the E-mail. We've been over this. She's not reporting this until we make an official statement."

"But I am reporting that the killer contacted me," Nikki cut in. She looked as tired as Morrisette felt. Dark smudges showed up beneath her eyes, her lipstick had faded and her hair was a tangled mess. But she was still feisty as hell. That probably came with being Big Ron Gillette's daughter.

"I'd like to see the article before it hits the stands."

"Too late." Gillette trapped Morrisette in a sharp, green-eyed glare. "I left one draft at the paper with orders to print it if I didn't get back with additional facts."

Morrisette's frayed temper snapped. "You're impeding the investigation."

"No, Detective, I'm helping it." Nikki Gillette opened her voluminous bag, pulled out the notes, encased in plastic sacks, and tossed them onto the table. "These are copies. Reed has the originals."

"Jesus," Cliff muttered and wiped a hand over his mouth like some kind of pansy. He was an odd one, she decided, though Morrisette didn't have time to analyze what was going through her new, scowling partner's brain. All the same, she found herself longing to be hooked up with Reed again. Him, she understood. Or did she? From the corner of her eye she saw him fold his arms over his chest and lean one shoulder against the door frame. It bothered her that he'd linked up with Nikki Gillette. In Morrisette's estimation, Reed was fraternizing with the enemy. Hadn't he said a hundred times how he hated the press?

And now he was in bed with them . . . or one . . . or soon to be, if she read the signals right. What the hell was he thinking?

She read the message:

> WILL THERE BE MORE?
> UNTIL THE TWELFTH,
> NO ONE CAN BE SURE.

"It *is* like the one you got," she said to Reed.

"More than that. It's a continuation."

"What do you mean?" Nikki asked, but Sylvie Morrisette was on Reed's wavelength.

"I get it. One line repeated . . . to link 'em . . . 'Now, we have number four. One third done, will there be more? Will there be more? Until the twelfth, no one can be sure.' "

"Singsong like a child's rhyme," Nikki said.

Siebert looked at the reporter and there was something in his eyes, a familiarity that he quickly disguised. "So what does the twelfth mean?"

"The twelfth of December?" Nikki said. "That's so soon."

"What about number of victims?" Reed ventured and Siebert sent him a look guaranteed to kill.

"Twelve? There will be twelve?" Gillette, to her credit, seemed horrified.

Morrisette ended the speculation. "Let's not throw theories around. And remember, everything you heard here is off the record."

"For now," she said. "Once the investigation is over—"

"Let's just solve it first," Siebert cut in.

Amen, Sylvie thought. It was the first time she'd agreed with her new partner. She figured it might just be the last.

Twelve.

That was the key. Nikki's brain was too tired to think what it could possibly mean, but there was something important in the number, something she'd have to research she thought as she drove to her parents' house. She'd called her father from the station, explained only that she needed a place to crash, and knew she'd get the third degree upon her arrival. Which was fine. Better her parents hear what was happening from her lips rather than through the gossip mill that churned out fact and fiction twenty-four hours a day in Savannah.

Twelve, twelve, twelve. Half of twenty-four. Half a day? Twelve numbers on a clock face? Twelve dough-nuts in a dozen, twelve members of a jury, twelve days of Christmas . . . The song popped into her brain as it was the season.

"On the twelfth day of Christmas my true love gave to me . . . twelve . . . oh, drummers drumming . . ." she sang off-key, then glanced in her rearview mirror. The street was deserted aside from the twin headlights behind her.

Detective Pierce Reed.

On the job.

Following her.

Making certain she was safe.

Somehow the thought that he was nearby made her feel safer as she drove down the cold, lonely streets and watched the play of light from her own beams splash against the boles of trees, white fences and the road winding ahead of her. She saw a few cars going the opposite direction and her beams had caught the eyes of an opossum before it lumbered beneath a hedge of azaleas and ferns. In a weird, all-too-needy way, Nikki was touched that Reed had elected to escort her home. It was the kind of emotion she usually detested.

But then, she was dead on her feet. Not thinking clearly. That explained her odd feelings for Reed. Had to. Nothing else made sense. Even though in a few hours her page one story would hit the stands, she couldn't wait up for it. She pulled into her parents' tree-lined drive and parked. Reed's Cadillac glided into the spot next to hers. He rolled his window down. "I'll wait until you get inside," he said.

"Thanks." Waving, she hauled her bag to the garage, punched in the code for the doors to open and walked past her mother's fifteen-year-old Mercedes and her father's new BMW convertible—a midlife crisis except for the fact her father had sped past midlife ten or fifteen years earlier. As she opened the door to the kitchen, she nearly ran into her mother, frail thing that she was, all wrapped up in a fluffy yellow bathrobe and matching slippers.

"My God, Nicole, what's going on?" Charlene asked, worriedly fingering the diamond cross that forever hung around her neck. "It's this Grave Robber thing, isn't it?"

Nikki couldn't lie. "Yes. Please, Mom, don't panic, but since you're going to read the papers in a few hours, you may as well know that the guy contacted me."

Charlene gasped. "The killer?"

Her father filled the doorway to the den. "Contacted you?" he repeated gruffly, his voice still deep from recent sleep, his thinning hair mussed, eyeglasses a little angled over his nose. "How?"

"It's a long story, Dad, and I can't keep my eyes open. I'll tell you all about it in the morning."

"Are you in danger?" he demanded.

"Oh, God." Charlene rubbed the diamond cross as if in so doing she could ward off the devil. "Of course she is. She courts it and now . . . if that monster is contacting you . . ."

"I don't know that it's him for certain," Nikki answered honestly. "It could be someone else just jerking my chain, but I don't think so." She lifted a weary hand. "So, it's okay if I crash here?"

"Of course."

Her father managed a smile as he engaged the alarm system. "Always, Firecracker. You know that. If anyone tries to mess with you here, he'll have to deal with me."

"And your personal arsenal." Nikki unbuttoned her coat.

"That's right."

Her father was ex-military, but took the Second Amendment to the nth degree. His right to bear arms was one he'd fight for to the death. His life had been threatened on more than one occasion. And he'd been on the bench long enough that criminals he'd put away for life, were now, thanks to prison rehabilitation or trusting parole boards, on the streets again.

Big Ron believed in being armed and he had the shotguns, revolvers and AK-47s to prove it.

"I'll see you in the morning." She made her way up the stairs to the room she'd grown up in and snapped on the bedside lamp. Warm light illuminated walls papered in a floral pattern she'd helped her mother choose over twenty years earlier. The maple bed with its matching desk and bureau were situated exactly as they had been when Nikki was growing up.

"Jesus, this is almost spooky," she thought aloud as she fingered the tennis trophies she'd won in high school that were mounted on a shelf. The corsage from her senior prom was still pinned to a bulletin board and there were snapshots from high school as well as her college years. The faded tassel from her mortarboard hung over the corner of a mirror, hiding a picture of Andrew and Simone Nikki had tucked into the mirror's frame. She pulled it out now and stared at the image.

Andrew, so vital and alive, his arm slung around Simone's shoulders. Dark-haired, willow-slim Simone with her trace of Mediterranean ancestry evident in her dark eyes and deeper skin tones, and Andrew, tall and fair, built like an athlete, reminiscent of a Norman warrior. In that frozen instant in time, when the camera had flashed, Simone had stared up at him as if he were a god. Or a fallen idol, Nikki thought, chewing on her lower lip and wondering what it was that bothered her about the picture and coming up blank.

"You're just tired," she muttered, replacing the photo to glance around her old room. Obviously Charlene Gillette was a firm believer in holding on to the past, no remodeling or updating or redecorating her children's rooms into sewing centers or mini gyms or even guest rooms.

At the desk, Nikki opened a drawer and found a dusty photograph album. Her album. Inside were her favorite snapshots from grade school, high school and college. She flipped the pages quickly and saw pictures of her family and friends. Andrew, of course, was predominate. His smiling image leapt off the pages, whether he was clowning around or posing in a football uniform. His hair was always cut short, his face clean shaven to show off a square jaw that was identical to their father's.

Andrew had been built like Big Ron, strong as an ox, yet fast enough to play tight end or quarterback on the football team. Though smart enough, he'd lacked the ambition and dedication of the man who had sired him and had taken the easy path too often . . . unlike herself. She was the one of Ronald Gillette's children who had inherited the old man's drive. Lily and Kyle were in many of the family photographs, but it was Andrew to whom the camera gravitated and Nikki wondered if it was just that her eldest brother had been so photogenic, or that the eye of the photographer had always been looking for him.

There were others in the pictures as well. Cliff Siebert was sprinkled into the snapshots, clowning with Andrew, making faces at the camera, occasionally mugging and leering at Nikki. Simone appeared in the later shots, either laughing with Nikki or hugging Andrew. A stunning couple, they'd been so much in love.

Or so it had seemed.

But it had been a lie. Andrew had broken up with her.

"You're making too much of it," Nikki whispered, realizing she was dead on her feet. Yet she continued to flip through the pages, to shots of college and the summers between, including her first real newspaper job at the *Sentinel*. There was a picture of Nikki and Sean, their arms wrapped around each other's waists, the wind catching their hair as they stood on a sand dune, beach grass ruffling at their bare feet. Sean had looked younger then, his face clean shaven, his smile more boyish and innocent, but he'd been fit and strong, about to join the navy and probably already involved with the other woman. Nikki wondered what had happened to that girl . . . what had her name been? Cindy Something-Or-Other. She hadn't lived in Savannah and Nikki had never heard what happened to her, though she didn't care enough to take Sean up on his offer of a drink or to catch up. It had been too painful a time in her life; not only had Sean dumped her, but she'd nearly screwed up her career and ruined her father's reputation all because of the LeRoy Chevalier trial. She didn't want to think about Chevalier, how he'd butchered a family, his *girlfriend's* family.

And now he was out . . . not because of Nikki, but because technology had caught up with the crime and DNA testing had suggested there might have been another murderer, that the case against LeRoy Chevalier was much weaker than originally thought.

Nikki shuddered. She remembered the lifeless eyes of Chevalier as he'd sat in the defendant's chair, never showing any emotion, not even when the photographs of his girlfriend and her two dead children were shown to the jury. Not even when the one surviving boy had testified and shown his brutal wounds.

So, he'd served only a few years of his life sentence. So much for justice.

She continued to turn the pages. There were no further snapshots of Sean Hawke, and those of Andrew suddenly ceased altogether. In the remaining few pictures the faces that the camera caught after that Christmas had lost their sparkle, the smiles seemed forced, the images sober.

Nikki had kept the card from Andrew's funeral and it, now fading, was pressed into the album. How gruesome, she thought now, removing the faded card . . . a few lines dedicated to his brilliant, if short, life. Nikki felt the same old sadness steal over her as always when she considered how tragically his life had ended. Such a waste. She wadded the damned reminder in her fist, then shoved it into her purse rather than leave it in the trash for her mother to find.

A floorboard in the hallway creaked and she heard her father's quiet cough. Hastily she shoved the album back into the drawer and turned just as Big Ron, backlit by the corridor lights, filled the doorway. In his hand he held a gun.

Her heart nearly stopped.

"I thought you might want this," he said as he came into the room.

"A pistol? You thought I'd want a pistol?"

"To protect yourself." He handed her the small caliber Colt.

"Is it loaded?"

"Yes."

"Damn it, Dad, this is scary."

"The safety's on. It's not cocked."

"I hope not. Dad, I don't think this is a good idea. In fact, I know it isn't! I don't even have a gun license."

"You know how to shoot." He wrapped her fingers around the pistol's grip and the cold metal felt surprisingly familiar. "At least, you did. I took you bird hunting. You were a good shot."

"That was about a billion years ago. With a shotgun."

He chuckled. "Don't make me any older than I am. Besides, I took you with me when I went target shooting. You used a handgun."

"I'm really not into weapons, Dad. I'm not gonna run around with a loaded pistol in my purse or strapped to my leg like you do."

He grinned widely, lines bracketing the sides of his face. "I'll have you know that I don't keep any guns in *my* purse. Now, promise me you won't print that."

"Very funny."

"But this isn't, Firecracker," he said, turning sober again. "This business with the Grave Robber is serious. Keep the pistol or let me find you something you're more comfortable with."

"No. No more." She had images of her father handing her a semiautomatic weapon with clips, or one of those ammunition belts that the bad guys wore in all the old Spaghetti Westerns he watched. "This will do just fine, but let's unload it." She did just that, taking out the bullets and dropping them into her pocket.

"What're you going to do if you're attacked? Pistol-whip the guy?"

"Let's hope it doesn't come to that." The gun was suddenly heavy.

"I'll sleep better knowing you're protected." He offered her another, weaker smile. "Be careful, Nicole. Your mother and I . . . we love you and we sure as hell don't want to lose you."

Her throat closed and tears burned the back of her eyelids as he gave her a bear hug. The scents of cigar smoke and whiskey, a combination that had been a part of him for as long as she could remember, clung to him. "I love you, too, Daddy."

"You're a good kid." Releasing her, he walked into the hallway and she heard the stairs moan under his weight as he made his way to the den.

Nikki sank onto the edge of the bed and held the unloaded pistol in one hand. She hated the thought of it, was radically against handguns in general, but with the

Grave Robber breaking into her apartment, she did need to protect herself.

She slid the Colt into her purse.

CHAPTER 21

It was time to move. He could feel it. The restlessness. The need. The hunger, a craving he could satisfy only one way. He turned on the tape player, listened to the screams. Barbara Jean's were desperate, panicked, shrieking and begging, while the old lady's were reduced to mewling and prayers. . . . He'd blended the two together and as he sat at his table, running his fingers over the plastic coated pictures—graduation shots, business photographs, even a prom picture, he closed his eyes, imagining what it would sound like when all of the damned had been captured, buried and recorded. His eyes moved rapidly beneath his eyelids, his hands shook and yet he smiled as he imagined their fear, sensed their terror, wondered if they would ever understand why they were being punished, why the retribution.

Twelve years had passed . . . and now all twelve tormentors would pay . . . one or two at a time . . . they would live his hell, feel his pain, experience the torture that he had suffered. Some had died already, others had no idea that their days on earth were about to end. Some lived nearby. In this very neighborhood, living their lives without concern, others had drifted to more distant vicinities, but he knew where they had landed and they could not hide. No, they were not safe.

The tape clicked to a stop and he closed his scrapbook.

It was time.

Leaving the televisions glowing, he slipped through his private entrance and up the vine covered brick stairs to the brisk air of the night. The storm was coming. Ice and sleet headed south from Tennessee and the Carolinas. Unusual for this climate. But perfect. He felt its breath, coveted the chill it would bring to his victims.

The drive to the river was uneventful. The night quiet. He hid his truck nearly a mile away from his boat's hiding spot, parking in a lane overgrown with brambles. Then he jogged back to the sandy dunes where he'd tucked the rowboat with its specialized equipment. Quickly, he stripped off his street clothes and pulled on a wet suit that was as black as the night. It was now or never, he thought, knowing the risks, anticipating resistance from a security guard or dogs. As much as he hated guns, he was prepared, the Glock in a water-tight pouch. Shoving off, he glanced to the stars, high above thin clouds, and a slice of moon barely visible. With even strokes he paddled against the current, his eyes trained on the shoreline and the point that jutted into the river.

Stroke, stroke, stroke, the little boat knifed through the water as he sweat inside the tight suit. Around the bend in the river, closer to the shore, to the old Peltier

Plantation. Once renowned for the rice it grew, the plantation was now home to a private cemetery and one very special plot. He guided his craft to the shoreline, donned night-vision goggles and saw the path that curved upward to the higher ground to the graveyard. Carefully, he removed his tools from the boat. Creeping silently, he made his way up the smooth dirt trail and walked unerringly through the graying headstones until he found the grave he was looking for.

Then he began to dig.

The woman was writhing beneath him, whispering his name, sweating and hot. White, slick skin, breasts with dark areolas, legs that wound around his as he made love to her. "Pierce," she whispered against his ear, and his blood sizzled in his veins. God, she was hot. And slick. The scent of her perfume mingled with the heady, musty odor of sex.

Her back arched and he opened his eyes, staring down at her dark eyes. She licked her red lips, her tongue flicking outward. He pumped harder. Faster.

"Don't leave me," she whispered and he felt a niggle of doubt. As hard as he was, he sensed something wrong. "He'll kill me."

"What?"

Oh, God, he was gonna come. He held onto a breast, felt it shift and looked into her eyes again, but they were no longer a deep, warm brown, but green, her hair a red-blond, a dusting of freckles bridging her nose. "Nikki?"

She smiled up at him, a naughty provocative smile,

her eyes nearly laughing. He felt a moment's confusion, but she reached up and wound her arms around his neck, dragged his head down to hers, kissed him hard, her mouth opened to him, inviting more. Her tongue found his, twisted and mated. God, he wanted all of her. He lifted her legs to his shoulders and plunged deeper into her moist warmth.

"That's it, Reed," she whispered throatily, moving with him, her heart beating wildly, her breath as rapid as his own. "More . . . more . . ."

Dear God, he was lost inside her.

"Help me! Pierce, please . . . I'm cold . . . please . . ." She screamed beneath him, but not the wild, abandoned cry of passion. It was an ear-splitting, terror-riddled shriek that tore through his brain. She changed then, morphing from Nikki to Bobbi in his arms, and her eyes, so recently burning with desire, widened in terror and glazed over, her face becoming a death mask. He tried to move and realized that he couldn't. That they weren't making love in a bed, but a box . . . a coffin, and someone was bolting down the lid.

His heart seemed to stop. He tried to move, but couldn't as the coffin's lid was pushing downward, against his shoulders and back, pressing him into Bobbi, now dead, her flesh disintegrating beneath him, the stench overpowering . . . "No!" he yelled.

His eyes flew open at the sound of his own voice.

Heart thudding, he found himself in his dark apartment, only the ghoulish light from the television giving off any illumination whatsoever. "Damn it," he muttered, running a shaking hand over his chin. Sweat dried on his body as his erection withered, thankfully, but his muscles were still tense. His half-drunk beer was on the side table where he'd left it as he'd clicked on the eleven o'clock news. Which was now long over. Instead, Jay Leno was interviewing Nicole Kidman. Reed clicked off the set, then snapped on a table lamp. Jesus, where had that dream come from? His skin crawled when he remembered the feeling of sheer panic at being locked in the coffin . . . and why had he pictured himself making love to Bobbi, then Nikki, then Bobbi as a corpse . . . as if they were all one woman?

He'd been working too hard, that was it. The case was consuming him. He rubbed the kinks from his neck and picked up the can of beer. It was now warm. He downed it anyway.

Though he wasn't officially on the Grave Robber case, he spent all his time away from the office trying to piece the clues together. Morrisette was reticent to give him much information and Cliff Siebert was worse, clamming up whenever Reed was around, glaring at him as if he were somehow the enemy.

Why?

They were all on the same team.

Or were they?

Reed had done a little digging on the younger detective and discovered that over ten years ago, before he was on the force, Siebert had been friends with Andrew Gillette, Nikki's older brother, who, from all outward appearances, had taken a leap off a deck at a frat party. Suicide? Accident? Who knew? All the reports Reed had sifted through had been inconclusive. But Siebert was connected to Nikki Gillette and, at least according to one of Siebert's college roommates, had been "hot" for her.

Well, join the club, Cliff.

Reed would hate to examine his own feelings for the wild-haired reporter. Lately, they'd become blurred. Confused.

To the point that now he was having erotic dreams or, more correctly, erotic nightmares about her.

That couldn't be good.

Rather than go to bed, he decided to do some more work. He had a few loose ends to tie up, some information to double check before morning. And he didn't trust himself to sleep right now. Not when the dream about Nikki Gillette still lingered and the effect of it was still evident in the hardness pressing against his fly.

Man, he was pathetic. Nikki Gillette was the last woman he should be lusting after. The very last one.

The Survivor gritted his teeth. It had been a long, drawn-out night. One where he'd had to hide within the mask that was himself, where he'd had to pretend, to watch, to wait . . . and then, rowing and digging . . . The exercise had been good, but now he needed sleep. It was almost dawn. He had precious few hours to rest and regain his strength.

But first he had one last duty.

Safe within his private space, he sat at the table and as the smell of damp earth permeated the walls, he pushed the rewind button on his tape player, then hit play and listened to the damning words again.

"Well . . . look what we have here . . ." The female voice that came in through the microphone was that of one of the cops who had searched Nikki Gillette's apartment the night before. He'd seen the cop cars and the vans, even caught a glimpse of Nikki huddled next to Detective Reed, that prick. Reed had been protective of Nikki, his hand had been curled over her arm, as if he owned her.

"See that, here in the fan . . ." the woman cop was saying. She sounded smug and overconfident. The Survivor hated her.

"Yeah, right there . . . clever, huh? . . . another mike. Wireless. Looks like the same kind we found in the coffins. The bastard's probably listening to this right now."

That's right, bitch. It is. And now I'm listening again, and you know what? You can't find me.

"What a sicko," the cop said, and her voice bothered him, grated on his brain.

"Too bad, the party's over you useless piece of shit," the cop said, directly to him. "No more free radio. You'll have to get your jollies somewhere else. *Say-o-nara.*"

There was rattling and a scraping and then the microphone went dead.

You useless piece of shit. No-good, lazy, scumbag. What're you good for? Nothin' that's what . . .

The Survivor quivered inside, wanted to run away and hide. As he had so long ago, hearing the voice that

336

had haunted him for years ricochet off the walls of his brain.

Stupid, stupid, stupid . . . I'm gonna teach you a lesson, boy. One I promise ya, you'll never forget . . .

Rage roiled up inside him.

He wasn't stupid. He was smart. IQ tests had said so and they don't lie, right? But maybe he'd screwed up.

You are a screw-up. Worthless. No good.

He flung himself away from the table, toppling over his chair as he threw his hands over his ears to shut out the noise, the recriminations, the accusations. "I'm not stupid. I'm not!" he yelled, his chin wobbling.

So, now ye're gonna cry. Little girlie-boy. Go ahead, cry . . . show me what a stupid little girl you are.

"I'm not a girl. I'm not stupid!" he yelled, gasping, his breath flying in and out of his lungs.

He was lying. To himself.

He had been foolish. Again.

He slapped his forehead with the heel of his hand over and over again and his hairpiece fell off to lie like a small, denuded dog on the floor.

The cops weren't supposed to find the microphone and figure it out. At least not so quickly. Nikki Gillette, that blabbermouth cunt, had told someone and she was ruining everything. He'd have to up his schedule. That was it. Accelerate.

Slowing his breathing, forcing his heart rate to lower, he climbed off the dirt floor. Picked up the toupee and hung it on a hook. With the others. He had to remain calm, remember his agenda, never falter. Already the next grave was being readied . . .

Calmer, he removed the contacts that turned his eyes from a clear blue to an impenetrable brown. It was time to trim his goatee to a moustache and grow out his sideburns.

His disguises were many. They fooled most people. No one seemed to remember him as he was and that was the way he wanted it. Of course, he'd been much younger then.

He pulled out his scrapbook and found the picture of Nikki—she'd been younger, too, freshfaced and green as a reporter. Her red-gold hair had been longer, her eyes bright and vibrant. Without fear. A daughter any man, even the bastard judge, should take pride in.

But fathers rarely did.

Born of privilege, athletic and beautiful, Nikki Gillette had never had to struggle. "Cunt," he muttered and slammed the book shut.

You expected her to go to the police once she got the note, didn't you? Everything's fine . . . stay calm . . . stay focused.

He reached into his pocket, pulled out a handkerchief and wiped the dots of sweat from his forehead. He couldn't lose it now. He had too much work to do. And it was all coming together. He slipped his fingers into his pocket again and withdrew the tiny cell phone. Neat. Compact. A flip phone. Kind of sexy. Just like its owner.

CHAPTER 22

"Just tell me you're not the fuckin' snitch, okay?" Morrisette was mad as a wet hen as she strode into Reed's office. It was late morning and she had obviously gotten up on the wrong side of bed.

"You know me better than that."

"Do I?" she demanded, slamming the door shut behind her. "The truth of the matter is that I don't know shit. Well, that's not entirely right. I do know that you are off the Grave Robber case, and yet you were with Nikki Gillette last night, and both your and my asses are gonna be in slings if you don't get smart. So tell me again and repeat it slowly, 'I'm not the snitch, Sylvie.'"

He stared at her. "Bad night?"

"Christ, yes. You were there." She ran stiff fingers through her hair, making it stand even farther from her head. With a look over her shoulder to make sure the door was still closed, she lowered her voice, planted both hands on his desk and leaned closer to him. "You and I both know that in order for you to be anywhere near this case you had better keep a low profile, and I mean low. You might want to risk your job, but I don't. I have two kids to support, Reed, so don't fuck with me!"

"This is getting us nowhere."

She stopped short. "Okay. You're right. I just want to nail this bastard."

"So do I."

"Well, do it from the sidelines, will ya? No, better yet, don't do it at all. Leave it to me. I need this job, though, sometimes, I gotta tell ya, I'm ready to take my retirement and run. I do have a life, you know, outside of this place."

"How's it going?"

"Just swell. Bart's decided that he shouldn't have to pay a nickel. Not one nickel, and so we're going to court. Well, you knew that. Priscilla's talking about living with Daddy, and my son . . . well, some kids in preschool are giving him trouble. And then there's this fuck—er, effin' Grave Robber case I'm supposed to crack." She thumped a finger on the paper tucked on the corner of Reed's desk. "You know—the one in which one of the victims was pregnant and involved with my partner and—" She must've read something in his eyes, because she came up short. "Jesus. I need coffee. At least two gallons. Maybe three."

"Don't you want to know what I've found out?"

"You're *not* a part of the investigation. Remember?"

"Last night Sheriff Jed Baldwin got in to see the kid who was attacked in the woods, Prescott Jones. Baldwin faxed me a copy of his interview. It's not much more than we already had, but it's something." Reed slid the three sheets across the desk. "Also, I got hold of Angelina, the maid for Roberta Peters. Here's the address." He slid another sheet onto the first three.

"Also, I've got addresses for most of the people who had access to Nikki Gillette's apartment—filled in the ones she couldn't remember. Some have phone numbers." Another sheet skidded onto the ever-growing pile. "And I was finally able to connect with Reverend Joe. I left a message and he called me back, none too happy about being phoned at five A.M.—it was meditation hour or some such garbage—but when I got through all the double-talk, I figure the mission was taking Roberta Peters financially, but they weren't beneficiaries on her insurance policy. Turns out she has a niece in Charlotte, North Carolina, who gets the bulk of her estate, including Maximus, that's her cat. Here's the name of Roberta Peters's lawyer and the address and phone number of the niece." He pushed those papers onto the pile. "I've also come up with a list of my enemies, people I've wronged and those I've put away. Jerome Marx is number one."

"Airtight alibi."

"I know, but I still included him along with the creeps that I sent to prison and are now out. Take a look at this—there are twelve."

"What?" Morrisette froze.

"Twelve who've gotten out since I've been back in Savannah." He pointed to his compiled list.

"That's downright scary."

"Mmm. The last guy is our good buddy LeRoy Chevalier."

"Shit." She picked up the paper, scanned the list of lowlife bastards who should never have been allowed back into society. "You have addresses for these guys?"

"Got calls into the parole officers, but I gave them your name. As you pointed out, I'm off the investigation. Start with Chevalier, though, his conviction was twelve years ago. The twelfth guy, in the twelfth year.

It could be nothing, but there was something about that trial that bothers me."

"What?"

He glanced out the window where Morrisette saw the usual group of pigeons crowding the ledge. "First of all, the judge was Ronald Gillette, Nikki Gillette's dad."

"He presided over a lot of cases."

"But Nikki was just working part-time and she nearly got the case thrown out of court."

"If we looked up all the cases where a reporter was out of line, we'd fill this room."

"I know, but there has to be some connection. I think we should, no, *you* should find Chevalier. His parole officer will have an address."

"I'll check out all of these jokers. See that they're walkin' the straight and narrow," Morrisette agreed. "Twelve of 'em. In twelve years. You don't suppose they're in this together . . . I've been considering the apostle angle, but it's not fitting."

"Farfetched."

She eyed the typed pages. Ran her thumb along the edge of the stack. Looked up at him and let out her breath. "Jesus, Reed, don't you ever sleep?"

"When I have to."

"Should I know anything else?" she asked, obviously mollified.

"Yeah." Skewering her with his gaze, he reached for his jacket. "You should know one final thing. I'm not the fuckin' snitch."

"So, now the killer's talking directly to you?" Norm

Metzger didn't bother hiding his skepticism as he hung his bomber jacket on one of the pegs on the coatrack near the back door of the *Sentinel*'s offices.

Dealing with Norm was the last thing Nikki wanted to do. It was nearly noon and even though she should have been keyed up because her story had hit page one again, she was too tired to feel her usual rush. Metzger only made her lack of enthusiasm worse. She hooked her raincoat over a peg and hoped he would shut up.

No such luck.

"A dialog with the killer." Unwrapping his scarf, he added, "That's damned convenient."

"Convenient?" she fired back. "Oh, yeah, right. Real convenient when the guy breaks into my place." She was tired and grouchy from a short, sleepless night in the bed she'd slept in as a kid. Her body had been weary, but her mind had raced, as if she'd downed eight cups of coffee before trying to burrow under the covers. She'd kept thinking about the Grave Robber, about the victims, about her house, about the number twelve, about Simone and Andrew and about Pierce Reed. Her mind had been a revolving carousel of images that had whirled faster and faster and driven sleep away. When she'd finally dozed she'd had dreams of corpses filling her apartment only to disintegrate in front of her eyes. The skeletons had turned to dust while somewhere in the shadows a killer had laughed, a chilling sound that had caused her heart to race and a cold sweat to cover her skin.

She'd forced herself out of bed only to face her parents, creeping down the stairs to hear the tail end of an argument that evaporated the minute she walked into the kitchen and her tight-lipped mother had caught sight of her. Charlene had shot her husband a *don't you say a word* glare and then managed a smile.

In the next hour, while guzzling coffee and trying to wake up, Nikki had heard a dozen times over all the reasons why she should give up her interest in crime reporting. Even her father had suggested she go back to school, get a degree in law, follow the old man's footsteps . . .

No way. Law had been her father's dream. Andrew's ambition. But now, facing Norm's petulant diatribe, she wondered if maybe she should take her mother's advice.

"The killer broke into your apartment?" Norm demanded.

"A couple of days ago."

"That what was going on last night?" he said. "I heard about it on the police band, but I was tied up and . . . Wait a minute, are you all right?"

"The truth?" she asked, hiking her purse strap higher on her shoulder. "No, I'm not all right. Not by a long shot. Contrary to what you might think, I'm not willing to"—she held up one finger—"A. Sell my soul"— another finger shot up—"B. Sell my body"—she raised another finger—"or C., allow some creep to break into my place and touch my stuff just for a story." She started to walk away then when she noticed Kevin Deeter, earphones in place, hanging out near the candy machine. He was eyeing the display as if the vending machine were dispensing the word of God, backlit in neon, all for a dollar. As she started to walk by she saw his reflection in the glass covering the Snickers bars, Cheetos and red licorice. His expression was dark, his eyes sliding to one side, as if he wasn't interested in the snacks at all, but had been listening to her conversation with Norm.

What was that all about? Edging closer, she poured herself a cup of coffee from the glass pot still warming on a hot plate nearby. As she stirred a little cream into her mug, she pretended to peruse the offerings and whispered, "What looks good?"

"What? Oh. Uh, everything."

Lowering her voice further still, she swirled the stir stick and said, "I'm thinking about M&M peanuts, but they're all out."

"No, they aren't." He tapped a thick finger against the glass. "See there? E-5. M&M peanuts."

Frowning, she took a sip of coffee and stared at the snack machine where his pudgy finger was putting an oily print on the glass. "You're right."

" 'Course I am. They're right there."

"Mmm. So how can you hear me?"

"What?"

"Even though you're supposedly plugged in to your music, you can hear what I say no matter how quiet I whisper. I find that a little peculiar. So, what's with the earphones . . . Are they not working or are they just part of a disguise so that you can listen to everyone else's conversations?"

"Man, are you paranoid, or what?" A red flush stole up his neck, blooming through his patchy beard shadow. "Norm's right about you."

"Is he?" She blew across her cup but kept her eyes trained on him.

"Yeah. I–I was just taking a break from the music."

"Most people do that by taking off their headsets, Kevin."

"I'm not like most people."

"I'll second that."

His flush deepened and a vein throbbed over one eye. His jaw tensed and for the first time she was aware that beneath his baggy shirts and jeans, he was a fit, able-bodied man. A young man. One who outweighed her by nearly a hundred pounds. One who could possibly have a rage problem.

"I didn't mean it that way," he said, defending himself.

"Take it whatever way you want." She narrowed her eyes at him. "I bet you know everything that's going on here, don't you? You pretend to be in your own little world all the time. But when you work on people's computers, you're eavesdropping on conversations and reading other people's E-mail."

"I don't—"

"Save it for someone who believes it, okay?" She walked away then, making a beeline for her desk and sloshing some of the hot coffee over her wrist and onto the sleeve of her shirt. "Damn." Celeste waved some messages frantically at her and she collected three scraps of paper indicating that Dr. Francis had called.

"She wouldn't leave a voice mail," Celeste said, tossing her streaked locks over one shoulder.

"Hey, where the hell have you been?" Trina rolled her desk chair away from her cubicle. "Wow, Nikki . . . you look like you haven't slept in a week. Make that two weeks."

"That's probably being kind." She pulled a Kleenex from the box on her desk and dabbed at the spill. "I feel like it's been forever."

"So, being a crime reporter is killing you."

"Something like that." She tossed the tissue at her wastebasket and missed. From the corner of her eye she noticed that both Kevin and Norm had retreated to their own desks. "So, what's been going on around here?"

"I think you have a secret admirer."

"A what?" She took a sip of her coffee.

"Look what came for you today." Trina reached around her monitor and retrieved a glass vase filled with an explosion of red and white carnations.

"You kept them?"

"Who knew when you'd get here. No reason for them to go to waste."

"I suppose." Shoving aside a ridiculous, fleeting thought of Pierce Reed, Nikki opened the small envelope and read the note.

Congratulations on all your success. Dinner soon?
Love,
Sean

Her stomach turned sour. "Man, he's laying it on thick," Nikki whispered, adjusting a few of the blooms and setting the vase on her desk.

"Who?"

"Sean."

"He's back in the picture?"

"No way, but he claims he wants to be."

Trina lifted an eyebrow. "Maybe he's truly sorry for being such a jerk and now that he's sown his wild oats and realized that not all women are as cool as you are, he's making his play."

"Doesn't sound like the Sean I know."

"Oh, give the guy a chance."

"So you don't believe in the 'once burned, twice shy,' adage."

"Isn't it 'once bitten, twice shy' . . . oh, whatever, it doesn't matter. As for me, I believe in love. I'm totally an incurable romantic."

"Who's never married."

"I said I like 'romance,' not drudgery." Trina's cell phone jangled with a Latin tune.

"I don't even believe in the romance part," Nikki said, though a part of her suspected that she was stretching the truth a bit. She didn't like to think of herself as one of those clingy, lovelorn single women looking for a possible husband in every man she met. And she wasn't. But if the right man happened to cross her path, she might just sing a different tune. She just couldn't cop to it. At least not now, not before she proved herself.

Trina rolled into her cubicle and whispered into her cell phone while Nikki sorted through her mail and E-mail, finding nothing out of the ordinary, no other notes from the Grave Robber. Her voice mail was filled with congratulations from some friends for her latest story on the Grave Robber and she had a few calls from reporters at rival papers and local news stations, all of whom hoped to cozy up to her and get an interview.

"Nikki, this is Stacey Baxter, remember, we went to school together. I'm with WRAW in Louisville and I'd love to talk to you about what's going on with the Grave Robber. Give me a call back at . . ."

"Nikki Gillette? Max O'Dell, WKAM. Heard about the break-in. Call me at . . ."

"Ms. Gillette. Steve Mendleson with *The Spirit*. My number is . . ."

So, now she knew how it felt to be hounded by the press, she thought, eyeing the flowers and plucking off a few petals that had already started to turn brown. No doubt the flowers had been on sale, a bargain basement bouquet. It was just the way Sean had always operated she thought as the voice mail messages streamed into her ear.

"Nikki, it's Lily. Okay, I was out of line last night. Way out of line. Sorry. I'm gonna be out today, so I'll catch up with you later."

"Nicole? This is Dr. Francis. I saw your article and it was fine, but I think it should be part of a series about the school district. Call me."

"Wow, look who's on the front page all the time!" Simone's voice was a breath of fresh air. "Pretty soon you'll be getting a swelled head and you'll forget the little people like me. Let's celebrate. We could go out right after class tonight . . ."

Damn, Nikki thought, tired to the bone. The last thing

she wanted to do was anything more strenuous than lying in front of the television with a bag of chips.

". . . I can safely assume you'll make it tonight, right? Maybe, with your newfound celebrity you'll be able to convince Jake to join us? I'll buy. *Again.*" She laughed. "Hey, it looks like I might move to Charlotte, after all! Well, unless I can make something work with Jake. Call me and I'll fill you in on all the details."

Nikki didn't want to think about Simone moving away. It was too damned depressing. Nor did she want to have to admit to Simone that she was considering blowing off kickboxing. It would be better to call her tomorrow, once the class was over. Nikki was a firm believer in asking forgiveness rather than permission. Tonight, Simone would be disappointed, maybe even angry about Nikki skipping out, but tomorrow, especially if things went well with Jake, Simone would have forgotten all about the fact that Nikki had stood her up again. She only felt a little niggle of guilt as the next message began to play. "Hi, Nik. It's me. I'd really like to see you again." Sean's voice. She dropped her hand, letting a few petals fall on her desk. There was something about the timbre and expression in Sean's voice she found unnerving. Though she didn't care for him any longer, just the fact that he'd dumped her seemed to make her overreact to him. "I heard about what happened, the break-in and all," he'd recorded. "Pretty scary stuff, Nik. Hope you're okay. Why don't you give me a buzz?" It would be a cold day in hell before that happened. "My cell number is . . ."

She didn't bother to write it down, nor did she intend to call him or anyone else for that matter. Not even Simone. Not today. She didn't have time. She had another story to write about the Grave Robber, one with more information . . .

The recorder beeped, indicating there was another voice mail message. She listened, but no one left a message. Whoever had called must've thought better of it because there was a pause with some low-level background noise, then the distinct sound of a phone clicking as it was hung up.

Whoever it was would call back she figured as she turned her attention to her computer to recheck her E-mail before digging into her next story. She found more of the same kind of well wishes and requests that had been on the phone. But there was no new message from the Grave Robber. No dancing coffins or twirling, disintegrating corpses.

She tapped her pencil on the desk.

For the moment, the killer seemed to be silent.

Which was good. Right?

Or just the calm before the storm?

"Nikki? I can't hear you. You're cutting out." Dashing out of her apartment, trying to put up her umbrella while hauling her athletic bag and cradling the phone between her shoulder and ear, Simone was having a helluva time hearing her friend. Nikki's voice was breaking up and garbled, impossible to understand over the whistle of the wind and splatter of thick raindrops.

"Simone . . . meet at . . ."

"Meet where? You're coming to the class tonight, aren't you?" Simone stepped around a puddle and caught the edge of her umbrella on the hedge that surrounded the parking lot. Raindrops slid icily through her hair. "Damn it." The trouble with her best friend was that Nikki was a flake. Pure and simple. But Simone loved her and not just because Nikki was Andrew's sister and the only member of the Gillette family who would speak to her, though that, in and of itself, was something. "Don't tell me you're trying to weasel out of exercise."

"No!" Nikki's voice sounded weird. Stressed. She seemed to be whispering. "Meet me . . . Galleria . . . parking lot, third floor . . . Important . . . about . . . Andrew."

"What? What about Andrew?" Simone asked and the wind and rain was instantly forgotten. "Nikki." Oh, geez, she'd lost her. Then she heard a spurt over the rush of the wind. "Let's . . . a drink . . . Cassan . . ."

"A drink before class at Cassandra's?" Simone said, feeling the rain run down her neck. "I'll be there. Around seven. In the restaurant. *Not* in the damned parking lot. Are you nuts? There's a killer on the loose, remember?" She managed to unlock her door. "If you get to Cassandra's before I do, order me a martini. Vodka. Two olives."

Her umbrella turned inside out.

"Shit. Nikki? Are you still there?"

But the connection had faded. She tossed the phone into her car, did a miserable job of folding the umbrella and left it to drip on the backseat near her sodden athletic bag.

Leave it to Nikki to be overly dramatic, Simone thought as she slid behind the wheel. Checking her reflection in the rearview mirror she decided the damage was minimal. She reapplied lip gloss so that the sheen was perfect, then pulled at a strand of her damp, now windblown hair to make it look even less "done" and more carefree, which was probably better. She had the impression that Jake liked athletic, strong women who weren't "high maintenance." Self-confident women attracted him, she was certain. "Gay, my ass," she said, starting the BMW and pulling out of her parking spot.

Rain pelted the car as the storm swept through the city streets, and from the corner of her eye she saw motion.

Goose bumps raised on her skin.

For a second she had the sensation that someone was watching her. Hiding just out of her line of vision. Instantly, she remembered the creep in the restaurant the last time she and Nikki had gotten together. But that had been days before. Biting her lip, she stared hard at the corner where she'd seen the movement. A bedraggled dog, head and tail down, loped across the street and fled between two tall buildings. Simone's heart rate slowed and she berated herself for being such a silly goose. Nonetheless, she glanced around the alleys and buildings. She saw no one through the BMW's rain-spattered windows, nor in any of her mirrors—no unholy monster, no dark figure, no hulking boogey man ready to pounce on her. In fact, there was nothing out of the ordinary. Just a few cars, and a couple of skateboarders hurrying along the sidewalk trying to outrun the storm. All was as it should be.

Her case of nerves was just because of Nikki's incessant talk about a serial killer, the Grave Robber, for God's sake. It was nothing. Still, Simone's hands felt clammy around the steering wheel as she drove first to the bank before it closed and then to the dry cleaners. She even managed to stop and pick up a prescription and a few groceries before it was time to meet Nikki and placed a call to Nikki's cell phone. Of course, Nikki didn't answer, so Simone called her friend's apartment and left a message on her recorder.

Fortunately the storm passed quickly, leaving in its wake a thickening mist. Wet streets glimmered under the street lamps, and leaves and debris clogged the sewer drains in the roads. Rush hour was over, traffic was thankfully thin, and only a few people had ventured onto the sidewalks. Here and there, Christmas lights winked merrily through the fog, a reminder of the season. She passed a church with a nativity scene posed beneath the spreading branches of a live oak. Instantly, she experienced that same old pang of longing for Andrew, the pain that didn't lessen with each passing Christmas season.

"Get over it," she muttered and decided she really did have to move. There was a possibility of a job in Charlotte and she should just take the plunge and move. Cut all ties to this place with its bad memories.

Simone pulled into the parking lot of the Galleria

and had no trouble finding a space on the first floor. Forget the third. Why walk any farther than she had to?

The lot was fairly deserted, only a few vehicles parked in the spaces. Though this was normal and she and Nikki parked here on a regular basis, she was still a little edgy. Making certain no one was lurking near the stairwell or elevator shaft, Simone grabbed her purse and locked the car behind her, then jogged to the restaurant. No murderer leapt from the shadows. No one was hiding near the exit. Simone walked the half a block to the restaurant without anyone accosting her.

Inside, Nikki wasn't waiting for her. No surprise. Nikki's M.O. was to always run late. *Or bag out completely.*

Surely, not tonight.

Simone slid into a booth near the front door and ordered two drinks—a martini for herself and a lemon drop for Nikki—from a sunny waitress with a thick drawl and braces. The girl looked barely seventeen, surely not old enough to serve liquor, though she cheerily reappeared with the chilled, stemmed glasses within minutes.

Cassandra's wasn't doing a banner business tonight. Only a few other patrons sat at the tables and booths that filled the small space with its black and white floor tiles and matching tabletops.

Simone studied the bar menu while sipping her drink and listening to Christmas carols from the jukebox. Elvis's rendition of "Blue Christmas" seemed to be the favorite as the minutes passed and a breathless Nikki Gillette didn't sweep into the restaurant. Simone plucked the olives from her martini with her teeth and looked at her watch. Fifteen minutes had passed. She finished her drink. Twenty minutes. Wonderful. Late again. "Come on, Nikki," Simone muttered under her breath.

The ebullient waitress stopped by and flashed her perennial schoolgirl grin. "Can I get you anything else?"

"A new best friend."

"What? Oh." The plastered-on smile chipped away. "So . . . do you want another drink or . . . something from the bar menu?"

Simone hesitated, but decided she had nothing to lose. "Sure. Why not? Another drink, I think." She tapped a fingernail on the rim of her empty martini glass. "Another one."

"And . . . ?" The girl glanced at Nikki's untouched glass. The rim of sugar was unbroken, the clear liquid unmoving around a curl of lemon rind.

"Just leave it. She may still show up. This is kind of a constant problem with her." Simone glanced at her watch and sighed. Nikki was nearly half an hour late. Not good news. Simone could almost hear the excuses already. She imagined Nikki flying into the kickboxing class after it had already started. She would be breathless as she explained about a "rewrite" that she wasn't satisfied with, a "deadline" that couldn't be ignored, or "research" that had to be done "ASAP."

Fifteen minutes later, Simone finished her second

drink. The lemon drop was still sweating across the table from her. "Great," she muttered and thought about downing Nikki's favorite drink herself, but decided against it. She did still have to walk to the gym and then be able to perform the exercise routines. One more drink and she wouldn't be able to do anything more than fall on her butt when she tried to strike a target with her foot.

She signaled for the bill, left the waitress with a ten dollar tip and, carrying her bag, started jogging toward the gym. The mist had turned into a thicker, shifting fog in the time that she'd been inside, the streets seeming darker.

Damn Nikki. She was always leaving Simone in the lurch.

It wasn't that Nicole Gillette wasn't responsible, just not reliable. But she was good-hearted. Nikki's downfall was that she was totally obsessed when it came to her job or what she perceived as her job. She was so hell-bent on becoming an ace crime reporter that she lost sight of everything, and everyone else. Even now, Simone guessed, Nikki was probably ferreting out clues as to the identity of the Grave Robber.

It would be a good change to move away, make new friends, connect with people who weren't related to or had known Andrew.

A stab of sadness cut through her. She'd loved him so much and he'd broken up with her, after vowing to adore her, after asking her to marry him, after learning that he'd been rejected by Harvard. Why? Had he thought he couldn't measure up to what she'd wanted in a husband, or had it been more . . . another woman?

Who knew? Who would ever know? The sorry part of it was she doubted she would ever love a man the way she'd so passionately and ardently fallen for Andrew Whitmore Gillette. She'd given him her heart, her virginity, and her self-respect. A part of her figured she'd never get any of them back.

"Oh, stop it," she muttered, angry at herself. "All those years of counseling and you still feel this way? Get ahold of yourself."

Light-headed from the martinis, she noticed for the first time how thin the traffic was, how deserted the street. Not that it mattered. She was so close to the class. As she rounded the final corner, she spied the lights of the gym burning warmly in the night. Beacons in the empty, foggy street, the patches of light from the windows were a bit blurry, probably a combination of the surrounding mist and the alcohol creating a warm fuzz in her brain. Somewhere in the distance she heard the sound of Christmas carols and she was reminded again that it would soon be Christmas, the time of year when she'd fallen so head over heels in love with Andrew Gillette. Why she hadn't stopped thinking about him, she didn't understand. What was it that Nikki wanted to tell her about her brother, now, a dozen years after his death?

Squinting, she thought she could make out Jake's SUV, which was parked under a street lamp. Simone grinned. Jake Vaughn wasn't the first man she'd been interested in after Andrew. Since Andrew's death, she'd dated, gone with and slept with a few other guys. None had captivated her the way Nikki's brother had, but Jake had possibilities. Serious possibilities. He certainly was the most challenging man she'd met in a long, long while. If he would take the bait and show some interest in her, she might not have to move after all.

She increased her pace. The gym was only a block away—just past the alley. She heard a strange sound, a hiss, like something slicing through the air. Turning her head toward the windowpanes of a darkened storefront, she saw her reflection and . . . something else . . . the shadowy, menacing figure of a man lurking between two parked cars. He sprang upward, pulling hard against something.

A rope?

No! She bolted. Adrenaline pumped through her blood. Fear shot through her brain. The man jerked hard. That same moment, her shin encountered something taut and invisible and thin enough to slice through her jogging pants and cut into her flesh. Pain screamed up her leg.

"Oooh!" she cried, pitching forward. The ground rushed up at her. She put out an arm to catch herself and hit the ground hard.

Snap!

Agony jettisoned up her arm. Her bag flew out of her hand to land on the pavement.

"Oh, God!" Whatever had caught her feet was tangling her, cutting into her flesh, a sharp spiderweb snaring her, eating into her. And her arm. It ached so badly she nearly passed out. "Help!" she screamed, writhing in agony. "Someone help me!"

"Shut up!" a deep voice snarled. A sweaty palm covered her mouth and she tried to bite, to roll away. To escape. But the more she squirmed, the more enmeshed she became. Oh, God, who was he? Why was he doing this? Twisting her neck, she caught a glimpse of his face in the darkness . . . a face she recognized. The guy in the restaurant . . . but even so, now she knew who he was. Realized he wasn't a stranger at all.

Oh, no! Oh, Jesus, no! Vainly she tried to free herself, but he was strong, determined. Muscles like steel, holding her against the wet sidewalk, his body pinning hers. Writhing, she prayed for help. Surely someone would see her . . . come to her aid . . . other people should be going into the gym . . . or driving by. *Please, please, help me!*

"Remember me," he whispered against her ear, and she felt terror burrow deep into her heart. "Remember what you did to me? It's time to pay." Then she spied the needle, a fine, thin weapon glinting evilly in the fog-shrouded night.

Her blood turned to ice.

No!

Vainly she tried to kick, to swing at him, to escape whatever horror he had in mind, but she couldn't scoot away and she watched in sheer terror as he plunged the vile needle deep into her shoulder.

Simone fought, but his weight pinned her down and her arms were suddenly heavy and useless, her trapped legs unable to move. Panic tore through her as the sluggishness invaded all her body parts. She tried vainly to scream but couldn't. Her tongue was thick, her vocal cords immobile.

The streetlights dimmed, the fog thickened in her mind, and merciful blackness dragged her under.

God be with me, she thought desperately and only hoped that death would come swiftly.

CHAPTER 23

"Wait up!"

Reed, jacket collar hiked around his neck, was leaving the station. He didn't break stride but Morrisette dashed through the puddle-strewn lot and around two parked cruisers to catch up with him.

"Jesus, what crappy weather," she growled.

Night had already fallen, streetlights glowing through the thickening fog, headlights few and far between. Rush hour was over; traffic no longer snarled and slowed. "Look, Reed," Morrisette said as they reached his El Dorado, "I thought about it and I guess I came on a little strong this morning."

"You guess right." His keys were already in his hand.

"So, you're pissed, right?" She was reaching into her purse, digging, presumably, for her pack of Marlboros.

"You're batting a thousand." Unlocking the car, he didn't bother to glance in her direction.

"Hey, I'm just doing my job."

"I know." He swung the car door open and the interior light flashed on. "So, do it. You don't need to apologize."

"Come on, Reed, when did you get to be so thin-skinned?" She found a crumpled pack and shook out a cigarette. "You know what the drill is."

"Was there something you wanted to tell me?"

"Yeah." She clicked her lighter to the end of her filter tip and drew in hard. "First of all, we haven't got much out of Nikki Gillette's apartment. No fingerprints or any other hard evidence." Morrisette blew out a cloud of smoke. It dissipated into the gathering fog. "She was right. The door and windows weren't forced, so we have to assume whoever got in had a key—he either had it made, stole it, or borrowed it from someone who had one, most likely Ms. Gillette.

"The microphone we found in her bedroom is identical to the two we found in the coffins and we're checking with stores and distributors who deal in all that electronic shit, including on-line dealers. All the mikes are wireless, kind of sophisticated, so we figure our guy is probably a techno geek. We're looking for anyone who bought at least three of that brand and make of microphone and the listening devices that go with them."

"Good."

"So, I guess I'm telling you that we're done searching her apartment. We've got all we can get from there." Morrisette took another drag. "Siebert called her already. Gave her the green light. She can move back in."

"Why tell me?"

"Because I thought you'd want to know." She lifted a brow as smoke drifted from her nostrils. "Right?"

"Yeah." A cruiser rolled in and parked two slots down from the Caddy.

"And there's something else." He heard the tension underlying her words; realized she was about to give him bad news. She glanced back at the station before meeting his eyes. "The DNA results on Barbara Jean Marx's baby came back."

His shoulders tightened.

"It confirmed the blood test."

"Great." He felt as if he'd been kicked in the gut. Not that he hadn't expected it, but this was so final. So unequivocal. A blood test left a little doubt. DNA did not.

She looked at him hard, her eyes squinting against the darkness. "If it's worth anything, I'm sorry."

His jaw slid to one side. Cold air collected on his face.

"I know. It's a bitch." Morrisette flicked her cigarette onto the pavement. Its red tip glowed for a second before sizzling and dying in a puddle. A brief little light. Extinguished quickly. "Hang in there." Without so much as a glance over her shoulder, she walked toward the back door of the station.

Standing in the parking lot in the night, Reed felt suddenly alone. Empty inside. Hollow.

He shoved his hands into the pockets of his raincoat and stared up at the heavens. Above the glow from the city lights, there was nothing but cloud cover. He should have experienced something more than this gnawing vacuum within him, something akin to loss. But how can you lose something you never really had?

The baby hadn't been planned. Nor had it been wanted. It would have complicated his life immeasurably and yet . . . and yet he experienced a deep-seated desolation that would only be assuaged by vengeance. That, at least, he could fix. He planned on finding the son of a bitch who had done this and stringing the bastard up by his miserable balls.

Climbing behind the wheel of his El Dorado, he jabbed his keys into the ignition. A look in the rearview mirror reflected haunted eyes that were dry but seething with pent-up anger, a beard-darkened jaw that was set in stone, lips that folded over his teeth in new-found determination.

"Shit," he growled. "Goddamned son of a bitch!" He threw the car into gear and backed up, then rammed the gearshift into drive. He punched the accelerator. The Caddy shot out of the parking lot and onto the foggy street.

Reed considered stopping by the local watering hole for a drink or two or six. Tonight would be a great night to get blotto and have the barkeep pour him into a cab. Jack Daniels sounded like a pretty damned good friend.

But Jack couldn't help.

It wouldn't change a damned thing.

When Reed woke up with a hangover pounding at his skull tomorrow morning, Bobbi Jean would still be dead. The baby would still never have had a chance to breathe a single breath. And Reed would have to live with the fact that somehow, some way, their deaths were his fault. He was the connection. The damned Grave Robber was talking to *him*. And killing with ease.

But what about Roberta Peters?

How is she connected to you?

He remembered walking through her home and sensed something . . . a feeling he couldn't identify. Like déjà vu, but that wasn't quite it. An unformed idea nagged at him and wouldn't gel . . . What the hell was it—something to do with Nikki Gillette? Had Nikki written an article on Roberta Peters? Known her? There was only one way to find out.

He eased off the gas and maneuvered the big car through the city streets, past shops bedecked with Christmas greenery and a few pedestrians on the sidewalks. At the offices of the *Sentinel* he found a parking space near the employee lot. Nikki Gillette's Subaru was parked near a short hedge. So she was working late. Again. A fact he'd learned long ago when she'd dogged him on other cases. Ambitious to a fault, she spent more time at the newspaper than at home. But she wouldn't work all night. Rather than be seen in the offices of the *Sentinel* where he could again be accused of being the police department's leak, he decided to wait outside. There was already enough speculation about him as it was. Morrisette wasn't the first cop to suggest he might be the rat who was filling the press with inside information.

Last summer he'd been a damned hero solving the Montgomery case, and now, less than six months later, he was under suspicion of being a snitch. A classic case of damned if you do and goddamned if you don't.

He slid the seat back, stretching his legs, and waited, his gaze glued to the front door as people drifted in and out of the brick building where the offices of the *Sentinel* were housed. As it was late, more people left the building than walked inside.

Reed recognized a few faces. Norm Metzger, wrapped in a wool coat and scarf, drove away in a Chevy Impala while Tom Fink tooled off in a restored vintage Corvette. A kid he recognized as Fink's nephew . . . what was his name? Deeter, that was it, Kevin Deeter, arrived in a truck with a canopy and walked into the offices. He wore an oversize Braves jacket and a baseball cap pulled low over his face. Reed watched the kid and noted that Deeter paused just outside of the light mounted over the front door, then fiddled with a cassette and donned earphones. He jammed the cassette into a pocket of his baggy jeans, then pushed open the door and stepped inside.

He was an oddball.

But the city was filthy with nutcases of one kind or another.

Reed settled onto his back and wondered why the Grave Robber was communicating with Nikki Gillette. He had half an ear turned to the police band that he kept at a low volume. What was the connection? Did the killer inherently know that she was hungry, that she was determined to make a name for herself? Had he been watching her? Or did he know her personally?

Condensation collected on the windshield.

What was the significance of twelve?

Gaze never sliding from the doorway, he thought of all the combinations he'd come up with during the past few days. Twelve what?

Months in the year?

Hours in a day? Or conversely, hours in a night?

He bit his lip, eyes narrowing.

Apostles?

Doughnuts in a dozen?

Members of a jury?

Signs of the zodiac?

Inches in a foot?

One, two, buckle my shoe.

Three, four, lock the door.

Five, six, pick up sticks.

And so forth. . . . What was the twelfth part?

Eleven, twelve,

Dig and delve.

Was that right? Hell, it had been years since he'd thought of that. Delve for what?

For bodies in coffins.

He zeroed in on that. Maybe there was something to the old nursery rhyme . . . or maybe not. The killer hadn't mentioned it in any of his pathetic communiques.

A group of six carolers strolled by, harmonizing on "Silent Night." Christmas lights twinkled in the shrubbery surrounding the buildings. Men dressed in Santa suits rang bells and collected for charity on the street corners.

Christmas.

Could that be it?

The twelve days of Christmas?

They started on December twenty-fifth and ran to January sixth, Epiphany—or at least he thought so. It had been a long while since he'd gone to Sunday school, hadn't heard a bit of Bible instruction since he was a kid up near Dahlonega. But he was fairly certain that was right.

How did the carol about the twelve days go?

Twelve lords a-leaping, no, no wrong. Twelve drummers drumming. That was it. Twelve damned drummers. But, so what? Big deal. What did drummers have to do with anything?

Before he could analyze the song, he spied Nikki Gillette as she strode through the glass door with a slim black woman Reed didn't recognize. They paused under the building's overhang, Nikki hiking up the collar of a tan raincoat that cinched tight around her small waist, her friend adjusting an umbrella.

Nikki's face was alive. Animated. Beautiful in a way that disturbed Reed. She was talking wildly as the wind blew her red-blond hair around her face. Together the women hurried to the parking lot, then got into separate cars. The black woman's Volkswagen Jetta sped away quickly while Nikki's hatchback took a little while to start. Once the Subaru kicked into gear, Nikki hit the throttle full-bore and barely stopped before entering the street.

Reed followed.

He had no trouble keeping up with Nikki's silver car, nor did he try to hide the fact that he was tailing her down the narrow streets leading to her apartment, through the historic district, past large homes with raised porches, tall windows, and ornate grillwork festooned with garlands and wreaths. Her little car bounced down cobblestone streets and paved roads until she pulled into the alley behind her apartment house.

Reed parked behind her, turning off his headlights as she opened her car door. "Well, well, well. Detective Reed. My new best friend. You know, for years you wouldn't even return my calls and now, here you are in the flesh. Again. You weren't kidding about this private bodyguard stuff, were you?"

"I rarely 'kid.'"

"I've noticed. But you might want to give it a try." She winked at him and offered the hint of a dimple, which was nearly his undoing. "Lighten up."

"I'll keep that in mind."

"Yeah, right," she said as if she didn't believe it, but even in the darkness, he noticed that her eyes twinkled a bit as she baited him. Flirted with him.

Don't even think this way. This is Nikki Gillette you're thinking about. Ronald Gillette's daughter. A hungry reporter always looking for an angle and a story.

She pushed open the gate and it creaked upon old hinges. "Detective Morrisette wouldn't give me any information about what's going on with the investigation."

See, what did I tell you? Always on the job. Don't let yourself get involved, Reed.

"I don't think there is anything. We're still checking things out."

"You, too? I thought you were off—"

"Let's not go into that," he suggested. They passed by a fountain that gurgled near the bole of a huge magnolia tree.

"There you are!" Reed recognized Fred Cooper, the landlord. An oval-shaped man with a falsetto voice, Fred bustled around the corner. His nose was too big for his face and his rimless glasses were a little tilted over the bridge of a small nose. Reed was reminded of all of the pictures he'd seen of Humpty-Dumpty. "I wanted to talk to you." Thin lips pursed.

"What is it, Fred?" Nikki paused at the bottom step. "You remember Detective Reed."

He stopped dead in his tracks. "Yes. Oh." Some of his gumption evaporated. "Don't tell me there's more trouble!"

Reed said, "I'm just escorting Ms. Gillette home."

"Why?" Fred asked nervously, his gaze darting around the yard as if certain dead bodies would pop out of the ground at any second. "Do you think whoever broke into the apartment is back? Oh, my God, that would just be the worst. I've got to tell you that everyone in the building is nervous. *Extremely* nervous." He adjusted his glasses and focused on Nikki. "They don't like the fact that you're attracting the attention of this killer, this Grave Robber, with your articles about him. It makes the tenants jumpy." His hands were moving quickly as he gestured wildly to an apartment doorway. "Brenda Hammond on the first floor wants stronger locks on the doors and even more bars on the windows, and Mrs. Fitz, in 201, is considering moving. Can you believe that?" He wrung his hands in agitation. "She's been here thirteen years and now, after last night, she's ready to jump ship. Already packing."

"I don't think anyone else is a target," Nikki said calmly, though the corners of her mouth were tight.

"But how do you know?" Fred demanded. "And what's this 'anyone else'? Do you think *you're* a target, because if you are, that would mean he'll be back. For the love of God, we can't have a murderer stalking around the premises looking to get at you. Or . . . or anyone!" He was really upset now. He turned his fearful gaze on Reed. "Are the police providing round-the-clock protection for Ms. Gillette? Will there be extra patrols in this area? Surveillance?" He glanced nervously toward the street where several cars had been parked.

"The department is taking all the appropriate steps."

"'The appropriate steps?' Meaning what? That just sounds like the company line to me." He folded his arms over his ample chest.

"Believe me, Mr. Cooper, we are doing everything possible to get this guy. Just advise your tenants to be careful, use their heads, don't go out alone and keep their doors and windows locked. Those who have security systems should use them. Those who don't should get them installed."

"And who will pay for that? Me?" Cooper was shaking his balding head, the horror of spending money edging out his fear of the killer. Temporarily. "Wait a minute." He refocused. "Oh, dear God, you *do* think he'll be back!"

"I don't know what he'll do, unfortunately. I'm only giving you the advice I'd give anyone in the city."

"This is all your doing," Cooper said, his features pinching as he glared at Nikki. His lips were pursed so tightly they turned white. "I warned you once before when you had that problem with that Sellwood boy."

"It was my problem, not Corey Sellwood's. I made a mistake." She was getting angry now. Reed sensed the full-blown fight before it erupted.

"But he threatened you. Ever since then I've wondered if he'd try to get revenge by doing something outrageous. Or ugly. Or . . . or horrible. I've even thought he was the kind that might try to get even by torching this place."

"Fred," she said, holding up a hand, trying to rein in her temper, "you worry too much."

"And you don't worry enough. I'm serious about this, Nikki. I can't have all the tenants here worried that someone might break in and kill them. It's damned irresponsible of you to bring this kind of terror here."

"All right. You've made your point. You've warned me," she snapped. "So, now what? Do you want me to move? Are you suggesting that you're going to evict me? Because some creep broke into my apartment?"

"Evict? Oh . . . no . . . I would never . . ." Cooper glanced anxiously at Reed. "I, um, just wanted to let you know that the other tenants are upset."

"Fine. You've done your duty. I got it." Leaving the manager standing on the walkway, Nikki stormed up the stairs. "I can't believe it," she muttered under her breath. "Like I'm *trying* to have my place broken into!"

"He'll get over it."

"You don't know Fred!" she said, loud enough for the manager, still hovering at the base of the stairs, to hear. "He never gets over anything! He's beyond anal!"

Two steps behind, Reed swallowed a smile and while following her, attempted not to notice the back of her leg peeking through the slit in the back of her raincoat as she climbed.

"Here goes nothing," she said, reaching for her keys.

Reed caught hold of her wrist, then wrested her key ring from her fingers. "I'll go first."

"Wait a minute." She turned affronted green eyes up to his and he noticed the way they were shaped over a sturdy, straight nose, the way they darkened with the night. "This is my house, Detective. You don't have to act like I'm a damsel in distress or anything." Her hair was damp, her lips shiny from the mist, her anger at the manager, Reed and all men in general, palpable. And ridiculously sexy.

"Damsel in distress? Nikki Gillette? Trust me, I *never* think of you in those terms."

"Good."

"But I'll go in first, anyway. Consider it part of my job." He slid the key into its lock, then pushed the door open. Reaching inside, he switched on an overhead light and surveyed the living room and kitchen just as a fat yellow cat streaked its way through the door.

"Jennings!"

The apartment seemed empty. Sounded unoccupied. Carefully, Reed stepped inside. Nikki was right behind.

In the kitchen she bent on one knee and cooed to the striped feline, "So you finally decided to come home, you bad boy." She scooped up the tabby. He let out a soft yowl before rubbing the top of his head under her chin and purring loudly enough for Reed to hear. "Did you miss me, hmm? Or just your dinner?"

Nikki rid herself of her coat, draping it over the back of a chair, leaving her in a slim gray skirt and fitted black top that showed off her curves. Jesus, why was he even noticing? This was Nikki Gillette, a woman who would only get close to him to use him for information. Sexy. Tough. And the adversary.

He searched the rest of the small apartment while she fed her cat. Her home was still messed up from the investigation, but no one was lurking in a closet or behind a door or under the damned bed. Reed checked every nook and cranny, but he didn't linger too long in Nikki Gillette's bedroom, didn't study the antique-looking bed, nor touch the soft blue linens that covered it. Doing so would bridge an emotional gap he thought better left unspanned and bring images to mind, mental pictures of Nikki in a nothing nightie on the bedclothes that he'd rather not face.

"You know," she said when he returned to the kitchen area, "I've been thinking."

"Always a good sign."

"Don't be smart."

"You'd rather I be stupid?"

She grinned, flashing white teeth and showing off her dimple again. "So you do have a sense of humor."

"Upon occasion."

"Well, let's be serious for a sec, okay?"

"Okay."

As the cat ate noisily, Nikki pushed some paperwork to the side of her café table, clearing a working space, then reached into a zipper pocket of her bag and withdrew some folded sheets of paper. Carefully, she smoothed the pages over the Formica. Reed recognized copies of the notes she'd received from the killer.

He leaned closer, caught a whiff of her perfume.

"Look at these. Two of the notes are basic. Simplistic." She pointed to the first two letters she received. "They're kind of a 'heads up, Gillette. Pay attention. I'm going to do something. Something big.' They remind me of a little kid who's jumped into the pool and is yelling at his parents, 'Watch me. Watch me!'" She shifted the two simple notes to one side of the table. The words: TONIGHT and IT'S DONE seemed stark against the white paper. "These are obviously in reference to a killing, probably the second one, but the next communication I got"—she moved her hand to the final note—"is much more sophisticated. It's lots different from the others. It's a rhyme, in the same tone as the ones you received. Right?"

"Yes," he agreed, eyeing the note, listening to her logic.

"It's another tone of voice, a bigger hint or broader clue: 'Will there be more? Until the twelfth, no one can be sure.'" She tapped her finger on the poem as Jennings hopped on the table and began washing himself. Without losing her concentration, she placed the cat on the floor. "It's not so much bragging as the first ones seemed to be. Uh-uh. It's *meant* to be a clue, a seduction, almost a dare that begs me to solve the mystery. Just as the notes to you are. Look at the third line, 'No one can be sure.'" Deep in concentration, her eyebrows yanked together, her teeth gnawing at her lower lip, she thought aloud, "First of all, the words 'more' and 'sure' don't really rhyme, so I do think that this entire letter is supposed to be read after yours. But why repeat the line, 'will there be more?' Yours already had the 'will there be more' question. And check out 'no one.' Two words. Not 'noone' all put together as some people misspell it."

She looked up at him with her intelligent green eyes and it clicked. He reviewed the other notes he'd received.

> TICK TOCK,
> ON GOES THE CLOCK.
> TWO IN ONE,
> ONE AND TWO.

Then,

> ONE, TWO, THREE, FOUR . . .
> SO, NOW, DON'T YOU WONDER HOW
> MANY MORE?

And finally,

> NOW WE HAVE NUMBER FOUR.
> ONE THIRD DONE,

"They all have twelve words," he said, "including the one you received. That's why the meter's off and the first line of your note repeats the last line of mine."

"Exactly!" Her expression was serious, but her eyes glittered with anticipation and he noticed striations of gold punctuating her dark green irises. "And when we put the two together, it makes sense. The way I read mine was that on December twelfth, something would happen, and it may still, yet. You know, twelfth month, twelfth day, but really, the killer wants us to tie the two notes together, making the meaning entirely different. Your half didn't indicate a date at all, but by saying a third was done with four deaths, gave you the clue that there will be twelve victims, and that probably both people in the coffins were part of the master plan."

"Except he didn't kill Thomas Massey or Pauline Alexander."

"But they were chosen for a reason."

Reed agreed and let her run with her theory. "And that is?"

"I don't know but I keep coming back to the apostles. Thomas is one, Pauline or Paul the other, Barbara Marx, as Mark, and Roberta Peters obviously for Peter. Could he possibly be killing people he considers somehow represent Christ's disciples?" she mused, frowning. "Perhaps that's how he chooses the people already in the coffin, because of their names."

It was possible, he thought, though far from solid.

"He has to prove he's smarter than everyone, especially the police. That's why he's taunting you and showing off to me. I can get him press coverage and he's chosen you, because you were the brains behind cracking the Montgomery case last summer and therefore the most challenging adversary. He might not have even known about you and Barbara Marx." She held up a finger. "No. He did know! Don't you see," she said, getting more excited as she talked, "the Grave Robber wants us to work together. It's the best of both worlds. He contacts me and is assured of a page one spread. He contacts you and he knows, because of your involvement with Barbara Jean Marx, that you'll try your damnedest to expose him. He's laughing at us both because this is a game. His game. And he expects to win."

"I agree with you about the reasons he's contacting us," Reed said, turning everything over in his mind and stepping backward to put some space between them. He needed to focus. Concentrate. "But I'm not sure I buy the apostle angle. At least, not yet."

"It only makes sense."

"If the killer wanted to get to me with Bobbi Marx, then he's killing everyone else just to link them to a biblical reference?"

"Who knows what's going on in his sick mind?"

"So far, it's just a theory."

"But a strong one. You have to admit."

"One we'll consider, but," he added, realizing the basis for her enthusiasm, "you're not going to print it."

She hesitated.

"Whoa, Gillette. Until you have the facts and the go-ahead from me or the department, you will not report any part of this. Nothing about the notes, nothing about the victims, nothing about your hypothesis or the killer's M.O."

"But—"

"Nikki," he said, leaning forward again. His nose was less than an inch from hers. "I mean it. If you go off half-cocked and any of what we've discussed here is in the newspaper, I'll personally see that you are arrested."

"For?"

"Hindering an investigation, to begin with."

"Damn it all, Reed, I thought we had a deal."

"We do. When it's all over, you get the exclusive. The inside view. If we capture the guy alive, I'll see that you can interview him, but until then, you have to be very careful what you say. And I have to approve it."

Little lines pulled her eyebrows together and she seemed about to protest, but eventually let out her breath and acquiesced. "Okay. Fine. But I get credit for this twelve-word thing and you keep me abreast of the investigation."

He lifted one side of his mouth. "I'm not involved in it anymore, remember."

"Shove it, Reed. I want to know what you know, when you know it." She scraped her chair back. "Oh, geez, I forgot." She was looking at her phone, focusing on the message light that was flashing dimly on an older-model answering machine. "Just a sec."

Leaning a hip against the counter, she punched a button.

A mechanical-sounding techno voice stated, "You have three new messages. First message."

There was a click and then a hang up.

"Great. Another one," she said. "I got a hang up at work today."

"At the office?" He didn't like the sound of that.

"Yeah. It happens sometimes. People are impatient."

"Second message," the mechanical voice said.

"Hey, Nikki, are you avoiding me? Come on, give me a call." A decidedly male voice gave her his phone number and Nikki frowned.

"Old boyfriend," she said and Reed felt an inexplicable spurt of jealousy. "Sean Hawke. He dumped me several years back and doesn't get it that I'm not about to come running back to him."

"Maybe you should," he said, testing.

"I'll think about it. The day after hell freezes over."

"Third message."

"Nikki?" A woman's voice. "I had a helluva time deciphering the message you left earlier. If it wouldn't have been for Caller ID, I wouldn't have guessed it was you, so get rid of that piece of junk that you call a cell phone, would ya?"

"Simone?" Nikki whispered.

"Anyway, I guess we have time for that drink, so I'll see you at Cassandra's! Maybe after a couple of martinis I'll have the nerve to ask Jake out again. He wouldn't turn me down twice, would he? See ya at seven."

"Seven? Shit!" Nikki's face turned white as she looked at her watch.

"What?" Reed demanded. "Don't tell me you stood her up."

"There are no more messages," the machine informed them.

Nikki's face was suddenly white as death. "It's eight-fifty. That was Simone. Simone Everly. I . . . I never called her and I blew off the class." She checked her watch again and replayed the message. "Damn it all to hell. She's talking about the kickboxing class we take together. It'll be over in ten minutes." Nikki searched wildly in her bag for her phone. "I didn't call her. Not on my cell. Not on *any* phone. Where the hell is it?" She was pawing through the purse wildly. "Oh, God. It's not here. But it has to be. It has to!" In a full-blown panic she dumped her purse upside down. Pens, notebook, makeup case, recorder, change, stamps, and brush fell to the table, clattering, rolling to the floor, but there was no phone. "What did she mean, I called her? I haven't used the cell!" She searched the clutter, as if the phone would suddenly materialize beneath a pile of stamps and hair doodads.

"When's the last time you used it?"

"I don't know . . . last night, maybe . . . Oh, damn, when was it? . . . I . . . talked to my sister while I was driving." She hesitated. "I remember Lily hung up on me and I dropped the phone into the cup holder in my car. That's where it is!" Nikki was already scooping her things into her purse and grabbing her coat.

"You haven't used it since the call last night?" he asked and felt that familiar, sickening sense of doom that came upon him right before bad news.

"No. I couldn't find it at the office today and just thought it was in the car, then I forgot all about it . . . I couldn't have called her. . . . I didn't . . . this has got to be a mistake . . ." She was racing out the door and down the stairs into the foggy night.

Reed locked the door, then was at her heels, catching her at the parking lot.

Fumbling with her keys, she tried to peer through the driver's side window. "I don't see it. Jesus! Please, please . . . don't tell me . . ."

"Don't you have an electronic lock?"

"It's broken." She finally jabbed the key into the lock and flung the door open. Quickly, she slid into the driver's seat. Reed watched as she cast about the car. Her fingers scrabbled in the empty cup holder, console and floor mats. "Oh, God," she whispered. "It's gone." Turning horrified eyes up at Reed, she choked out, "My phone's not here and . . . and . . . I didn't make that call . . . you don't think . . . I mean, if someone stole my phone or . . . found it and then called Simone . . . it couldn't . . . wouldn't be the Grave Robber, would it?" Her face was twisted with a hideous fear. "He wouldn't have called Simone and arranged a meeting?"

"I don't know," Reed heard himself say, though the bad sensation he'd felt in her apartment was deepening. "Here, let me look."

She found a flashlight in the glove compartment and they shined it all through the interior of the little car. Reed checked under the seats, on the floor, in the side pockets, on the visors, in the glove box, then swept the flashlight's weak beam under the car.

Nothing.

The phone was definitely missing.

"It's not here."

"No," she cried, her chin wobbling. "Oh . . . no."

He placed an arm around her shoulders. "Don't borrow trouble," he said, but he felt it more intensely than ever in the dark night. The dawning of a new, profound terror. If Nikki hadn't left her cell phone at her parents' house, or her office, Simone Everly was in trouble.

CHAPTER 24

Not Simone . . . please, God, not *Simone!*

Nikki's world turned black and desolate. She leaned heavily against her car, the fog sliding around her, fear burrowing deep into her heart. The Grave Robber couldn't have stolen her phone and called Simone to set up a meeting. No, no . . . she was jumping to conclusions. Just because *someone,* most likely the killer, had broken into her place didn't mean that he had her phone and had set up an appointment with her best friend. "This has got to be a mistake or a prank or something," she said to Reed, willing her fear to subside and trying to think logically. "Someone got hold of my cell phone, probably at work . . . maybe Norm Metzger or Kevin Deeter, and whoever it was they called Simone because she's on speed dial, so . . ." So why set up an appointment? Pretend to be Nikki. Her insides turned to water and she sank against her car. No one would do that.

"Let's go to the gym. See if she made it to class. Come on." Once again Reed threw a strong arm over her shoulders, then shepherded her toward his Cadillac. For once Nikki didn't resist letting a man guide her. For once she was grateful for a strong arm to lean on. Adrenaline shot through her bloodstream. Guilt gnawed at her brain. How could she have lost her phone? Shaking, she dropped into the passenger seat of the El Dorado, then leaned against the door.

"It's the Sports Center in the Montgomery Building on West Broadway."

"I know the place."

"But we're probably too late," she said, checking her watch. "The class is over in a few minutes."

"If she's not there, we'll try her apartment." He handed Nikki his cell phone as he nosed his Caddy into the street and gunned it. The big car shot forward through the dark streets. "Call Simone," he ordered, taking a corner fast. "She's got a cell, right?"

"Yes."

Nikki was already punching out the numbers. Her fingers were shaking, her mind filled with dread. The phone rang. *Please answer,* Nikki silently prayed. *Come on, Simone.* Two rings. *Pick up. Oh, please, God, let her be safe.* Three rings and Nikki's fear crystalized. Simone always had her cell with her, always answered. "Come on, come on . . ." Four rings and then the taped message with Simone's voice on it. Nikki felt sick inside. "Simone, it's Nikki. Call me ASAP." Then she hung up and dialed Simone's apartment. On the fourth ring, the answering machine picked up. Again Nikki left a message.

"No luck?" Reed asked grimly as he sped through a yellow light.

"No. But I'll try her cell again. Maybe she didn't hear it over the noise of the class. Jake always has music playing and, well, you know." She punched out Simone's cell phone number again, but deep in her heart she knew her friend wouldn't answer. Might never return Nikki's call. A dark corner of her brain feared Simone was with the killer, maybe already dead, or waking up in a coffin with a dead body. . . . Nikki shuddered as she listened to Simone's voice instructing her to leave a message again. *Please let her be all right,* she silently prayed. *Please!*

Maybe her cell phone was out of battery life. Maybe even now she was lingering after class, flirting with Jake, inviting him out for a drink.

Please let Simone be there. It doesn't matter how angry with me she is, just let her be safe.

She clicked off the phone and stared into the dismal, dreary night.

Reed drove as if possessed, and yet it seemed to Nikki that it took forever to drive down the street where the gym was located. Reed double-parked and Nikki jumped out of the car. She was up the steps of the gym and through the doors before she could think twice. Jake was at the front desk, talking to the receptionist.

"Was Simone Everly in class?" she asked. "You know, my friend with the dark hair who asked you out the other night."

Jake shook his head. "Not tonight."

No. This can't be. "You're certain? We were supposed to meet here, but I got hung up and . . ." her voice dwindled away as she heard Reed catch up with her.

"I would have noticed. This is the first class she's missed."

"Oh, God." Nikki leaned heavily against the reception desk. She thought she might break down altogether as Reed flashed his badge, asked the same questions and got no further.

"Is something wrong?" Jake asked.

"We don't know yet," Reed said. "But if Ms. Everly comes in, would you have her call me?" He slid a card out of his wallet and thanked Jake, then helped Nikki to the door. She walked on wobbly legs, leaned on him as he whipped out his phone and made a call. "I thought you should know that Nikki Gillette's best friend may be missing . . . Simone Everly . . . No, we're not certain, but here's what happened." He repeated the events of the night. "We'll check out the restaurant, then her apartment . . . No, but I'm not waiting twenty-four hours if she does turn up missing . . . Yeah, I know." He clicked off. "I called Morrisette. She agrees with me that we'd better find Simone." He helped her into the Caddy and drove to the parking structure where Nikki had often parked, the place she and Simone had met. There, on the first floor, bold as brass, was the BMW convertible.

Nikki's heart tumbled. "It's her car," she said and climbed out of the Caddy as it rolled to a stop. There were only a couple of other cars, an ancient Volkswagen bus that had once been green, and a dirty white compact, both parked several spaces away from Simone's sleek convertible. No one else was visible and aside from the hum of traffic outside, the parking lot was silent and one of the fluorescent lights sizzled and flickered overhead.

"Don't touch anything," Reed warned as Nikki reached the BMW. He was only a couple of steps behind.

Heartsick, Nikki peered through the windows and noticed Simone's umbrella in the backseat along with a couple of beat-up paperback books, a sack of groceries and a coffee cup in the holder.

"So, we know that she made it this far."

"And it was a trap," Nikki said, but saw no signs of a struggle near the convertible, no traces of leather where shoes had scraped on the concrete, no drops of blood that were visible, thank God. Maybe she'd gotten away, or never met whoever it was who had pretended to be Nikki. If only! Nikki crossed her fingers and sent up another prayer.

Reed suggested, "Let's check the restaurant."

Dread pulling at her, she nodded and headed through the open door. Reed kept up with her and managed to make another call. The streets were foggy and damp, light from the street lamps shimmering oddly against the wet sidewalks, moisture blurring the windows of storefronts.

Cassandra's red and yellow neon sign burned bright.

Nikki threw open the doors. A hostess who had been studying her seating chart looked up and smiled.

"Two?" she asked with a glance at Reed.

"We're not interested in a table. I'm looking for my friend," Nikki explained. Christmas music was playing and the tables and booths were half filled with customers. Waiters and busboys bustled in the narrow aisles. "I was supposed to meet her and got hung up. Her name is Simone Everly and she's about five foot six with dark hair and—"

"She was here," a young-looking waitress said as she cruised by with two cups of coffee on a tray. "Had a couple of drinks, martinis, and bought a lemon drop for her friend who never showed up. Left the drink on the table. Was that you?"

"Yes." Nikki's heart plummeted.

Reed stepped forward, opening his wallet and showing his ID. "I'm Detective Pierce Reed. Was the woman with anyone?"

The waitress's mouth dropped open and she nearly lost her tray. "You're a cop?" she asked, righting the wobbling cups of coffee.

"Yes. Did anyone meet her tonight?"

"No. She just waited, watching the clock."

Nikki cringed inside.

"She drank two martinis, then left the lemon drop on the table and took off. She was pretty upset though . . . at you . . ." Round eyes rotated to Nikki. "If you were the one who stood her up."

"What time was that?" Reed asked.

"I dunno . . . an hour and a half ago . . . around seven, maybe a little before."

Nikki felt dead inside. Simone had been here. Had

left her car. Because she'd been lured by someone posing as Nikki. Then, she hadn't made it to the gym. What had happened? Had someone pulled her into a car at gunpoint?

Reed asked a few more questions, again left his card, with instructions to call, then eased Nikki out of the restaurant.

"Do you think she's with *him?*" Nikki asked.

"Don't know." He guided her toward the parking lot as he dialed his phone again.

"But she could have gone somewhere else. This doesn't mean that she's with the Grave Robber. . . ." She nearly stumbled with her next terrifying thought. Simone's name. A derivative of Simon. Another apostle. *Don't get ahead of yourself. Reed doesn't think that there's a connection.* Then, what else? Twelve apostles . . . *what the hell else?* Her head was pounding as they reached Simone's car again just as a police siren cut through the night. Within minutes a cruiser sped into the lot and stopped inches from Reed's Cadillac. Detective Morrisette flew out of the car. "Still nothing?" she asked, and slid a scathing look at Nikki.

"No," Reed said. "We left several messages on her phone."

"Then, let's rope this off. You been to her house yet?" Morrisette asked.

"On our way."

"Hold up a second. You know the address?"

"Yes." Nikki rattled it off.

Morrisette glanced around the deserted parking lot with its cement pillars, tire marks and a few oil stains.

Two other cars were parked. "I'll get someone to rope this off, but we really can't do anything more because we don't know that a crime's been committed. I'm sticking my neck out on this one, Reed."

"But not too far."

Another police car entered the lot. Morrisette instructed the plainclothes to cordon off the vehicle and stay with it until she had more information.

"Okay, I'm going to Ms. Everly's house. I know I can't persuade you to stay away, so keep it at a distance."

Reed didn't answer.

"Oh, hell. You just don't get it, do ya?" she asked Reed, then asked Nikki, "I don't suppose you have a car here?"

"No."

"She's with me."

Morrisette raised a studded eyebrow, but didn't say whatever it was that was on her mind. "Then let's go. Follow, but keep it low-key, okay?"

"So where's your new partner?" Reed asked, and for the first time Nikki realized that Cliff Siebert was missing.

"Off duty."

"So are you," Reed pointed out.

"Yeah, but I'm dedicated."

"Siebert isn't?"

"Let's not go into that one, okay?" she muttered irritably as she lit a cigarette. "Okay, let's do this thing, but it better not be a wild goose chase, Reed."

Simone Everly kept a key hidden on a hook beneath the porch of her condo. Nikki found the spare and they walked into the foyer to be met by a little scrap of a dog that yapped and barked from the top of the stairs.

"Come on, Mikado, it's me, Nikki."

The dog kept up his vigil on the upper landing. Only when Nikki climbed the stairs and picked him up did the noise stop and the wiggling begin. Aside from the useless pet, the condo was devoid of life. Most of the rooms were so tidy that vacuum tracks showed on the cream-colored carpet and there wasn't a speck of dust to be found on furniture that looked old, but was obviously new. It all was color coordinated and appeared expensive.

There were no messages on the answering machine except for Nikki's panicked and breathless call. Nothing stored in the memory. When Morrisette called for the last number dialed, it was Nikki's cell phone number. But there were phone numbers on a Caller ID list and Morrisette quickly wrote them down. "You recognize any of these?" she asked Nikki who was still holding the dog. Now Mikado was wagging his tail and washing her face feverishly.

"No, but then, Simone and I really don't run in the same circles."

"Why not?"

"We never have."

"You've been friends a long time."

"Yeah. She dated my brother and was going to marry him . . . at least, that was the plan until he broke up with

391

her. That was right before he died."

"How'd they meet?"

"I introduced them."

"She go to school with you?"

"No . . . I met her in another exercise class . . . kind of jazz dance. It was right after the Chevalier trial and I found out she'd been one of the jurors. I tried to get close to her, you know, for a story, but that didn't pan out. I'd already been burned on that one." Rubbing the back of Mikado's neck, she felt some of the old embarrassment. "Anyway, we hit it off."

"The Chevalier trial," Reed said, and he was deathly serious.

"Yeah."

"She was impaneled?"

Nikki nodded and saw his expression change. "Do you know the names of any of the other jurors?"

"No, but . . ." Her heart stopped. "Oh, God . . ."

"Can we get a list of everyone who was on the jury?" Reed asked, looking at Morrisette.

"Now, wait a minute. Just because this woman is presumably missing, doesn't mean that it has anything to do with LeRoy Chevalier."

"But he's out now, right? Have you heard from his parole officer?"

"Yeah, he made his appointment last week."

"Let's go check with him. Make sure that LeRoy's been a good boy. And we'll need to find out the other jurors who were on that trial."

"What about Barbara Jean Marx. Did she ever mention it?"

"Not to me," Reed said, "but our relationship was brief . . . kind of in the moment. We didn't do much discussing of what had happened a long time ago." He pulled out his cell phone and notepad, then dialed quickly, waiting a few seconds until the other party picked up. "Mrs. Massey, this is Detective Reed, Savannah police . . . Yes, I was there the other day . . . I'm fine, but I need some information about your husband. Can you tell me if he was ever on jury duty? The case I'm concerned about is the LeRoy Chevalier trial. He was convicted of killing his girlfriend and two of her children."

Nikki waited, her heart drumming. She hadn't known who the jurors were during the trial and the judge had ordered no cameras in the courtroom. It had been so long ago, she didn't remember the names. . . . Slowly, she set the dog down.

"Thank you, Mrs. Massey . . . Yes, yes, of course I'll let you know. Good-bye." He hung up the phone and looked at Morrisette. "Bingo."

"Shit. Let's go find him. I'll call for backup. You get her home or somewhere safe." Morrisette hitched her chin at Nikki.

"No. I'm coming."

"Reed isn't even supposed to be coming," Morrisette said, whipping out her phone.

"I'll stay out of the way."

Morrisette advanced on her. "Look, Gillette, this isn't your big chance, okay. I don't know what kind of a deal you worked with him"—she hooked her thumb at Reed and the little dog growled—"but it doesn't hold water with me."

"This isn't about a story," Nikki whispered, horrified. "It's about my friend."

"I don't have time to argue," she growled, then looked at Reed. "Keep her in line." A second later she was on the phone. Reed, too, had dialed another number. His conversation was short. As he hung up, he said, "That was Beauford Alexander. His wife Pauline served on the jury."

"That's three that we know of," Nikki said, chilled to the bone.

"So Chevalier's picking off the jurors, one by one?" Morrisette asked. "After he got out on a technicality? Does that make any sense? Doesn't he know we'll nail him?"

"He's spent twelve years fantasizing about this," Reed said. "My guess is that he doesn't care."

"I don't know. He couldn't have killed Thomas Massey and Pauline Alexander."

"Because they were already dead, but if they'd been alive when he was released, they'd be on his hit list."

"I hate arguing with you," Morrisette said. "I'll call the station and get hold of Siebert. We'll get a unit out here and someone figuring out who was on that jury who's still alive."

"If he hasn't gotten to them in the last couple of days."

"He hasn't. He would have bragged," Nikki said.

"That's why I think there's a chance Simone isn't dead yet."

Isn't dead yet. Dear God. The horrid words reverberated through her brain and she inwardly recoiled.

"We have to find her. No matter what."

"Absolutely." Reed touched her on the shoulder. "When we find Chevalier, we'll find your friend."

"Then, let's go," she said.

"She can't be involved. I'm not arguing about this, you got it?" Morrisette was adamant, her sharp chin jutting forward with authority. "This is serious business. Police business. If you show up and mess things up or get hurt, I can't be responsible. Oh, hell, Reed, would you deal with this?"

"Nikki, she's right," he said, and the hand on her shoulder gripped her a little more tightly. "It's not safe."

"I don't care. Simone's my friend."

"All the more reason!" he said sharply. Dropping his hand he looked skyward and ran stiff fingers through his hair. "Look, Nikki, please. You can't be involved in this, not at this level. It could be dangerous. We'll drop you off at the station. You'll be safe there. And I'll let you know the minute we find her."

"But—"

"This is the best way for you to help. We'll need a list of all of Simone Everly's friends, family and acquaintances. Work friends, siblings, anyone you can think of who might have seen her or know where she is. You can call and ask if anyone's heard from her, okay?"

"You're patronizing me," she accused.

"I'm just trying to keep you safe and play by the rules as much as possible."

Morrisette snorted at that. "We don't have any time for mollycoddling. You do what he says or we take you home."

"That's not an option." Reed's gaze fastened on Nikki's. "Just go to the station. I promise, the minute I know anything, I'll call. And as soon as we're done with Chevalier, I'll be back." He squeezed her upper arm. "Work with me for once, okay?"

"I don't like this."

"Neither do we," Morrisette said.

"Fine. I'll go to the station." *Where I'll go out of my mind waiting for news about Simone.*

"Good. We have to work fast." Pointing at Morrisette, he added, "We need to contact everyone who was on that jury. Offer protection. See if anyone strange has contacted them, staked out their homes. Get the most recent picture of Chevalier that we have, print out a million copies, then fax one up to McFee and Baldwin in Dahlonega. Have one of them show it to the kid who fell down the cliff. He's the only person we know who's seen the killer's face."

"You mean the only one who's still alive," Nikki whispered as she stared at her friend's home with its cheery, pastel décor. Everything was neat. Tidy. In its place. Just the way Simone liked her life.

"I meant he's the only one we can talk to readily," Reed said. "But I want a BOLF bulletin sent out throughout the state, maybe even farther. Every cop on the southeastern seaboard needs to be on the lookout for this fucker."

"Amen," Morrisette agreed. "We need to find this

396

sick bastard and shut him down. Now."

But Nikki had the feeling it was too late. Too many hours had passed. What were the chances that Simone was still alive? She picked up Mikado again and held him close. Hearing the little dog's heart beating was some comfort. "I'm taking him with me," she said, and for once, neither cop objected.

It's dark.
And cold.
So dark and cold and . . . I can't breathe.
And I hurt. Worse than I ever have in my life.

She was floating, trying to wake up and not aware of anything other than the darkness and some awful smell that made her want to retch. She felt a dull ache all through her body and her arm . . . God, her arm hurt like hell. Her mind was so damned fuzzy and . . . and she couldn't move, could barely breathe. She tried to turn over and her shoulder hit against something. Pain ripped down her arm. Had she hurt it? She couldn't remember. She coughed. Tried to sit up.

Bam! Her head thudded against something hard. What the hell was it and why couldn't she drag in a breath to save her soul? And the stench . . . Her stomach quivered as the cobwebs in her mind were cleared away by panic.

She suddenly realized why she couldn't move, why she couldn't breathe, couldn't move. Oh, God . . . oh, no . . . She felt the cold, rotting flesh against the back of her bare legs and buttocks and shoulders.

She was in a coffin.

397

With a dead person.

Terror shrieked through her.

She screamed as if being impaled. Pounded frantically on the sides and top of the coffin.

It seemed to shrink around her, pressing against her, creating a space so small she could barely move.

"No! Oh please, no! Help! Someone help!" She was crying and coughing, the fetid air burning in her lungs.

The son of a bitch who had captured her was the damned Grave Robber! Why, oh, God, why? Within minutes, possibly seconds, she'd run out of air. "Let me out," she yelled frantically, wailing and shrieking and pounding at the sides of the coffin with her good hand. She kicked. Hard. But the steel liner didn't give, only clanged dully as intense pain rocketed up her ankle. Oh, no, oh, no, oh, no . . . Now she understood. Now she remembered jogging to the gym, thinking of the class, not sensing the evil that had been lurking, not realizing that the monster had set her up and tripped her.

She'd seen his face as he'd wrestled her to the ground and thrust the needle into her arm. That's when she'd recognized him, when she'd realized the depths of the evil she faced. Though he'd aged and his looks had altered, she knew who had done this to her.

Fleetingly she remembered the trial. The testimony. The horrid pictures of the crime scene. The chilling murders of a woman and her children.

Leroy Chevalier was an animal. He'd beaten Carol Legittel and her kids mercilessly. He'd raped them all, then forced them to have sex with each other, with their mother. There had been hospital records submitted at the trial, which only seemed to prove how sick and twisted he was. He'd deserved prison. Or hell. Or both.

She'd known when she'd learned of his release that there would be trouble.

But she hadn't expected this.

No, no, not this.

"Help me, oh, God, help me," she screamed, her mind running in a crazy, wild kaleidoscope of jagged images. Torturing her while the feel of rotting flesh made her skin crawl. She had to get out. Had to!

Surely someone would hear her.

Certainly someone would come to her rescue.

"You have to do it yourself!" she said aloud, or was it the other person in the grave with her. Oh, God, did she feel him moving beneath her? Touching her. Running a bony, rotten finger up her spine.

Her shriek was the keening wail of an inmate in an asylum, the desperate, psychotic howl of a person whose mind was jagged and torn.

Think, Simone . . . think. Don't lose it. As bad as the air was, it still existed and she thought—oh, Jesus, was she imagining it—that there was the hint of fresh oxygen mingling with the sour, malodorous stench of decay. Again, she thought she felt something move—a worm or beetle that had bored into the coffin, or the ghost of whoever it was she was entombed with, touching her, breathing against the back of her neck?

She screamed and clawed, swearing and crying, feeling claustrophobia grip her, knowing her mind was fragmenting. *Hold on, for God's sake hold on . . . someone will save you . . . or will they?*

If she ever got out of here alive, she'd kill the bastard with her bare hands.

You'll never get out, Simone . . .

Did someone say that? Or was it her own terrorized mind.

You're going to suffer the same fate as the others and die slowly and miserably.

She heard it then, the spray and rattle of dirt and pebbles falling upon the lid of the coffin. She wasn't yet buried. There was a chance.

"Let me out!" Again she pounded, her wrist throbbing, panic spurring her. "Please, please, let me go. I won't tell anyone, oh, please, don't do this!"

More clattering as another scoop of dirt rained upon her tomb. But if she wasn't yet buried, someone besides the sick bastard might hear her. She screamed wildly, kicking, pounding, scraping, pleading. "Help me! Oh, God, someone, help me!" But still the dirt thudded above her and the smell of fresh air seemed to fade with each mind-dulling shovelful. He was going to kill her slowly. There was no escape.

The darkness seemed more complete. The air so thin it burned. The stench unbearable and the corpse beneath her seemed to move . . . to touch her in the most unimaginable places.

That was impossible, she thought for a fleeting second, but that bit of sanity was soon destroyed as the voice in her mind jeered back at her. *You're doomed, Simone. Just like the others.*

Her shrieks were muffled, her pleadings muted as he filled the yawning hole, but The Survivor was hearing Simone Everly's pitiful cries in stereo, not only listening to her screams from the coffin itself, but also hearing very clearly her every breath from the earpiece he'd lodged in one ear. He couldn't resist. Though it would have been safer to fill the hole and listen to her recorded cries later, the temptation to hear her as she was actually experiencing her fate was too great. Usually his victims didn't awaken until he was well away from the scene, but Simone Everly had been stronger than he'd anticipated and the drug he'd used to control her had worn off early.

Which was just as well, he thought as he scooped the damp earth. There was something purely sensual about knowing she was just below him, lying in the coffin beneath a few inches of earth, pleading with him to free her. Oh, she would plead and cry and offer him sexual favors, but even the thought of actually fucking her wasn't as thrilling as what he was experiencing now, the adrenaline rush of hearing her plead and gasp and cry.

A soft rain was falling, offering a veil for his actions should anyone climb the locked gates of the cemetery. He was alone, aside for a creature or two that scuttled through the foliage. If he looked through his night-vision goggles, he saw them, raccoons, skunks and opossums, huddled beneath the shrubs on the edge of the graveyard, peering at him with wide suspicious eyes.

Go ahead and watch, he thought of the furry witnesses to his crime. He was sweating as he threw the dirt into the grave, her voice fading in the damp cloud-covered night. He had to work fast, just in case some teenagers or vagrants showed up, but for now, they were alone.

He and Simone.

She was crying now, babbling incoherently, shrieking occasionally, prattling on about someone touching her and breathing on her—as if she were in the coffin with a ghost.

Man, she was really losing it.

Which was perfect.

Let her fears drive her crazy in the last few minutes of her life, let her think that there is no way out, that no matter how hard she struggles, pleads and fights, she's doomed.

See how it feels, you rich bitch.

CHAPTER 25

"I tell you, the creep hasn't been around for a couple of days." Dan Oliver, the manager of Chevalier's apartment building, was more than eager to let them inside. He looked to be around fifty and wore the bitter, I've-never-caught-a-break-in-my-life expression of a man who had lost his youthful dreams years before. Beneath the brim of a dirty baseball cap, his small eyes glittered in a face that carried too much flesh, and he'd barely cast a glance at the search warrant Reed and Morrisette had managed to procure. It seemed that Danny Boy had been anticipating them as he led them down a crumbling brick path and down a few steps to a basement. The apartment was nearly subterranean, a small space that had obviously been the work of a handyman hoping to make some extra bucks by taking in a tenant.

"Does he have a job? Keep regular hours?" Reed asked, though he knew the answer.

"Yeah, he's got a job. If you can call it that. Over at the video store. The guy's a perv, man, he's probably just been watching porn flicks all day. His hours vary, I think, but I don't keep tabs on him. It's not my job. That's what the parole officer does, right?"

"But you haven't seen anything out of the ordinary?" Reed pressed.

"He's a fuckin' murderer. Everything's out of the ordinary."

"Can't argue with that," Morrisette said as the door opened. Oliver stood outside and lit a cigarette while Reed and Morrisette entered what was little more than a tomb with dingy, cracked walls, bare wires and two tiny windows that were not only covered with dirt, but barred. No light could possibly reach the interior where a patchwork of carpet was matted and stained and a recliner held together with duct tape sat in front of a television with drooping rabbit ears adorned with bits of aluminum foil. The TV sat upon a battered bookcase that housed old record albums, though no phonograph was in sight.

"Cozy," Morrisette muttered under her breath as she

looked at the kitchenette—which consisted of a hot plate and half-refrigerator. A toilet was in the closet. "Right out of the pages of *House Beautiful.*"

"He's only been out a little while. Hasn't had time to consult with a decorator," Reed replied as he studied LeRoy Chevalier's bed, an army cot pushed into a corner and covered by a sleeping bag. Above the cot was the only decoration in the entire apartment—a picture of the Virgin Mary, beatifically looking down, as if at Chevalier's bed. Though fully dressed, her heart was visible, her expression kind. Loving.

"So what did he do? Hack up another family?" Oliver asked, then sucked hard on his cigarette.

"We just want to talk to him."

"Sure."

"Did he have any visitors?"

"I don't know. He keeps mostly to himself. Most of his buddies are in the big house."

"No phone?" Reed asked, looking around. "No computer?"

Oliver laughed so hard he started coughing. "He's not exactly a high-tech kind of guy."

That much seemed true and The Grave Robber had contacted both he and Nikki through E-mail, had installed wireless microphones in the coffins, had used technology to his advantage.

"Look at this." Morrisette had donned a pair of gloves and pulled a scrapbook from the bookcase holding the record albums. She laid it on the recliner and began flipping through the plastic-encased pages. News clippings, now yellowed with age, had been clipped and pasted carefully in the scrapbook. "He's obsessed with it."

"So where is he?" Reed said, and felt even more uncomfortable. Something was wrong here, something he didn't understand. Unless Chevalier was a chameleon; unless he was faking them out with this hovel of a living area. Unless he was playing them for fools.

Reed didn't like it.

He was missing something.

Something important.

Something that could cost Simone Everly her life.

The police were closing in.

The Survivor had heard the information on the police band. Could sense them getting closer, felt their collective hot breath on the back of his neck. They'd found the apartment, just as he'd expected. Just as he'd planned. He anticipated their next steps.

Rounding a corner, he crossed the street and walked down the narrow alley where trash cans were piled and a suspicious cat glowered at him from the top of a fence. He found his truck parked in a public lot. In plain view. This time, rather than take a chance that his vehicle would be recognized, he'd dumped a drugged Simone and his tools beneath the shrubbery at the grave site. He'd hidden his truck and returned to the cemetery later, before Simone had awoken, to finish his work. He found his keys and climbed into his truck. Satisfaction stole through him. He'd delivered his package; it was what he'd expected, what he'd wanted. He knew they'd soon figure out his clues. Unless they were complete morons. But he'd fooled them again. All that nonsense with the number twelve was just to whet their appetites, point them in the right direction but keep them blind to his real target.

He drove the speed limit, not encountering any trouble, and parked in the alley. Certain he hadn't been followed, that no one suspected where he'd hidden his lair, he hurried down the steps and slipped into the room where he found his solitude. His peace.

Glancing at the pile of Simone Everly's clothes, he smiled. Remembered undressing her. She'd been unconscious, of course, while he'd pulled off her warm-up suit and shorts and T-shirt beneath. He'd taken off her jog bra, quietly fondling a breast. God, it had been beautiful with its fading tan lines indicating she'd sunbathed in a small bikini. On the whitest part of her skin, in sharp contrast, were her nipples. Dark. Round. Perfect. He couldn't stop himself from caressing them and then he'd pulled off her jogging shorts and found the treasure.

A scarlet thong.

Barely covering any part of her and wedged up into her ass to show off the tight, round cheeks. He'd thought about biting her on the rump, of mounting her from behind, of forcing his hard cock deep into her, but he'd restrained himself. His hands had quivered as he'd removed the red piece of nothing she'd thought were panties. He'd smelled it and touched it with his tongue while he'd taken the time to get himself off. And then he'd put the thong away, hog-tied Simone and wrapped her into a tarp with breathing holes. He'd been careful to gag her just in case she'd woken up during the ride or in the half hour he'd had to leave her hidden in the dense foliage surrounding the cemetery.

Then, he'd hauled her to her final resting place.

Quickly, he sat down and listened to the tape of her screams, heard her beg for mercy and felt her terror. Perfect, he thought, listening to the sounds over and over. He indulged himself, walked to the bureau, rubbed the bloodstains on the surface, then reached into the drawer where his keepsakes waited. Silk and lace slid through his fingers.

He got hard.

Real hard.

Nikki was slowly going out of her mind. She'd heard nothing. It had been hours and Nikki was tired as she sat at the barren desk she'd been assigned at the police station. After whining for an hour, Mikado had curled into a ball at Nikki's feet while she tried to reach Simone's family and friends. A tall, efficient-looking officer named Willie Armstrong was seated near enough to her that she wondered if he'd been told to "baby-sit" her and keep her out of trouble. Such was her reputation, she supposed, though she didn't care as she watched the hands of the clock tick off the minutes and hours with no word from Reed.

What had they found at Chevalier's apartment? Surely, if he and Detective Morrisette had found Simone they would have called.

No such luck.

Her heart heavy with fear, her brain creating mind-numbing scenarios of sheer horror for her friend, she'd watched the police department in action from the inside. Even though it was the dead of night, the crew that was working took care of the BOLF bulletin and had copies of LeRoy Chevalier's likeness distributed. Nikki had called all of the friends and family of Simone that she could reach. Unfortunately her parents weren't home, but maybe that was for the best. Why worry them unnecessarily?

If it is unnecessary.

Finally, she heard Reed's voice and his footsteps on the stairs. Ludicrous as it was, her silly heart skipped a beat. She was on her feet in an instant but his dark expression when he walked up the steps stopped her cold. Her heart nosedived. "Did you find her?"

"No."

Morrisette was with him. "No trace. Not of her. Nor Chevalier."

"He wasn't home?"

"No. Nor did he show up at the video store where he works. We checked. And that's not to be printed, you got it?" Morrisette said.

Reed asked, "Did you find out anything?"

"No. No one's seen her since the restaurant."

"Hell."

Morrisette's phone chirped and she pulled it out of her bag as Reed and Nikki walked into his office.

"He's got her, doesn't he?" she asked as she stood at the window and stared into the dark, relentless night. Mikado had roused and was whining at her feet.

"I don't know. Nothing's certain."

"But you think so."

He started to argue with her, but stopped himself. The corners of his mouth drew tight. "Yeah. You're right. That is what I think."

"I knew it."

"I could be wrong."

"Yeah, right." She leaned over and picked up Simone's dog. "And the Pope could suddenly get married." She rubbed the crick from the back of her neck. "We have to find some way to get to her. Before it's too late." But she knew it probably already was, that there were probably few grains of sand left to run through Simone's hourglass.

Clicking off her cell phone, Morrisette returned. "They're handling everything here. I checked. We've got a BOLF out and if anything pops, they'll call me or Siebert."

"Where is he?" Nikki scratched Mikado behind his ears.

"On his way. He spent the day up in Dahlonega—said he left me a message I never got. Talked to the kid who saw the killer, but the kid couldn't finger Chevalier. Claimed he wouldn't know the guy if he ran into him." She shrugged a slim shoulder. "Who knows if the kid is lying? Siebert thinks he's too afraid of what might happen to him. And his old man wasn't very cooperative—thinks his boy might have a story that some rag will pay money for . . . Gee, maybe you can convince the *Sentinel* to ante up."

"We don't pay for news," Nikki snapped.

Morrisette snorted as she opened her purse and rooted around in it. "No, you just rake up the muck, get people agitated and get in the way." Nikki opened her mouth to protest, but Morrisette cut her off. "And don't give me any crap about freedom of the press and letting the people know, because it's all bullshit."

"I think she gets it," Reed cut in.

"She'd better." Morrisette found a pack of cigarettes and shook the last one out. "Be smart, okay?" she suggested to Reed as she crumpled the empty pack and tossed it into the trash.

"I try." His tone was cold as ice and his ex-partner seemed to get the message.

"Okay—maybe I came on a little strong, but I'm beat and I don't need anyone telling me how to do my job. I'm gonna go home to my kids. Who are, presumably, sleeping, and don't even know I'm not there . . . This is no damned job for a mother, let me tell you." She placed the unlit cigarette between lips showing only a hint of lipstick that had been applied hours earlier.

"But you can't just stop looking for him tonight," Nikki protested, worried sick about Simone. The dog whimpered and she set him on the ground. "Not now . . ." Turning pleading eyes on Reed, she said, "Every second counts. Right now Simone could be in a coffin, trying to get out, hearing shovelfuls of dirt being rained upon her. Dear God, can you imagine what she might be going through? We have to find her. We can't give up."

"No one's giving up!" Morrisette turned swiftly and stared Nikki down. Her already hot temper flared. "If

410

you haven't noticed, Ms. Gillette, we've been working our asses off on this one, and all you've been doing is getting in the way. If you can come up with one sound reason why I shouldn't go home, give me an idea of how to handle this any better than I have, then, shoot." She waited, cigarette twitching.

"Slow down, Sylvie," Reed warned. "We've all put in a long night."

"Just keep her in line, okay?"

Nikki said slowly, "No one keeps me in line."

"That's the problem. You're the loose cannon, Gillette, and frankly, I don't have time for it." Morrisette glared at Reed. "I'm surprised you do." Retrieving a Bic lighter from her pocket, Morrisette stormed out, her boots ringing with each furious step, her anger radiating in nearly visible waves.

The entire world seemed to crash down on Nikki. She stood in Reed's office feeling bereft, Simone's little dog pacing the office. "This is my fault," she said, wounded that anyone, even the prickly woman detective, would think she placed her ambitions or a story before her friend's life. "I didn't come here for a story," she said, and the weight of the night settled deep in her soul. "I just want to find Simone." Tears filled her eyes. "I just want to do everything possible so that she's safe."

"I know." He was impossibly kind, the look in his eyes compassionate, and she knew he felt her pain. Hadn't he lost those he'd held dear, a woman he'd once loved, a child he'd never gotten the chance to meet, to this twisted maniac?

"I'm sorry," she said. "For your loss and—"

"Shh." He folded her into his arms and rested his chin on her head. He felt so strong. So male. So dependable that she sagged against him and fought the tears that seemed determined to flow. Crying wouldn't help Simone. Nor would moping and worrying. She had to take action. Find the bastard who did this and stop him. Fast.

She felt Reed stiffen and the supporting arms around her dropped as someone cleared his throat. Instinctively she took a step backward and turned to find Cliff Siebert in the doorway.

"Ms. Gillette," he said, his voice flat. "You're the last person I expected to find here."

"Just on my way home," she replied. "I'm here because my friend is missing."

"I heard." His hard features softened a bit. "I'm sorry."

"I just hope that you find her. And soon. Come, Mikado!"

Cliff nodded curtly. "We'll do our best."

"Thanks," she said, nearly calling him by his first name and giving away the fact that she was close to Cliff Siebert. Reed didn't know they were friends, had no idea that Siebert was her source within the department, and she wanted to keep it that way. She scooped up the little mutt.

"I'll give you a lift," Reed offered and she managed a weak smile. He motioned to Mikado. "The dog can come, too."

"That would be great." She felt Cliff's gaze upon her as she and Reed walked out of the station, but she was too distraught and tired to worry about what he thought. Not that it was any of his business. Outside, the night seemed to close in on her, the dampness reached her bones, the darkness touched her soul. No one was on the street and the deserted city seemed to take on a sinister hue. Blue light from the street lamps danced eerily upon the wet pavement.

She climbed into the El Dorado and, with Mikado on her lap, leaned heavily against the passenger door. Without a word, Reed got behind the steering wheel and wheeled out of the parking lot, nosing the Caddy in the direction of her apartment. She felt so tired, her muscles aching, but her mind was in overdrive as she petted the dog and tried vainly to keep guilt at bay. Where was Simone? Did that horrid animal have her? *Please keep her safe. Keep her alive. Don't let her die a horrible, mind-numbing death.*

Outside, the city was quiet, the streets nearly deserted, only few interior lights in the grand old homes shining in the darkness. Inside the El Dorado, Reed held his silence and all Nikki heard was the rumble of the engine, whine of spinning tires and crackle of the police band with its short, staccato bursts of conversation. Simone's little dog, front feet on the window ledge, nose pressed to the fogging glass, didn't bark or whimper. Nikki tried not to think about Simone, attempted vainly not to envision the horrors of what she might be going through.

Finally, Nikki could stand the thick silence between them no more. "God, I wonder where she is?"

"Don't beat yourself up thinking about it," Reed said

as he maneuvered through the back alleys and narrow streets. A startled cat jumped out of the shadows and scurried through a wrought-iron fence. "It's not your fault."

"I should have met her."

"You couldn't. Didn't know you were supposed to. Someone stole your phone, remember?"

"But I was careless."

"Didn't matter." He guided the car around a final corner, then pulled into the lot and took the empty space next to Nikki's Subaru. "He would have found a way to get to her. Your phone provided the vehicle, but if he hadn't been able to use your cell, he would have found something else. This creep has a plan." Reed turned off the ignition and the engine died, ticking as it cooled.

"I still feel responsible," she admitted, reaching for the door handle as condensation blurred the windows, building a flimsy barrier to the outside world.

"So do I."

"You aren't her best friend." She petted Mikado and his stub of a tail wiggled.

"No, not her friend. Didn't even know her. I'm just a cop. Trying to nail the son of a bitch. It's my job. So far, I've failed."

"A wise man once told me 'Don't beat yourself up thinking about it.'" She forced a humorless smile as she threw his words back at him.

"Not so wise, I think, but I do try to take his advice."

"You'll catch Chevalier."

He nodded, but rubbed the back of his neck and

scowled into the darkness beyond the windshield. "Yeah, he can't get far." There was a hint of doubt in his voice—one Nikki hadn't heard before.

"But . . ."

"But what?" she asked and saw the consternation tightening the skin over his face, the hesitation in his eyes as he squinted into oncoming headlights. "There's something more bothering you about this, isn't there?"

"There's a lot that bothers me."

"Come on, Reed, spill it. And don't give me any guff about not reporting it, because we're way past that, okay? I know whatever we talk about here is 'off the record.'" As if to add emphasis to her words, Mikádo growled and yipped, his breath fogging the passenger window even more. When he didn't answer, she said, "Come on. What is it? Something's bothering you."

"Oh, hell." Reed's fingers gripped the wheel so hard his knuckles blanched. "Something's not hanging together with this one. I want the killer to be Chevalier in the worst way. I want to nail his hide to the wall and I'm sure Chevalier's tied up in the murders. They're all about him and the jury panel that convicted him, but I remember LeRoy Chevalier as a brutal, useless piece of shit. He was secretive. Nasty. Dark. A person who would terrorize members of his own girlfriend's family. Torture them. I don't see him writing little poems, childish poems, really, and taunting us into a game, if that's what you'd call it. He wasn't the least bit cerebral. And unless he's spent the last twelve years honing his computer skills, I can't see him as having the brains, nor the means, nor the desire to bait us. He got out.

Picked up the 'get out of jail free' card, so why throw it all away? Nah, I'm missing a piece here. I just can't figure out what it is."

"I don't understand," she said as she ruffled Mikado's fur. But inside she felt cold as death. If Reed was right . . . this was worse. She wanted to believe that LeRoy Chevalier was behind the murders. She needed to pin a face and a name on the twisted creature stalking the streets of Savannah.

"As I said, Chevalier was, and probably still is, a brute and a bully. Perverted and sick, and without any refinement. What surprised me about the entire case was that Carol Legittel, an educated woman, ever hooked up with him."

"It happens all the time. Think of the women lawyers who get involved with their clients. Rapists. Murderers. Doesn't matter. They get sucked in."

"It's still stupid."

"I won't argue that, but if I remember right, Carol Legittel had lost her job, got no child support from her ex and was taking care of three teenaged kids. She was in debt and teetering on bankruptcy when she met Chevalier. He had a good job with benefits as a trucker. In my opinion, she was desperate."

"It just seemed that she could have picked someone who swam a little higher in the gene pool."

"Maybe that's what attracted her—that he was rough-and-tumble. Who knows?"

"Yeah. Who the hell knows?" Reed muttered.

"Probably no one will ever be able to figure it out. Good night, Reed." She opened the car door and the interior light blinked on.

"Wait." He grabbed her arm before she could step outside. "I don't like the idea of you being here alone tonight." His voice was low, a whisper that caused an unlikely tingle to run up the back of her neck. Strong fingers curled over her arm.

"Is that a come-on?" she asked, trying to ease the tension.

"I'm just concerned."

"I'll be fine."

"Will you?" From his expression it was evident he didn't believe her.

"So, do you want to come in?" she asked. "Or not?"

He hesitated. Glanced up at her turret apartment. "That wouldn't be such a good idea."

Disappointment cut through her, but she managed a wry smile. "Then, don't."

"Isn't there anywhere else you can stay?"

"This is my home. I changed the locks." She managed a thin smile. "And now, with Mikado, I've got a guard dog."

Reed snorted as he glanced at the mutt. "Yeah, he's major protection, all right. Can't you stay with your folks?"

"I'm not thirteen, Reed," she said, remembering the sleepless night she'd had in her old bed with shards of her parents' fights running through her head. "And I wasn't on the jury of the Chevalier trial, so I'm not an intended victim. I don't think I'm in any danger."

The hand around her sleeve tightened and the skin of his face drew taut with concern. "No one's safe. Not

417

while he's on the loose. What about staying with your sister?"

Nikki shrank from the thought as she imagined overbearing, petulant Lily. The I-told-you-sos wouldn't be so much spoken as intimated. "Let's not even go there. Lily is about three steps up from the Grave Robber. And my brother Kyle is a head case as well as allergic to dog dander. Neither of them will want me knocking at his or her door in the middle of the night. Besides, I can't let anyone force me from my home." Grabbing her purse, she pulled free of his grasp. "Not even the Grave Robber."

"He's more than a name in one of your stories, Nikki. He's a cold-blooded killer. A guy who gets his jollies by burying people alive. I know you replaced the locks, but big deal. He got in once before. We just assume he had a key, but locks can be picked."

"Now I've got a dead bolt."

"Which isn't a guarantee."

"You're trying to scare me."

"Damn straight, I am."

"Okay. You've done your job. But I'm staying here. In my home." She looked down at the fingers still wrapped around her sleeve. "So what's it gonna be, Reed? Are you coming up, or what?"

They were together. From the bell tower of the church a block away, The Survivor adjusted his binoculars and watched as Reed climbed out of his car and walked Nikki Gillette and that stupid little mutt up the stairs to her apartment.

The Survivor wondered if the cop was going to spend the night.

If they'd yet become lovers.

He'd seen the sparks fly between them, had known that it was only a matter of time before they would end up in bed together, but it galled him nonetheless.

Nikki Gillette was just another cunt. Like the rest. He felt more than a little bit of envy, even jealousy that Reed was with her. But it would be short-lived. No matter how torrid the affair was now, it would die quickly. He'd see to it. Holding the binoculars with one hand, he reached into his pocket with the other, past the thick packet he intended to deliver, to the jumble of fabric below. Alone in the bell tower, he rubbed the silken panties he'd taken from his drawer, Nikki's panties. It was a luxury he seldom afforded himself— to remove a treasure from the bureau, but tonight he felt it necessary.

The wisp of silk and lace felt like heaven beneath his rough fingertips and he licked his lips as lust invaded his blood. He itched to screw her, to throw her onto a bed, or, better yet, into a coffin and fuck her over and over again. Her screams of protest would turn into moans of pleasure and then she'd beg him not only to spare her life but to thrust into her again and again. In his mind's eye he saw her beneath him, sweating, writhing, begging . . .

With one hand he rubbed her panties and felt his cock grow ramrod-stiff in anticipation. Sweat broke out on his forehead and made his hands slick on the binoculars.

Through the powerful lenses he saw Reed take the keys from her hand and unlock the door, swinging it open carefully, reaching for the light switch.

Unaware that they were being observed. Even through the binoculars it was difficult to see clearly as Nikki's porch light was dim, the street lamps casting little illumination on the turret, but still, he caught Reed's intimate gesture. After checking the interior, the cop placed his hand on the small of Nikki's back, gently propelling her inside, leaning close and no doubt whispering to her that it was safe.

Reed probably even believed it.

But he was wrong.

Dead wrong.

CHAPTER 26

He shouldn't stay.

No way. No how.

But Reed couldn't leave Nikki Gillette's apartment. Not when he had the feeling that she was a target. He'd lost the woman he was watching on the stakeout in San Francisco, had seen her being killed and could do nothing about it, and then, the Grave Robber had murdered Bobbi Jean and the baby.

He wouldn't let the same fate happen to Nikki, no matter how hard she protested. So he stood in her small living room feeling uncomfortable and out of place as she placed the dog on the floor. Her cat had hopped onto the counter and, back arched, eyed the interloper as Nikki shed her coat and dropped her purse and computer onto the floor near her desk where she eyed the answering machine.

"No messages." Her voice caught and she suddenly felt so weary she could barely stand. "Simone didn't call back." She slammed a fist onto the top of the desk. "Damn it all, Reed. He's got her," she whispered, her tiny fist curled so tightly the cords in the back of her hand were visible. "The bastard has her right now."

"Don't think about it."

The look she cast him cut him to the quick. "How can I think of anything else?"

"I don't know, but try."

"I have. But it's impossible." She stretched her fingers and sighed loudly. "What do you think he did to her? How did he lure her? Even if he pretended to be me, didn't she know? Where did he get her? In the parking lot? As she came out of the restaurant?"

"Don't do this," he warned.

"I can't stop." She jabbed her fingers through the wild riot of curls that had fallen over her eyes. "I see her. In that coffin. Waking up. Trying to get out."

That did it. He crossed the space between them and wrapped his arms around her. "Shh," he whispered against her ear. "Don't torture yourself. It's not helping."

"But I feel so guilty."

"Fight it. You need to pull yourself together. It's the only way to help her. Why don't you . . . take a bath . . . go to bed . . . try to find some way to relax," he suggested, feeling the tension in her muscles. "You need to sleep. You'll think more clearly in the morning. . . . We both will."

"You're staying?"

"Unless you throw me out into the street."

She snorted. It was almost a laugh. As if she found the image ludicrous.

"And then I'll camp out in the car."

"It's cold out there."

He lifted a shoulder. "Not that cold. I lived in San Francisco. Remember?"

"Yeah." She pulled her head back so that she could look him in the eye even though his arms were still holding them close. Too close. His hips touched hers through their clothing, her legs were nestled inside of his. "I don't think it'll be necessary for you to bunk in the Caddy."

"Thanks."

Studying him as if she were seeing him with new eyes, she added, "And I'll try to take your advice . . . to . . . try to think positively, about saving Simone. I'll try not to freak out or be a damned basket case."

"All I can ask."

She arched a skeptical eyebrow. "Oh, I think you could ask for a lot more." She was so close he noticed the slight dusting of freckles bridging her nose, watched the play of emotions on her small face as she struggled to pull herself together.

"And that would be a mistake."

"Undeniably." But she didn't pull away. Her lower lip trembled a bit and he felt the unlikely urge to kiss her.

Hard. To force her thoughts away from the pain of this night.

To where? Don't do it, Reed, don't open a door you can't close. "Let's just . . ."

"Yes, let's."

". . . keep things in perspective," he said, though his pulse was quickening with the nearness of her, his blood running hotter, the urge to kiss her, to hold her, to touch her, strong.

"And focus on what we need to be doing," she added, though he thought he detected a note of reluctance in her voice.

"Yes, focus." He stared into her eyes and saw the hint of desire in her gaze. Or was it desperation? It would be easy to make love to her, so easy. And he knew that tonight, because of everything she'd been through, because of her need to be comforted, she'd give in to him. Easily. Even eagerly. But in the morning with the light of dawn everything would change. "Focus," he repeated, damning himself for his lust. Women had always been his downfall. Probably always would be. But he didn't want to make another mistake. Not with this woman. "Focusing is good." He kissed her crown and released her.

"I don't know if it's good or not." If she was disappointed, she hid it and forced one side of her mouth into a half smile. "Okay." With a shrug, she turned and walked the few steps to her kitchen. "So . . . would you like something to drink? I've got beer, I think . . ." She opened the refrigerator and, leaning over the door, frowned at what he assumed to be meager contents.

"Make that I've got *one* lite beer and a bottle of semi-cheap wine."

He was about to protest when she said, "Don't give me any of that garbage about you being on duty, because we both know you're not, nor are you officially on this case, nor should you be in my apartment, anyway, as it's kind of like consorting with the enemy, right? So a glass of California's not-so-finest shouldn't be a problem."

"I'm not much of a wine drinker."

"Indulge me," she suggested as she kicked off her shoes and left them in the middle of the kitchen floor. "Since you're staying anyway, why don't you take your coat off?" Even though she attempted another smile, there was no amusement in her voice and her dimple failed to appear. Her eyes, when she looked over her shoulder at him, were dark. Haunted. Worry and fear evident in their green depths.

He tossed his jacket over the back of one of the kitchen chairs and did the same with his shoulder holster and pistol. "You wear that all the time?" she asked, but knew the answer. She'd noticed the bulge of his weapon on more than one occasion.

"I like to be prepared."

"A regular Boy Scout, are you?"

He snorted. "Been a long time since anyone even suggested it."

"Then, forget I said it." Some of the tension had eased out of her face as she eyed the contents of her refrigerator. "So . . . back to business. Now, let's see . . . here we go." She retrieved a chilled bottle, let the door swing closed, then rummaged around in a drawer, making a lot of racket before coming up with a corkscrew. "I'm really lousy at this," she admitted. "Maybe you should do the honors."

Grateful for something to do, he rolled up his sleeves, opened the bottle and poured two mismatched goblets of chardonnay. "Here's to . . . better days." He touched the rim of his glass to hers.

"Much better days. And better nights, too."

"Amen." He took a swallow. The wine wasn't half bad and Reed felt himself unwind. The tension in his shoulders eased a bit; his jaw wasn't as tight. Nikki, too, seemed to relax, if just a little. The haunted look didn't leave her eyes but the lines of strain around the corners of her mouth faded and she managed to change into a nightgown and robe somewhere between the first and second glasses of wine.

Even the cat had mellowed out, taking up his vigil on the desk as the dog, after a small meal of dry cat food, had finally settled onto a bed of blankets Nikki had arranged near the door.

"So, where do you think Chevalier is?" Nikki asked as she finished her second glass of wine. She hitched her chin toward the window. "Outside."

"Somewhere." But he was bothered.

"You're still not convinced he's the Grave Robber?" she asked around a yawn.

"Would he be so stupid? Get out of prison and start knocking off the jury who sent him up the river?"

"Some killers can't control themselves. The killing's the thrill. It has nothing to do with logic. God, Reed,

I'm dead," she said, then cringed. "Sorry. Bad choice of words."

"Go on," he said.

"What about you?"

"I'll crash here." He slapped the pillows of the small couch.

"You don't fit."

"I've had worse. It beats the El Dorado."

She almost laughed as she crossed the room and placed a kiss upon his cheek. "For a crusty old cop," she said, "you're really a very sweet man."

"Don't let it get out. My reputation at the station would be ruined."

She did laugh then, and he tried not to notice the way her robe gapped to show a gauzy nightgown, nor the hollow between her breasts, nor a bit of nipple that peeked out as she leaned over him. "Don't worry. I'm fairly certain any reputation you've already earned is black as tar."

"You're probably right."

"There's no probably about it."

He kissed her then. Grabbed her, pulled her close, and as she tumbled onto him, pressed his lips against hers with an urgency he hadn't anticipated. She didn't fight, but opened her mouth to him and returned his fervor. Closing his eyes, he felt the blood rush through his veins, the heat on his skin, the hardness in his groin.

Don't do this, Reed.

Haven't you learned your lesson?

Think of Bobbi Jean.

Remember what happened to her. To the baby.

His hands tangled in her hair and he forced her head to loll to one side so that he could brush his mouth across that seductive spot where her neck joined her shoulders, and felt her shudder.

Her arms surrounded him and she sighed loudly. "Reed, I . . . don't know . . ."

"Shh, darlin'," he whispered into her hair. "I just wanted to say good night."

"Like hell." She pulled her face away from his "We both wanted something a lot more than a good night kiss."

He smiled. "Well, yeah . . . I suppose."

"There's no supposin' about it, Detective."

"I can wait."

"Can you?" Her eyes glittered a sexy shade of green. Her skin was flushed, and for the first time since she'd realized Simone Everly was missing, she showed just the hint of a dimple as she dropped another kiss on his forehead. "Are you sure?" Her voice had taken on a deeper, naughty tone.

"Yeah, but you're not making it any easier."

"Which was all part of my diabolical scheme," she teased, sighing and pushing his hair from his eyes. "You and me? Who woulda thunk?"

"Not me," he said.

"Me, neither. I wasn't sure I even liked you."

"I *knew* I didn't like you. Now, I think we should get some sleep. Before we both do something we'll regret." As he straightened, he gave her a playful swat on the rump.

"Tease," she said, opening an antique armoire where

she pulled out a quilt and pillow, then tossed them both to him. "Knock yourself out," she said as she walked into the bedroom. He was left with a lasting impression of her hips moving beneath the white bathrobe and a tangle of strawberry-blond curls hanging past her shoulders. And a hard-on that wouldn't quit.

She shut the door and Reed heard the latch click. Jesus, what was he thinking? Nearly making love to Nikki Gillette. Not a good idea. Not a good idea at all. He was a fool to consider her as anything but a reporter for that rag, the *Sentinel.* As she'd so aptly stated earlier, she was, in fact, the enemy. But the image of her leaning over him, flashing him a tantalizing view of her breasts, lingered.

Sleep was bound to be impossible.

He'd never be able to put it out of his mind that she was only a few feet away, lying on a bed with her hair fanned out around that incredible, intelligent face, her tight body naked and willing beneath a thin, gauzy nightgown.

Yep, it was gonna be a long night.

Stacking his hands behind his head, he forced his testosterone-pumped thoughts away from Nikki Gillette to LeRoy Chevalier and his trial twelve years ago.

Chevalier's lawyer had changed his defendant's wardrobe. Gone were LeRoy Chevalier's jeans and work shirts, replaced by a smart navy blue suit, white shirt and conservative tie. Chevalier's unkempt long hair and straggly beard were suddenly history. He was now clean shaven with a neat, nearly military haircut that framed a newly visible face that included a square jaw, prominent nose and big, expressive eyes beneath a ridge of dark eyebrows. Chevalier had shed a few pounds, losing his gut and slovenly appearance. In the courtroom he looked more like an executive or a member of a country club than an independent trucker with a marred history of barroom fights and domestic violence.

LeRoy Chevalier had once broken a pool cue over a man's head, another time been arrested for breaking his live-in girlfriend's nose and collarbone, compliments of his steel-toed boots, and in yet another instance had been hauled in for the attempted rape of a fourteen-year-old girl, another girlfriend's niece. In each and every case, he'd gotten a slap on the wrist, serving little time.

Chevalier was mean, angry and a brute who, in the murder of Carol Legittel and her children, deserved no less than the death sentence. Between the judge and jury, he'd ended up with three consecutive life sentences for the deaths of Carol, Becky and Marlin Legittel.

At the trial Chevalier's defense attorney had attempted to blur the facts, insisting the children's biological father, Stephen, a known cocaine addict with a history of violence all his own, was to blame. Though Stephen hadn't had much of an alibi—just an old friend who'd insisted they'd been on a hunting trip together—the evidence pointed too strongly toward LeRoy Chevalier.

And Carol's youngest child, Joey, who had survived

with serious wounds that had hospitalized him for several weeks, had haltingly testified against his mother's boyfriend. On the witness stand, Joey had been embarrassed, afraid to look at Chevalier during the trial, sometimes whispering his testimony so quietly that Judge Ronald Gillette had asked the boy to repeat his answers.

Joey Legittel and Ken Stern's testimony had hushed the courtroom. Along with Chevalier's past history, some of which had been documented and allowed "in" the courtroom, and the physical evidence at the crime scene, including a bloody boot print from Chevalier's work boots, had sealed the bastard's fate.

Until DNA had proved otherwise.

Well, not really proved, but at least created a reasonable doubt. And that's all it had taken to set the monster free.

Reasonable doubt, my ass.

So, why now, after getting off for the murders, would Chevalier start this rampage, daring the police to catch him? It didn't make sense.

Reed listened to the wind slap the branches of a tree against the window and wondered if Nikki was getting any sleep on the other side of the door. He considered checking on her, but decided against it. No need to tempt fate any more than he already had.

Where am I?

Simone's eyes flew open. She'd been asleep or . . . or drugged and had the feeling of oppression, a huge weight was laying heavy on her chest. She was so

430

uncomfortable and she was gasping for breath. The nightmare had been so real . . . and then she knew, she hadn't been asleep at all. She'd passed out. Inside the coffin with the body.

Oh, God . . . Her mind slipped in and out of consciousness as she tried to fight, tried to think of a way out, but the corpse beneath her, the small space and lack of oxygen played upon her, tricked her mind.

Screaming frantically, she recoiled as the sound rebounded back at her, ricocheting like a million lunatics railing upon her. She thought something moved against the back of her neck and she squealed again, her scream echoing and reechoing through her brain.

There was no hope. No way out. Something squished beneath her. Bones scraped her naked skin and her mind fragmented into a thousand painful shards. Memories of Andrew skittered through her brain.

Far in the distance, somewhere in the darkness where her soul had run to, she knew she was going to die. What remained of rational thought shriveled at the thought of the dead person beneath her, the sharp ribs and fleshless fingers that were scratching up at her. Trembling, she felt the slimy soft tissue clinging to her skin, rubbing into her hair.

Tears streamed from her eyes. She coughed and tried vainly to drag in enough air for her tortured lungs. Feebly she kicked at the sides of the coffin as the oxygen ebbed.

In a last fit of sanity she realized she was doomed. To die like this.

Horribly.

She thought of Andrew one last time and gave up a final, harrowing scream.

The smell of coffee and a dog yapping in the distance roused Nikki from a heavy sleep laden with nightmares. A dull ache throbbed behind her eyes and a heavy weight, like an anvil, pushed down on her chest. It was just the effects of the bad dreams, that was it.

Her eyes flew open. Oh, God, Simone was missing. And Pierce Reed was in the living room . . . it wasn't part of a nightmare. The dog was Mikado. She flung back the covers, walked to the bathroom, used the toilet and flung water from the sink over her face. She looked like hell. Black smudges of mascara rimmed her eyes and her hair was even more unruly than ever. Not that she could do anything about it now.

She snapped her hair into a ponytail, scrubbed her face and slid into a pair of khaki pants and a knit top before opening the door and having Mikado launch himself at her. "Hey, how are you?" she asked, rubbing the dog behind his ears.

"Not glad to see you," Reed observed sarcastically. The little dog streaked around the coffee table, running in fast, furious circles as from the top of the bookcase Jennings eyed the rambunctious white tornado with feline contempt.

She finally caught the dog and was rewarded with an enthusiastic face wash. "Slow down, you," she said, giggling despite her worries.

"Coffee?" Reed poured a big mug from a pot he'd obviously brewed this morning. A dark beard shadow covered his jaw, his hair was mussed, the tail of his shirt hung outside his pants and his feet were bare, but he still looked sexy as hell as he glanced at her over his shoulder. "Black?"

"Today—yes. The blacker, the better." She remembered drinking more wine than she should have, kissing him on her little couch, then nearly making love to him only a few hours earlier. It seemed foolish now in the light of day. She put a wiggling Mikado down on the floor and he immediately walked into the kitchen, inspecting Jennings's empty food dish.

"Don't let him fool you. I already fed him and took him outside for his morning constitutional."

"*And* brewed the coffee."

"Efficiency's my middle name." He handed the steaming mug to her and she took it gratefully.

"I guess, but you're in trouble, Reed, because now I know your secret," she said, blowing across her cup.

He arched an eyebrow, silently encouraging her as he leaned his hips against the counter and drank from a chipped cup she'd bought years ago at a garage sale.

"Hard-boiled ace detective at night, domestic goddess in the morning."

He nearly choked on a swallow. "Yeah, that's me, all right."

"You could hire out."

"I might have to," he admitted. "After this case, I'll probably lose my badge."

"The police department's loss is Merry Maid's gain,"

she quipped, referring to a local housekeeping service. She took an experimental sip. The coffee was hot and strong.

"Just as long as you don't print it."

"Moi?" she mocked, splaying the fingers of one hand over her heart. "Never!"

"Yeah, right." He drained his cup, tossed the dregs into her sink, then slid into his socks and shoes. "It's been fun, but duty calls." He tucked in his shirt, slid one arm through his holster and grabbed his jacket.

"Keep me posted," she said. "If you hear anything about Simone."

"I will." He started for the door, then turned quickly and cleared his throat. "About last night . . ."

"Don't." Holding up a hand, she said, "Let's just forget it."

He felt a slow smile spread from one side of his mouth to the other. "Just for the record, let's get something straight."

"What?"

Though he knew he was probably making a mistake he'd regret for the rest of his life, he crossed the short distance between them, removed the cup from her fingers, wrapped an arm around her waist and dragged her body tight against his.

"What're you—?"

He kissed her. Soundly. So there would be no question about what he felt. She squeaked a bit of a protest before her lips molded to his and she melted against him, locking her arms around his neck before he finally lifted his head. "Now, do we have an understanding?"

She raised slumberous green eyes to his. "And how, Detective. And how."

Sylvie Morrisette punched the accelerator of her little car and tore around a corner on her way to work. She'd just dropped her kids off at school and preschool. For once, both her daughter and son were healthy and in school, seemingly not suffering from the lack of "quality time" with their mother. Fortunately Bart, their unemployed, broke father was pinch-hitting in the care department and for that, Sylvie was grateful. At least he seemed to understand that until the Grave Robber was nabbed, Morrisette would be logging in hours and hours of overtime.

But she missed working with Reed.

Cliff Siebert was a pansy-ass and a hothead. Smart enough, but flawed. Morrisette's friend Celia had once made the comment that all men were seriously flawed, it was just in their nature, but Sylvie thought it went further than that. They were fatally flawed. Period.

As proved by Reed.

What the hell was he thinking?

She slid in her favorite Alabama CD and cranked up the bass as the country music filled her car. What the hell was Reed thinking, getting involved with Nikki Gillette? He could protest it to the heavens, but Morrisette recognized what she'd witnessed last night when they were together. The guy was getting crotch-deep in trouble. Hadn't he learned anything with Bobbi Jean Marx?

Morrisette poked in the cigarette lighter as she braked

for an amber light that was about to turn red. She'd never thought Pierce Reed was a fool, but she'd been wrong, she decided, picking up her pack of Marlboro Lights and shaking out a cig. When it came to women, Reed thought with his dick. The lighter clicked and she lit up just as the traffic light turned to green. Rolling down the window, she made a final turn toward the station.

Her cell phone beeped. "Great. Just give me two minutes, will ya?" she growled as she pushed the mute button on her CD player and flipped her phone open. "Detective Morrisette."

"Where are you?" Cliff Siebert.

"In the lot. I'll be up in half a minute."

"Don't bother," he said. "I just got a call from the caretaker at Peltier Cemetery."

"Don't tell me. Our boy's been busy."

"You got it. A unit's already been dispatched and Diane Moses has been called."

"Okay, hotshot. Let's go check it out."

"I'm on my way down," Cliff said and hung up.

Morrisette took a long drag on her cigarette and wished to hell that she was waiting for Reed instead of Siebert.

Just as Reed's El Dorado wheeled into the lot.

Nikki dashed around the puddles in the parking lot and held her purse over her head as a cloudburst drenched the city. She fumbled with the lock on her car door before she realized the Subaru was open. "Stupid," she muttered, feeling raindrops slide beneath the collar of her coat. In her haste yesterday, she must've left the damned car unlocked, inviting anyone in. She was lucky she still had her stereo.

She dropped her purse and laptop onto the passenger seat and finger-combed her hair as she slid behind the wheel. She looked the wreck she was. She'd slept fitfully and only a few hours. But she had to go into work and try to sort through all the clues she had on the Grave Robber. That bastard had her friend and Nikki intended to ferret him out. She'd search the Internet, the archives at the paper, talk to anyone who knew anything about LeRoy Chevalier and the damned trial. Especially the jurors who were still living. Maybe one of them had seen Chevalier recently . . . and she'd talk to the kid in Dahlonega. And Ken Stern, Carol Legittel's brother, along with Stephen and Joey Legittel and anyone else connected with the original trial. She'd leave no stone unturned.

Deciding her hair and makeup were a lost cause, she plunged her key into the ignition when she noticed her cell phone in the cup holder.

Her hands froze over the wheel. The phone wasn't there last night. It wasn't. She and Reed had looked . . . Her stomach twisted at the thought that someone had been watching. Waiting. She swallowed hard, glanced through the foggy windows and saw no one. Double checked the backseat and hatch area, but the car was empty. Telling herself not to panic, she picked up the phone and checked for messages . . . none. But when she looked at the menu for missed calls she saw Simone's number. "Oh, God." She bit her lip and pressed the menu button for recent out-going calls. The last one was Simone's number.

"Shit." She blinked hard and was about to call Reed when she noticed the corner of a padded envelope sticking out from under the passenger seat. Some old notes that had slid from her briefcase. But she didn't remember losing anything.

It was unfamiliar.

Probably left when the phone had been returned. By someone who had been watching her place. Someone who had probably seen her return. With Reed.

Her heart pounded with dread.

Tugging the packet out of its hiding spot, she felt a cold, deadly premonition, a sliver of fear slide down her spine. The packet wasn't sealed, nor addressed, nor did it have any hint of postage. Inside was a single cassette tape.

From the Grave Robber.

He'd been in her car, not once, but twice. Once to steal her cell phone, the other to return it with this package. All the spit dried in her mouth. Again, she peered frantically through the fogging windows, but she caught no glimmer of anything out of the ordinary on this gray December morning. . . .

She thought about taking the envelope back to her apartment, locking the door and calling Reed. Instead, she locked the car doors. *As if that'll do any good. He's got the key, remember? Unless you left it unlocked.*

She turned on the ignition and backed out of her space. There was a chance he might be watching, might be hidden in the mist of early morning. With shaking fingers she eased the hatchback out of the lot and headed toward the police station.

At the first red light, she popped the cassette into the tape deck. For a second there was only silence, the hum of the tape running and then a few muffled scratches and scrapes. A sharp bang, the tape hissing, and a woman's voice.

"Oooh." A long, lonely, soul-wrenching moan.

The hairs on the back of Nikki's neck stood on end.

There was a second of silence . . . then another painful groan.

The spit in Nikki's mouth dried.

A scrape and more intense moaning.

"Jesus," Nikki whispered, her heart hammering. "No." Her mind was racing, her fingers clenching the wheel in a death grip. It couldn't be. It couldn't!

More moaning and scraping, frantic clawing and then . . . oh, God . . . she heard Simone's voice as clearly as if her friend were seated in the seat next to her.

"No! Let me out . . . please . . ." Simone pleaded.

Nikki's hand flew to her mouth. She let out a horrified cry. *No, no, no!* Her eyes and throat burned. Not Simone! *NOT SIMONE!*

"Help me! Help me! Oh, God, please help me!" Simone screamed above a frantic pounding and scraping.

"Please, no," Nikki whispered, imagining her friend's terror, the horror of being locked in a coffin underground.

A loud bang. Then a snap and a yelp.

Nikki jumped. Her foot slid off the brake.

The car jerked forward before she tromped on the brake again. But she didn't see the traffic nor hear the horns blasting at her. All she heard, all she imagined was her friend. Naked. Cold. Scared out of her wits.

There was more pounding and frantic breathing on the tape. Mewling. Crying.

Nikki's skin crawled and she began to cry, tears running from her eyes.

A horn blared. Startled, Nikki saw that the light had changed. She punched the accelerator, tires squealing through the intersection, barely noticing the trucker who held out his hands as if asking her what she was thinking. Her concentration was on the horrific noises, the scraping and mewling and sheer panic emanating from the speakers. She could barely maneuver her hatchback into the next alley.

Trembling, she threw her little car into park.

Tears rained from her eyes as the Subaru idled. The hideous clawing, banging and crying poured from the speakers.

"Help me . . . please . . . Andrew? Nikki? Someone . . . I'll do anything . . . where am I?" Nikki began to shake uncontrollably. Simone was crying, whispering incoherently, but still Nikki heard her despair. Her fear. Her abject horror.

"Oh, no . . ." Nikki whispered to the empty car. "No! No!" Angrily, she pounded an impotent fist on the steering wheel.

There was a gap in the tape, silence for a while, then Simone's voice again. Frailer now, fading. Gasping. "I can't see . . . please, let me out," she pled and Nikki squeezed her eyes shut as if she could block out the ghastly image of Simone lying in a coffin somewhere, no doubt wedged onto the top of a decomposing dead person while the air slowly seeped out of the tomb. ". . . Oh, God, help me . . ."

"I wish I could," Nikki said, knowing in her heart it was too late.

A tortured scream ripped through the car's interior, a shriek of fear so horrifying Nikki knew it would be with her for the rest of her life. She threw open the door and retched at the side of the alley, all the while hearing the last pitiful sounds coming from the stereo.

As she straightened in the seat and wiped her sleeve over her mouth, she closed her eyes. Imagined the horror her friend had experienced.

"Please God . . . don't let me die alone . . ."

A scream of pure agony ripped through the speakers and Nikki sobbed out loud.

"No . . . no, please, Simone . . ."

She strained to listen, but heard nothing more.

Just the cold hiss of the empty tape.

CHAPTER 27

"Trouble at Peltier Cemetery," Morrisette said as Reed climbed out of his Caddy. She was standing in the department parking lot, the driver's door to a cruiser open and waiting, taking a final drag on her cigarette, Cliff Siebert ready to ride shotgun. At the news, Reed tensed. Imagined the victim was Simone Everly. Knew Nikki would be destroyed. "A grave disturbed last night."

"Damn." Reed's jaw ached.

"Hey! He's not on the case," Siebert reminded her sullenly. "Let's go."

"Hold on a minute, bucko." Morrisette looked pissed and tired as hell as she flicked the remains of her filter tip into a puddle where it sizzled and died. This case was getting to her, to them all. "We've got a little time," she flung over her shoulder. "Dispatch has already sent a car and Diane Moses's people are on their way, right?"

"Yeah, but this is our case."

"We're going. Just give me a minute." Morrisette slammed the cruiser's driver's-side door shut as the younger cop slid into the passenger seat. "Overanxious idiot," she muttered under her breath as she and Reed met. "Look, we don't know yet, but our best guess is that Simone Everly is in that coffin. You might want to come along and then, if so, contact Nikki Gillette yourself. I know they were close and oh, hell, I gotta go, but I laid into her pretty bad last night."

"Let's not jump to conclusions."

"What are the odds that it's someone else?" Morrisette asked.

Reed didn't want to think. "I'll meet you there," he said as his cell phone beeped. Caller ID indicated Nikki was on the line.

Or someone who'd taken her phone.

His gut clenched. "Reed," he answered as Morrisette

climbed into the cruiser and wheeled out of the lot.

"Thank God. Pierce . . . oh . . . he contacted me," she said, her words barely gasps.

"Who?" But he knew. He was already on his way to the El Dorado.

"I got a package. A recording . . . oh . . . God, it's Simone. He killed her. That damned bastard buried her alive and sent me the recording." She was crying. Hiccuping and sniffing.

"Where are you?" Holding the phone to his ear, he found his keys and started the engine.

"In an alley. Not far from home." She gave him the cross street and address.

"Are you safe?"

"What do you mean?"

"Did anyone follow you?" He nosed the Caddy into traffic.

"Oh, Jesus," she whispered and there was a pause. "I don't know."

"Lock the doors and stay on the line with me. I'll be there in ten minutes."

"Good."

He made it in seven and Nikki was never so glad to see anyone in her life. She threw open the car door and flung herself into his arms. "That son of a bitch. That goddamned son of a bitch killed her." She wanted to sink into the strength of him, to close off the world, to find some kind of solace in someone stronger.

"Shh," he whispered into her hair as raindrops fell from a gray Savannah sky. He held her close. So close and it felt so right. "I'm here."

She shuddered, trying to erase Simone's screams from her mind, knowing, rationally, that she couldn't help her friend by falling apart and yet emotionally splintering into a million painful pieces. "He left it in my car," she said, sniffing and finally pulling her head back to look up at him and see the concern etched upon his features.

"Was the car locked?"

"No, but maybe I forgot . . . I don't know . . . he's been in the car before. Got my cell phone."

"Do you have an extra key?"

"No . . . well, yes. I left one with my dad years ago, with the house keys. You know, in case there was a problem. Kind of a backup?"

"No one else?"

"No, I don't think so . . ."

"Simone?"

Nikki snorted as she thought of her friend's sleek BMW. "She never borrowed it, no."

"What about that old boyfriend?"

"Sean?"

"Yeah."

"Not recently. But maybe. Oh, I let lots of people use it over the years. It's old enough to have a cassette player rather than a CD player."

"Can I see the tape?"

She nodded.

"Listen to it?"

"Oh, God."

"It can wait."

"No . . . it's all right." Reluctantly she pulled out of his embrace and they both got into her car. Nikki started the engine and rewound the tape, then played it for Reed. Again, Simone's voice filled the small interior, again, horrid images cut through Nikki's mind. Finally, there was only silence.

"Jesus," Reed whispered and it almost sounded like a prayer.

"She's dead . . ." Nikki felt the tears again, tears borne of sorrow, pain and guilt. Overwhelming guilt. If only she'd met her friend last night. If only she'd called . . .

He grabbed her hand. Laced his fingers through hers. "There's been another disturbance at a cemetery."

She felt the blood drain from her face. "You found her?"

"Don't know yet. A team's been sent to Peltier Cemetery just outside the city."

"We have to go there. Now."

"I won't be able to let you inside the scene," he said, his eyes dark, the fingers holding hers tightening. "You can stay in the car or join the rest of the press, but that's as far as it'll go."

"But you'll let me know if the body is Simone."

"Absolutely."

She leaned back against the headrest, closed her eyes and drew in a big, calming breath, the kind Jake Vaughn insisted they take before and after kickboxing class. "Okay," she said. "Let's go."

"First, Nikki, I need the tape."

She opened her eyes and nodded.

"And your cell phone?"

"But—" She started to protest, then didn't. The police needed anything the killer had touched, for evidence.

"You touched the phone and tape without gloves?"

"Unfortunately, yes. I'm sure my fingerprints are on them both, but the police have my prints on file." When he looked at her, she added, "There was another incident, years ago. I think I told you about Corey Sellwood. When he was a kid and, I thought, stalking me, the police needed my prints to compare to others in my house."

"But no one else touched the phone or the tape since you found them this morning?"

"No."

"Hold on a second." She watched as he walked to the Caddy and retrieved two plastic bags from his glove compartment. Once he returned to her car he used a handkerchief and placed the phone in one bag, then carefully extracted the vile recording from the player and dropped it into the other bag. She showed him the envelope and he took it as well, sealing it in the plastic envelope with the tape.

"You know I'm going to have to impound the car," he said, "just in case the son of a bitch left any evidence behind."

"Now, wait a minute Reed, I can't be without a car." As distraught as she was, she couldn't imagine that she would have to give up the Subaru.

"Nikki," he reproached and she didn't argue.

"Fine, fine. Just take me to a rental agency, *after* the cemetery."

"You're sure you want to go."

446

"Absolutely."

Reed called for someone to retrieve her car and once the officers and tow truck arrived, Nikki signed all the appropriate papers, then climbed into Reed's Caddy and, as he drove through the rain-washed streets toward the outskirts of town, she was silent, her heart filled with dread, her world darker than it had been only a day before.

What would she do once she knew the truth? Race to the office and write an intimate story as she was close to the victim, work hard to edge out the competition on the most recent killing by the Grave Robber?

She barely noticed the change of scenery as they reached the bend in the river where Peltier Plantation had once stood. Now, police vehicles, news vans and unmarked cars clustered around the main gate where a uniformed police officer stood guard, waving through other cops, but keeping the public and press at bay.

Reed passed the WKAM rig and parked behind the crime scene van. As Nikki stared out the window she noticed Norm Metzger arriving in his Impala. Thankfully, he didn't even glance her way as he joined the crowd at the gate. To Nikki the media frenzy was suddenly personal. And ugly. These people with their recorders and cameras were her peers, her contemporaries, and they were rabid for news, any kind of sensational news, regardless of the tragedy involved, not caring that Simone Everly had been a living, breathing, loving and charismatic individual. A person, not just a story.

How many times were you one of them? How often

would you have done anything *for a story? How many bereaved people did you interview looking for that little gem in their personal catastrophe, that unique angle that would push you onto page one.*

Her stomach heaved and she thought she might be sick. If there was any way that Simone could have survived . . . if the Grave Robber had just once shown some mercy . . . but she knew better. The tape proved it all.

She stared through the watery drizzle on the windshield as Metzger and the others craned their necks for a better view and shoulder cameras were elevated in hopes of a glimpse of the Grave Robber's work. Overhead, the sound of a helicopter's blades indicated that a television station was going airborne for a panoramic shot of the graveyard with a zoom lens focusing on the police sifting through the evidence, exhuming the coffin, perhaps opening it. Grief and guilt tore at her soul.

Her stomach roiled again and she flung open the door and threw up on the bent grass. She didn't care if anyone saw her. Didn't even notice the tears streaming down her face as she coughed and wiped her mouth. She was too focused on what she had to do. She couldn't just let the bastard get away with this. Couldn't let him terrorize the city and kill again. The damned Grave Robber was communicating with her. Using her. It was time to turn the tables.

She had to find the son of a bitch and nail his sick hide to the wall. No matter what it took.

• • •

They had to wait until all the evidence had been collected around the grave site before they could remove the coffin. Shoe prints were measured, photographed and cast, the surrounding grounds searched and the dirt sifted for anything that might lead to the Grave Robber's identity. Savannah police officers worked side by side with the FBI. Along with an agent named Haskins, a skeletal-looking man with a freckled pate and hooked nose, Morrisette directed the investigation, Cliff Siebert in close attendance, his expression dark and unreadable. At the sight of Reed he visibly tensed.

Reed stood nearby in the hastily constructed tent, knowing with a steadfast certainty who shared the grave of Tyrell Demonico Brown, one more juror in the Chevalier trial.

Tyrell Brown, Morrisette had already informed him, had died barely a month earlier. Single car accident on the interstate. A blown tire coupled with a high alcohol content in his bloodstream and lack of a seat belt had combined to send the thirty-seven-year-old father of two to this grave.

"I assume you're videotaping everyone who shows up here," he said to Morrisette.

She shot him a look that told him he should know better. "Yeah. And we'll compare it to the other tapes we've got of the other crime scenes to see if we have any special guests."

"Good. And you've checked out Sean Hawke and Corey Sellwood."

"Still working on those, but yeah, we're looking into

them." Her lips tightened over her teeth as she added, "Even though we know Chevalier is our man."

"Right." Reed couldn't disagree. Chevalier was the glue that held this case together. And it made sense that Chevalier would be contacting him because he helped with the collar. The senior detective, Clive Bateman, was already dead, alcoholism having sent him to an early grave at fifty-eight.

Reed remembered the case all too clearly and the incidents leading up to Carol's brutal slaying. How many times, before he'd been assigned to Homicide, had Reed or some other detective been called out to the Chevalier home, a small, run-down cottage with an overgrown yard and a dog tied to a tree? How many times had he seen Carol or her children battered? How many times had she refused to press charges? He remembered vividly one incident as he had stood on the porch of that little house.

Flies and mosquitoes had buzzed around his head, the dog had barked and Carol's three children had been hanging out. Marlin, the eldest boy, had been working on a dilapidated old Dodge that had been rusting in the driveway. His hair had fallen over his eyes and he'd studied Reed suspiciously and wiped his hands on an oily rag. The younger boy, Joey, had been at his brother's side, peering beneath the hood at an engine that, Reed had guessed, hadn't started in a long, long while. Joey, too, had turned his eyes on Reed as the detective had urged their bruised mother to press charges.

Carol's daughter Becky had been insolently smoking

a cigarette on the porch and swatting at the flies. "She won't do it," Becky had interrupted, tossing her streaked hair off her shoulders.

"Hush. This isn't your business." One of Carol's eyes had been swollen and bruised, the white part bloody and red. Her nose hadn't been broken that time, nor her jaw, but she'd still looked like hell.

"Not my business?" Becky repeated, smoke filtering out of her nostrils. "I suppose it's not my business when that fat old turd—"

"Stop it!" Carol had turned back to Reed. "Please leave, Detective. You're just upsetting my family."

"I'm not what's upsetting them." Reed's gut had churned. He was certain the whole damned family was suffering under Chevalier's quick temper and heavy fists.

"Get the hell out." Marlin had strode to the porch and placed himself squarely between his mother and Reed. "She don't want any help from the police."

"But he's right," Joey had said. He was thin and gawky and had crept up the porch steps behind his brother. His eyes were round with worry. "The detective's right."

"Ms. Legittel, for the sake of your children and your own safety, please don't back down now."

"Just leave, Detective Reed. This is family business."

"Dad wouldn't do this to you!" Joey said stubbornly. "He wouldn't make us—"

"You don't know what your father would do," Carol burst out. "He's a psycho."

"But he wouldn't—"

"Shut up, Joseph! You don't know your father. Not the way I do."

"I want to go live with him."

"Do you? Oh, for the love of God, you'd last ten minutes with that son of a bitch. He's a druggie. He threw us out, remember? All of us. He doesn't love you, Joey." Her stern face softened as she reached out to touch her youngest son's face. The boy jerked away. "Stephen Legittel doesn't understand love. He only knows hate."

"And what does LeRoy know?" Becky said. "He's sick, Mom. A perv."

"He takes care of us."

Becky snorted and squashed her cigarette in a pot where petunias were busy dying. "He sure does." She looked at Reed. "Don't come back here again. It's a waste of your time." She pointed to her mother with her chin. "She's not gonna listen."

"That's right," Marlin agreed, scowling down at the floorboards, his dirty hands clenched into fists. He'd been suffering from guilt, Reed had assumed, the eldest boy unable to save his mother from the monster she'd tied herself to.

"No! He can't leave!" Joey turned big eyes on Reed. "You can get rid of him. You can send him away."

"If your mother presses charges."

Spinning so fast he nearly stumbled, Joey glared at the woman who had brought him into this hell of a world. "You have to do it. You have to."

"Joey, please."

"He's gonna kill us, Mom. He's gonna kill all of us!"

"Then just run away, you little chicken," Becky muttered.

Reed said, "Ms. Legittel, this has to be stopped. I can help." He reached into his pocket and withdrew a card. "Call me."

"Don't leave," Joey pleaded.

"I could call child services."

"Like hell, Detective. You won't take my children away from me. Joey, hush!" She placed a protective arm around her son. "My kids are all I have, Detective Reed. Please don't try to take them from me."

"I just want to protect you. And them."

"You can't," she whispered, a tear tracking from her bad eye. "No one can. Come on in, kids." She'd shepherded them into the house and Reed had felt bleak inside.

"I'll be back."

"Don't bother." The torn screen door slapped shut and the dog started barking loudly. Reed stood on the steps and felt impotent. The door behind the screen shut with a slam and he noticed his card was still on the floorboards of the porch. Carefully, he tucked it into the windowsill and noticed the slats on the blinds move. Someone from the inside was watching him. Good. Something had to be done, or Joey's prophecy might come true, he'd thought at the time, not understanding completely the depths of depravity Chevalier had wallowed in. Only at the trial had he learned how he'd abused the children and their mother, molested them and made them touch each other for his own vile entertainment.

LeRoy Chevalier should never have gotten out of prison. Never.

Now, as he stood in the tent, waiting for the coffin to be removed from the grave and opened, he realized why the killer was contacting him. He'd collared Chevalier and been a part of the trial.

Judge Ronald Gillette had presided. And Nikki was Big Ron's daughter as well as a reporter for the *Sentinel* during the trial. The pieces were beginning to fall together. There was some logic in all this chaos.

LeRoy Chevalier had to be the killer. Had to be. He could almost convince himself and decided his reservations were clearly because he was a skeptic by nature, never believed anything until he saw it with his own two eyes.

Theories were just that—all conjecture.

Hard evidence, that was what counted.

Reed edged to the tent's doorway. He looked at the area beyond the gate, to the parking lot half filled with cars parked haphazardly beneath huge live oaks. He noted that Nikki was still inside his car. Seeing her huddled there, looking small and frail, he felt a pang of empathy that went bone deep. Guilt was eating at her, torturing her, and as strong as she was, Nicole Gillette might not survive the horrendous death of her friend. She felt far too responsible.

No telling what she'd do. He saw the car door fly open and then she was hidden from view as she leaned over. No doubt losing her breakfast. He waited and she eventually sat up again and wiped a sleeve over her mouth. He wasn't able to define her features through the foggy glass, just her small silhouette.

He'd always considered her a pain in the butt. A privileged brat with brass balls to accompany her brains, a pushy reporter who got under his skin and a person to avoid. Now, he didn't want to think too closely about his conflicted feelings for her. Nor did he have the time.

He only hoped she'd brace herself and, despite all of his previous grumblings about her, mentally crossed his fingers that she was as strong and tough as he'd once thought. He stepped back into the tent and stood near one of the plastic walls.

Show time.

The coffin was being hoisted out of the grave and into the tent. Diane Moses barked orders, kept a log, and made sure that nothing was damaged, no evidence lost, destroyed, or tampered with as the exterior of the casket was photographed and examined for tool marks, fingerprints or scrapes.

Reed waited, his stomach in knots as the coffin lid was raised. The stench of death rolled out of the tomb and caught on an easterly wind.

"Shit," Morrisette said, turning away from the two bodies.

Cliff Siebert took a long look, then dragged his eyes away. "Son of a bitch."

"You know this woman?" Diane asked.

"Simone Everly." Reed turned his back on the open casket, unable to gawk at the bruised, naked body and unblinking eyes of Nikki's friend. Her hair was matted and wild, caught in the remnants of flesh beneath, and her skin where it wasn't contused was the pale gray shade of death. Once beautiful features were marred and broken where she'd banged her head on the lid and her fingers, as Bobbi's had been, were covered in blood, the skin rubbed off, bare flesh exposed. "She went missing yesterday."

"There's something in here . . . a microphone and some kind of note." One of the officers of the crime scene waited until the photographer had done his job, then carefully pried an envelope from the side of the coffin where it had been taped near Simone's head.

"Don't mess with the tape," Diane warned sharply. "It could have fingerprints."

If the guy's stupid or careless, Reed thought, but didn't say it. He didn't have to. Morrisette stepped up to the plate.

"I doubt that Chevalier would make that kind of mistake."

"Anyone can get distracted and slip up."

The investigator removed the envelope and Reed's name was written in block letters.

"This guy's got a hard-on for you," Morrisette muttered. Reed donned gloves, extracted the single sheet of paper and read:

FOUR ALREADY GONE,
TOO MANY MORE STILL ALIVE.
NO LONGER TWELVE,
NOW TEN AND TWO AND FIVE.

"What the hell does that mean? Four already gone?" Morrisette growled, motioning toward the open

456

casket. "What four? I count six."

"He's talking about a total number of victims. Seventeen. Look at the last line. Ten, two and five. Seventeen." Reed's mind was spinning ahead as he read the note again and again, comparing it to the others that had been received.

He thought hard. Why up the tally? Were they barking up the wrong tree? This had to be Chevalier's work. All of the victims had been jurors . . . so far. What if he'd expanded his list. But who . . . or why?

"I don't get it," Morrisette grumbled.

"Some of the people died of natural causes, right? Maybe that's what he's talking about. He's going to kill twelve, but four were already dead."

"Three, Reed." She held up three fingers and dropped them one at a time as she said, "Brown, Alexander, and Massey."

"There could be someone else we haven't found yet."

"We checked. We're all out of dead jurors. Everyone's alive and accounted for. Kinda blows your whole jury panel theory then, doesn't it? Unless the freak is so hung up on the number twelve, why not just kill the remaining jurors who were alive? Why isn't the number nine? Seventeen? Crap! This doesn't make any sense."

"He's giving us a clue," Reed insisted.

"Or just messing with us!" Morrisette said irritably as wind lashed at the flaps of the tent.

"No . . . I don't think he would bother. The words on the note add up to seventeen. That's the number he's working with now."

"Well, since you seem to think you know how this perv's thought processes work, you'd better figure out what he's talkin' about, and fast."

She was right. Reed rubbed the back of his neck and wished he understood the cryptic note. As far as the police knew, Pauline Alexander, Thomas Massey and Tyrell Demonico Brown were the only three jurors who'd died of natural causes. Another three, Barbara Marx, Roberta Peters and now Simone Everly had been buried alive. At the Grave Robber's hands. The other six jurors were alive and under police protection. And that total was only twelve. Why up the score by *five*? What was the significance of that particular number? He thought of Nikki and how the Grave Robber had chosen her to contact. To terrorize. The creep had been in her apartment? Bugged her? Why? And why contact Reed as well?

Because you both were involved in the Chevalier trial. This all has something to do with what went down then when Chevalier was arrested and sent to prison.

Reed had already gone over all the notes of the trial, had requested all the prison records on the guy and found nothing that would help. Maybe if the senior detective who had helped collar Chevalier were still alive, he would remember something about the trial that would help. But Reed's ex-partner was dead.

"I tell ya, the guy's messin' with us. Ten and two and five?" Morrisette cut in.

"It's his way of telling us there will be seventeen bodies, and, check it out, the note had to be seventeen words long."

"What a crock," Siebert cut in.

Morrisette glared at the note as if it were pure evil.

"Listen, this just doesn't make any sense. The guy's way off." Cliff was obviously not buying into Reed's line of reasoning. "There weren't seventeen jurors."

"What about alternates, or other people involved in the trial?" Reed asked, thinking aloud. "We're not talking about a rational guy, you know."

"Shit, no," Morrisette muttered under her breath, lines creasing her forehead.

The new note from the Grave Robber meant more death. More killing. More work and more frustration.

"There aren't five alternates on a jury panel, you know that. And why up the score now?" Morrisette wondered aloud and Reed could almost see the wheels turning in her mind. "To confuse us? Jesus, this is one sick prick." She stared at the damned note. "I hate to say it, but I think you're right. For whatever the reason, the bastard's definitely talking about seventeen."

"Son of a bitch," Siebert growled.

Haskins stared at the note. "I'll check with our profiler. See what she says about this guy."

"This guy? Meaning you don't think it's Chevalier?" Morrisette exchanged looks with Reed.

The FBI agent held up a hand. "I'm just covering all the bases, but yeah, I think it's Chevalier. Everyone who died suspiciously who was on the jury—even good old Tyrell here—kicked off *after* Chevalier was released. Coincidence?"

"I don't believe in coincidence," Morrisette said. "I'm an 'everything for a reason' kind of girl."

Reed's cell phone beeped. Turning his back on the crowd in the tent as the wind tugged at the flaps, he answered, "Reed," seeing from Caller ID that the call was long distance.

"Rick Bentz, New Orleans P.D. You asked me to call you when we located Vince Lassiter."

"I did."

"We found him today in a hospital in San Antonio. Drug OD, no ID on him, so it took a while for us to piece it all together. According to hospital records, he was admitted five days ago, comatose, only regained consciousness late last night. Doesn't look like he's your boy."

"It sure doesn't," Reed agreed. He'd already struck Bobbi Jean's brother from the list of suspects.

"How's the investigation coming along?"

"Unearthed another body today. Same M.O. Buried alive."

"Hell."

"Yeah, that's what it's been around here."

"Let me know if there's anything else I can do."

"I will," Reed agreed before hanging up and deciding he had to face Nikki. He slipped through the vent in the tent and saw her stiffen in the passenger seat. Other reporters, all clustered near the front gate, started hurling questions at him, but he ignored them, didn't even bother acknowledging their presence. No doubt he was being filmed from the news chopper overhead and from the handheld cams on the other side of the iron bars. He only hoped that the footage would be edited out before the story aired and that Nikki Gillette wasn't recognized as the woman sitting in his car.

What were the chances of that?

Without a word he opened the car door, slid into the driver's seat and started the engine. "I'm sorry," he said and she let out a weak gasp. She looked away, through the passenger window as he drove away from the cemetery.

"Who was Simone with?" she asked.

"A man by the name of Tyrell Demonico Brown."

"A juror?"

"Yes."

She sniffed loudly and from the corner of his eye he saw her chin tighten as if she were willing herself to be strong. In more ways than one she was Ronald Gillette's daughter.

"Get him, Reed," she said, dashing away her tears. "Get the son of a bitch."

"I will." He turned onto a road leading away from the city. "That's a promise."

Nikki wanted to believe him. Desperately she wanted to think that justice would be served, that Chevalier would rot in hell for his crimes. "Did you find any other evidence?"

"Another note."

"Oh, God, no."

"Addressed to me."

"What did it say?"

He explained and she listened, horrified. "More? More than twelve? Seventeen," she whispered as they drove across the bridge to Tybee Island. "Where are we going?"

"Someplace quiet. Just for a little while. To regroup."

"On Tybee?"

"Got a better idea?"

"I wish."

They stopped at the beach and walked along the dunes and beach grass, not saying a word, smelling the salty sea air as a thick mist rolled in from the sea. Reed draped an arm over her shoulders and she huddled close to him as her pain lessened and the guilt she clung to so tightly eased a little.

"Are you going to be all right?" he asked and she nodded, squinting up at him, feeling the wind snatch at her hair and pull at the hem of her coat.

"I have to be. We Gillettes, we're survivors . . . well, except for Andrew." She sighed and admitted something she'd held in for twelve years. "I think he committed suicide. There was talk of an accident and that's what Mom and Dad choose to think, but when you examine the facts, Andrew hated to lose and the fact that he couldn't get into the law school he wanted, even with Dad's pull as an alumnus and a judge, Andrew decided to flick it in." She plunged her hands deep into the pockets of her coat and stared out to sea where the gray water met the dark clouds.

"But you're different."

"I hope." She managed a weak, watery smile. "Okay, Detective, so you brought me out here to help me shake off the guilt and, I assume, to be away from the prying eyes of the other cops and journalists. So, now what?"

He drew her closer still and lowered his head to hers,

kissing her so hard, with such desperation that she couldn't resist him and kissed him back. Over the rush of the sea she heard his heart, steady and strong, felt his heat at odds with the weather, and realized that in the past few days she'd started to fall in love with this brusque, hardheaded cop.

He pressed his tongue against her teeth and she opened to him, clinging to him, feeling his body, hard and wanting beneath his clothes. The winter air swirled around them, the sea pounded the surf, and for just a few vital minutes Nikki forgot about everything, all the pain, all the guilt and grief, everything except this one lone man.

It felt so good to forget. If only for a few minutes.

With a groan, he lifted his head and loosened his hold on her. "I hate to cut this short, really, but I have work to do."

"*We* have work to do," she corrected. "And I'll take a rain check."

"You'll get it." His tone was soft, his gaze concerned. "You're sure you'll be all right?"

"Not all right. But as right as I ever was."

"Then, I'll drive you to a car rental agency."

"That, Detective, would be an excellent idea." She slid into the Caddy's interior and knew that she'd have to face Norm Metzger and Tom Fink and all their questions. Metzger had seen her with Reed. Hence she'd have to endure the third degree, but so be it.

She'd do whatever she had to to help bring Simone's killer to justice.

Now is the time.

Everything is in place.

The Survivor glanced at the unmoving body on his floor. Not dead. Just out cold. Death would come soon. Around his room, television screens flickered with images of Peltier Cemetery. The police and FBI had been there *en masse*. He knew. Just as he knew they would be. Looking in the other direction.

That had been earlier today and the stations had been replaying the footage over and over again. He was pleased. At least the media was finally taking notice. Giving him the proper respect.

Two of the televisions were playing DVDs. His favorites. The two with which he could identify most closely. *Rambo* filled one screen and he noticed Sylvester Stallone in the title role, silently eluding the army, and on another screen, a sleeker avenger, Neo, in *The Matrix*.

He, too, was an avenger. A seeker of justice. A victim of the system and one who would right the wrongs cast upon him.

Turning his attention from the screens, he crossed the small room and ended up at his dresser. With the glimmering blue light from the screens as a backdrop, he saw his face reflected harshly in the cracked mirror. He'd aged so much in the past few weeks, he was nearly unrecognizable to himself. Which, he decided, was good. For he wouldn't be easily recognized by others. With or without his elaborate disguises.

Besides, it was time to unmask himself.

To face the world.

To make his ultimate point.

He glanced down at the stained top of the bureau and remembered how that blood had been spilled, how this dark spot in the wood had become sacred to him. Delicately, he touched one drop, then another, using a swirling motion, feeling the oak finish and the blood, once hot, that had pooled there. It was almost as if it pulsed beneath his fingertips. Faster and faster he rubbed the stain. Sharp images of the past, of spraying blood and shrieks and dying rushed through his head.

So much blood.

So much pain.

Twelve-year-old screams resounded in his ears, echoing eerily, urging him on.

Closing his eyes, he mentally focused on his mission.

All the recent killings were only practice.

Now was the time for the coup de grâce.

The clues he'd sent had been a smoke screen. There had been enough truth in the notes to keep the cops interested, but also to throw them off. They were busy protecting and offering surveillance to the remaining jurors in the trial, but they were wasting their time, disbursing manpower to remote locations.

He smiled. Rubbing the bloodstains gave him strength.

Power. Reminded him of his purpose.

Now.

Tonight.

It had to be done.

For the first time in a dozen years, he unlocked the

top drawer. His eyes remained closed, his heart pounding rapidly, his pulse leaping in anticipation as he pulled. The old drawer stuck, but he yanked harder and it squeaked open.

Gingerly, he reached inside.

His fingers encountered the long leather sheath and he unbuckled it eagerly, suddenly anxious, knowing the end was so close. He had to force himself to slow down, extracting as much pleasure as possible as he slid the hunting knife from its case.

Then he opened his eyes.

Gazed down at the shiny honed blade, then tested it on his own palm.

A thin crimson line appeared upon his skin. Blood oozing. Another scar in the making.

It was perfect.

CHAPTER 28

"I thought I made it clear that you were off this investigation," Katherine Okano stated angrily from the throne that was her desk chair. She was polishing her glasses so furiously that Reed thought the lenses might pop out of the frames. "Or did you conveniently forget, Detective?"

"I remembered," he said tightly.

"And yet, there you are, big as life, caught on film. When we nail the killer what do you think his defense lawyer is going to come up with? Footage of one of the victim's lovers at a crime scene and proof that you were there when Barbara Marx's body was found along with the little nugget that you were her baby's father. Won't *that* be the reason you might contaminate or embellish the evidence to convict?" She stopped rubbing her glasses long enough to give him a long, hard stare. "You know I gave Morrisette specific instructions about you, so it's not just your ass that's in a sling right now. She's jeopardizing the case by keeping you privy to what's going on."

"The Grave Robber addresses his notes to me."

"Big deal. Just stop, Reed, and stop now or I'll have to ask for your badge."

"That won't be necessary." Searching his pocket, he came up with the wallet that held his police ID and badge. With a flick of his wrist, the leather case slid across her desk to land in front of her trademark glass of some iced-coffee concoction. "It's not Morrisette's fault. I coerced her."

"My ass." She settled her glasses on the bridge of her sharp nose. "You're not getting off this easy, Reed." She pushed the wallet back to him. "Just lay low. I'll see how I can handle this."

"And here I thought you didn't care," he mocked.

"Don't push me."

Picking up his ID, he started for the door. "Wouldn't dream of it, K.O.," he said, knowing he was lying through his teeth.

The day had been hell. After renting a car, Nikki had driven home and walked an excited and uproariously enthusiastic Mikado. Watching the dog scamper, chase squirrels and eagerly bark at strangers only reminded Nikki that she'd never see Simone again. Never hear her voice. Never stand her up.

But you can do something. You can help catch this creep. Put him away. He communicates with you.

And you can take care of her dog. She would have wanted that.

Though Jennings had been obviously miffed with the new little interloper, Nikki had decided that Mikado was to become a permanent addition to the family.

Leaving the dog and cat to sort things out, she finally drove to work and upon arriving was accosted at the coatrack by Tom Fink. "Nikki," he said in a hushed tone as she draped her scarf over an empty hook. "Can you spare a minute?"

"Of course."

"Good. Let's go to my office."

As they walked through the cubicles, she felt everyone's eyes upon her, sensed the curiosity in their gazes. Trina didn't even look up as she passed. Norm Metzger eyed her as if she were the enemy and Kevin studied her from beneath the rim of a baseball cap. Even the ever ebullient and inefficient Celeste stared openly as Tom escorted her into his office. It seemed to Nikki that all clicking of computer keys, ringing of phones and gentle buzz of conversation ceased as she walked by. The newspaper offices sounded more like an elevator with only the soft chords of piped-in music disturbing the silence.

"What's going on?" she asked as Tom waved her into

a side chair and took his seat behind the desk.

"That's what I'd like to know." He tented his hands in front of him and balanced his chin on his thumbs. "Something's up. Something major. You're getting notes from the killer, your apartment was broken into and now one of your best friends has become a victim of the killer you named the Grave Robber; have I got that right?"

"I thought the police weren't releasing the names of the most current victims until the next of kin had been notified."

"They have been. Simone Everly's parents have already heard the news as have Tyrell Demonico Brown's sister, kids and ex-wife."

"Bad news travels fast."

"Yes."

"Because we make sure it does."

"We, as in the paper? Oh, God, Nikki, don't tell me you've suddenly developed a conscience."

"I like to think I always had one."

"To report the news one has to be unbiased. Completely," he said and she sensed something bad was coming at her. Something with the velocity of a freight train. "Simone Everly was a friend of yours, wasn't she? Engaged to your brother years ago?" he asked, then, as if he were suddenly aware that he was coming on too strong, added, "For what it's worth, I'm sorry about what happened."

"Are you?" she shot back.

"Of course. This is an awful thing. Awful. It's no wonder you feel defensive."

"Defensive?" Where was this coming from?

"I wouldn't blame you if you threw in the towel."

She didn't respond, just waited. Sooner or later Tom would get to his point, the reason he'd pounced upon her the minute she'd walked into the office and started taking off her coat and scarf.

"Because of your relationship with Simone Everly and the Grave Robber, we have a unique opportunity here at the *Sentinel*."

"We?" she repeated.

"Mmm. Let's turn the tables around a bit," he said, moving his hands rapidly in two circular motions. "Instead of you doing the interview, you'll be interviewed."

This was getting worse by the minute.

"Norm can do an in-depth article about Simone, you, and the Grave Robber, kind of a full-circle thing. It'll focus on your relationship with the killer and one of his victims."

"No way. Tom, don't—" But he was already on his feet, tapping at the glass window and motioning someone in. A second later Norm Metzger slipped through the door. He was carrying a recorder, a pen, and a thick, virgin notepad without so much as an apostrophe on the pages.

"Nikki," he said, dipping his head but unable to conceal his smarmy smile.

"Tom told me about the article," she said and forced a replica of his grin.

"Great."

"I think I should start with a statement."

470

"Good idea," he said, though there was a new wariness in his tone. "What kind of statement?"

Nikki stood and kicked back her chair. "It's pretty simple and straightforward."

"Nikki—" Tom warned.

"Here it is, Metzger. When Ms. Gillette was asked about the death of her friend Simone Everly, her only response was a clipped, clear 'No comment!'"

And then she was outta there.

Reed stopped by the station, then drove to the funeral home where Barbara Jean Marx's life was being reviewed and relived by a young preacher who pronounced her name incorrectly and had to keep checking his notes as he spoke about her. It was a pathetic service. Low-budget and low-key despite the bevy of reporters camped outside the small chapel. He recognized most of them, including Norm Metzger from the *Sentinel,* but the one he was searching for wasn't around. Apparently Nikki Gillette couldn't stomach a funeral so soon after Simone's murder.

He didn't blame her. But Reed thought that the least he could do was pay his respects to the woman who'd been pregnant with his child and surreptitiously scan the mourners to see if any of the grief-stricken might be the killer. Morrisette and Siebert were in attendance as well, checking for a party crasher, a guy who got his jollies by killing his victims by dumping them into already-occupied coffins, then attending the funeral to check out the ravages of his deeds and feel superior in the knowledge that no one but he knew that he was the reason the victim was dead, the catalyst for the funeral itself.

But he didn't know many of Bobbi's friends or acquaintances. He spied Jerome Marx who seemed less sad than annoyed that he had to attend the service, a couple of undercover cops, some of the people she had worked with, but that was all.

It was a small, straggling, nervous group that listened to the inept preacher, bowed their heads in prayer and struggled with the words to a couple of obscure hymns. All in all, it was a depressing affair.

Afterwards, he decided not to approach Morrisette. There was just no reason to drag her into deeper trouble. She was already wading knee-deep in that particular muck as it was.

Outside the chapel, the wind was blowing full force, holding the rain at bay but stinging as it hit his face and hands. He drove to the graveyard where, once again, Barbara Jean Marx was buried. Fewer mourners gathered at the grave site and he observed them silently, wondering how they knew her, if some of the men had been her lovers, if any of them knew her killer.

". . . God be with you," the preacher said finally and Jerome Marx approached the casket, placing a rose and something shiny—the ring that the kid had found in Dahlonega—upon the flower draped casket. With that, he turned and left and the mourners dispersed just as the rain began to fall.

She was steamed as she cleaned out her desk. The

gall of Tom Fink. In league with Norm Metzger, that slimeball. Why she had expected more, she didn't know, but she had.

"This is a mistake," Trina said, rolling back her chair. "You're tired. You've suffered a tremendous loss and yeah, Norm and Tom are jerks, but you don't want to quit."

"That's where you're wrong." Nikki threw a jumble of pens and a notepad into the smallest of the three dilapidated boxes she's procured from the mail room. "I've wanted to get out of here for a long time. Now I have an excuse."

"But you need this job."

"No one needs this job," she said as she tossed in two coffee mugs, a nameplate and her Rolodex.

"What's going on?" a male voice asked from behind her and she nearly jumped out of her chair.

Kevin, earphones in place, was only a foot behind her. "God, don't you ever knock?" she said and when he didn't get the joke, didn't bother to explain.

"Nikki quit," Trina said.

"Quit? You?" His dark eyes flashed.

"That's right. Time for a change," she said and noticed Norm Metzger lurking on the other side of the stub wall.

He peered over the top, only his eyes and forehead showing.

"I've thought a lot of things about you over the years, Gillette, but I never figured you for a quitter."

She was bristly. Tired. On the edge, but she bit back a retort about what he could do with himself. "Guess you were wrong," she said as she swept some papers and files from the last drawer and dumped them into the largest of the boxes surrounding her desk chair. She dusted her hands. "That about does it."

"Don't you have to give two weeks' notice?" Kevin asked and she offered him a pained, I-don't-believe-I-just-heard-that expression.

"If Tom wants, I'll come in every day and warm this chair, but, really, I imagine he'll be glad I'm not here in his face."

"I just can't believe you're going." Trina's usual smile was missing and her eyes were stone-cold sober. "Things won't be the same."

"Maybe they'll be better." Nikki winked at her.

"Yeah, right."

"Need a hand with the boxes?" Kevin asked and Nikki nearly took him up on his offer, then thought better of it. "Thanks. I think I can manage."

"That's what I like about you," Norm said. "Belligerent to the end."

"Stuff it, Metzger." She slung the strap of her purse over one shoulder and picked up the largest of the boxes, then met Trina's gaze. "I'll call you later," she promised and vowed that she would do just that as she marched down the hallway and to the outside door where the afternoon was already dark, evening quick approaching.

She finished loading and started out of the parking lot just as her cell phone rang. Wondering if Reed were calling, she checked Caller ID and saw her parents' number on the display that also indicated her battery life was nearly depleted.

"Hello?" she said as she eased out of the parking lot for the last time.

"Nikki?" her mother asked, her voice faint, the connection faltering.

"Hi, Mom."

"Nikki . . . it . . . it's your father."

Charlene sounded so tenuous. So unsure.

"What about Dad?"

"I . . . I don't know."

"Is he sick?" Her heart rate kicked into high gear. "What about him?"

"I . . . Please . . ."

"Mom, call nine-one-one!"

"No! No!" Her mother sounded urgent, frightened. Oh, God, her father's heart. That's what it was.

"Then, I'll call."

"No, Nicole, don't."

"For crying out loud. Then call Lily or Kyle. I'm on my way. Mom?" Her cell phone died, the battery exhausted.

"Crap," Nikki said, and punched the accelerator. She only hoped she could get to her father in time. The drive was only ten minutes, but that time could be critical. She punched out 911 on her cell, was connected, then heard the operator answer.

"Nine-one-one. Police Emergency"—before the connection failed.

"This is Nikki Gillette. Please send someone to my father, Ronald Gillette's, address." She yelled the address into her phone, then told the dispatcher to get

475

hold of Pierce Reed, but it was to no avail. Her phone was dead.

Reed tried Nikki on her cell again. No answer. He left another message, then called the *Sentinel* and was told by an icy receptionist that "Nicole Gillette" was unavailable. When he pressed for a time he could expect her to return, the receptionist said she had no idea.

It didn't feel right.

But then, nothing did.

He dialed her apartment and got the answering machine. For whatever the reason, Nikki was under the radar and he didn't like it.

At all.

He grabbed his jacket and stopped by Morrisette's desk.

She was going through a pile of paperwork but looked up at the sound of his footsteps. "I heard you tried to turn in your badge."

"Good news travels fast."

"Don't do it, Reed."

"Why not?"

"She's not worth it."

He waited.

"Look, I'm not blind, okay? I saw the two of you together. You've got it bad for Nikki Gillette, but she's just playin' you, man. Using you for all she can."

"You're sure about that?"

"Yeah. I am. And don't ask me about the Grave Robber case, okay, cuz I can't tell you anything."

"Maybe I should try Siebert."

"Be my guest." Morrisette wasn't about to budge.

"So, did you check out Corey Sellwood and Sean Hawke?"

"I warned you." She glared up at him and shuffled some papers, then sighed. "Okay, I don't see what this will hurt. They're clean, all right. Iron-clad alibis. Not suspects, so forget them. When we find Chevalier, we'll have our boy."

"Then find him," Reed said. "Fast."

"We're working on it." He turned to leave and she cleared her throat. "I'm going outside for a smoke."

"So?"

She looked him dead in the eye. "You'd better get out of here, Reed. I don't need this kind of trouble."

He got it then. Understood the unspoken message in Sylvie Morrisette's determined glare. "Fine. I'll see ya around."

"If you're lucky."

He hurried out of the building and hunched his shoulders against a rain so cold it stung the back of his neck and chilled his skin. Where the hell was Nikki? What if the Grave Robber were playing with them—twelve jurors and three more people. Him, Nikki and an unknown. There had to be a reason for the killer to keep contacting Reed and Nikki . . . but who would be the third? The connection was the Chevalier trial, so who besides the jurors . . . The Judge.

Had to be.

Seventeen. Twelve jurors. The detective who was alive who had made the collar, the reporter who had reported on the trial and the judge.

Except the reporter nearly got the case thrown out. Maybe she was safe.

But she didn't get it thrown out, did she? She failed Chevalier. As had Reed. As had the jurors. As had the judge.

Judge Ronald Gillette.

More certain than ever, he climbed into his El Dorado. He hadn't gone two blocks when his cell phone rang. "Reed," he answered crisply.

"Look, I'm sorry to give you the brush-off, but I'm walkin' a fine line, here," Morrisette said. "Okano tore me a new one this morning, okay?"

"Got it."

"But I thought you should know that the nine-one-one dispatcher called me. Nikki Gillette called in about ten minutes ago, identified herself and then the connection was lost. They called back to the number dialed in, but she didn't answer. It was her cell phone. I tried her home and office and got no answer and a strange response at the *Sentinel*. I was just about to call you when you stopped by my desk. You might want to check up on her."

"I will," Reed said.

"I've already got a unit sent to her apartment and another one to the *Sentinel*. If she's located, I'll let you know. To hell with Okano."

"Thanks. I think Nikki Gillette's a target. One of seventeen," Reed said, his voice devoid of emotion as he told Morrisette his theory.

Morrisette listened. "You sure?" she asked and he heard her making the sounds of lighting up.

"It's all I've got. As I said, it's not perfect."

"Shit. Nothing is."

He didn't want to believe his theory himself as he watched the wipers slap away the rain. He silently prayed that this was just a mistake, that was all. He ached to think that Nikki was fine. A part of him trusted that she was okay. But the other part, the logical cop, knew better. A darkness settled in his heart and he felt a fear as deep as he'd ever known.

"Mom! Dad!" Nikki yelled, throwing open the garage door of her parents' house and bursting into the kitchen, but no one answered. Aside from the clock on the wall ticking and the refrigerator droning, there was total silence. Sandra wasn't in the kitchen cooking, but then, Nikki realized, this was her day off. The TV wasn't blaring, nor did she hear her mother's off-key humming.

So, where were they? And why were the lights so dim?

"Mom?"

Had they gone to the hospital?

Both cars were parked in their respective spots in the garage; Nikki had checked on her way inside. So, unless they'd called an ambulance or a friend . . . Anxiety tensed her muscles. "Mom?" she said again, shaking the rain from her coat.

Again, no response.

Something was wrong. Terribly wrong.

It's only your case of nerves because of the phone call.

She reached for the phone as she noticed a flickering light from the den. The television. But no sound.

She carried the portable phone with her. Rounding the corner to the den, she felt an instant's relief. Her father was half lying in his favorite recliner, his feet propped up, the television on but muted. He looked sound asleep. Dead to the world.

"Jesus, Dad, you scared me," she said softly, hoping he would rouse. She set the phone on a table. "Where's Mom? She called frantic a while ago." When he didn't respond, she walked to the chair and touched him lightly on the shoulder. "Hey, Pops." No response. She felt a new niggle of worry. "Dad? Wake up." His head was lolled to one side and his breathing was so shallow. Or nonexistent? Her heart slammed against her ribs. "Dad?" she said more loudly, leaning over him, bending close, listening for some sign of life as she shook his shoulder.

But there was no whisper of breath from his lungs. "No . . . oh, God, no . . . Dad! *Dad!*"

Then, she noticed the blood. Not on him, but from the corner of her eye she spied what appeared to be a trickle of red running from the hallway.

"Mom?" she said, her heart in her throat. *Oh, dear God, no!* Why the blood? Why? Was her mother wounded? Every hair on the back of her arms raised as she heard a low moan. Her mother's soft voice. "Mom, I'm coming. I'll get help," she called, running toward the hallway when she heard something behind her, a footstep that had come from the direction of the kitchen.

She whirled.

And saw him.

Bloody and wet. His face set and hard, eyes glittering beneath a high forehead and a hank of dripping hair that fell over eyes so cruel she screamed. In one hand he held a hypodermic needle. In the other a bloodied hunting knife.

The Grave Robber.

Icy fear scissored through her as she recognized him. "Where's my mother?" she demanded, backing up, her pulse thundering loudly.

No answer. Just a glitter of satisfaction in his gaze.

"If you hurt her, I'll kill you, you sick, twisted son of a bitch," she hissed, backing up. There were loaded rifles in the gun closet, carving knives in the kitchen, the phone receiver only inches away on the table. Only three more steps.

"Your turn, Nikki," he said with a cold, sardonic smile that was pure evil. And the blood. All the damned blood. Whose? Her mother's?

Oh, God. She couldn't outrun him; he'd be on her before she'd gone three steps. Somehow, she had to beat him, trick him.

She whipped around, turning as if to run.

He sprang, his weapons clenched in his fists.

Instantly, she dived, spinning on one leg, kicking up hard with the other.

Her boot connected with his groin.

"Oooh!"

With a yowl, he went down. The knife clattered to the floor, but he grabbed it quickly and managed to hold fast onto the needle. She kicked again, aiming for his nose, but he drew back his head and she crashed the heel of her boot into the side of his face.

"You bitch!" he roared, dropping his needle and scrabbling at her boot, his fingers raking down the leather as she started to run, fast, snatching the hand-held phone on the fly.

He was on his feet in an instant, bearing down on her. She punched nine, snagged a photo from the wall and hurled it at him. She hit one and one again as she flew out of the house and down the two short steps into the garage. "Help!" she cried, gasping into the receiver. "I'm being attacked! By the Grave Robber. My mother's hurt. The bastard killed my dad. Send someone to—" But the phone was dead, too far from the base to pick up a signal.

Damn! Her keys! Where the hell were her keys! She fumbled in her pocket, found the single key to her rental car. He was in the garage, his face enraged as he stumbled, running. She slid into the rental, slammed the door and locked it with shaking fingers. Her cell phone! Where was it?

He leaped, pounded on the windshield.

Frantically, seeing his bloody face smashed against the windshield, she jammed her key into the ignition. The engine turned over.

He was only inches from her. Separated by a thin layer of glass.

The engine caught and she jammed the car in reverse, gunned the throttle and glanced in the rearview mirror to see a pickup, a huge pickup blocking her path.

No! She jammed on the brakes.

He must've been waiting for her in the next alley, his lights dimmed, and rolled quietly behind her while she walked into her parent's house.

She reached for the cell. Maybe there was a little life in the battery.

Crash!

Glass splintered everywhere as the driver's-side window smashed.

Nikki screamed and jumped, but it was too late; she saw the deadly needle a split second before it jabbed hard into her shoulder. "You can't get away," he said with chilling calm. An evil smile slid from one side of his bloodied face to the other. His eyes glittered maliciously.

She screamed at the top of her lungs.

Tried to fight through the shards of shattered glass.

But it was useless.

She could barely move. The door to the car opened and he was there, looming in the night, the bloody knife a testament to his killing. Fleetingly, she thought of her mother, of her father, her family and Pierce Reed before the darkness dragged her under.

CHAPTER 29

With each passing minute, Reed's panic increased. He'd stopped by Nikki's apartment and found no sign of her, even after coercing that lame-brained manager Fred Cooper to let him inside. Everything looked pretty much the same as it had when he'd left this morning. The cat regarded them suspiciously from the top of the bookcase and the little dog danced around his feet.

"She has another pet, you know." Cooper said. "She knows better. There are no dogs allowed in this building. I told her the cat was even iffy when she moved in."

"It's a friend's dog," Reed said, then listened to the messages on her answering machine. Messages, Cooper told him, the other officers had already heard.

There were two. "Hey, it's Sean. Come on, Nik, cut me a break, would ya? Give me a call. You know the number." Reed's jaw clenched at the sound of the guy. There was a pause before the next message played. "Nikki?" a frail woman whispered. "Nikki, it's . . . it's Mom . . . call me . . . it's, um, it's urgent." Another long pause. "It's about Dad."

The message on the phone was timed at four-seventeen. A couple of hours earlier.

He called the number listed on Caller ID for Ronald Gillette. The phone rang until an answering machine picked up and Judge Gillette's voice boomed through the wires, instructing the caller to leave name, number and message.

Reed complied. "This is Detective Pierce Reed of the Savannah Police Department. I'm looking for Nicole Gillette. If you hear from her, please have her call me." He left his number and hung up.

"I just don't know what I'm going to do about this dog," Fred Cooper said, his lips pursed as he stared at the little mutt. "I already said as much to the other officers who were here a little while ago."

"I do. You're going to leave him right here for now. Until you hear from Nikki."

"But, I have a legal obligation to . . ." He sighed and backed down. "All right. For now, he stays. But the minute she gets back, the *minute,* I want to speak to her."

Reed only hoped Cooper got the chance to ream Nikki out, but as he drove through the rain and gathering darkness to the *Sentinel*'s offices, he couldn't shake the sensation that something was very wrong. No one had called him, even though Morrisette had promised that if the units she'd sent to Nikki's apartment and the newspaper offices had found anything out, she would call. Reed couldn't sit around and wait. He decided to check things out for himself.

He didn't feel much better once he was at the newspaper. Nikki had been there, but had cleaned out her desk and no one, not even her friend Trina, had heard from her since.

Not that it was all that odd, he supposed, and yet as he stood at her empty workstation, looking at the crime scene wallpaper of her computer monitor, he experienced and ever increasing sense of anxiety.

However, Tom Fink, the aptly named editor, wasn't worried. "Look, as I told the other cops, she got her knickers in a knot, cleaned out her desk and stormed out." A pompous ass if ever there was one, Fink leaned a hip against what had been Nikki's desk and folded his arms over his chest. "She's a hothead."

"Why'd she leave?"

"Didn't want to do a story I assigned her."

"And what was that?" Reed asked.

"Another installment on the Grave Robber."

"And she objected?" Reed knew what was coming. "Let me guess . . . it was a story around the latest victim, right?"

Fink shrugged. "We heard that he got Simone Everly. She was a friend of Nikki's. It seemed like a natural."

"To sell more newspapers."

"That's our business, Detective." Norm Metzger, the *Sentinel*'s smarmy crime reporter, sidled up to the group. He'd obviously been eavesdropping from behind the stub wall. "She should have been objective. Sure, she lost a friend, but how can she help her or save the next potential victim if she doesn't tell her story and warn the public? We just wanted to do a tribute to Simone Everly and report what had happened to her. It's news."

"It's always news until it's someone close to you. Then, it's personal and called sensationalism."

"As a reporter, she should remain objective," Fink stated.

"No wonder she walked out."

"Listen, Reed, you do your job and I'll do mine. I don't need any bullshit from the police department."

Reed felt the cords on the back of his neck stand out and it took all his strength to keep his hands from curling into fists. "And we don't need any pseudo-sanctimonious crap from the press." He turned his gaze to the next cubicle where a wide-eyed Trina had listened to the entire exchange. "If you hear from Ms. Gillette," he instructed, "please have her call me ASAP."

"Absolutely." She took down his cell number, sent a withering glare in Fink's direction and rolled her chair toward her desk.

"I'll be calling your superior," Fink threatened.

"Please. Do," Reed invited. "Show her what a stellar, public-serving individual you are!"

Reed left the *Sentinel* with a worse opinion of journalists than he'd had when he'd walked in. Which, considering his viewpoint, was damned near impossible.

Scum.

Maggots.

Vultures.

Tom Fink and Norm Metzger fit right into the pathetic mold, he thought, ignoring the rain as it swirled from the sky. He'd nearly reached his car when Trina, shoulders hunched against the cold, ran to catch up to him. "Detective Reed," she called, waving to flag him down, her slim skirt and high-heeled boots making her steps short and quick. She was breathless and soaked by the time she reached him. "I just wanted you to know that Nikki was really upset when she left. I don't know what went on in the meeting she had with Tom, but she was furious. I tried to talk her into staying, but she'd made up her mind."

"Do you have any idea where she'd go?" he asked and Trina lifted a shoulder.

"Only home. She had all the stuff from her desk with her. But she did get a couple of calls that were inadvertently sent to my voice mail." She lowered her voice to a whisper, her teeth chattering. "Celeste, our receptionist, is an idiot." A streak of lightning hissed through the sky. Trina jumped.

"So, who phoned?"

She handed him a wet note with numbers that had begun to run. "The first one is from Sean, he's an old boyfriend who doesn't seem to know how to take a hint, and the second is her mother." Trina's dark eyes clouded as thunder pealed over the rush of traffic. "It was an odd call. Mrs. Gillette sounded upset."

Reed was reminded of the message left on Nikki's home machine. "Thanks."

"If you . . . no, *when* you find her, will you let me know?" Trina asked. "I'm worried. The Grave Robber was contacting her directly."

"I'll have Nikki call."

"Thanks." She started toward the office and Reed was left more anxious than before. He tried Nikki's cell phone again, but there was still no answer. The same with the Ronald Gillette home. Maybe one of her parents had taken ill and she'd rushed them to the hospital—no, that didn't explain why her cell phone wasn't working. Unless it was out of battery life.

He dug through his notebook and located her brother and sister's phone numbers. As he drove, he first called Kyle, who sounded irritated about being pulled away from the television blaring in the background and who informed him that he hadn't seen Nikki since Thanksgiving. Another strike. Reed then called Lily. Another piece of work.

"I haven't heard from Nikki since she stood me up. Again. I wanted her to baby-sit and she bagged out on me, which is par for the course. Her M.O. All Nikki really cares about is her job, or more specifically, her ambitions. . . . She wants to be the best damned crime reporter this town has ever seen and it really pisses her off to be on the town meeting desk or whatever it is she does. So now she's hot on the trail of the Grave Robber, just like she was last summer when that other serial killer was running around. I'm telling you, if she keeps this up, she's going to end up dead herself. God, she's just so . . . so Nikki!"

Reed waited until she'd quit ranting, then asked, "So what about your parents? Have you heard from your mother today?"

"No . . . why?" Instant concern.

"Your mother left several messages for her. She sounded worried. But she didn't call you?"

"That's odd," Lily said, all of her anger suddenly vanishing. "I mean, usually, if Mom needs anything—and I mean *any*thing—she calls me. Nikki's convinced my parents that she's too busy, so they don't rely on her. But I've been home all day and Mom never called. Not once."

The muscles in the back of Reed's neck tightened. "You're certain?"

"Of course I am. But I'll call right now."

"Good. Keep trying. I phoned earlier and left a message. No one's called back."

"Oh, my God, you don't think something awful has happened, do you?"

"Probably not," he said, not believing it for a minute. "I'll go over there."

"It would be best if you stayed by the phone. I'll dispatch a unit," he said.

"If you're sure."

"Absolutely. I'm already on my way."

"Then you'll have Mom call or you'll phone me, right?"

"Yes." He hung up and floored the Cadillac, heading straight to the upscale neighborhood of three acre lots where Judge Ronald Gillette had retired. Traffic was light, the streets dark with winter dusk, the intense rain slamming against the windshield and blurring the red glow of taillights.

He pulled into the driveway and his heart nosedived when he recognized Nikki's rental car parked outside the garage where the door was left wide open, two vehicles visible in the wash of his headlights. An older Mercedes sat next to a sleek new BMW convertible. But the house and garage were dark.

No lamplight glowed through the windows of the graceful old home, not even a porch light was lit. The other houses on the street were separated by fences, hedges, dense shrubbery and rolling acres.

Reed didn't like what he saw. Not at all. He punched out Morrisette's cell phone number and explained what was going on as lightning forked and thunder clapped.

"Jesus Christ, Reed, wait for backup," Morrisette ordered. "This could be some kind of trap. Chevalier probably knows we're on to him."

"I'm going in."

"No way. Don't do it. We'll be there in less than ten minutes."

"Make it five." He hung up. Going against all of his training, he followed his instincts. There was a good chance Nikki was inside. He intended to find her.

No security lights blazed as he approached. No face appeared in a window. No sound escaped from the two stories of white clapboard and green shutters. Steeling himself, he crept through the garage, then pushed open the door. "Police!" he yelled. "Drop your weapons!"

From far in the distance he heard the wail of a siren, but inside, the house was silent as death. Dark.

Heart pounding in his ears, he snapped on the switch. The mud room was suddenly illuminated. No one. No sound. He took a deep breath, then moved quickly. Stealthily. Two steps to the wall. He reached around the open door casing and flipped on another light. The kitchen was now illuminated and still no one moved, there wasn't a sound.

"Police!" he yelled again. "Drop your weapons and kick them into the kitchen. Then come out with your hands over your head where I can see them!"

Again, all he heard was silence and the low hum of the furnace forcing air through the ducts while the wind kicked up outside. If he stepped into the light now and the killer was waiting around the corner, he'd be a sitting duck.

He could wait a few more minutes.

"Ummph."

The low moan sent a shock wave through him.

His ears strained. "Is anyone there?"

Another muffled groan over the sound of a siren splintering the night. Tires screeched outside and he heard Morrisette barking orders.

Seconds later she was at his side. "We've got the place surrounded," Morrisette stated. "What the hell's going on?"

"Not sure. But someone's over there." He motioned across the room to a doorway hanging slightly ajar about the same time that Cliff Siebert joined them in the mud room. "Cover me."

"You got it," Siebert said and Reed sprinted across the kitchen, then flattened to the wall beside the open door.

"Police!" he yelled again and the muffled cry increased. It sounded like a woman's voice. He could barely breathe. "Nikki?" he yelled and the response was another muted cry.

"Don't go in there!" Morrisette warned. "I've got a man outside and he's reported that he can't see through the window. The shades are pulled down."

Tough.

Weapon drawn, Reed whipped around the corner, kicked open the door so hard it banged against the wall and snapped on the light. He stared in horror at the scene before him and yelled over his shoulder, "Get an ambulance! We need EMTs. NOW!"

Inside, bound and gagged, was a frail woman Reed recognized as Charlene Gillette. Her eyes were wide and terror-riddled and she was shaking, whimpering behind the gag. All around the woman was a dark, coagulating pool of blood.

He bent over her and tore off the gag as footsteps pounded behind him. "I'm Detective Reed with the police department, Mrs. Gillette. Hang in there."

"I'll take over." A young EMT with a military haircut, whip-thin body, and commanding attitude had snapped on gloves and knelt beside the shivering woman. "No visible wounds," he muttered as he unbound her.

"But all this blood?"

"Holy shit!" Morrisette appeared in the doorway. "Okay, we need to preserve this scene. Touch as little as possible!" Her eyes moved from the woman to one wall where Gillette family memorabilia hung. "Jesus Christ," she whispered and Reed turned to the wall where awards, certificates and pictures were hung neatly.

His stomach clenched. "That son of a bitch." Portraits of the family, snapshots of crucial moments blown up and mounted, even some pictures with pets were framed and placed side by side. It was the pictures that held his attention. There was a message hurriedly scrawled on the wall beneath a blown up snapshot of Nikki Gillette and her father at her college graduation. It was a clear summer day, Nikki's wild hair was tousled in a breeze, her father's arm draped over the shoulders of her graduation gown, her mortarboard at an angle as she smiled and squinted into the camera. Judge Ron towered over her, grinning proudly.

The single word message that ran and streaked down the knotty pine wall read: *LE BLANC.*

French for "The White."

And the name of a cemetery on the north side of town.

Nikki opened a bleary eye and felt pain jarring through every bone in her body. But it was too dark to see and she was disoriented, her mind thick, her mouth tasting foul. She had the sensation of movement, but that was ridiculous, right? She was lying in her bed . . . no . . . where was she? Thoughts drifted in and out of her mind in restless waves, as if they were carried upon a sluggish, murky sea.

She remembered that Simone was dead . . . Oh, no . . . maybe that was a dream and . . . She lifted her head.

Bang!

Ouch!

Her forehead rammed into something hard.

Tears sprang to her eyes. Dear God, what was happening? She tried to raise her hand to rub the knot on her forehead but she could barely move . . . it was as if she were wedged into a box . . . a tight box and . . . and . . . Oh, dear Lord, something was wrong, something she should remember. *Think, Nikki, think! Where the hell are you? You should know.* She willed her brain to concentrate, but she kept wanting to fall back to sleep.

You can't! Something is terribly, terribly wrong. . . .

She tried to reach around her, but could barely move and the panic she felt was fuzzy and far away. She felt the mattress beneath her. Lumpy. Soft and cold and uneven pressing into her back and on her shoulders. When she moved her head, the back of it connected with something hard . . . and . . . and . . . Oh, no!

Her eyes fluttered open. Her mind was so foggy, she had to strain to think. Where was she? She'd been looking for someone . . . and . . . and . . . . Oh, God, was she, like Simone, packed into a coffin? With a dead body beneath her!

She should try to fight, to scream. She was going to be buried alive. That part she remembered. She had to do something fast. But still her mind was like molasses, the drug she'd been given pulling her under again. She tried to scream, but couldn't. It was as if she were slogging through quicksand and her mind wouldn't clear. She remembered the needle and blacking out.

Maybe this was all just a dream, a really bad dream. She tried to grasp onto conscious thought, but the drug in her system kept working on her, dragging her back into the blissful blackness . . . and with terror lurking in the dark corners of her consciousness, she quit fighting and let go, slipping once again into the void.

The bitch had hurt him. His crotch still throbbed where she'd nailed him in the nuts and the side of his face ached, compliments of her sharp-heeled boots.

But she hadn't gotten away. No. She was getting everything she deserved. Finally. Like the rest.

Nikki Gillette was already in a casket. Soon to draw

her last breath, soon to know the fear and pain, the sheer terror of being helpless, at the mercy of someone stronger. She, like the others, had crumpled before him, always underestimating his strength and cunning.

As he drove outside of the city, The Survivor swiped a bloody hand over his forehead, catching a glimpse of himself in the rearview mirror. Blood covered a face streaked with mud, compliments of Le Blanc Cemetery. His hair was wet and plastered to his head, his muscles sore from the hard work and the wounds she'd inflicted.

But he'd suffered worse and survived. Nikki Gillette's pathetic attempt at harming him was nothing.

His mission for the night was nearly accomplished. Soon, the police would arrive and he imagined the look of horror on that bastard Reed's face as he opened the coffin buried deep in the mud of Le Blanc Cemetery.

"Too late," the Grave Robber said aloud as he headed steadily north, wipers slogging through the rain that pummeled his windshield. Past the lights of the city, he saw a flash of lightning sizzling through the night sky. Rolling claps of thunder followed.

It seemed fitting.

A storm was raging as Nikki Gillette breathed her last.

Unfortunately he couldn't finish all of his business. Not right away. He would have to lay low for a while. Now, for certain, the police would know who he was and it would take time, after tonight, for him to be able to continue his quest. But the principals had been punished. Those who'd been most influential at the trial.

The other jurors, had, he'd sensed even then, been weaker, not as strong of personalities, their opinions more easily swayed. They wouldn't get away. He'd find them, one at a time, and when they least expected it, he'd spring. He'd have to make the first couple look like accidents in a year or so, just so he wouldn't arouse any suspicion. He smiled to himself as a police car drove past, flying down the road in the opposite direction.

"Go get 'em," he muttered, watching in his mirror as the cruiser's lights flashed on and disappeared around a corner.

Chuckling to himself, he felt invincible.

He only wished he could witness Pierce Reed opening the coffin lid and discovering that he was too late. By the time the casket was pried open, Nikki Gillette would be dead.

CHAPTER 30

Reed's gut clenched with fear. Had the blood in the Gillette home been Nikki's? What had that twisted bastard done to her?

His headlights cut a wide swath of light through Le Blanc Cemetery, illuminating the old gravestones and plots and he told himself to hang in there, to have faith; he couldn't help her if he went off the deep end. And yet, terror unlike any he'd ever known tore at him.

Other police cars followed him through the intricately designed iron gates that the caretaker had opened a few minutes before.

"Please, God, no," he whispered as he parked the El Dorado and the rain poured from the sky.

He saw it as he climbed out of the car. A fresh mound of mud already collecting puddles near the back wall. He started running. Oh, God, was he too late?

No, no, no! She couldn't be buried here, even now trying to claw her way out.

"Over here!" he yelled, his pants wet over his ankles. Flashlights bobbed, people shouted as other cops wearing slickers and carrying shovels and picks and crowbars poured over the area.

A big cop tossed Reed a shovel and they began digging frantically, trying to save a life, each cop knowing what they were up against with the Grave Robber.

To hell with the crime scene, Reed thought, shoveling faster; all that mattered was to get Nikki out alive! He strained to hear any sound from the earth below, barely noticed that other cops, radios crackling, cell phones jangling, were roping off the area and starting to make a grid.

He dug frantically. Fearfully. Knowing that every second that passed could cost Nikki her life.

Hold on, darlin', he thought, throwing shovelful after shovelful of the muck over his shoulder. *I'm coming. Just you hold on!*

Faster and faster he flung mud over his shoulder as rain pounded down in sheets that shimmered on the tombstones and danced in the beams of flashlights. He didn't bother with a slicker, just kept throwing his weight into each scoop of muck he could loosen.

What were the chances that she was still alive? God damn Chevalier. God damn his soul to hell! If she was dead, Reed would take the law into his own hands. That bastard would never have a chance to get out of jail again.

Come on, Nikki, hang in there, he silently said and remembered another night in San Francisco, recalled sitting in the dark on the stakeout, watching what he'd thought was a sex game through the shades until he'd realized the silhouette he was viewing had turned from a game into a violent struggle for her life. Reed had raced into the building, taking the stairs two at a time to her apartment, but it had been too late.

But not this time.

It couldn't happen again. Not to Nikki. Not Nikki. Reed sent up another quick prayer. And still he shoveled. Sweat ran down his back, cold rain peppered his head. Voices shouted. Diane Moses was squawking about her crime scene.

Fuck off! Reed thought as his shovel struck thick wood.

"We got something!" another officer said, his shovel clunking against the top of a long box.

Wildly they dug with shovels and hands, scooping away the mud, uncovering the coffin's lid. Over the rush of wind and the splash of raindrops and voices around him, Reed strained to hear something, anything, coming from inside the casket. He heard nothing. He pounded on the lid. Stomped on it. "Nikki!" he yelled. "Nikki!" Oh, Jesus, was he too late? Like before? Had the blood on the wall been hers?

"Don't mess up the coffin," Diane Moses warned. "That's evidence, Reed. There could be tool marks or fingerprints or—"

"Open it up. Now!" he yelled, ignoring Moses, his fingers raking at the casket's mud-slickened top. "Now!"

It was sealed tight. Wedged into the hole.

His heart pounding fearfully, he and a burly cop used crowbars to wedge into the top, using their weight against the handles of their tools, blinking against the rain, straining in the night.

"It's no use, we'll have to lift it," Cliff Siebert yelled down at them.

"We don't have the time," he screamed, flinging his weight harder against the bar.

"We'll get the equipment."

"For God's sake, we have to open this fucker now!" He and the big man leaned on one bar, their muscles flexing, cords of their necks visible, jaws set. He felt the bar give. Just a little.

The big man roared and pressed harder and there was a cracking sound as the seal gave way. They both straddled the coffin, their legs sinking into the mud as they forced open the lid and the smell of blood and death seeped out.

"God, no," Reed whispered, hearing nothing. "Nikki?" He pulled the flashlight from his pocket and, heart thudding in dread, shined its thin beam through the crack to the bloodied, mutilated corpse within.

Reed thought he might be sick as he stared into the

glassy eyes of a very dead LeRoy Chevalier.

Nikki dragged in a breath. Opened an eye to the intense darkness.

Her mind was foggy. She reached up and hit her hands.

Just like before. You thought it was all part of a macabre dream, but it's not.

"No!" she cried, trying to sit up and cracking her head again. It couldn't be. She couldn't be trapped in a coffin! This was a sick dream.

Adrenaline pumped through her blood.

Instantly her mind cleared.

There was something beneath her, something that felt like a big, lumpy body and . . . and . . . She touched her leg with her hand, then her hip and her chest. She could barely move but she realized she was naked and definitely pressed into a box . . . No . . . oh, no . . . this couldn't be a casket! Whatever she was in was moving. She felt the bumps as it bounced. Or was being transported. Faintly she heard the whine of an engine. Probably a truck carrying her to what the Grave Robber thought was her final resting place.

With a dead body beneath her.

That was it.

Terror cut her to the core and she nearly threw up. She couldn't be buried alive in a coffin, and oh, please, God, and not mashed into a rotting, dead body.

Panic strangled her. She began clawing, pressing against the top of her cage. The lid didn't budge.

This was insane. She had to get out! Had to! This

small dark space . . . Her mind tried to turn to jelly; she'd always been a little claustrophobic, but she wouldn't die this way. Couldn't. As long as she wasn't yet buried, she had time. She could escape.

Think, Nikki. Don't lose it. Do something! Do something smart!

She forced herself to concentrate, to keep the panic at bay.

She remembered going to her parents' house without the gun her father had insisted she carry. If only she had that weapon now, she might be able to save her life, but no, she hadn't had it with her when she'd found her father and come face to face with the Grave Robber.

Sick, detestable bastard.

And to think she'd once felt empathy for him.

How foolish she'd been.

He'd duped them all and now she was his captive, his next victim along with the corpse on which she'd been placed. Her skin crawled and it was all she could do not to cry out, but she knew that would be to no avail. Hadn't she heard Simone's pathetic wails? No doubt the animal would record her screams should she cry out, getting his rocks off listening to her terror as she realized she was trapped in this casket with a dead, rotting cadaver . . . but there wasn't a stench, nor the sickening scent of weak, decomposing flesh. Just the slight smell of cigars and whiskey, the same blend of scents that had surrounded her father, the aromas she equated with safety and trust and . . .

She froze. Her mind wandered to a forbidden territory more bizarre than what she already knew to be true.

Her throat clutched.

The bastard wouldn't have . . . couldn't have been so cold-hearted, so diabolically sick to have forced her into a coffin with . . . with . . . her father!

NO!

She couldn't believe it, *wouldn't* believe anything so disgusting.

And yet?

Wasn't her father dead or near death in the house? Wasn't the corpse beneath her fresh . . . still not cold? And whoever was beneath her was large and smelled like . . . *Oh, Daddy.*

She swallowed back tears, forced her fear and anger at bay. Gingerly, her skin crawling, she touched the clothing on the body beneath her. She felt the stiff weave of slacks and the cold buckle of a belt, the hands beneath hers were big with hair upon their backs.

Oh, Daddy, no . . .

Bile burned up her throat. She nearly heaved as the stark, horrid realization hit her. She was trapped in a coffin with her dead father! Her fists clenched in rage. Tears filled her eyes. She wanted to scream and rant and kick, but she fought the urge to cry out, to say anything as much as a whisper. That's what the bastard was waiting for. That's how the sick son of a bitch got off.

Nikki refused to give him the satisfaction of so much as a whimper, not even though the air was thin and breathing was getting harder by the minute, not even when panic screamed through her and she wanted to kick and claw and pound her way out of her prison.

You twisted, bilious piece of shit!

She was shaking violently. Her mind splintering between fury and fear.

Think, Nikki, think. You have to hold it together. It's your only chance. Get this bastard. Find a way to nail him. Turn the goddamned tables!

How? She was trapped.

The only weapon you have against him is your brain.

He's stronger.

He's athletic.

He's determined.

He's psychotic.

But if he's not satisfied, if you don't give him the crying, begging, pitiful sobs he's expecting, he may open the lid. . . . You have to be patient. No matter how badly your lungs are burning, you have to wait it out. . . .

Her fingers dug into her palms. Her lungs burned. There was a damned good chance she was about to die. A damned good chance.

She was probably waking up. Feeling the effects of the drug but at least realizing where she was, what would be her fate. The Survivor smiled to himself as he drove.

And now she knew that he'd survived. Beaten the system.

It was so dark in this part of the country that he nearly missed the turn-off to the old, forgotten, overgrown cemetery, even though he'd been here earlier—but there had been a bit of daylight to guide him. But now, with the storm raging, his wipers could barely clear the windows and visibility was poor.

Which was perfect.

He eased off the gas and stopped the truck at the old family plot. Leaving the pickup's door open, he stepped outside and into the maelstrom. Rain and wind lashed at him as he walked up the overgrown ruts that had once been a gravel road. The rusted gate creaked as it swung inward. Earlier he'd found it unlocked and pre-pared the grave site—the final resting place—for Judge Ronald Gillette and his worthless daughter. "Rest in peace, you bastard," The Survivor muttered under his breath as rain drizzled down his nose. The man had been elected to mete out justice and he'd been a joke, an embarrassment to the court system.

LeRoy Chevalier should never have seen the light of day again. If not executed, then kept in a small dark cell until he rotted to death.

But there had been screwups from the beginning, with the arrest, with the crime scene, with Nikki's article in the paper. As The Survivor had watched it all play out, he'd seen the eyes of the jury, unconvinced that LeRoy Chevalier was the true monster he was. They heard conflicting testimony and with the murder weapon missing and only circumstantial evidence of a bloody boot print, the case wasn't as strong as it could have been.

Because Reed and his partner didn't do their job.

Because Judge Gillette didn't preside correctly.

Because Nikki Gillette blundered with her story.

Because the jury was weak.

So they had to be killed. One by one. Twelve spineless jurors, a worthless judge, two inept detectives, a bungling reporter and of course, the monster himself—LeRoy Chevalier, the worst kind of scum that had ever walked the planet.

Even now he heard Chevalier's raspy voice: *What are you a girl? A stupid girl?* Just before the belt would snake from its worn loops.

Never again! *Never!*

With all the mistakes at the trial, it had been a miracle he'd gotten three life sentences in prison.

But it hadn't stuck, had it? And now, all those who hadn't done their jobs, those who had sworn to protect the victims and justice, the jurors, the judge, the cops and even a reporter who almost blew the whole damned trial were paying. Along with the monster.

After swinging the gate wide, he drove through the muddy grass. His throat tightened a bit as he noticed the three twelve-year-old graves. Carol Legittel and two of her three children, poor Marlin and Becky. So foolish. Where had they been when he'd needed them? Why hadn't they stopped the sickness? In his mind's eye he remembered Chevalier ordering him onto his knees, then into bed . . . with . . .

He pounded a fist on the steering wheel and tears burned in his eyes.

Don't think about it. Don't think about what he forced you to do. Don't think about the pain and humiliation and the fact that no one helped you. Not your mother, not your brother, not your sister, not even the police.

Pierce Reed, coming to the house, feigning concern, offering his card . . . his damned card . . . when he suspected what was going on! What a joke. What a fucking pathetic joke.

In his mind's eye he saw the sweaty, scared bodies of his sister and brother and mother, the naked skin, the twisted bedsheets and he heard Chevalier's wicked grunts and laughter.

No more. *NO MORE!*

He caught a glimpse of his reflection in the rearview mirror and saw the redness in his eyes. The useless tears.

Maybe he was a stupid-ass girl after all.

Blinking rapidly, he turned his attention to the small cemetery and did a quick U-turn. The deep hole he had dug was visible in his backup lights and he rolled across the graves of his mother, brother and stupid sister before stomping on the parking brake and cutting the engine.

He didn't have much time. Reed would figure out what was happening as soon as he uncovered LeRoy Chevalier's body at Le Blanc Cemetery.

He had to work fast.

All motion ceased.

The drone of the engine was extinguished.

The coffin stopped moving.

Nikki's muscles froze.

Every nerve ending jittered.

She didn't have to be told that he'd brought her to a cemetery. That within minutes, perhaps seconds, he'd start burying her alive. She was shaking. Now was the time to act. But what?

A loud creak and bang, like a tailgate of a truck opening. Suddenly the casket was moving again, scraping, being pulled out of its transport.

God help me!

Should she call out to him? Beg him to let her go? She knew it wouldn't do any good, but she had to do something. *Any*thing.

A sharp rap.

"Hey, Nikki, you still awake?" the bastard asked.

She bit her tongue.

More rapping. "I know you're awake."

No . . . no, he didn't. And she didn't tell him, didn't utter a word.

"Oh, fuck it."

The coffin was moving again and she heard the muted rattle of wheels, like those on a hospital gurney. Rolling, rolling along bumpy terrain . . . no doubt taking her to the pit where the coffin would be dropped and buried. She had to do something!

All motion ceased.

No doubt he'd reached the grave. *Her* grave.

"Who would have done this?" Morrisette demanded.

Reed, worried sick about Nikki, remembered staring into the bloodied carcass of LeRoy Chevalier. They'd pulled out the coffin and opened it up, revealing a naked and slashed body. Chevalier's head had nearly been severed and there were dozens of wounds upon his body made by a sharp, deadly weapon. Finally Reed understood that the Grave Robber had no doubt also hacked up Carol Legittel and her children. Two dead. One brutally wounded. "This was done by someone who hated him. Someone with a dark rage. This isn't like the other killings where the deaths occurred without a lot of violence . . . No, Chevalier was chopped to death and then his body mutilated." Reed knew enough about serial killers to realize that Chevalier's murderer was someone close to him, someone he'd mistreated, someone whose hatred and need for vengeance was white-hot. "This one is someone who's enraged that he got out of prison and he's blaming everyone involved. The jurors, the judge and the woman who almost got the case thrown out years ago, Nikki Gillette."

"Who the fuck is that?" Morrisette asked.

Reed was thinking hard as the storm swirled around the soaked officers working the scene. Time was running out. Nikki was trapped with the monster somewhere. "It's someone like Ken Stern, Carol Legittel's brother. He hated Chevalier, promised to kill him—and as an ex-Marine, he would know how—or Stephen Legittel, her ex-husband and father of the children Chevalier abused, or Joey Legittel, her son, the only one who survived the killings."

"Chevalier beat him and forced him to have sex with his mother, right?" Morrisette said, eyeing the carnage. She visibly cringed at the crusted, dark purple slash surrounding Chevalier's throat.

Reed nodded, felt the icy rain run down his collar. "According to Joey. Along with his siblings. It was kind of a sadistic sexual free-for-all with Chevalier holding the whip."

"Deserved what he got," Morrisette muttered, turning away from the open casket as Diane Moses's team worked the area as they had at the previous crime scenes.

Cliff Siebert hung up his phone. "I got through to the hospital. Charlene Gillette can't tell us anything. She's traumatized. An officer tried to speak with her but she won't or can't say a word. Nearly catatonic. Whatever she saw pushed her over the edge."

"Shit." Morrisette glared up at the sky. Blinked against the rain.

Reed felt as if Nikki's life were in his hands and she was slowly, irrevocably, slipping away.

"Wonder why the asshole was buried alone?" Morrisette asked, jabbing her chin at the coffin.

"Again, not like the others," Reed thought, panic surging through him as the seconds ticked by. Where the hell did he have Nikki? "Send a unit to every grave-yard in the city," he said, but his mind was turning wildly, remembering the trial twelve years ago. The bleak courtroom. Judge Ronald Gillette sitting imperiously above the proceedings. The jurors watching raptly as the prosecution laid out its case. There was a clue here . . . there had to be. The killer had tricked him, steered him off course, but he had to . . . Lightning forked the sky. Suddenly he knew. As surely as if Lucifer had whispered the answer in his ear.

It was what this entire case was all about.

"Where was Carol Legittel buried?"

"Don't know." Morrisette shook her head.

Siebert said, "I do. I saw it in the file. She and her children are in Adams Cemetery, a small plot east of town."

That was all Reed needed to hear. "Let's go." He was already running through the spitting rain to his El Dorado. "We don't have much time."

Nikki was sweating, her heart pounding wildly. She had to find a way out. Pushing on the lid didn't do anything. She needed a weapon. Something she could use to pry the thing open from the inside out, but what? She had nothing. She was naked.

But her father was still wearing his clothes.

Her heart nearly stopped. Unless the killer had discovered it, Big Ron kept a loaded pistol strapped to his ankle.

Nikki's hopes jumped at the feeble possibility. Getting to the gun, and fast, seemed impossible.

But it was her only chance.

And, by God, she was going to take it.

The pounding started again. "Wake up, bitch!" His voice was raw. Anxious. Good.

He could damn well rot in hell before she uttered a word. Her lungs could turn to dust before she gave him the satisfaction.

It was so hard to breathe, nearly impossible to move and panic had her in a stranglehold, but the only chance out of this trap was to reach her father's weapon. *Please let it be there,* she thought, but knew the chances were slim. Surely the Grave Robber had found the small gun.

But there was a sliver of a chance that he'd over-looked it in his haste. She had to find out.

Using all her strength, she pressed down against her father's body, compressing his flesh, making herself smaller so that she had room to scoot down and bend her knees. The soft flab of her father's stomach gave way and she shuddered, her heart hammering, a horrid taste crawling up her throat. She slid. Possibly an inch. Maybe less. But she could barely move and as she stretched her hand along his pant leg, gathering the fabric, she knew her chance of survival was small.

Infinitesimal.

You bastard, she thought. *You goddamned animal.*

She felt the top of her father's boot. That was a good sign, right? Maybe the killer thought the ankle strap was part of her father's shoes.

She strained. Hard. Every muscle aching, her finger-tips brushing the top of the holster.

She heard a chain rattling, a lock clicking, then the sound of a small motor. She had the sensation of the coffin being lifted off the cart or gurney that had brought her here.

Bang!

"Hey, Nikki. Can you hear me?" The killer's voice was muted, but the words clear and her skin crawled. "How do you like sleeping with your father? It bites, doesn't it. Kinda like it bites when you have to kill your own family because they sold you out!"

She didn't answer. Felt ill. She pictured the Grave Robber not as the grisly, obsessed ogre he'd become but as he was twelve years ago. Then, seated in the courtroom at that gawky awkward age, Joey Legittel was ashen-faced, obviously scared to death, abused, forced to do terrible acts at the whim of LeRoy Chevalier. And then the court had made him tell about it.

Now, belatedly, she realized that he'd become a killer. He'd murdered his mother, sister and brother. He'd wounded himself, self-inflicted the wounds so cleverly that no one had guessed, then managed to hide the murder weapon and frame Chevalier with his own work boots. Now, he was crazed. Obsessed. No doubt because his tormentor had found freedom.

"Hey! You awake? Damn it. You nearly blew it, you know, you stupid bitch. And your old man, why the fuck didn't he sentence the bastard to die? Why?"

Her lungs burning, she considered talking to him, trying to reason with him, but then remembered again all too vividly the tape with Simone's hoarse, desperate voice as she pled, begged and bargained for her life. No matter what, Nikki wouldn't give him the satisfaction. Her shoulders straining, every muscle in her body cramped, she concentrated on easing the gun from its holster.

"Hey! *Hey!*"

More thudding. Wild. Crazy. As if he were losing it. The coffin jerked and spun.

Nikki concentrated on the weapon.

"Guess what I've got out here with me, Nikki," he taunted, and Nikki froze. She couldn't imagine. Didn't want to. "Something of yours. And Simone's."

Not Mikado. Not Jennings!

She nearly screamed, wanted to scratch his eyes out.

"Right here in my pocket. Your panties, Nikki. I took 'em out of your drawer. My, aren't they naughty? And Simone's . . ."

Nikki thought she might be sick.

"You hear me? I've got them all. Little treasures from all my victims. You know who's in there with you, right? Daddy dearest? Know what I got of his?"

She didn't want to know.

"And old jockstrap. Looks like it was made a billion years ago. What do you think of that?"

Go blow, you stinkin' pervert, she thought, anger surfacing beneath her terror.

"I've been planning this for years . . . but I wasn't gonna do it, not as long as LeRoy was behind bars. But he got out and so . . . too bad for all of you who failed me."

He wanted pity? Was he kidding?

"Did you enjoy the tape of your friend?" he asked and Nikki's skin turned to ice. "Did you hear her? How she begged."

Nikki wanted to scream at him, but held her tongue. That's what he wanted.

"They all did." He waited. "You awake?" He pounded again, the sound echoing through the coffin and cutting into her brain. "Hey, Nikki!"

Tune him out. Don't let him get to you! She stretched until her muscles and tendons screamed. Her fingers touched something cold and hard. The tiny pistol! Tears filled her eyes. Now, if she could just get it into her hand!

"Oh, fuck it."

The coffin began to move again.

This time it was descending into a pit Nikki could only imagine in her worst nightmare.

Reed pushed the El Dorado to the limit. Seventy miles an hour, eighty . . . ninety. His radio crackled and he figured he could be at the cemetery in less than fifteen minutes.

Would it be enough time?

God, he hoped so.

The thought of Nikki trapped in a casket and buried alive sent a chill as cold as all death down his spine. He stepped on it and the night flew by, the beams of his headlights cutting through the curtain of rain and bouncing on the slick pavement.

Only a maniac would drive like this on such a bleak night.

Sirens wailing, blue and red lights flashing, a cop car caught up with him and passed him on the fly.

Morrisette was at the wheel.

"Go get him, Sylvie," Reed ground out. "I'm right behind you."

Within minutes he saw the turnoff to Adams Cemetery and he braced himself. What were the chances that she was still alive?

The gun slipped away as the coffin swayed and swung, ever slowly making its descent into the grave.

No! Oh, no! Not buried alive!

Frantic, gasping for breath, her fingers scrabbling, searching, glancing off the butt of the gun, Nikki tried to think of another way to free herself.

There was none.

This was it.

If she could only reach the pistol before six feet of sodden earth covered her. *Come on, come on, Nikki, don't give up. Grab it, grab it now!*

Her middle finger felt cold steel, then her index finger. Straining, concentrating, she slowly eased the small caliber weapon from its sheath.

Now—if only it was loaded.

Dirt rained onto the top of the coffin.

Give me strength. Please, God . . .

She dragged in a breath that only made her head swim. Blackness closed in. Oh, no . . . she couldn't lose it now. If she blacked out, she'd never awaken. She'd be doomed.

More pebbles and clods clattered above her.

Gritting her teeth, she forced her body lower, her knees scraping the top of the casket. It was there . . . If she could just force the handle into her palm.

The noise in the coffin was deafening as rocks and dirt hit the wooden sides.

Come on, Nikki, grab the damned gun. But her thoughts were disjointed and slow. *Don't lose it now, Nikki. You can't. It's now or never.*

Sirens! Shit, he'd have to work fast. How had Reed figured it out so quickly? Shit, he'd spent too much time trying to get a response from Nikki! The Survivor looked into the darkness and concentrated. The sirens were screaming far away, still in the distance, but

516

heading in this direction. He had to get his work done fast and disappear. He already had another car parked on the far side of the fence. All he had to do was scale the wrought iron, make his way down a path, across a small river and there was another vehicle waiting.

Even dogs wouldn't find him.

But first he had to finish here. Only a few more scoops, but his microphone wasn't picking up much, just a few scrapes and kicks, but that didn't indicate Nikki was alive. Or conscious. Those sounds could be from the movement of the coffin.

He felt unsatisfied.

Empty.

He'd so wanted Nikki Gillette to know her fate.

She deserved to realize what was happening to her, that there was no way out, that she would suffer, that she wouldn't survive. Not like he had.

But he didn't have time to open the lid and check on her.

The police were getting closer. He heard their sirens, saw the lights strobing the night sky.

Too late, Reed, he thought, throwing in one final shovel of dirt.

Dragging in a breath of stale air, she extended her fingers, nudged the tiny weapon into her hand and pointed the barrel at the roof of the coffin. There was a chance the bullet wouldn't go through, that it would ricochet back at her or lodge in the earth above.

She had no other option.

And her thoughts were thick. Time and air were running out. She gasped. Coughed. Tried to think straight.

Reed. If only she could see Reed one last time . . .

Hand slick with sweat, body cold as ice, she forced the muzzle of the gun upward, she wrapped her finger around the trigger, sucked in what was left of her air and squeezed. "Die, you son of a bitch!"

Pain.

Hot searing pain shot up his leg and the sound was deafening. What the hell had happened? The Survivor looked down at his leg and saw the blood oozing, felt the burning. Who'd shot him? He saw the lights now. The cops were closing in. He had to get away.

He started hobbling toward the back fence, but his damned leg buckled. Gritting his teeth, he turned, tripping, falling over himself. Shit.

Sirens screamed, tires crunched and headlights cut through the night.

"Shit!"

He was cornered.

But not beaten.

He dropped back into the pit and waited.

A gunshot had echoed through the graveyard.

Reed, weapon drawn, sprang from his car.

Nikki, he thought, *oh, please be alive.*

He saw the truck and the fresh grave, mist swirling up from the wet dirt, the rain having abated to a fine drizzle.

"Police!" he yelled. "Legittel, drop your weapon!"

Behind him, he heard footsteps, then Morrisette's

voice barking instructions. "Siebert, call for backup," she yelled. "Reed, don't do anything stupid."

Reed didn't listen. Eyes fixed on the open grave, he ran forward.

"Reed!" Morrisette screamed. "Don't! Stop! Oh, crap!"

He knew he was taking a chance, but didn't care. Nikki's life was being smothered from her and he had to do whatever he could.

"Police," he yelled again, advancing on the pit. It was so dark. He should wait for backup, should wait for a flashlight, shouldn't sacrifice himself nor put himself into a potential hostage situation, but he didn't have time to think of anything but Nikki.

He flung himself into the pit and saw the Grave Robber huddled in one corner. At the instant Reed jumped in, Joey sprang and Reed saw it then, the glint of a knife.

Pain jarred up his shoulder.

He fired, careful to aim level and not downward, not toward Nikki.

"You bastard," he growled as Joey hacked wildly.

"Kill me," he taunted, breathing heavily, teeth flashing, blood visible. Reed cuffed him with the gun. Joey gave up a yelp, but fought back, surprisingly strong, muscles honed, dark eyes flashing with rage.

"You promised," he squealed as Reed placed the gun to his head and pulled one hand behind his back. "You lying bastard, you promised to come back and you didn't."

"Get up, Joey. It's over."

"Shoot me."

"No way, you piece of shit. Put your hands on your head and—"

Joey flung himself away, his wet clothes slipping through Reed's fingers. Whirling on his good leg, he slashed wildly with his knife.

A gun barked. Joey's body jerked and the knife clattered away.

"I'll live with it," Morrisette said. "Now, let's get that piece of shit out of here."

Reed was already on his knees. Digging frantically with his hands. "Nikki!" he yelled. In a scene of déjà vu he pulled at the dirt with his bare hands and heard something . . . scratching? Coughing? . . . from inside the buried coffin.

"Nikki? Oh, God, Nikki, hang on." He was digging furiously, flinging mud over his shoulders. "I need help here!" His fingers touched solid wood, then splintered wood and a small hole in the casket from the bullet that had incapacitated Joey Legittel. Another officer jumped into the pit with him. Together they scraped off the mud, found the microphone and tore it out, allowing air into the coffin.

"Get me out of here!" she cried, gasping and coughing from inside. He thought it was the most beautiful sound he'd ever heard. "For the love of God, Reed, get me the hell out of here!"

Within minutes he'd scraped the mud away, pried the coffin open and Nikki, frantic, eyes wide, body shaking, flung her naked body into his arms. She was gasping and crying and choking and screaming.

Reed looked into the casket and cringed.

The other body was that of her father, the Honorable Ronald Gillette.

Christ, what a mess.

Throwing his wet coat over her shoulders, he carried Nikki through the mire to his waiting El Dorado. How close he'd come to losing her. How damned close.

EPILOGUE

Nikki sipped coffee and stared out at the gray light of dawn. The sky was cloudless, the coming morning in sharp contrast with the dark events of two weeks earlier and that harrowing night where she'd nearly died. If she thought too closely about it, she would feel the fear again. The darkness. But she wouldn't allow herself to go there. At least not yet.

She'd healed physically and mentally she was improving daily, enough to gain some perspective about the rest of her life.

Christmas was only a few days away and Nikki hadn't yet put up a single strand of lights, nor had she found a little tree to dress up her apartment. It would be a difficult season this year, without her father, with her mother still recovering.

It was Saturday and she felt lazy, finishing her first cup of the day. Jennings was curled on his perch upon the bookcase, Mikado at Nikki's feet and the monitor of her computer screen said nothing but Page One.

The beginning of her novel.

About the Grave Robber, a tortured soul who had named himself The Survivor, according to the police. Joey Legittel, a boy who had suffered at the hands of Chevalier before snapping and killing his family and framing the man who had tormented him. From there it had been foster homes and an adulthood that had been filled with no relationships and piecemeal jobs usually at video stores where he had purchased the movies of vengeance.

It was all so horrid. He'd even realized that his last name was an acronym for Gillette and had scribbled her name and his all over his scarred table where he'd kept a scrapbook of the trial.

Now, the exterior steps squeaked and Mikado began to bark and run to the door. "I think it's someone you know," Nikki said just as a sharp rap on the door caused the dog to go into conniptions.

Her pulse quickened as she scraped back her chair. The cat stretched as if bored and Mikado twirled crazily.

After rescuing her from the coffin, Reed had held her close and insisted she go to the hospital. For most of the night he'd been with her, at her bedside, only taking time off to fill out reports or converse with the other cops. His own wound had been virtually ignored.

The Grave Robber was no more.

He'd died that night. Morrisette had put him away before he'd had the chance to kill Reed with the very knife that he'd used to butcher his family twelve years

522

before, a knife he'd somehow hidden, then retrieved and held in a drawer in the lair the police had found, a small dugout room with recording equipment, televisions, movies, and a bloodstained bureau wherein underwear from his victims had been stashed. The lair was in the home of an elderly woman who'd paid him to house-sit. He had barely used the rest of the huge manor deep in the heart of Savannah. But now he was dead. After having taken so many lives. Including Simone's.

Casting off the brutal memories, Nikki reached the door and pulled it open.

Clean shaven, in jeans and a sweater, Reed stood on her porch. He was juggling two cups of coffee and a bag of pastries and his eyes lighted as he spied her. "Mornin'," he drawled.

Mikado launched himself at Reed's legs and Jennings shot outside, escaping.

"Back at ya, Reed." Standing on her tiptoes, she brushed her lips across his beard-roughened cheek. "Come on in. What brings you up here?" she teased.

"Just doin' my duty, ma'am," he drawled.

"My ass."

"And a fine one it is." Lifting a dark eyebrow he took an exaggerated look at her bottom though she was completely covered in a thick bathrobe.

"Always nice to know." She took the sack and cups of coffee from him so that he could pet the dog for a few minutes as she cut up the pastries—a cinnamon roll and honey drizzled croissant.

"So, how are you, really?" He was suddenly serious.

"I know it's been a couple of weeks, but you haven't really said."

Which was true. Since the murders they'd kept conversation between them light. Teasing. Getting to know each other.

"Traumatized, of course, but I think I'll survive." Hearing her words, she cringed inwardly. Joey Legittel had also survived—once. Only to end up a serial killer who'd terrorized her and this town.

"And your mom?"

"She went home two days ago, but a nurse stops in daily and I visit every day. So do Lily and Kyle." Nikki sighed and leaned a hip against the counter. "I don't know if Mom will ever be right. She saw such horror and she was frail to begin with. Lily and Phee, my niece, plan to move into the house for a while, and Sandra's there to help out with the cooking and cleaning, so we'll see how it goes. It'll take time."

She wiped the knife clean with her fingers. "So, your theory is that Joey Legittel not only killed Chevalier, but his mother, sister and brother as well because they didn't protect him."

"Yep. He was the youngest and thought everyone had sold him out. He was beaten and forced to do unthinkable acts as well as have them performed on him. With members of his family. The only way to free himself from Chevalier was to set him up. So he killed all his family, and tromped through the blood in Chevalier's boots, even managed to slice his own arms, legs and shoulder without hitting anything vital and somehow hid the weapon, then claimed Chevalier was to blame."

"But to kill your own mother, and your siblings." Nikki felt a chill as cold as death.

"They were the enemy. They didn't protect him. He contacted me, sent me up to Dahlonega to get my attention and throw us off. I was the junior detective who had collared Chevalier, but I didn't have enough evidence to send him to Death Row. Neither did your dad or the other jurors."

"And he accused me of nearly causing a mistrial."

"Right."

"So, does this mean you and Morrisette get big promotions for exposing him?" She placed the plates on her small table and shoved her laptop to one side.

"No, but I might get to keep my badge. And even Cliff Siebert might get to keep his. He fessed up, you know. That he was the leak."

"I'm sorry."

"Don't be. No one twisted his arm."

"Yeah, I kinda did."

"He's a big boy. So, what about you? What are you going to do with your life?"

"Write that book you promised me the exclusive on. I started today. Since Joey's dead, we won't have to worry about a trial."

"So, you'll stick around?"

"Mmm." She picked up a sliver of cinnamon roll and popped it into her mouth. "Tom Fink called. Wants me to come back. Has offered me the crime beat."

"And?"

"And it'll be the proverbial cold day in hell before that happens." She laughed and licked her fingers. "I also got a call from a newspaper in Chicago and one in Atlanta, but . . . I don't know. Chicago gets awfully cold in the winter."

"And Atlanta?"

She lifted a shoulder.

"I thought you wanted the big break. To work for a real, respected newspaper." Bracing himself on the counter next to her, he held her gaze with his. Thoughtfully, his eyes narrowed. "Just what the hell is it you're really looking for, Gillette?"

"What do you mean?"

"Out of life. What do you want? You've always been so damned ambitious, always talking about going to the big city to make your mark. What now?"

"I'm not sure."

"Really? That doesn't sound like you."

"Well, then, how about a big, burly, brusque cop to keep me in line?" She took a piece of cinnamon roll and playfully fed it to him.

He grinned around the morsel. "Yeah, right. *That's* what would make you happy, all right," he said sarcastically. "It would last five minutes. Ten, tops."

"Well . . . it just so happens I have five minutes."

He stared at her, then glanced at the bedroom door. "You mean . . . now?"

She winked and twined her fingers through his. "Exactly. See . . . you figured that out all by yourself. You really are an ace detective, aren't you?"

Center Point Publishing
600 Brooks Road ● PO Box 1
Thorndike ME 04986-0001 USA

(207) 568-3717

US & Canada:
1 800 929-9108